CHURCHGOERS
DON KURTZ

"Isn't He Good"
Words and music by Stephen Altrogge
© 2004 Sovereign Grace Praise/BMI
All rights reserved International Copyright Secured Used by permission

COOL OF THE MORNING PRESS
2751 Hennepin Ave South, Suite 254
Minneapolis, MN 55408

ISBN: 978-0-9795563-0-2
Printed in the United States of America

10 9 8 7 6 5 4 3 2 1

For Ann

I wondered why, since I had gone so deep, I had seen nothing of the *love* of God, but only His relentlessness.

J. A. Symonds

Isn't He good, isn't He kind,
Hasn't He blessed us time after time?

Christian Praise Song

ONE

There was little indication early on that the ground rules had changed. A chill along his spine and at the tips of his fingers. A brush of perspiration at the small of his back. An acuity, too, of sensation; a strange sort of *sharpness* he simply chose not to notice — his lab was large and the competition stiff, the sprawling Midwestern campus familiar to him, his interest fully engaged by the tasks he had at hand. Ahead was the old Campus Church; normally he cut through a small alleyway behind it on the way to his car. On a warm September afternoon Mitchell paused at its entrance. He let a group of students pass by on the sidewalk, then trotted up the steps to the door.

Prairie Grove was a town of fifty thousand or so, dominated by the University, a landgrant school in the center of the state. Behind him were the low shops of campustown, a copy center and photographer's studio, the Warrior Jitters coffee shop shining brightly in the sun. Inside, the church foyer was dark. As his eyes adjusted, he picked out an empty coat rack, along with two large bulletin boards flanking an entrance to the parlor. A stairway led to a small classroom above the foyer, where two days earlier he had come to give his talk.

On one of the bulletin boards, a flyer still remained:

> The men's class on Sunday morning welcomes Dr. Mitchell Chandler. His research is world-renowned, especially for his identification of the "Lazarus gene," believed to govern the regeneration of severed limbs in amphibian species.
>
> Professor Chandler received his doctorate from Stanford University and was a fellow at the National Institute of Health. He is former director of the Chandler Laboratory at the University of North Carolina and a co-founder of LazTec, Inc. of Rahway, New Jersey. His mother Edie was a member of this congregation for many years.

He had been recruited for the class by old Walter Eller, a Prairie Grove neighbor when he was a boy. His audience was small, consisting of a half-dozen retired faculty members in narrow neckties and baggy trousers, laminate name tags hanging from cords around their necks. Mitchell had brought along his slides and a one-page handout that he used for less technical presentations, complete with a cartoon Lazarus emerging from the genome in rags.

Salamanders are among the few species that possess the ability to regenerate a severed limb or tail, with nerves intact and full functioning restored. His achievement had been to identify Lazarus, a gene that "came back to life" in response to trauma. An endowed chair and new lab were among the fruits of that breakthrough, the only reasons he would ever have returned to his childhood home of Prairie Grove.

The town itself was as placid and uninteresting as ever. There had been nothing out of the ordinary, certainly, at that Sunday morning men's class. If anything, there was a flatness to the occasion — the stuffy church classroom and dull clank of the projector, his circle of aging listeners — and before long he had found himself ranging further afield, into a kind of gloss on the neurological correlates of human thought. It was the *Astonishing Hypothesis*, more or less — even if hardly that astonishing anymore near the end of the millennium

— the notion that our identities are essentially biochemical. Our thoughts, our passions, our meanings, our gods: all arise from a complex assembly of neurons and their related activity, activity that would, with the individual, pass away. It was a thesis intended, on a Sunday morning, to be provocative, but the oldtimers seemed barely to notice. Instead, they had questions about his work.

"What about other proteins?" asked a man whose tag read 'Fitzgerald.' "I assume they have a role in this as well."

"I'm interested," from another class member, "in how the gene was introduced. What kind of vector did you use?"

A small man in red suspenders was the next to raise his hand. "What are you finding in vivo? That seems important to know."

Mitchell turned to him. "I assume you're asking whether we have observed regeneration in mammals. So far the results have been mixed."

"Why should we even accept," Fitzgerald asked, "that Lazarus is the engine? It may well be a factor, but with much less importance than originally believed."

Mitchell had felt himself growing testy. "The gene has been proven over the past fifty years to be the primary agent in biological development. Lazarus' significance is hardly in doubt."

"But what about *in vivo*?" the suspendered man insisted. "Isn't that where the payoff will be?"

During the last of his slides there had been a rumbling from the sanctuary, the whine of an electric guitar as it wound up the stairs. Before he could respond to his questioner, a loud wave of rock music swept into the classroom, joining amplified calls of "Jesus, Jesus" that rattled against the walls.

"Uh-oh," one of the men said. "Our co-religionists."

Fitzgerald slid the handout back to Mitchell. "Well," he said, "might as well see if the coffee is ready. We won't get much further today."

Apparently the class was over: there were grimaces and resigned smiles as the men climbed to their feet around the table, mouthed words of thanks beneath the clanging of the chords. "Jesus, Jesus," came the call up the stairway, but the man in suspenders wasn't done.

"What about *in vivo*?" he kept insisting above the racket, and in the confusion Mitchell had left his slides behind.

Now he was back, on a Tuesday afternoon, to retrieve them, another of a long series of annoyances that robbed him of his day. There had been a difficult phone conference with LazTec's board — the investors were restless. He had renewed his passport for an October conference in Copenhagen. A tedious meeting with the Research Council had taken two hours, followed by a twenty-minute wait for a flu shot on his way to the lab.

The Campus congregation's few remaining members still conspired to keep busy — besides his own flyer there was a posting for a Long-Term Care lecture, and a Senses Alive! class that met afternoons at four. The Senses Alive! class was apparently in session: through one of the parlor doors, Mitchell glimpsed a small group of elderly women clustered around a young man in a tee shirt. Blankets at their feet, they stood with their eyes closed, passing what looked to be a billiard ball from one to another around the group.

In the dark foyer, he had begun to feel chilled. There was a sharp tingle along his spine as he came past the parlor. The second bulletin board was labeled "The Justice Corner," and he paused before it. A fading sign with a peace dove staked out a Nuclear Free Zone. There was the obligatory poster of a laughing peasant child. "People are not mascots," was spelled out above a dancing Chief Cheehaha, while in a second photo a middle-aged man — mild Harry Applebee, the Campus Church preacher — stood with a young girl at the stadium, both smiling as they held placards in the sun.

On a nearby table his slide tray, as promised, was waiting. Just beyond were the doors to the sanctuary, and on impulse he pulled one open to slip inside.

The last time he had been in the sanctuary had been for his mother's funeral, almost two years earlier. What he recalled was an unassuming plainness, bare white walls and a high, arching ceiling, the walnut pews plain and polished on either side. A huge projection screen now graced the choir loft. Spotlights framed an acrylic podium at the front of the church. The pulpit had been pushed aside in favor of a shiny drum set, with a bank of speakers stacked high on either side. Behind the podium there was a wooden cross, easily eight feet tall, its heavy beams lashed together with rope.

Some sort of video program was running on the projection screen, scenes of distant mountains and a tree-lined autumn valley. Just beneath the podium, a small, thick-haired man in a sport shirt talked insistently to a woman with a ponytail. The small man gestured and the woman shook her head, but by that time he had caught sight of Mitchell, standing alone at the back of the church.

"Geoff?" he called out, a grin breaking across his face. He hurried up the aisle. "Geoffrey, praise God, is that you?"

"No," Mitchell said. "I'm afraid it isn't."

"Geoffrey Chandler? It sure looks like you."

The man had arrived to greet him, hand extended. Reluctantly, Mitchell took it. "I'm Mitchell Chandler. A professor at the University. You must be thinking of my brother."

"*Mitchell* Chandler, then, a professor at the University. We're both glad to meet you just the same. I'm Pastor Randy Overmeyer, and this is my wife, Lee. We've got a kingdom-based mission, Spirit Rising, where we heal through the sovereign power of Jesus Christ. Any time left over, we spend praising the Lord."

These aren't University people, Mitchell thought instinctively, and slowly the reason came to mind. Campus Church, its membership dwindling, had decided to rent space to Spirit Rising, a freelance ministry from town. It had elected to share its sanctuary with the same crowd whose frenzied shouts had drowned out his Sunday-morning presentation, whose wooden cross and shiny instruments stood high above the pews.

Mitchell recoiled from the pastor's eager handshake, his wide grin and sharp smell of cologne.

"So, Mitchell Chandler, brother of Geoffrey Chandler, what brings you to us this afternoon? Are you looking for a faith family of your own?"

"I'm not looking for anything," Mitchell said. He held up the tray. "I came for my slides. "

"The last time I saw Geoffrey, he was headed out west on an old Honda 600 he had. Where did he end up, Venezuela or someplace?"

"Guatemala. He's been there for over twenty years."

"We used to send money to a mission down there somewhere, maybe he's run across it. What was the name of that guy from Nebraska, honey, we met at a conference? Maybe he and Geoff —"

"I doubt it," Mitchell said. "None of us is involved in religion in any way."

Beyond the walls of the old church lay the mammoth state university with its tree-lined quadrangle and colonial architecture, the sports facilities, classrooms, and dorms. High-stakes research formed the heart of the enterprise: a half-dozen Nobel laureates had made their names in Prairie Grove. It wasn't inconceivable that Mitchell, too, might one day join their ranks. That is, if he could get Lazarus to pay off in mammals, an achievement still elusive; even as the chill from the church foyer followed him into the sanctuary, and he felt a fresh patch of perspiration beneath his shirt. The tingle along his spine reached the base of his neck.

The little man put his hand on his arm. "I don't know what it is, but I got this funny feeling going on inside me. You ever have that happen? I got this question that keeps wanting to be asked."

"Look, I'd better be going."

"It's a question about Professor Mitchell Chandler. It's a question about how Professor Mitchell Chandler might be standing with the Lord."

His wife had come up to join them, attractive in her pastel sweatshirt and ponytail, standing with arms folded a short distance away. Mitchell had little choice but to confront, then, a nagging feel of *strangeness*, strange in itself — little beyond his work held the power to distract him. All day long he had been absorbed by Lazarus, going over its expression sequence as he sat in the Council meeting, later at the Health Center as he waited for his shot. He had been running through it yet again afterwards, striding impatient through the reception area, when abruptly he fainted dead away.

He had been out barely a minute — if that — before regaining consciousness. A trivial incident, almost certainly, except for its residue, a peculiar sense of resonance that had steadily deepened. The moment itself, there in the sanctuary, seemed oddly *known* to him — the Jesus woman wasn't just attractive but deeply familiar, as if encountered before in some place he'd never been. Careful makeup smoothed the skin around her eyelids. A strand of hair had slipped down across her ear. She looked at him coolly.

"He isn't interested, Randy. He has all the answers he needs."

Still smiling, the man shook his head. "I must have missed that, honey. I didn't hear him say he wasn't interested. I never heard him say he has all the answers he needs."

"I'm not interested," Mitchell said, pulling his arm free. "I have all the answers I need."

Nature scenes were unfolding in the choir loft, and Mitchell felt the pastor's hand creep back to his elbow as they looked at the screen. Two gulls glided low along a seashore, the image fracturing into a pair of ragged bands that moved steadily apart. A brook framed by yellow aspens followed, only to dissolve in bright static. Pastor Randy shook his head.

"All of a sudden that crazy system doesn't like us. I wonder why. But maybe we could take a minute to pray here, together, before you leave."

As Mitchell tried to move away, Pastor Randy's fingers tightened.

"Father God, speed our brother Mitchell's understanding. Let him know we'll be here as he moves to your side." The man looked up at him appraisingly. "I thought it was Geoffrey, but you turned out to be Mitchell. It's always a surprise to me what God decides to do."

The resonant feeling contended with a headache that had steadily worsened; Mitchell felt the man's fingers on his arm even after he managed to break away. His escape was delayed briefly at the edge of sanctuary: the Senses Alive! class had ended, and women strolled from the parlor with their blankets, chatting easily. Watching them, Mitchell felt the same odd sense of familiarity he had experienced with the pastor's wife. And, as he suddenly realized, he *did* know two or three, their faces resolving through wrinkles and years into the mothers of childhood playmates: Mrs. McNeil who had been his den mother for cub scouts, Mrs. Cobble whose car he had thrown up in at ten. Elements of a Prairie Grove that slumbered in prehistory — intimations of himself before Hopkins and Stanford, the NIH and Chapel Hill — a Mitchell Chandler he barely knew.

A Mitchell Chandler whose consciousness still, on a sunny September afternoon, hadn't quite set in right: as he came out into the alcove, student chatter burbled from the sidewalk. The copy shop's neon sign gently smoldered across the street. A fanfare from the marching band practice field joined a 40/7 ratio — odd as much for its fractional notation as sudden insistence — a ratio that had abruptly appeared, unbidden, in his mind. A boy ran as if pursued across a winter landscape, gaining speed beneath a low prairie sky.

Mitchell took a deep breath, craning his neck; he could bum a couple of Tylenols off one of his post-docs at the lab. Even then, an image surfaced to distract him, a man glimpsed a moment earlier as he hung back with his slide tray, the churchwomen before him and the Christians at his back. Of all the impressions, it was by far the most anomalous — hallucinatory, almost — especially since the man had looked so much like his father. His father in church, the last place he would expect to see him; squeezed improbably into a sweatsuit and shiny white tennis shoes, his own blanket tucked high beneath his arm. A man broad-shouldered and with silver glasses flashing — again, disturbingly like his father — a man who ducked his head low as he hurried across the entryway, scuttling without a backward glance past the women to the door.

Two

The leaf had a paper-like texture beneath his fingers. There was the tug of the branch against his arm muscles, a layer of air that rested lightly against his face. Austin Chandler, no longer in his sweatsuit and tennis shoes, and far from the Campus Church parlor, was doing his homework. He closed his eyes only to be confronted with his arthritis as it throbbed beneath his knee caps, a stubborn heaviness at the center of his chest. When his jaw loosened, it was with a painful sort of cracking. He had just made his way back to the leaf when a voice broke in.

"Looking a little peaked, I'd say."

Startled, he whirled to find Walter Eller at his elbow. Walter had come across the lawn to join him, and Austin Chandler let go of the branch as if scalded.

"Good God, man, you don't need to come creeping up on people like that."

"Sorry, Dean Chandler. I didn't mean to startle you. I thought you'd picked up on the chlorosis in those leaves."

Smiling easily, Walter stood before him in a shapeless summer shirt and necktie, a terrycloth tennis hat sagging low around his ears. Austin Chandler nodded sagely toward the tree.

"Right, chlorosis. A lack of potassium, I'm calling it."

Walter nodded. "Could be," he said. "Could very well be. Funny, though, but I'd almost be inclined to say ferrous oxide. A lot of this ground was leveled off when they made room for the addition. Without the topsoil, you often lack iron."

The late-summer grass was thick around them, the parking lot and his Buick a full twenty yards away. Austin Chandler had felt vaguely furtive when he'd stepped away from the pavement; now he stood like a fool beneath a pin oak, the limb above them bobbing faintly in the air.

"Bah," he said, "it's probably iron. You're the soils man, not me. And good God, you could at least call me Austin. We've known each other almost fifty years."

Both men lived on Washington Street, their houses a block apart, so Austin Chandler was more likely to run into Walter there, rather than on the front lawn of the Cooke-Davis retirement village, set among trees on the south edge of town. To their left rose the trim row of apartments that made up the Senior Life section, with the common area and Assisted Living units spread out along the base. The entrance to SkilCare lay before them across the grass.

"Out to see the inmates?" he asked, nodding toward the door.

"Oh, well," Walter said, "I like to keep up with friends. Mostly, though, I come to see Vic Jacobs. He's been failing some, and I like to..."

"Jacobs is still here? I thought he'd been dead for years."

Walter was still smiling good-naturedly. "Oh, I wanted to tell you," he said. "I enjoyed Mitchell's talk the other morning at the Men's Class. The recap of his work was quite impressive."

Austin Chandler couldn't help noticing his face tighten — that damned Senses Alive! class — as he felt himself scowl. "I'm sure it was. Mitchell is very capable. Why he came back to Prairie Grove is the mystery to me. Probably all the money the University threw his way. The Governor flew down to meet him, I probably told you that. Yes, I'm quite certain that I did."

"Genetic factors in neurogenesis," Walter said, nodding. "It reminds me of the work Dick Frederick used to do in the seventies, over at the animal science lab. I wonder if Dick was moving that way?"

"I doubt it," Austin Chandler said curtly. "Dick Frederick never knew his right foot from his left. He should have been put out to pasture a dozen years before he was."

It was a source of some irritation that he had to do the same job over again, long after they retired — older profs like Eller still thought they had some kind of grasp of things, when even in their prime they'd been slipping behind. He disliked, too, being reminded of his close brush with his eldest son in the Campus Church foyer. What was Mitchell doing in church?

His indignation was interrupted by the sound of women's voices. Two chubby girls in salmon-colored uniforms had parked themselves on a bench outside the SkilCare entrance where they waved enthusiastically, calling Walter by name. Grinning beneath his bonnet, Walter waved back.

"Say there, Walter, it's none of my business, but what's the story with that Spirit Rising group up at Campus? I thought they'd be moved out of there by now."

Grin fading, Walter tugged at his ear. "That's what we thought, too. Apparently they've run into some snags on their building project."

"Hardly the kind of thing you'd expect from Campus in the first place, wouldn't you say, sharing space with an outfit like that? Faith-healing and miracles! Throw away your crutches and go for a walk!"

"Well, we didn't really go into their beliefs. They needed a place while their new building is going up, and we have more space than we need. Several of the older congregations are doing it. The Methodists downtown have the Koreans and there's a Buddhist group that meets at First Presbyterian. We thought —"

"But Spirit Rising, damn it, Walter, wake up! You've got to watch those holy rollers or they'll rob you blind."

"Well ..." Walter said mildly.

"Just look at it, man! How much do they pay to share the Campus facilities? Five hundred a month? That barely covers the utilities! And there they are at all hours, camped out in the middle of things, wailing on their microphones and pounding their guitars. You'd better be careful of that Randy Overmeyer. He's been a slick one all his life!"

Austin Chandler felt the heat rising to his face.

"And that preacher of yours, Harry Applebee! What's all this fuss about the Chief? We're talking about Chief Cheehaha, damn it, the symbol for the whole University. If that's not an honor, I don't know what is!"

Walter shrugged. "It's kind of become Harry's issue. He feels the University could be a little more sensitive. Apparently, some find the whole thing quite hurtful."

"Oh for God's sake." Austin Chandler waved toward the SkilCare entrance. "You think any of the people in there never had their feelings hurt? That's the nature of things, you take your knocks and move on. People love the Chief. Makes the church a goddamn laughingstock when they see Applebee on the news." The injustice of it pressed against his eyes. "The Chief has to be an Eagle Scout, damn it, too. A lot of people don't realize that. It's not like he's some fraternity boy out on a lark!"

"Well," Walter said slowly, "I'd better let you go. You probably need to get back to…things." He nodded toward the tree.

"Fine," Austin Chandler replied. "No use letting the morning get away."

Walter started toward the sidewalk. "Oh, I meant to ask if you got that writeup on Reldon Kemp for the archives. I stuck it in your screen door early in the week."

Austin Chandler snorted. "I got it all right. What did you write, twenty pages? Old Kemp couldn't have contributed that much if he lived a thousand years. I cut it to a couple of paragraphs and sent it in."

"Well," Walter said, "at least it's taken care of. Good to see you again, Austin." He backed away and then turned toward the entrance, leaving Austin Chandler on the lawn with his tree.

His wife, Vera, couldn't understand it, but Walter had never minded coming out to Cooke-Davis. He wished Vera wasn't so reluctant to sell their house on Washington: in the Senior Life apartments they could live like they always had, with Assisted Living close at hand for when trouble set in. The staff was pleasant too, which made a difference. He spent another ten minutes talking to the girls who sat smoking on the bench. Inside, he greeted the woman at the desk.

"Hello, Bettina, how's it going?"

"Fine, Mr. Eller, how are you?"

"Just fine. It's a pretty day."

A heavy-set woman with a clipboard joined. "Hi, Walter, what's new?"

"Hi there, Connie. How's your mom?"

"Ornery as ever," she said, patting him on the shoulder. "Mr. Jacobs's been eating a little better. I'll walk down with you on my way to the lab."

A resident or two shuffled slowly along the corridor and a group had been rolled into the cafeteria to sit nodding in their chairs. Connie struggled with her weight, like so many of the girls who worked there, rocking beside him as they walked. She led Walter into a room near the end of the hall.

"Hey, Mr. Jacobs, your old drinking buddy is here."

"Hi Vic," Walter said easily. "Looks like you're feeling spry!"

Connie pressed against the door to let him pass. "Yesterday he got into that box of candy you left for him. Ate the whole thing before we saw what he'd done."

"Oh my."

"It went straight through, about like you'd expect with all that chocolate. Seemed like we spent the whole evening cleaning up at the other end. He's a pill sometimes, Mr. Eller, he really is. All of us enjoy him a lot."

Vic wore a print shirt and a pair of denim pants as he sat slumped in his wheelchair. He blinked his eyes but was otherwise expressionless — the Parkinson's had slowly closed him in. He didn't have a roommate which made things a little nicer. A bright afternoon sun came in through his window, and a bank calendar from his home town in Minnesota hung above the bed.

"I ran into Dean Chandler a few minutes ago," Walter told him. "Out in front. Maybe he's considering moving into one of the apartments."

Vic looked back at him blankly. There was a gathering rumble and a man rode past the window on a lawnmower. He came by again in the other direction and Walter settled in.

He had to admit he had been concerned that morning as he

approached Austin Chandler on the lawn. It was the way so many people their age started out, wandering away from home or the shopping mall, ending up in their cars somewhere out on the highway without the slightest idea of what they were doing behind the wheel. It had been a relief to see that he was as prickly as ever, his jaw thrust forward like a bulldog's, and glasses flashing silver in the sun.

"I saw his boy Mitchell last week when he gave a talk at the church. He has that new Brightbill Chair in Neurobiology."

Vic looked back at him in silence.

"He's had quite a career for himself. You probably remember the writeup in *Newsweek*. Still, I couldn't help thinking that he might be a little stalled. All that money, the big lab, the special chair — it's the kind of position where expectations run high. I wonder if calcium might be affecting his neural outgrowth. There was a piece in *Chem Engineering News* about it just the other day."

Comfortable, Walter leaned back in his chair. It was always a pleasure to sit with Vic and talk science. His office had been just down the hall at the department, and Walter couldn't have counted the number of times he'd stopped in with a problem that the two of them would gradually figure out. He had liked going down to the coffee room where the Ag men used to gather. He learned more in those twenty minutes than he would have in a year working all on his own.

Still, the dean was right: times had changed. The last time he had been up to the department, the men stayed in their offices, tapping intently at their keyboards. The coffee room had been converted into a computer lab and the farmers they'd worked with were gone. When he heard a rustle he saw that Vic was leaning forward, chin tensed like he had something to say.

"Plaster," was what he finally got out.

"I'm sorry, Vic. I don't quite follow."

"Plastered!" he spit out, and Walter tried to think.

"Chandler? Dean Chandler? I saw him a few minutes ago."

There was a shine in his old friend's eyes, and his fingers were twitching. His lips had formed something like a smile. The gurgle that came next was encouraging, so Walter leaned forward to shout.

"Austin Chandler! Old man Chandler! I say I saw him outside on the lawn!"

Vic's throat trembled and his shoulders were shaking, all part of the struggle to push sound past his lips. There was a surprising clarity when he finally got it out.

"B-b-b-astard!" Vic sputtered and for a moment grinned wildly, before sinking back exhausted in his chair.

The Parkinson's had been hard on Vic, there was no doubt about it. Long before that, though, he'd begun to grow bitter; changes in the College had been hard on a lot of the men as disciplines changed. The old dean was still formidable, bristling beneath a pin oak, but Vic had been a battler too. There was no telling how many times the two of them had tangled. Vic was locked up again, his face and body rigid, but even so, Walter felt cheered. It was exactly what he often told Vera: there was a lot more going on there than anybody knew.

THREE

Pastor Randy Overmeyer could still remember the cold winter afternoon when he had walked with a trio of older boys past a line of boxcars in the freight yard, following the tracks as they wound out of town. A half mile away a wooden trestle spanned a dry ravine forty feet deep, thick with wild grasses and trash.

It was a ravine that served, on the prairie, as a hill; the previous summer he had watched from a distance as those same older boys — his brother Dike, Ralph Pitcher, Tommy Markland — balanced a bicycle at the edge of the dropoff. They took turns, as first one and then another tugged on a molded white football helmet, wrapped an old towel around his face, and pushed off, plunging to crash at full speed into the wall of brush at the bottom. When that rider had dragged the bicycle back to the top, he passed it on. Each waited patiently, shins and forearms bleeding, until it was his turn to go down again.

The bicycle was Randy's, but he could admire the group only from a distance. More often than not, when he ventured close, he was punched and pounded, made to eat dirt, reminders that they were seventeen while he was only twelve. That's why he'd been surprised to find them waiting when he got off the school bus a week before Christmas, motioning him to where they stood smoking at the back of the lot.

The neighborhood was called Darryl Chapel for an old Catholic parish that had served railworkers a generation earlier; now it was a string of bare frame houses spread out along the railroad. A silver guard rail divided their backyard from the tracks. Dike leaned against it, working at his nails.

"Hey, Squirt," he said, "how's it going?"

"All right," Randy said.

Ralph Pitcher flicked his cigarette across the guard rail. "So how's school? Going okay?"

Randy nodded. "I guess so."

"That's good," Tommy Markland said. "You always want to do good in school."

"Come on," Dike said, "let's go for a walk."

The snow was late that year but the afternoon was cold, the weeds along the embankment withered and brown. Randy settled in eagerly among them as they stumped along the tracks. Ralph gave him a drag off his cigarette and Tommy passed the pint bottle of whiskey he'd lifted from his father's liquor store. The railyard gave way to a single track bounded by a strip of scrub timber. From beyond it came the sound of trucks on the highway, downshifting as they came into town.

Just before the trestle a rusted forty-gallon barrel lay in the weeds. Randy stood with Dike as Tommy and Ralph wrestled it along the tracks to the trestle, and from there to the edge of the ravine.

Randy was still carrying his geography book and Dike took it from him. "You won't be needing this," he said, and sailed it across the ravine. They watched as it flew, pages fluttering, until it disappeared beneath the trestle. The older boys laughed and Randy did too.

It turned out they had plans for him: when the barrel righted, they lifted him over the rim.

"You're the only one small enough," Dike explained was all the persuasion Randy needed, crouching inside, drawn up and back pressed against the metal. A moment later they'd set the lid in place, pounding down the flanges to make it tight. Randy was still shifting his feet, trying to steady himself, when they dropped the barrel roughly on its side.

Through a threaded bunghole the outer world had been reduced to the oily cuff of Tommy Markland's jacket and a small disk of clouds. The Apollo moon mission had lifted off earlier in the week, so there was a countdown and more laughter. A moment later, Randy was launched.

It had never occurred to him to be scared. He felt only a quick surge of excitement as the barrel gained speed, rolling and pitching as the slope steepened. His small leverage, after the first few turns, couldn't hold him, and he began to be tossed back and forth, knees and elbows banging, his face grinding hard against the sides. His winter coat, new that fall, helped cushion him, and his stocking cap served as a kind of helmet, but otherwise he was unprotected, the shaft of light spinning wildly as he tumbled. The barrel bounced over rocks and stumps, gathering speed until it finally went airborne, landing with a thud at the bottom of the ravine.

The final plunge had knocked the wind out of him, but even as Randy lay gasping in a shower of rust, his excitement was intact. His temple was swelling and his shoulders and knees bruised, but the important thing was that he'd made it. Mission accomplished, he thought, and lay back quietly, like an astronaut bobbing in the ocean, savoring his moment of private triumph before they climbed down to let him out.

The bobbing feeling slowly faded, along with his dizziness. As the rust settled Randy moved uncomfortably, trying to find some way to lie back that didn't hurt. Through the bunghole he saw the base of the trestle, black steel scaffolding in a solid concrete base. When he heard voices, they were still at a distance, along with a shuffle and snickering that soon died away.

Squeezing one arm up to cradle his head, Randy smiled. He had begun to appreciate the elegance of the plan, pleased that they had bothered to fool him. They would wait until he called out in panic, crying and banging at the lid, but Randy knew himself better than that. He could already picture being allowed to hang out with them, a kid whose toughness they admired. A warm, club-house sort of feeling settled in as he waited for their footsteps through the weeds. He waited hopefully for fifteen minutes, and then, less hopefully, for a half hour more, fingers and toes numbing, his scrapes growing stiff from the cold. It seemed that Dike, at least, would have to account for him, reassurance that waned as the hours slipped away. The afternoon gave way and night deepened, the world outside the barrel gradually settling into black.

On an early September afternoon almost thirty years later, driving along the state highway in his shiny new Explorer, Pastor Randy could see at a distance the rail yard. He slowed to look south toward the trestle, speeding up to pass the new Manor Lake subdivision where he and Lee had their home. A mile east of the subdivision he turned right to cross the railroad, moving out onto the wide carpet of cropland that surrounded the town.

Though he was a city boy, the country roads east of town were like old friends to him. Randy still could have picked out the place where, one winter night, stoned and careless, he'd slid with a carload of friends into a creek. A little farther on was the field where he'd been flushed out half-naked from the back seat with Julie Schumacher, by a farmer having sport with his jacklight. Three miles from the railroad, he turned right at the old Glissendorf place, then left on a narrow county road. Just as the blacktop began its long rise toward the interstate Randy slowed, turning onto an overgrown lane that wound back along a ditch.

At the end of the lane he pulled over. With his engine cut, the world around him returned to life: a pair of crows renewed their squabble on a fence wire and there was a splash among the weeds along the ditch. Across a small meadow trucks nosed by on the interstate, past the wide lot of a John Deere dealer a quarter mile away.

From the first time he'd ever driven, easing his mother's Impala out of the driveway at fourteen, headlights off and motor ticking, Randy had always found comfort behind the wheel of a car. Later, when he needed relief from the ministry, he slipped away to trace a wide loop through the countryside, out along the Mud Fork to the airport, looping past an old gravel pit a dozen miles south. Over time, the meadow became the place he ended up, black soil stretching endless in winter, the explosion of green through the first weeks of June. Whenever he got most tired of himself as a pastor, back-slapping and cajoling, he found relief in the cicadas fiddling madly along the ditchbank, the trucks that moved with indifference on a calm summer day.

On some level he must have known the meadow's attractions. Though uneven, the ground would yield to a bulldozer. After a rainstorm, water seldom stood. Even in summer the site was clearly visible from the interstate. At night he had begun dreaming of rosewood trim and charcoal carpeting, an office and classrooms, details of the church God had decided he should build. He marveled sometimes that he had even found the place — a forgotten meadow, the grassy lane — all part of the illusion that he was the one driving, when there had been Another Hand on the wheel all along.

Even then, Randy had been — at least for him — cautious. The ministry that he and Lee built had grown steadily, over eight years moving from the Moose Lodge to the Marine Building on Springfield, and eventually to the old Lamplighter Restaurant in the strip mall next to Kroger's. With two packed services on Sunday and another Wednesday night, with Lee's Women's Ministry and the Praise Team, their plates were full. So he had been surprised at the elders' eagerness — he only had to mention the idea and excitement did the rest. God moved through them in His various ways: Carl and Darlene Huber talked to the farmer who was willing to sell. Danny

Harmon's brother-in-law was an architect who drew up the plans. Mickey Ellrod, through his car agency, knew a banker, and in no time, a note had been signed. Greeley Myers — a prominent builder in town before the booze had taken over, sending him stumbling through Randy to Christ — agreed to supervise construction, and Randy would serve as contractor himself.

In the Explorer Randy felt his arms tighten as they wrapped around the wheel. He couldn't say he wasn't warned; Lee had walked with the Lord a lifetime and knew how congregations could be. She had been against renting space on campus when they lost the lease at the Lamplighter — a loss that was just more of God's handiwork, he'd been certain at the time. A third of the people, though, hadn't followed, and the ones who did began to drift away almost immediately, uncomfortable among the students and bars.

By that time, he had been too busy to listen, rushing back and forth to the building site, his nose pressed into a maze of blueprints. His plan had been to be at Campus Church only a few months until the new building was finished, but from the start, almost nothing went right. Chords from the Praise Team clanged back in the stark sanctuary. The bank grew uneasy as collections began to lag. Even the altar calls became a weekly battle, Randy struggling with his own strange sense that the Spirit floated high against the old church's vaulted ceiling, unwilling to come down and lend a hand. The work parties had already dwindled when Greeley Myers stopped returning his phone calls. As attendance dropped and accusations mounted, the elders began to hear something different in their prayers. And along about then the real ugliness began.

In the long-ago December that Randy had ridden the barrel, his scrapes and bruises healed easily and his coat, after a few washings, came clean. In the days before Christmas he watched on TV as the astronauts moved closer to the moon. By Christmas Eve they had moved into orbit, and he sat up in the living room to watch.

Except for the television, the house was dark. When his mom

had joined the Jehovah Witnesses a couple of years earlier, Christmas had been one of the casualties, the tree and presents disappearing down the same black hole that swallowed the family's birthdays. After studying her *Watchtower* at the kitchen table she had gone to bed early. Randy made a batch of Whip 'n Chill during a stretch of commercials and by ten-thirty it had set. He was lying in the recliner, spooning it out of the mixing bowl, when the astronauts began their broadcast from space.

There was a rattle at the door and Dike slipped in with a pretty girl in a shaggy sweater and short black skirt, slender ankles flashing as he guided her to the stairs. Randy barely looked their way. As the camera grazed the lunar surface the astronauts were pointing out landmarks: the Seas of Tranquility and Crises, countless craters with their steep, terraced sides. Across the country millions were watching, but the black and white cabin had an intimacy that Randy recognized, as if his own recliner were jammed into the capsule with theirs. The astronauts took turns reading from the Bible, which made him yawn, and with that the broadcast was done. A moment later Houston reported loss of signal, as the capsule moved around the back side of the moon.

A single telescope shot of the sky was left hanging on the screen. An eerie sort of emptiness spread out through the house. It floated through the living room and kitchen back toward his mother's bedroom, up to the unfinished half-attic where he and Dike had their beds. From the open stairway Randy could hear the pretty girl's voice as she pleaded, Dike's own murmur low and insistent, the rustling of fabric. Eventually they were quiet too.

A few minutes later, Dike was back down. "Hiya Squirt," he said, leaning above his chair.

Randy was wary but his brother seemed relaxed. "Moon stuff, huh? A lot of people say it's bullshit. They shoot movies so we think it's all real."

"It's real," Randy said. "They're just out of contact right now."

"You want contact?" Dike asked, and seized his wrist. Twisting effortlessly, he soon had Randy dangling above the recliner, stocking feet flailing, the mixing bowl clutched against his chest. Usually his brother liked to hold him there, helpless, but instead Dike just shook him a couple of times and let him go, distracted by the girl in the shaggy sweater as she came down the stairs.

"Hey, Squirt, this is Candy. Candy, say hi to my brother."

Randy shrank back, rubbing his arm, but Dike had the girl to bully now. When she tried to move past he blocked her, so that she stood for a moment before Randy, one hand drawn across the front of her shaggy sweater, the other pressed tight against her skirt. In the TV's gray moonlight Randy could see she was crying. When they were gone he turned back to the television and the last of the Whip 'n Chill at the bottom of the bowl.

It wasn't long after that winter night that Randy discovered music, wearing out the grooves of his records on the stereo, his fingers callused from the strings of his guitar. On a Grand Funk poster tacked to the eaves he found his models: Don straining shirtless behind his drum set, Mel on bass, while in the center there was always Mark, with his fierce Fu-Manchu mustache and leather arm band, a fist clenched high above the crowd. He recruited Donnie Faber to play guitar while they were still in junior high school, Stan Wertz on drums the summer after that, and for the next dozen years Randy was no different than Dike or anybody else. He used people he met for his pleasure, scarcely believing they had life beyond his own. By the time he was twenty the band had moved to Texas. They opened for Aerosmith at the Astrodome in January, and a month later, in Arlington, for Ratt. Randy still had the promo picture they'd shot for their album: Donnie in eye shadow and a woman's sheer blouse, Stan in a flowing kimono, Randy at the center in his fringed vest and choker, his sleek Sunburst hanging low on his hip. He looked pleased with himself, and why not, wrapped in a dream-come-true world of music and girls, doping, more music, more girls, until God — tired of tapping him on the shoulder — had finally reached out to whack him in the head.

On that Christmas Eve of the Apollo orbit, though, he was still unguided, following the astronauts until the local station signed off.

While he was sleeping they turned toward home. By late the next morning Randy was outside again, making his way east along the tracks.

He was grateful to the sober Witnesses with their distrust of human holidays; otherwise he might have been trapped inside that Christmas morning like the other kids. While they sat cross-legged in pajamas with their families, clapping for presents, he crunched along the cinders of the track bed, a pair of stained coveralls under his arm. He stopped at the trestle to pull them on. Even the highway beyond the woodlot had gone silent, as he slid down the slope to the barrel. Unlike Apollo, it was still orbiting, so he climbed in and pulled down the lid.

He was surprised at the ease with which he adjusted to weightlessness, back arching from the side of the barrel, his glove floating inches above his chest. At first there were the routines of space travel: he ran through checklists and calibrated instruments, reporting back to Houston through his fist. Below was the bright lunar surface, while in the distance the earth lay suspended, marked by its two halves of darkness and light. His reports remained crisply professional as he approached the horizon. There were a few last exchanges while Houston counted down the seconds, and all at once the signal was gone.

It was hard for Randy to believe that even the astronauts, with all their training, were really prepared for it: the utter silence on the far side of the moon. His heartbeat swelled to fill the emptiness and gradually subsided. The air in the capsule grew colder, seeping past the bunghole to where he floated alone.

In orbit, memory seemed like somebody's daydreams: his mother at the kitchen table with the *Watchtower*, the pages of his geography book fluttering as it sailed beneath the trestle, the pretty girl flushed and eager as Dike led her to the stairs. Afterwards, as she stood crying in the living room, he'd seen something else. Randy had found himself abruptly knowing, directly and without effort, *who the girl was*. It was a talent that would never, over a lifetime, desert him, his ability to see past that gathered impulse of bare legs and ankles, shaggy sweater and short black skirt, all the way to a deeper brightness that made up her core. Disappointment and shame were layered in too, but only lightly, just as Dike's plain meanness served mainly to reduce him, like bands of steel twisted tight around his heart.

Randy had never minded that they tricked him with the barrel. Even locked inside, he had traced the older boys moving careless along the railroad, caught the faint scent of creosote as it drifted above the tracks. He remembered his pride that they had been waiting when he got off the school bus, the hopefulness that kept him company in the weeds. He had felt the strange pooling pleasure that filled him — half dread and half distant recognition — when he realized they weren't coming back.

It wasn't just Christmas day, then, but every afternoon after that, through the rest of vacation and into the school year, that he returned to the barrel. Even after the astronauts were home Randy maintained his orbit, circling the moon again and again. For a time he still worked the checklists, did his calisthenics and filed his reports, but more and more there was only one thing he cared for: the waiting silence on the dark side of the moon.

Below him lay the hidden lunar surface. Above were all the stars that litter frank infinity, unmediated by chattered reassurance in his ears. It was a long way to go to feel satisfied, but settled in his small container, Randy did. It seemed a small price to pay for the thrill of being out there, for the opportunity to make acquaintance with his courage, for a trajectory that even then bore him safely through the shadows, toward the waiting signals from Mission Control.

At the edge of a meadow thirty years later, Randy sighed. The bulldozer, at least, had done its job, leveling the ground for the building, clearing the acre and a half of parking he'd been certain they'd need. The cement slab had been laid, so the outline of his church was clear enough to mock him, the black dirt around it grown over with weeds. Unlike his Savior, Randy wasn't a carpenter: the two walls he'd managed to frame were already separating, the lumber brown and sagging from the rain.

Part of it, he knew, was simple embarrassment. He had never planned to be back in his hometown in the first place, let alone nearly forty years old with a failing ministry, and barely a penny he and Lee could call their own. The verdict on the building project was in, filtering back from Four Square and Calvary, River of Life and Final Harvest, that Randy Overmeyer's only glory was himself. It was something he had heard so often over the years that he seldom bothered to disagree. There was little doubt God had given him an ego, but it wasn't just for strutting across the stage at the Astrodome in a feather boa and tight leather pants. It took ego too to step up as God's holy vessel, and let the healing Spirit flow like fire through his hands. People were glad for that confidence when they came to him, desperate for the new life made abundant in Jesus Christ, so it was just as well he had some left when they later turned ungrateful, losing track of the deeper truth of who they were. And everyone did, it seemed — himself no less than the others — which is why he'd fallen into that oldest of pastimes, trying to decide for God how things were going to be.

Clouds clumped serenely above the building site, while the crows gave up their squabble to sail low above the meadow, winging across the cornfield to the south. He couldn't pretend he wasn't baffled, but his only job was to be faithful, listening for whenever God cared to speak to him again. So Pastor Randy leaned forward above the steering wheel to listen carefully through the drone of trucks from the interstate, through the sound of the cicadas wild along the ditchbank, through the cornstalks as they waved and rustled, whenever the wind moved lightly past their leaves.

FOUR

The girl at the table was struggling. "At the lesion site we would expect relumination."

"Right," Mitchell said, "but are we talking folding or cavitation? It can't be both. Which is more likely the case?"

"Embryonic processes imply cavitation. Folding would indicate repair. If it's true regeneration, we wouldn't see repair."

"Okay, good. Nicole knows her neural development. What did you find in the mice? Was there any kind of outgrowth at all?"

When she shook her head, Mitchell looked around the room. "So what's going on here? Pin Shen, you want to weigh in? How about you, Daphne? Want to give us a hand, Prakash, or are you just holding up the wall?"

His research team was arrayed for its Thursday afternoon lab meeting, doctoral students and post-docs around the table, undergrads and lab techs at the edge of the room. Brian, his lab director, had been with him from the beginning. Charlie Bates had come in June from MIT. Nicole, with her army drab tee shirt and studded ears, sat across from him, coiled tightly in her chair.

"All right," he said, "Brian, it's up to you."

"Nicole has the gene cloned and sequenced. The construct has taken, because proteins are there. But there still isn't any real regeneration. In terms of mammals, we're back to square one."

Mitchell nodded. "Even taking into account Dr. Kirby's characteristic pessimism I think we have a verdict. Lazarus expresses, but it expresses in vain."

It was hard to know how long they might have wandered, mistaken. A decade's work dismissed, but that no longer mattered. What Mitchell assessed instead was his lab team. Separate clusters of awareness shimmered around him at the table. A pool of shared attention had found a place above their heads. That intelligence bound them was hardly surprising. Being smart, at their level, was taken for granted, along with the unforgiving coursework and years of apprenticeship, the undisguised ambition that had brought them to his lab. What distinguished him, it seemed, was simple *willingness*: that rare determination to stay the course and prevail. For a time attention still buoyed them, grid-like and alive, but he watched it slowly fade as distractions took over — boyfriends and dinner plans, daydreams, self-doubt — and one after another the rest dropped away.

"Okay," he said, "that's it for today. Prakash, talk to Brian before your next set of trials. There's something else we have in mind for you to do."

When he came out of his office an hour later Nicole was waiting.

"So what's the deal? Should I vary the growth factors or take another look at caudal modeling?"

"Neither. Lazarus is a dry hole. We're done with it. We're packing up the tents and moving on."

"Hey Mitch, we're talking my dissertation here. I'm finishing in May. I can't switch areas this late in the game."

"Fine," he told her, "you don't have to."

"Really?"

"Sure, forget about it. Forget the dissertation, too. Go teach high school chemistry. Run assays for American Cyanamid. Let somebody else stake out the new ground."

"But —"

"Look, either you're in or out. We want the results to be one way, and they go another. We think our model works, and it turns out it doesn't. So what do you do? What do you do if you really want to know?"

She knew what he was after but shook her head.

"Come on, Nicole. In or out. What we do is follow the data. We follow the data…"

"Where they lead," she finally said grudgingly.

"Close, but no cigar. We follow the data wher*ever* they lead. That's when you're doing real science. Anybody can do the fill work behind."

"But —"

"Listen, I've got to get going. Talk to Brian. We've got something else in the works."

"Come on, Mitch, I…"

"Got to go, got to go. Talk to Brian."

Ginny Weeks, his chief lab tech, called out as he came past her door. "Mitch, there's some kind of contamination in the incubators.

I had to shut them all down in 503."

"Talk to Brian," he said, moving faster. "Got to go, talk to Brian, got to go."

His own ability had never been in question. His willingness to stay the course wasn't really in doubt. More novel was the powerful feeling of inevitability that seemed to accompany this breakthrough, the clear sense of trajectory that bore him forward in his work. Their mistake with Lazarus as it turned out had been a simple one: too narrow a focus on the gene as autonomous agent. It was a common enough practice, given the glamor of the field, when what had become abruptly clear in recent days was *context*, the complex cell environment where the gene did its work.

Transitioning was never easy, especially at their level, but he and Brian had set in immediately on a new round of grant proposals, both hinting at and obscuring the direction they planned to go. With evening settling in, he felt a rush of exhilaration — by early spring they'd be back in the game.

His momentum by that time had borne him to the tree-lined quadrangle at the center of campus. At one end stood the colonial student union, yellow lights from its study rooms fanning out across the grass. A smell of moisture floated in from the prairie. An Asian couple pushed their baby in a stroller and a single airplane moved slowly across the sky.

"I've got to get out more," he thought, but was already moving on again, past the quad toward the Math Building, with its weathered bell tower set high above the trees.

Excitement joined the tingle along his spine. Genes weren't free agents but at every moment guided, embedded within a larger pattern extending far beyond the cell. A traffic light blinked with special resonance as he crossed into campustown. Tavern beer signs glowed red across the street. His own progress, too, felt oddly governed: a half block further on, he found himself slowing on the sidewalk. He came to a stop in front of the Art Co-op's broad display window, bound by drawing boards and easels until it was time to move on. The next place to snag him was the grubby Wonton, where students awaited takeout under dim fluorescent light. He gathered speed only to be held up at Sixth Street as if someone's hand were pressing lightly against his chest.

Campus Church stood before him in the twilight. A late model green Lumina idled at the curb. Its driver, in a Warrior ballcap, barely glanced at him, raising his hand from the wheel to look at his watch.

Mitchell moved past the Lumina's low fender to cross the street. Hurrying again, he came briskly past the church. In this way he was delivered, right on time, to the alleyway where Lee Overmeyer had just closed her eyes.

Absent was the little pastor himself, with his crown of hair and eager grin. Instead, she stood alone, a cardboard box awkwardly balanced on her hip. The fingertips of her free hand rested lightly against her temple and her head was bowed low, as if in pain.

"She's *praying*," he thought, and retreated, moving back against the ivy along the wall.

Even in the fading twilight, the old church cast a shadow. Where she stood within it, the streetlight barely reached her, reflecting off a silver chain that hung at her neck. It was a moment of devotion that felt likewise inevitable: all had been in place as he rounded the corner, the battered Toyota at her side and a streetlight's coolness, the soft skin along her eyelids and gentle curve of her cheek. The only thing missing was the sound of a motorcycle, the very motorcycle that suddenly accelerated, as if on cue, along Sixth Street, the growl of its engine reaching back to where they stood. She opened her eyes to pick him out against the wall.

"I'm Mitchell Chandler," he said. "We met the other day."

"I know who you are. What do you want?"

"My car." He pointed past her to the parking garage.

"You'll have to excuse me," she said, "I've got to go."

Even as she juggled the box he was too late to help her — first the back door and then the front swung open to block his way. He already knew rather than saw her flush of anger, the long legs dipping low as she slid behind the wheel. The Toyota's dome light spread over torn upholstery and her Bible on the console, a pastel hair brush that lay jammed between the seats. An interior lost as she slammed her door shut, put the car into gear and pulled quickly away.

His own car was a classic Triumph purchased while he was still at Stanford. He squeezed into the front seat and rattled down the ramp of the parking garage. He reached for NPR but the radio was silent, victim of a short only a few days before.

He had been a guest himself a half-dozen times on *All Things Considered*, twice more on *The News Hour* on PBS. His expert tone had been matter-of-fact, the appropriate register — nature was simply nature, once fully revealed. Likewise his brief loss of consciousness at the Health Center had a ready explanation. Fainting spells were common after even routine injections, products of a sudden drop in blood pressure that hindered perfusion to the brain.

Less readily dismissed as it turned out were its aftereffects, so powerful that it was life beforehand that now seemed cluttered and dreamlike, minus a powerful sense of recognition that had followed in its wake. He had stood at the nurses' station with his arm bared. He had come across the reception area, tugging at his sleeve. Those last seconds were important, because even then he must have seen it — the Health Center's clear *logic* as it resolved itself around him. A boy with a bad complexion bent over his calculator. A thin girl with a magazine sat slouched in her chair. The next thing he knew he was on his back looking up at the ceiling, the tile of the Health Center pressing cool through his shirt.

It was unclear exactly where the difference lay if not in himself. His surroundings were exactly the same. Exactly the same, except stripped of their camouflage; a richness and self-evidence lay exposed underneath. A larger set of data had come into view. There was a kind of knowing, not wholly deductive, that was already proving so effective in his work.

Genetic expression is inseparable from its context — that much had been clear almost immediately — a context that only deepened as he left campus behind. Prairie Grove was an old town, and beyond the University, unprosperous. Its dark streets seemed to pulse alive with an eerie sort of fullness, a fullness only poorly constrained by convention and courtesies, sump pumps and storm windows, a tidiness that fell away as he moved toward the tracks.

At a stop light on Lincoln he came across the green Lumina again, the same driver who had been on Sixth Street as he crossed to the church. This time the man shifted to stare at him. When the light changed, Mitchell turned onto misnamed University, accelerating past its fringe of filling stations and marginal storefronts, flashing portable signs that stood chained beside the curb.

He glided to rest beside another stoplight at Five Points where the highway left town. A half block north was the candy-pink facade of the Chief Cheehaha, a motel that had deteriorated with the neighborhood. The Warrior Autoplex showcased a row of used cars behind a sagging cable, with a faded McDonald's just beyond. A tense sort of distraction seemed to reach out across the intersection, rising up to pool against the wheelwells of his car.

From Five Points he accelerated past an abandoned car wash and the National Guard Armory. A low row of houses lay scattered along the railroad, just before a ragged patch of brushland where "town" lost its hold. Beneath a black sky his headlights rattled above the pavement. He went a first mile and then a second, finally picking out in the distance the scattered lights of Manor Lake.

Brick columns with a pair of coachlights marked the subdivision's entrance. A wide boulevard carried him past high-peaked houses with broad lawns and driveways. When he climbed out at his own house the golf course lay before him, the lake a tarnished silver behind the house. As in all else his momentum proved decisive, bearing him up the walk to his family inside.

He had a family? Apparently so: beneath the high ceiling of the Great Room, Kai had his school books spread out across the dinner table, TV blaring, while Nick pummeled a Game Boy with his thumbs. At twelve Kai still struggled with reading; he glanced guiltily Mitchell's way as he muted the sound. Two years younger, Nick didn't bother to look up. Max, their fat labrador, raised his head only to drop it, sprawled on his belly across the floor.

"Aunt Betsy called," Kai reported dutifully. "She wanted to know if you've talked to Grampa."

Mitchell nodded as he set down his briefcase. The oven was on and there were saucepans on the stove. From the back of the house came the steady metal shuffle of the Nordic Trak, Maureen skiing fiercely through her workout at the end of the hall.

With exaggerated care Kai bent to his textbook. He was the more sensitive of the two boys and the reason Maureen had postponed a return to her own position at Santa Clara — she hoped to shore up the reading with another semester's leave. Mitchell himself had met with teachers at the middle school. He had attended soccer games and advised on school projects, taped crayon drawings above his desk in Chapel Hill.

All of this when he must have known, on some level, the truth. Even so it had, at the edge of the Great Room, the quality of revelation: his sudden realization of how little he really cared for his sons. When they were babies there had been nothing to interest him; now that they were older, he disliked their shrill voices and pathetic weakness, the way their heads lolled on slender, fragile necks. Necks he could snap, in an instant, if he cared to, an awareness the boys shared as well. It echoed before him in the hunch of their shoulders, the press of their lips — some relic gene still endured to code caution whenever the adult male had ventured too near.

From the floor came the jangle of a dog collar. Fat Max had climbed to his feet and stood watching him, eyes glittering and fully alert.

In the back room the Nordic Trak stopped. Maureen joined them a moment later, her face damp and flushed, a short white towel draped across her shoulders.

"Betsy called. She wanted to make sure you were keeping up with your dad."

"I know. Kai told me."

"Mother Betsy," she said sarcastically, toweling her arms as she walked to the kitchen. "Always keeping track of the brood."

Mitchell stood quietly beside his briefcase. Within a steadily deepening moment, only two questions seemed salient: who was this thin woman in leotards and why did she care?

The pathways involved in our sense of smell had long been articulated, a binding of ambient molecules to receptors in the nose. Pheromone release in mammals is closely linked with ovulation and across the room Max raised his muzzle in the air. Amidst the lush canine environment where Mitchell joined him — orange rinds and paper towels in the trash can, flesh browning in the oven and poorly-wiped boy — they tracked her together, man and dog. Maureen checked the stove, turning off the burner beneath a pan. She came past them on her way back to shower, a heavy spore of estrus trailing behind her down the hall.

Max was less indifferent than speechless; subordinate and a dog — it was no affair of his how the female was used. For better or worse, his fate had been entrusted to this family, with their sluggish reflexes and brittle, busy minds. Slack-faced, Kai tracked the Simpsons above his textbook. Nick grunted in disappointment and tried the game again. Max's eyes had never left Mitchell: at least the tall one was finally awake.

The tall one was awake and not without resources. Electric current flowed from power plant to wall plug, tamed for ready service through the house. Gas inched with silent pressure beneath their feet. Food materialized as if from nowhere in a dog dish; by that same hand the door was opened that led to Outside.

Access to adjacent pools of awareness no longer seemed so unusual. Harder for Mitchell to gauge, still, was which were his own thoughts, and which ones belonged somewhere else.

Max's stance, on the other hand, was more primal: only within a merged consciousness could Mitchell's forebrain lend it words. The tall one knew the genome and a few of its secrets. He had learned how to pay attention and not turn away. By these wiles and many others he fashioned the small band's protection, space for the unhappy woman, the two weak ones, a dog. A dog whose wordlessness, in the end, hardly mattered because what stalked them had nothing to say. It was older than they were and would easily outlast them. It had no interest in being appeased. It watched even then from the fields around the golf course, hungry and unimpressed, crouching quietly in the darkness beyond the ring.

FIVE

A four-letter word for 'Great Lake' was 'Erie,' while 'in the present' was undoubtedly 'today.' Pencil in hand, Vera Eller bent close above her crossword. One of the clues that still stumped her was 'Brazilian resort city,' five spaces across. She had gained two letters with 'haddock,' but fish clues were never her specialty and either one could have easily been wrong.

Vera straightened at the counter. The garbage man had come at dawn while she was measuring coffee, and now the sun spilled through her wide kitchen window. An early morning breeze floated in past the door. When she looked at the clock it wasn't quite seven, so she hoped to have a little time before the phone began to ring.

After all their years of faithful Sundays Vera didn't see why she couldn't play hooky now and then. By eight o'clock that Monday morning, though, the Campus Church people would be calling, wanting to know if she or Walter had been sick. They hadn't been, of course; Walter missed the service because he'd gone to the farm — what little was left of his family's old homestead in Indiana — while she stayed home to meet their granddaughter when she came over from the University. It was hard to imagine choosing one of Harry Applebee's plodding sermons over being in the basement with Maddie, folding clothes and laughing at her silly stories. For that matter, it was hard to imagine picking the dreary old church at all, especially over her bright, sunny kitchen. Walter's people had been the churchgoers, not hers; even after fifty years at Campus, it was hard to imagine any place she'd rather be than on her kitchen stool beside the microwave, working puzzles while the world came alive.

Her recipe box was next to the telephone and grudgingly she

pulled it over. Walter had run into Austin Chandler out at Cooke-Davis a few days earlier, and when he got home he said the old dean looked depressed. That was hardly a concern to Vera: Austin Chandler had always been, in her experience, a thoroughly disagreeable man. Still, Walter was determined to have him down later in the week for coffee, which meant some kind of dessert she had to come up with by then.

Even on such a pretty morning the thought of Austin Chandler could make her frown. Short-tempered and gruff, he hadn't really fit in with the other Ag men, who for the most part tried their best to get along. It had taken him down a peg when he lost out on the Vice-Provost's position but that just meant he stayed in the dean's office, tormenting Walter and the other men until the end of their careers. He was lucky there were people like Walter, good-hearted to a fault, to keep an eye on him. He wouldn't get a Hostess Twinkie if it was left up to her.

She listened for Walter in the back of the house. There were mornings she let him sleep a while, sometimes as late as seven-thirty. Even at that, she was forever rousting him from the sofa or rocker — he wasn't going to be one of those old people who slept their lives away. She got them out walking and kept a close eye on their diets: breakfast was a bowl of Grapenuts, lunch a half sandwich and small bowl of fruit. She couldn't help thinking the puzzles were a help, too, against the Alzheimer's. It would be a shame to end up like that Mrs. Murray, who'd had both the kids in grade school. Or poor Barney Washburn either, who had spent his last years at Harmony House, tied by a rope to his bed. It never hurt to find an edge if you could — it was amazing how all their friends had gone to pot.

Vera still found herself resisting as she pondered her desserts. A piece of cantaloupe would be easy enough: Austin Chandler looked like he could use a little fruit. A scoop of frozen yogurt with a sugar cookie was a possibility too. There was a recipe from the *Courier* that she pulled out to scan quickly, a pie with low-cal topping and a graham-cracker crust. It was more than she cared to do, but she had berries in the freezer. If she ran down to the basement she could see if there were enough.

On the way to the stairs she looked out to see Lacey Butler's little wire-haired terrier Jasper coming into their yard. He was followed a moment later by Lacey in her Warrior windbreaker and a ragged pair of shorts, a rolled-up newspaper in her hand. The dog trotted a few steps before sitting down to wait for her, and she just got the paper raised when he trotted off again. Vera watched as he made a wide circle around their lawn and back across the driveway, his owner hobbling painfully behind.

Vera listened for movement from the back of the house but Walter still hadn't stirred and she slipped out to their porch. Fat squirrels jumped from the phone wire to the garage roof. A blue jay swept low across the Tolleys' yard to settle high in Lacey's hemlock. That must have been where it had its nest because Lacey was hard at work with her garden hose, spraying down the pavement beneath the tree.

Vera had always loved their neighborhood, from the time Walter was hired onto the faculty and they could finally afford a house. The neighbors were working people, which made it more comfortable, and they had picked one of the new ones on Washington where the back yards ran together, which made it nice when their families were young. By this time on a week day the kids would have been outside already, running back and forth across the grass. Ted Butler and Harold Tolley would have been strolling to their pickups, toolbelts in hand, while in the bedroom Walter straightened his tie.

Things had changed, of course, especially now that the Tolleys were gone and Helen Meade had moved to Colorado to be closer to her son. The new woman in the Tolleys' house didn't care to neighbor, putting in a row of oleanders clearly intended as a hedge. Vera hesitated at the edge of her driveway. She scanned the drawn curtains in the Tolleys' bedroom, finally slipping between the bushes to hurry across the grass.

"Don't look," Lacey said, when she'd joined her beneath the hemlock. Vera didn't, keeping her eyes low as she stepped across the hose. After they had studied the pavement a while Lacey nodded toward the street. "Don't turn too quick. Make it seem natural. Is that a new briefcase he's got?"

The morning sun was high enough to create a glare from the Tolleys' garage roof, and Vera squinted through it to locate their new neighbor, Mr. Williams. He was across the street in his driveway, unlocking the door to his car.

"I can't tell," she said, eyes tearing.

"Does it hang from his shoulder?"

"No, it's more like a little suitcase with handles."

Lacey nodded with satisfaction. "It's new, then. That's what I thought. The old one he carried with a strap."

Vera rubbed her eyes. Just before he climbed into the driver's seat, the Williams man straightened, smiling as he waved across the street. Vera made a small wave in return, her hand low at her side.

"That's about right," Lacey said bitterly, snapping at the hose. "They've been here all of a month and he already has a new briefcase. You would have thought the old one was plenty good enough."

Vera had been worried when the Williams bought the Manner house — Lacey had always been so dead set against colored people coming in. For so long in Prairie Grove it had hardly been an issue, with the colored people settled north of University, while the white people lived to the south. Almost overnight, though, all of that changed. The first couple had bought in on Webber, three blocks east, followed by a policeman and his family on Anderson, and now the Williams right across the street.

For her part Vera hadn't thought much about it, because white families were moving in too, more and more as the older people died away. She liked seeing children in the neighborhood again, enjoyed the bikes and wading pools scattered out across the lawns. Walter had been over a dozen times at least to loan a ladder or wheelbarrow, help Mr. Williams rescue a rose bush that the Manners had almost lost.

As she watered Lacey inched closer to Jasper, the dog darting in and out at the edge of the spray. He was good company, Vera supposed, even little and ugly as he was, with coarse hair and a springy sort of mustache that covered his mouth. The mustache reminded her of the bangs that Lacey's daughter Lindy had worn back in high school, except on Lindy they'd been cute, while Jasper's glistened with slobber and half-chewed flecks of food. He jingled his way over to Vera, managing to plant his soggy whiskers against her ankle before she kicked him away.

Lacey shook her head. "He's going to put me in the poorhouse yet. Animal Control found him up on campus again, this time in one of the labs. I'll never understand it if I live a hundred years. I beat that dog, I beat that dog and I beat that dog, and he still runs away!"

Hose in hand, Lacey inched closer. When she lunged Jasper dodged nimbly, settling in again just beyond her reach.

It bothered Vera to see her old friend moving with such difficulty around the driveway, her joints swollen and belly bloated, the veins on her legs like little blue sausages tucked under her skin. The arthritis was what wore at her most — the only time she had ever been free of it had been a few years earlier when she'd gotten involved with that Randy Overmeyer who rented space at the church. In those days he was still at the Marine Building and Lacey had been out there almost every other night.

For a while it had been awkward for the neighbors. The Tolleys weren't church people to begin with and she and Walter were loyal to Campus, which wasn't all that demanding, if truth be told. The first thing they knew, Lacey had a Bible and was carrying on about the Holy Spirit, trying to get them to join her in prayer.

"Oh, I suppose we *could*," Mary Tolley said when Lacey trapped them on the Tolleys' back porch one evening, but overall it kind of put a damper on things, those pretty summer nights when they liked to sit out and talk. She and the Tolleys began avoiding their backyards after supper. Whenever Lacey cornered Vera there was an urgent look in her eyes. She wanted them to understand what had happened to her, how that little Randy had freed her from the pain.

And really, thinking back, it *had* been miraculous — all of them thought so. As the swelling in her joints went down Lacey began to walk easier, and before long was sleeping through the night. She threw away her pain pills and had even started bowling again, in a Christian league over at Western Lanes. The whole thing must have lasted six months or so before the arthritis came back strong as ever, along with the high blood pressure and varicose veins. That was the last they saw of the Bible. They didn't hear anything more about all Jesus could do for them or the plan that He had for their lives.

Lacey turned off the water, straightening with difficulty. She squinted at the Williams house across the street. "There was a white couple that visited last night. With a little boy. They were there until almost eleven."

Vera nodded.

"That's late on a school night."

"Oh yes," Vera said, "I suppose it is. Children go to school so early anymore."

"Did you see what they put in out back, under the Manners' oak tree? A gazebo! I couldn't believe it when I saw that. What are they going to do with a darn gazebo?"

"Well," Vera said, "I imagine they'll sit in it. I imagine they'll sit in it like anybody else."

Lacey threw the hose angrily to the ground. "You go ahead, Vera, and defend them. What do you care who moves in across the street? You and Walter will be out at Cooke-Davis before long and it won't matter. The only one stuck here is me."

"Oh Lacey," Vera said hurriedly, "we're not going anywhere. Not for a long time anyway. Maddie's only a junior at the University, and then her brother might come down. I don't want to give up my house!"

As convincing as she tried to sound, Vera felt her face grow warm. She was embarrassed too because Lacey had started crying, like she did so often anymore. It was hard on her, a widow woman who had gotten crosswise with her children — she stopped crying long enough to make another lunge for Jasper and to the surprise of all three caught his collar with her hand. She wiped across her eyes with her wrist.

"Now that I've got him I'd better get inside. I need to make a trip to the grocery store and then I've got a Booster Club meeting at noon."

"My goodness," Vera said, "I hope the Warriors can start doing better. It gets so tiresome every week to see them lose."

Blinking fiercely, Lacey shook her head. "Fifty-five to nothing isn't a loss, it's a slaughter. It's an embarrassment. And Louisville was hardly a powerhouse. Their RPI rating is even lower than ours!"

"Okay, I'll talk to you later," Vera said, and after a quick check of the Tolleys' windows hurried back across the lawn.

Vera didn't know how Lacey had found out they were on the list at the retirement village, but really, she supposed, it stood to reason: Cooke-Davis was where so many of the University people ended up. If Walter had had his way, they would be out there already, but so far she had been able to resist. She couldn't really imagine leaving their neighborhood on Washington Street, especially when she had her big freezer and pretty south window, and when the dew in the early mornings glistened so brightly on the grass.

She stood another minute on the porch looking out across the new woman's oleanders. Sometimes she couldn't quite picture Lacey jumping and shouting with the rest of the Spirit Rising people, waving her hands and rolling on the floor, but maybe if Campus Church were a little more lively they wouldn't be petering out. Still, it could have been worse. Her sister Jeanette had married into Church of the Brethren with all that foot-washing, and Vera counted herself lucky to have landed where she did.

She listened to see if Walter was stirring, but he wasn't — he had been up working on Jack Heineke's eulogy half the night. People counted on him to do a good send-off: he'd labored over Reldon Kemp's writeup for the archives for almost a month. She ran through the recipe from the *Courier*. She supposed the old dean could have his pie. Walter liked a piece of pie when he could get it and there was no use in punishing him, too.

By that time, at least, her day was taking shape. If she got the pie made she wanted to go by the hospital to see Tess Rohovec. On the way home, they could visit Lydie Bains, whose faucet was leaking

— she would make sure Walter brought along his tools. Then there was the pan of brownies she had baked for the Williams; she'd been waiting to take them over as soon as Lacey went out.

With the morning slipping away Vera turned a final time to her crosswords. She could always ask Walter, who had the advantage with his education, but in the end, she liked to solve them on her own. The answers were in the back, which helped, and Vera flipped back and forth through the pages, cheerfully filling in the blanks. By the end of the week she'd have another book done.

She had just made it to the basement stairs when the phone began to ring — if it was barely seven-thirty, it had to be Becky Hartzel. She would have to hurry if she was going to get Walter roused and fed, because after Becky there would be the Fullers and Mrs. Huntsberger, Sally Springer and Jenny Goran, all calling to make sure she and Walter walked the earth. As she reached for the phone, Vera sighed. That was one thing she had learned about church a long time ago: generally it was a whole lot easier just to go.

SIX

"The most difficult thing, many times, is simply to let go and let existence be. The breath we are taking, so essential to us now, will soon be gone. Another will take its place. It's remarkable, really, to think of all the breaths we have taken in a lifetime, each one so vital and precious, each giving way to the next."

His legs folded in front of him, his knees stiff and jutting beneath his elbows, Austin Chandler studied the small circle of his Senses Alive! classmates. The air conditioning had been turned off for the year so the Campus Church parlor was warm and airless. The soft wrinkles on Libby McNeil's face glistened as she sat across from him with her eyes closed, dutifully following their young instructor's directions as to what to consider next.

"Often," the boy was saying, "we pass through long periods of relative numbness, barely aware that we're alive. Instead, there's a web of stories that we are constantly revising, hour after hour through the day. Despite our best efforts we remain unconvinced, so we continue to defend and justify, justify and defend, while the breath that sustains us comes and goes. Let us move awareness to our hearts, so steady and faithful, as they beat right now in our chests."

He had been surprised when Libby called him, in the middle of August, to see how he was doing. He was wary at first, but flattered — he'd forgotten that he might have some resale value once Edie was gone. Libby wasn't the most attractive woman and something of a know-it-all, but a little exercise, which was how she described the class to him, was something he could use. He had found himself nervous that first day as he showered: it was his first time out with a woman other than Edie in almost sixty years.

Libby hadn't bothered to look nice for him, dressed in an old sweatshirt and pair of men's pants when they met outside the church. He tried, out of duty, to be attentive, sitting nearby as their teacher, a Swiss boy, explained the class. The boy asked them to examine their relationship with the floor and the pleasure in seeing, but what Austin Chandler found himself considering as he sat among the women were his advantages. He was tall and not entirely unpresentable; he was mobile and had all his marbles; most importantly he was still alive and a man.

These were valuable assets, especially with so many of his colleagues dropped in the harness. The next week it was Olive Giesseking who called to see if he was coming to class. The third week it was Billie Morrison, and the week after that Mary Kerwin. It didn't take quite that long for him to realize he was just the latest of their projects, that they were keeping an eye on him because Edie had been their friend.

As they sat in the circle he studied Libby, her gray hair sticking out like cobwebs beneath a faded baseball cap. From Libby he moved on to Olive, the widow of old Giesseking in Chemistry, who had done so much of the early work on polymers in the years after the war. Billie Morrison had shed her husband too, and Marge Cobble might as well have: he had seen old Cobble at the Warrior Pioneers banquet in March, where his stroke had left him staggering between the tables like a drunken mule. Sheila Williams kept herself feminine, at least, with a new hairstyle and lipstick, a crisp blouse and pressed lavender slacks. She sat directly across from him with her eyes closed and a "People Are Not Mascots" button pinned to her chest.

He came at last to their young instructor, Stefan, who looked back at him with interest. Austin Chandler felt a flood of irritation: their eyes were supposed to be closed! For the hundredth time he took the boy's measure, assaying the thin chest and mild asexuality, the clear foreignness and shaved, bony head. Stefan, for his part, considered him impassively, sandals to one side on the carpet, a single vein bulging as it traced the narrow bicep of his arm.

Austin Chandler shifted with difficulty, chest and belly damp beneath his sweatshirt. The damn church and its endless causes — he could hardly see how turning on an air conditioner meant the end of the world. Across from him Stefan had closed his eyes.

"Some of us may, at this time, be experiencing warmth. Perhaps we are uncomfortable. But what exactly is this discomfort we're feeling? What exactly is this thing we're so eager to avoid? Perhaps we feel the layer of warm air as it rests against our bodies. Perhaps we sense perspiration on the surface of our skin. This, we might think, is heat. And, over time, other sensations take their turn. This is hunger, we might say, or this is thirst. This is fear. This is loneliness. These too are aspects of our experience. Perhaps they can be of interest as well."

Austin Chandler snorted. "I imagine I know what being hot feels like after all my time overseas. I can remember what poor feels like too, and hungry. I bet a lot of us sitting here do!"

He looked around the circle for approval, seeking Libby first, then Billie Morrison and Olive Giesseking, sliding from Sheila Williams to the boy. Without exception, they simply looked back at him, their faces expressionless, while his voice hung aggrieved in the air. One by one they closed their eyes again, joining the Swiss boy as he considered the heat. This is ridiculous, he thought, but when he closed his eyes, it was his own ridiculousness that rose up to greet him, bumping and clamoring behind his forehead. He was relieved when the boy took over again, ushering them from the heat to the scattered sounds of campus, to the shadows of tree branches as they played across the floor. The afternoon settled back in around them, blissfully freed from the echo of his voice.

Their activities weren't much exercise really, and it was hardly an idea strong enough to build a group around, but Austin Chandler couldn't help noticing that he felt a certain buoyancy on evenings after class. That night, in his kitchen, he studied the deep red of a tomato on his cutting board, felt the resistance of its skin as it parted beneath the knife. The head of lettuce gave off a crack when he broke it between his hands. His steak sizzled smartly in the frying pan, dipping heavy against his fork when he swung it to a plate. When the timer on the microwave began to beep he noticed something that surprised him: the sound of his own humming as he stirred gravy in the pan.

That afternoon in class they had passed a wooden cylinder from hand to hand around the circle. He had sat on the parlor floor and experienced heat. At the kitchen table he didn't need the Swiss boy to guide him: there was the speckled sting where hot grease had spattered his fingers, the grains of salt tumbling like tiny dice across the steak. His first bite rested on his tongue, alien and unsettling, and the grind of his molars brought a sharp taste of blood.

It was the kind of thing he wasn't sure the churchwomen really followed, the boy's idea of facing each new moment as it came. They paid attention in class and did what they were told to, but as soon as class ended they were back gabbing about their families, all their different projects in the community and at church. They didn't know how to bear down on one thing and do it fully, one of the differences between a woman and a man.

Austin Chandler considered the lettuce as it glistened in front of him, the forkful of potato that clumped starchy in his mouth. As he had moved around the kitchen he couldn't help thinking back to his foreign work, his three months on the Sierra Leone program, and the rice project in the Philippines after that. There had been a world to feed and the money to do it, but what he found himself remembering was his tiny bungalow at Njala, where he had stood to fix dinner after the workday was done. He had *known* himself there in the same way he had recognized himself at work in the dean's office, his solid feeling of self-sufficiency as he went about his tasks. He hadn't needed any church class to locate his senses: he could still hear the secretaries' typewriters as they clattered outside his office, feel his own weight and presence as he walked down the hall. In Njala he had picked out the scent of rain as it moved in from the seacoast, heard the sound of thunder rolling low above the trees.

There were other things, almost certainly, that he thought about, one of them old Heineke's obituary that he'd seen in the *Courier*. He might have considered Edie and her fragility, the reason he'd left foreign work behind. The Warriors were a concern like always — they were going to have to decide if they wanted a top level program, or were content with the second division year after year.

He couldn't say where else his mind might have wandered, because it was only when it came back that he saw what had happened. Someone had eaten his steak. Stripped clean, its bone lay beside the mauled skin of his potato. The lettuce and tomato were gone. His hand guided a crust of bread clenched between thumb and forefinger, skillfully tracing a last smear of grease across the plate.

Austin Chandler wiped his hands and sat back at the table. It was what the Swiss boy always tried to tell them: the hardest task a person faced was to stay fully in the present. An overstatement, almost certainly — precision was hardly the boy's strong point — but still there was truth in what he said. He brought himself to standing, which was how the boy liked to say it. Wetness slid across his hands as he washed dishes in the sink. Outside the kitchen window, evening was deepening — the whole thing was a little spooky, if you really tried to do it — as Edie's gingham curtains lifted lightly in the breeze.

His dinner wasn't over, though, he was only arriving at the best part: a half-gallon of ice cream he'd picked up driving home after class. The feeling of buoyancy returned as he moved to the freezer, where a cloud of vapor floated out to steam his glasses. There was the carton's pleasant heft as he lifted it, the tingle on his fingertips as heat drained away. He used one of Edie's old wooden stirring spoons to heap his bowl high. At the kitchen table he came back to sitting and brought the first spoonful to his lips.

He closed his eyes as he took the first bite. The ice cream felt like a pocket of sweetness at the center of his being, especially set against the throb beneath his breast bone, the steady ache of arthritis in his knees. He sat with his head down and spoon hand in neutral, feeling the smooth glide of vanilla as it spread across his tongue.

He had always been a man who did his homework — he'd had no choice if he wanted to keep up. Nothing had come easily like it did for Mitchell, who'd had a running start to begin with and made the most of it later on. He had hoped he might see a little more of him once he was at the University, but a man at that level couldn't waste time sipping coffee with his dad. Not when the governor himself came down to recruit him and the University had finally decided to open up its wallet and pay him what he asked. LazTec alone had made him a millionaire, a far cry from the kind of money any Ag man would ever see.

Austin Chandler took another bite of ice cream, the kind of thing he finally had time to enjoy. As a boy he hadn't been able to afford it, and as a man there had been his family and career. Now and then he'd even made ice cream himself, cranking up the freezer on a long summer evening. It was something the children had liked, Mitchell and the twins; the grandchildren too, when Edie was alive. A damned nuisance, really, with the rock salt and ice, and thinking back, he felt a flush of embarrassment. He didn't imagine Mitchell spent his evenings spinning the crank on an ice cream freezer, not when so many new advances were being made in his field.

The dairy boys had pretty much worked things out on the commercial end by that time anyway, fine-tuning the milk fat and emulsifiers, ensuring the same smooth consistency batch after batch. They had figured out ice cream but raised hell about their pasturing program, blind to how the industry had changed. It was the same thing when he took on the experimental stations a couple of years later. The University had never minded having someone close at hand when it was time to play hardball, somebody willing to take off the gloves when push came to shove.

Plainspokenness was his style and people got used to it. They hadn't known what to make of him when he first joined the Dean's Council — it was a different class of men there than you met at the Ag College, quick on their feet and frank in their ambitions, men like Peltason from Liberal Arts with his horn-rimmed glasses and Neumann from Commerce with his dry, fussy ways. He could still remember the small smiles they liked to exchange when he spoke at the Council, the sound of their laughter afterwards as they strolled down the hall.

Mitchell had more polish, which helped. He knew how to cut his losses when it was time to move on. He had the right wife for advancement too, which made a difference — a woman didn't have to be a professor like Maureen necessarily, which brought its own problems, but even Vera Eller could put on a simple department party. The few times he'd tried one himself Edie was collapsed in tears before she had dinner in the oven, and he was on the phone asking everyone not to come. That only has to happen a time or two before the higherups begin to wonder, and they start looking past you to the next man in line.

Poor Edie wasn't cut out to be an administrator's wife — getting dressed and through the day was challenge enough. And then there was Geoff with his troubles as a teenager: by that time he had fallen in with Randy Overmeyer and his crowd of ruffians, the Darryl Chapel boys from over by the tracks. Their break-in at the liquor store had hit the *Courier* the same spring he'd gone up for Vice Provost, when it was all he could do to keep the boy out of jail. Even at that, Geoff might still have amounted to something. Instead, he hung around Prairie Grove another year, drifting in and out of trouble, until he finally ran off on his motorbike and broke his mother's heart.

So much, it seemed, had the power to gall him — the Vice Provost job and his thankless years in the dean's office, Edie's unsuitability and Geoff's damnedable wildness — resentments so profound that the Swiss boy's voice had a hard time even reaching him, with its small reminder of the moment at hand. Gradually, though, under that foreign urging, Austin Chandler did make it back to the kitchen table. He had his bowl in front of him and wooden spoon in hand. He was even alone, like he'd so often imagined, but when he looked down, all the ice cream was gone.

SEVEN

Lee was at her desk when she heard someone in the parlor. The creaking came close and then retreated, a short time later came closer again. She pulled open the door to find Harry Applebee, the Campus Church preacher, standing tentatively outside.

"Oh, hello, Mrs. Overmeyer. I wasn't sure anyone was here. I hope I'm not bothering you."

"It's no more bother now than any other time, Reverend Applebee. We're always busy with our work."

"Yes, of course. I won't be long."

"My husband spoke to Walter Eller of the liaison committee. We received assurances our rent could wait another month."

"Ah, the rent. That is a problem. I'm glad you're in touch with Mr. Eller." He moved his gaze fondly around the room. "Before the remodeling this was my office, you know. I composed many a sermon in this room. You might like to open the window, by the way. Sometimes it helps to get a little air."

Applebee sported corduroy pants and a worn shirt with a necktie, while Lee was in heels and a rose-colored suit, part of the busy corporate executive style Randy favored for the ministry. They looked together at the closed office window, with its hint of daylight beyond thick amber glass.

"I remember a breeze that often came up in the afternoon. It was quite a temptation, especially with the Karmelkorn shop just down the block." He chuckled. As Lee looked at him without comment, his smile began to fade.

"The rent is a problem, of course, but at the moment there's a more immediate issue. As you know, we've agreed that each congregation will remove its worship materials from the sanctuary after services."

"I saw the men breaking down the equipment last night. I'm sure all our literature was put away."

"Oh yes, and in general, you've been quite cooperative. The problem lies more in the cross."

"The cross," she repeated.

"The cross behind the pulpit. I've discussed this with your husband any number of times. After the service you need to move it to the choir room. We had a funeral service yesterday and it was quite upsetting for the family."

Lee felt the flush of anger as it rose to her cheeks. "The family was upset to see a cross."

"Well, yes, as a matter of fact they were. It's problematical for a number of our members. Reasons vary, of course, although I suspect the old Calvinist proscription against icons is one. And then there's the Puritan strain in our faith, with its distrust of adornment of any kind. Rather a stern tradition, really, for all the liberal leanings of the modern church. It's interesting how the issue has played out. I remember my first pulpit, right after seminary —"

"If not in a church," Lee interrupted, "then where does the cross have its place? Maybe the family could consider what it stands for, and the suffering that Jesus endured."

Applebee tried a smile. "The service was for Dr. Heineke, who was in the Agronomy Department for many years. He did some work for the AID in Sierra Leone, I believe. Wasn't that where your family served its mission?

"Ghana," Lee replied, "in the Ashanti region. My father there almost twenty years." Her face burned but her voice had grown cold. "I don't remember that the cross was ever an icon for him, Reverend Applebee. I don't think he saw it as adornment. It was a daily reminder of a Savior who loves him, who suffered and died so that he would have eternal life."

"Just so," Applebee said, coloring too. "There's certainly that perspective."

"His blood was shed for you, for me, and for all of us, whether we accept it or not. If that makes people uncomfortable, so be it. Some may get so uncomfortable they'll decide to change their lives."

Applebee was discomfited, but not by her faith: Lee knew there was little chance her words could ever reach him. She had grown accustomed, too, to the effect that she had on men, their quick deflation in the coolness of her gaze. The preacher, though, simply looked back at her. He looked back at her, and not without kindness, as campustown pressed in at the amber window, and she fought a familiar rising tightness in her throat.

"I'm sorry, Mrs. Overmeyer, but I must insist. A regular service would be one thing, but a funeral demands that I respect the family's wishes."

"Fine," she said. "I'll move it right away."

"I'd be happy to lend a hand, of course. It looks to be quite substantial. Some men from the congregation are coming by later to work on the gutters. Perhaps if we all pitched in…"

"Don't trouble yourselves. I can do it."

"It would be no trouble at all, Mrs. Overmeyer. Why don't we —"

"I said I'd take care of it, Reverend Applebee. Now if you'll excuse me, I still have my work."

"Yes, of course," he said. "There has been considerable adjustment for both congregations. We appreciate your sensitivity to our needs."

Almost eight feet tall, with rough rope looped tightly around its beams, the cross was the handiwork of Larry Hamm, a Prairie Grove fireman Randy brought to Christ five years earlier. It had dominated the stage at the Lamplighter but in the Campus Church sanctuary seemed oddly diminished, dwarfed beneath high walls and a distant arched ceiling. Even so, it towered above her as Lee came past the pulpit. She had seen the men handle it after services, so she knew what to do: reaching high on tiptoe, she wrapped her arms around the base. She rocked it toward her so it settled on her shoulder. She staggered but after a moment found balance, and began backing toward the edge of the stage.

Jesus had climbed with his cross to Calvary, weakened and stumbling, the Son of God mocked and taunted by the crowd. Her own journey, in contrast, was easy: Larry had made sure to balance the crossbeams carefully, the weight of the wood resting on a pair of casters in the base. Her heels snagged as they sank into the carpet and the fabric of her skirt bound her legs, but Lee felt reassured by the load on her shoulder, the wood that pressed rough against her cheek. She bumped down three steps to the floor of the sanctuary, dipping low to negotiate the entrance to the choir room. Once past the door, she tipped the cross upright, its weight settling back on its base.

The choir room was for the choir in name only, serving more as a large storage closet for the two congregations. Campus Church's few extra hymnals had been pushed to one side by the Praise Team's sound system and the huge computer console that barely fit through the door. Perspiring from her exertion, Lee let the door close behind her. There was a folding chair squeezed in beside the console, and with the cross safely stowed, she sat down to rest.

The choir room was narrow and windowless. Stacked in boxes were the fifty thousand studio portraits of her and Randy that he'd had printed on postcards, with a map to the new church on the back. Lee rubbed her temples as she sat quietly among them. The darkness felt cool and welcoming, and for a time she almost forgot where she was. Almost forgot that God's work lay before her unfinished — several times she tried to rouse herself before she was finally successful and, climbing to her feet, left the choir room behind.

Halfway across the sanctuary she heard someone call her name. When she turned to find a large woman in one of the pews, Lee felt her heart sink.

"Barbara," she said, "you startled me."

"Aren't we having Prayer Circle today?"

Lee brushed across her skirt as if to straighten it, squaring her shoulders as she located a smile. "If it's Thursday morning then we're having Women's Prayer Circle. Is it already ten o'clock?"

"Almost ten-thirty. I'm sorry I was late. Parking is so hard to find up on campus."

"Well, you're here now, and that's what counts. God bless you."

"God bless you too, Lee. May He always bless and keep you in his sight."

Lee slipped in beside her. "Maybe we can just meet out here where it's cooler. Would that be all right?"

Barbara moved heavily along the pew to make room. For all the warmth of the day, she was dressed in a velvet dress with a wide lace collar, and a bulky gold broach on her breast. Lee registered against her will the woman's heavy lips and unflattering hair style, the purple scars from long-ago acne that lay along her neck.

"We may as well get started," she said. "Is there someone you want us to remember?"

"I'd like to pray for my mother who had tests again this week. And my neighbor Cheryl, whose husband is drinking. I pray that God will work His grace on their lives."

"Jesus," Lee prayed, "Jesus, Jesus. Please cleanse us and make us holy in Your name."

"Jesus, " Barbara echoed, "Loving Savior. Know that You're always in our hearts."

Lee closed her eyes and raised her hand. "All-powerful and living God, extend Your peace to Barbara's mother, who has always lived in accordance with Your will. Be with Cheryl, who suffers from another's sinfulness. Guide her to find comfort in Your name."

"Jesus," Barbara murmured, "help us know You. Be with us in Your most perfect love."

By that time, their two prayers had intermingled under murmurs of "Jesus, Jesus" that rose around them. The Women's Prayer Circle had occasionally possessed, under Lee's leadership, a surprising power, as women shouted out in joy or broke down in tears. In spite of herself she felt embarrassed at that intensity of feeling, the intimacy of the problems they felt moved to discuss. Even as her voice rose in praise, her mind drifted to the choir room, with its stacks of boxes and cool plaster walls. It came to her only gradually that she was praying alone. When she opened her eyes she found Barbara looking back at her.

"I'm sorry," she said, "I'm not sure where I was just then. The Lord must have taken me away." Lee checked her watch. "We may not have that big a group today. Lynn is back at work, I think. I don't know about Katie Claymore."

"Katie's at Full Harvest. So are Bob and Shirley Wright."

"Andrea Walker sometimes comes, and Mary Paulson when her boys are in school."

"Andrea's at Full Harvest, too. Mary has stopped going to church."

"I thought Becky Sellers might be here now that her daughter's made it through her surgery, praise God. Randy was at the hospital with them, praying every night. Well, you're here, Barbara, and so am I. There's you and me…" Lee counted on her fingers. "Let's see, now. There's you and there's me, and there's…" Stalled, she looked at Barbara, who shook her head.

"There's you and there's me, and that's it, Lee. The Thursday morning meeting of the Barren Women's Club. The only ones Pastor Randy never healed."

Lee wasn't certain at first she had heard right. Barbara managed to meet her eyes before looking away. When she turned back there was real anguish on her face.

"I'm sorry, Lee, please forgive me. I don't know where that came from."

Lee kept her own voice even. "Maybe we've been wasting your time here at Spirit Rising. Maybe you should be over at Full Harvest with everyone else."

"No, please don't say that. I love you guys, I really do. That's why God doesn't like me. He knows I've got this meanness in my heart."

"They meet at the old Ward's building across from the courthouse. They have services the same time as ours. Besides, God doesn't like you, He loves you. He has a special plan for your life."

Barbara nodded unhappily. "I know that He does."

"And Randy doesn't heal us, God does. All that He asks is that we trust Him. That we know He loves us and answers our prayers."

Barbara closed her eyes. "Please God, know that I need You. Teach me to prosper in Your Word."

"Jesus, sweet Jesus, bless us."

"Please loving God, hear our prayers!"

They had moved back into the current of prayer again, their voices merged into a buzzing sort of cadence. This time it was Lee who faltered. After a time Barbara fell silent as well. They looked at their hands until Barbara spoke up.

"I'm sorry, Lee, I really am. I know Pastor Randy prays for us. I know he does what he can."

"That's what they say, though, isn't it? How can Randy help someone else when he can't heal his wife?"

Barbara squirmed uneasily. "They say all kinds of things. You know how people are."

When she spoke up again, her voice was low. "I had another appointment last week with Dr. Bronson."

Lee nodded.

"He doesn't think the treatments are working."

"What are you taking, Pergonal?"

"I couldn't stay on it because I was building up fluids. We're going to do another IUI early next week. After that, we might try St. Louis."

"Dr. Kelleher? We saw him a couple of years ago."

"And?"

"And nothing," Lee said. "We did two cycles and I never conceived."

Barbara paused, their voices almost a whisper. "How about Randy? Is he okay? I mean, Royce didn't even want to get tested, but…"

Lee shook her head wearily. "Randy's not the problem, it's me. Somehow my body's not receptive. And now that I'm older…"

"It's not just the count, it's the volatility. When Royce got his results…"

Lee was surprised to hear her own voice as it rose up between them. "With Randy and me," she said and stopped, stomach tightening. "With the ministry…" she began, and stopped again.

"Lee, it's okay. I know it's been hard. I always see the pain in your eyes."

"No, you don't."

"Yes, "Barbara told her, "I do."

Lee had come to church that morning prepared, in her suit and heels, for ministry, ready to proclaim God's promise and the glory of His Word. Instead it seemed she was crying. She was crying, which was the last thing she wanted, turning her face away so Barbara wouldn't see.

God created and sustains the universe. He opened His hand every day to give her life. The first tears on her cheeks served mainly to shame her. Instead of gratitude, she felt a deep surge of anger: anger that Applebee might presume she needed kindness, that fat Barbara ever thought of her at all. She was enjoined to love but could find only hatred: she despised the Women's Prayer Circle for all that it was and ever had been, erratic Lynn Waller and stuck-up Katie Claymore, ungrateful Becky Sellers and her healed little girl. Too stupid to know how she loathed her, Barbara reached along the pew to take her hand.

Unable to escape, Lee gave in and wept. It hardly mattered, with the ministry collapsing — there was little need to protect Randy or the church. There was more than enough, anyway, to indict her: an ungrateful heart filled with judgments and hatred, her pride and ceaseless preference for herself. It was the failure at motherhood that still cut most deeply, a despair so powerful that it had surged up to stop her in her tracks, earlier that week, in the alleyway. It was only when she opened her eyes that she found the tall professor watching, looking out from the shadows of his mocking, empty world.

Jesus might have had compassion for that arrogance. He had walked among them, fully human except for sin. Unlike her father, though, Lee was a poor evangelist. In the pew she had swiped at her cheeks with her jacket sleeve, until at some point Barbara produced tissues from her purse. Five or six now lay soggy between them. She hazarded a glance at her companion who sat back beside her, Lee's hand cradled lightly in hers.

"I was just remembering," Barbara said, "last Mother's Day. A couple of months after we first came to campus. Randy had bought white petunias and set them out out along the stage. There were little ones with us still, sitting with their mothers, and when they went up to get those flowers I thought I'd die. I *wanted* to die, I felt so all alone. But that's when I looked up and saw you. I saw you up in front with Pastor Randy, so faithful and full of praise. I felt so much love for you that it almost scared me, just like God was looking at you through my eyes."

"No," Lee said, "You're wrong. I'm not…"

Barbara squeezed her hand. "I know Pastor Randy tries to help us. It's not even that I haven't felt the Spirit, because I have. The first time Randy touched me it was like a bolt of lightning, a surge of God's power that knocked me off my feet." She shook her head. "It's just that sometimes it doesn't work like Pastor Randy says it will. I call out to Jesus just like he does. I lift my heart in wonder and praise. I'd be a good mother, I know I would. Why can't I have a baby too?"

Lee didn't know, but for once she didn't have to. A moment later Barbara went on.

"That's one of the questions I ask Him. That's one of the things I ask God when I pray. Sometimes when I can't sleep I go down to the basement. There's an old rocking chair that sits by the furnace. There's a blanket I put on my legs. I read the Bible and I rock in my chair.

"It's so peaceful that it's easy to listen. Gradually the quietness settles in. And once it's quiet enough I finally hear it. I get to hear what God has to say." She turned to face Lee in the pew. "'No baby.' That's what He tells me. That's what He's been trying to say. It comes right in time with the rocking. 'No baby, no baby, no baby, Barbara.

There won't be a baby for you.'"

Weakened by tears, Lee sat helpless beside her. This was the danger when women gathered alone. Randy would have come up with something, a stray Bible verse or story to tide them over, but Randy was out ranging in his Explorer, unable to face the truth that Spirit Rising was done. Even Applebee might have lent a hand, but he was closed up in his office, which meant that Barbara could finally have her say.

"No baby. That's what He tells me. No baby, no matter how hard I pray. And sometimes I can even accept it. I accept that God is God, and He gets to decide. It's the other times that start to undo me. It's the other times I begin to lose heart. I'm not sure we'll get through this together, Royce and me. It's like he can't even bring himself to touch me. It's like he can't stand to look at me at all."

It seemed to Lee that she had never looked at Barbara either. When she did, what she saw was a living person, another woman in pain like herself. Her reluctant breakdown and rush of tears had changed something — there was human life, deeply precious, at her side. The heavy cheeks and strong features no longer mattered. The purple welts brought fresh tears to her eyes. Ashamed, Barbara had lowered her head. When she raised it a moment later, she was beginning to smile.

"Of course, right about then is when it always happens. Right about then when I'm feeling the lowest. Right about then when I'm ready to give up. That's when Jesus comes to me, down in the basement. That's when He sits down and holds my hand."

Lee was still listening, but the words hardly mattered. Instead there was that strange, unaccustomed sense of another person's realness, the warmth of Barbara's fingers as they wrapped around her own. The world, through teary lashes, seemed brand new to her. The tightness in her throat had finally eased. She was free to simply be there, without mission or purpose, one of two women together in a pew.

A single window was propped open at the edge of the sanctuary. Through it came the sounds of a September morning: a boy's eager shout from the alleyway, the rolling slam of a van door parked somewhere on the street. A beam of sunlight had broken in above the window, bright and warm through amber-tinted glass.

The beam was still narrow as it entered the sanctuary, growing wider as it stretched across the pews. As they sat together, it moved slowly toward them.

"Can you feel Him?" Barbara said in a whisper. "Can you feel Jesus with us right now?"

For all of a long moment, Lee could pretend she didn't hear. If she didn't hear then the moment would continue. She could sit with Barbara and never have to move. The Light was insistent, though, lapping at their ankles, rising to cloak them in the fullness of Its glow.

That Jesus had come to join them was hardly the miracle; far more wearing to Lee was that He never went away. Before she was born, He had already redeemed her. Without sin, He suffered for hers. She was never so lost that He hadn't quickly found her. She had never fallen so far that He didn't reach to pick her up. There was never a time that He hadn't known her better, loved her anyway — no direction she could ever turn where He wasn't there waiting, doe-eyed and disappointed, her only Lord and Savior Jesus Christ.

EIGHT

Three sharpened pencils were on his blotter, a yellow legal pad lay in front of him, and his iMac hummed quietly at his side. The Common Lectionary and its attendant commentaries were close at hand. The office was quiet and his desk chair comfortable, but still Harry Applebee — the Preacher — was stuck. After three hours, he not only had made no dent in his Campus Church sermon, he was unsure even how to begin.

Bert Heineke's funeral had thrown him behind schedule: the time he normally spent on Wednesday, blocking out his Sunday morning message, had been given over to preparing for the service.

Too, a particularly vivid dream from the night before still distracted him, pulling at his attention again and again.

In it, he had been moving across a wide plain covered with peach-colored gravel. There were countless others walking in the same direction, among them a fair number from his Campus congregation: the Nesbitts and Schallers, Billie Morrison and Olive Giesseking, Libby McNeil, fresh from her latest project with Habitat, a sprinkling of sawdust in her hair. He possessed, it seemed, some need to address them, so he had begun to call out and wave his hands. Two or three paused and then a few more, until most of his people heeded him, coming to a stop and turning his way.

He felt a continuing affection for Joanne Meyer, who had chaired his hiring committee fifteen years earlier — he had been recently divorced and uncertain he would find another post. Walter and Vera Eller were strolling in tennis shoes as if on one of their evening walks. Dori Maple stood impatient, petitions in hand. His own parents were at the edge of the group, floating somewhere near middle age. They stood with his Uncle Curt, killed on a rain-slick highway decades earlier, bound for New London with a calf.

His task, it seemed, was to frame their journey somehow, to offer perspective on how they had ended up together on a plain of peach gravel, moving toward a horizon they could barely make out. It was only when he had their full attention, good-natured and indulgent as always, that he realized he had nothing to say.

The Preacher sat at his desk, tapping the blotter with his pencil. The dream wasn't such an unusual visitation from the pastoral unconscious, akin to nightmares where pages of text fluttered away beneath his fingers or he found himself behind the pulpit abruptly naked, robe and trousers swept away. Nor was it uncommon for modern clergy to struggle, especially in the mainline denominations, in the attempt to develop a message meaningful for an educated audience. What nagged, though, was something else — the powerful feeling of self-consciousness that had seized him. It seemed related to the self-consciousness he had felt earlier that morning in the Spirit Rising office, as he stood with young Lee Overmeyer and wrangled about the cross.

It was still difficult to refer to it as the Spirit Rising office. He had been opposed to sharing space with the Overmeyers' congregation from the time the idea had first been hatched at a Board of Deacons meeting the winter before. He could have predicted the inevitable tensions, with the townspeople little used to the relativism of the university setting, and the Campus members embarrassed by the emotions of a more primitive brand of faith. At first the older congregation had been simply overwhelmed by Spirit Rising, with its electric guitars and prayer meetings, its Bible groups and healing circles, by the pickups and late-model cars that clogged the alley on Sunday mornings, so that Campus people couldn't even find a place to park.

On a more personal level, he distrusted the young pastor's sharp suits and shiny new Explorer, all part of his "gospel of prosperity," a spiritual entrepreneurship so powerfully at odds with their own tradition. The man's theology, such as it was, seemed to combine positive thinking and Biblical ignorance in almost equal measure, supplemented by the notion of the Holy Spirit as some kind of ethereal administrative assistant, eager to respond to the smallest of human needs. To be honest, too, there was his own resentment. The old brick building at the edge of campus was, from a professional standpoint, *his* church, for better or worse, and he couldn't deny a certain guilty pleasure when the other ministry began to fail. He had approached the Spirit Rising office that morning with the easy condescension of the victor, only to see that advantage slip away. Instead, he had felt a disconcerting awareness of himself — and of Mrs. Overmeyer as well — as they enacted their small drama. A self-consciousness successfully concealed, perhaps, but surprisingly powerful, as he had stood with her babbling about Karmelkorn, and she had lectured him like a child about the cross.

Some portion of his unease no doubt had to do with Mrs. Overmeyer herself. Unlike her husband, who had never quite shed the image of huckster in his mind, she obviously held her beliefs with great sincerity. That she was from a missionary background commanded a vestigial respect as well. The Preacher looked at his writing pad lying blank on his desk. The sluggish progress of his own thoughts only underscored their unimportance, a sentiment which had no doubt contributed, richly, to his dream.

He had found himself, the winter before, deeply affected by the arrival of the Spirit Rising contingent. The Campus people might shake their heads at the altar calls and slayings in the Spirit, but what was Christianity meant to be if not transformative? He had the same basic story to work with, after all, only drained, over time, of its mystery. What was it he was trying to accomplish? It was no wonder he had reacted so strongly to the Overmeyers' presence. They had sounded a more general uneasiness deep within him, a funhouse mirror parody of Campus Church's own well-worn rituals and tepid faith.

So it was that he had arrived, in his fifty-fifth year, at a full-fledged crisis in his ministry. He had no complaint with the Campus Church members themselves, good and considerate people whom he respected in every way. He enjoyed the intellectual challenge of the the campus community. He liked the University's many lectures and fine performing arts. Still, he felt largely superfluous to the lives of his congregation. Their beliefs were, for the most part, intensely private. Their lifelong habits of attention to one another would clearly continue whether he preached another sermon or not. They sang hymns to God's wonders on Sunday mornings, every six weeks shared grape juice and bread. In funeral services — depressingly more frequent in an aging congregation — he commended their souls to Christ, whatever that meant.

He had even gone so far, one slushy afternoon in March, to write out a letter of resignation. He had put it in the top drawer of his desk for a week's consideration, his custom when pondering a difficult decision. That would have made it the following Tuesday that Em Freyfogle and Meg Willem showed up at his office. They had formed a group to oppose Chief Cheehaha, the University sports teams' Native American symbol, and they were looking for someplace to meet.

The Preacher sat back in his chair, looking out the window of his office. It had already grown difficult to imagine his life before he had become involved with the Justice Coalition. It seemed incredible, too, that Em and Meg could have seemed virtually indistinguishable to him at first, especially since Em was much smaller, with dark curly hair, while Meg was willowy and distracted, pining for a boyfriend at Purdue. Others in the group quickly sorted themselves out as well: Debbie Tsosie was a young Navaho from New Mexico, Salim Podila a young Pakistani from Chicago who worked well with the press. They had set up a website that Em ran off her laptop from a tumble-down house shared with other students only a few blocks away.

As nearly as he could tell, none of them had been formally churched. Their instinctive sense of justice, though, never failed to impress him, along with the ease they displayed among themselves. He and Clare had labored, in the first weeks of their courtship, to even sit down together over Cokes in the campus malt shop; when they did, they talked earnestly about Buber and Heidegger, popular topics at the small religious college where they studied. That kind of earnest stiffness seemed to have passed away with the malt shop and saddle shoes — the great chasm between the genders seemed largely unknown to the young people who gathered for Coalition meetings, leaning easily around and into one another as they sprawled in the parlor. Other coalition members became distinct as well: there was Carrie Easterbrook, her arms and fingers tattooed in strange henna patterns, and Stephanie Cole with creamy, brown skin and large oval eyes, her face framed by a clump of matted dreadlocks.

Racism's casual cruelties had been deeply impressed on him as a child growing up in northern Virginia, but surprisingly, his own congregation, which had risen to the challenge so faithfully over the years, rallying against the Gulf War and in favor of affordable housing, marching to close the War College and take back the night, was less than enthusiastic about his campaign against the Chief. Old traditions died hard, even among people of good will, but that, too, he found deeply invigorating. He had been given the opportunity to truly minister again, to recall them to the prophetic tradition that had long defined their faith.

And gradually the Campus people did begin to pick up buttons and bumper stickers and several made it to the open forum held on campus in May. The real energy, though, came from the young members of the Coalition, as they met in the church parlor to plan. An egalitarianism defined their interactions at the meetings: everyone got to speak once before any spoke twice, and no interruptions were allowed. In a twist, the order of speaking went against the grain of societal privilege: women of color were first and then men of color, followed by white women and finally white men. That he was among the last to speak was, from the first, oddly freeing — by the time the discussion came to him, everything of importance had been said. A demonstration had been planned for the first football game in late August, and as game day approached, the old church was alive with the painting of posters and copying of press releases, the coordination of a series of teach-ins leading up to the event.

There were probably forty in all, on a sunny Saturday morning, who gathered at the stadium, standing in silent witness as fans drifted from their tailgate parties to the gates. After his experience in other campaigns the Preacher was better prepared than his young companions for the hostility they encountered. Otherwise placid faces twisted in rage at the sight of them. Drunken fraternity boys surrounded them in a tight circle, chanting "Chief, Chief, Chief," with an aggressiveness that was truly unsettling. Em and Salim, in the forefront, faced the brunt of it, and the Preacher moved quickly to join them, in case violence broke out.

Later, as the hecklers grew weary and game time approached, the group had been left alone on the concourse along with a press contingent that had come to cover the protest. Near the front already, the Preacher found himself pushed forward to join Em before the cameras. Though he had prepared no remarks, the right words came to mind without difficulty: he found himself speaking eloquently about the need to respect other cultures, to honor ideas of the sacred that might differ from our own. Em was next, her pretty face troubled, clearly rocked by the ferocity they'd provoked.

"I know people are upset," she said, her voice high and clear. "But Native Americans are people too. Sure, we have our traditions at the University. But how can we just ignore it when those traditions cause pain?"

Afterwards, they had gathered at the Wigwam still giddy from their bravery. The Preacher hadn't been in a tavern in years — he could barely remember the last time he'd had a beer — but he felt a camaraderie as he sat among them, half-hidden in the booth. The little band cheered when he and Em appeared at halftime on the TV screen above the bar. He hadn't done such a bad job, all things considered, while Em was radiant beside him in her tee shirt and khaki overalls, cheeks glowing red from the sun.

At the next Justice Coalition meeting spirits were high. Em, as usual, ran the meeting, and as usual she had some small activity at the beginning that served as warmup. On that particular evening she had asked them to share something unusual about themselves.

Blushing, Salim confessed a weakness for country music. Wendy had spent a year living on a game preserve in New Guinea. Stephanie Cole passed the summer backpacking in Morocco, while Carrie Easterbrook had worked on a fishing boat in Maine. The Preacher sat listening to them with relaxed admiration, as the question made its way through the accustomed hierarchy to him.

"Okay, Harry," Em said, "It's your turn. What can you tell us about yourself?"

They sat in the same parlor where he had been interviewed by the Campus Church hiring committee. He had expressed hopes at the time for a vibrant student ministry; perhaps this, at long last, was it. He was pleased at how easily they had made themselves at home in the old church building, felt deeply renewed by their freshness and youth.

"I'm not sure if you know," he said, "how honored I've been to work with you. How much I enjoy your good will and enthusiasm. It wasn't easy taking on an issue like this."

It was inevitable, too, perhaps, that he would feel special kinship with Em. It helped that she often stopped by to have lunch with him, or just to visit, in late afternoon. She hadn't worked on a fishing boat or trekked across North Africa; instead she passed the summer at her parents' home, dipping ice cream at a local Baskin-Robbins. He had received three separate postcards from the Chicago suburbs, quick notes of greeting in her wide girlish script.

"Thanks," she said, "but that's not the question. You're supposed to tell us something unusual about yourself."

"Something unusual about me," he repeated. "I'm not sure there's really much to say. It seems like I've always stayed pretty much…, that I've always…" As he paused, searching for words, he felt their eyes upon him. They had come and gone all spring while he went about his business at the church. Now that it was fall they had gathered once again. They were less than half his age, but for a moment he felt oddly *seen* by them, by Salim and Debbie, by Stephanie and Carrie and Meg. He was Harry to them, not the Preacher, a word that had always conjured up in his own mind the image of a stout squire in a frock coat, his cartoon mouth stretched open to shout.

"I'm grateful," he said, with real feeling, "that you came to my office door last spring. I'm pleased to be accepted as your friend."

"Okay, Harry, " Em said, smiling, "I'll let you off the hook. But next time we get to hear about you."

That would have been the first time, then, that he had acknowledged this new feeling of self-consciousness, a growing reacquaintance with his substance in the world. He had found Em's frank brown eyes meeting his above the microphones, felt her warmth beside him at the Wigwam as they sat crowded in their booth. She was a woman — a female, a girl — while he, Harry Applebee, was a man. It was a polarity largely missing from his life in the years since his divorce, but one which had come back to him again with Lee Overmeyer that morning. He had experienced that same self-consciousness — an awareness of himself and this young woman in the office — a self-consciousness that for all its awkwardness had felt surprisingly bracing, and a great deal like being alive.

The Preacher leaned back at his desk, considering. The encounter with Mrs. Overmeyer had been uncomfortable, but hardly fatal.

For that matter, wasn't a certain awkwardness inherent in the acknowledgement of another's personhood, especially a personhood co-existent with our own? And what was self-consciousness, anyway, if not a subset of a larger Consciousness? Had Jesus ever urged us to be less than fully aware? Wasn't his invitation, on the contrary, toward an ever-expanding presence, with the assurance that God would meet us there, too?

He reached for the pad of paper before him. Poor, conflicted Paul was likely to be helpful — he never forgot that earthen vessels hold our souls. Luke's injunction from the Lectionary seemed newly appropriate, finding its place within a block letter outline that soon filled the page. At some point the Preacher moved from his outline to the computer, fingers moving lightly across the keys. The familiar rhythm of his style could finally assert itself: a question and our first easy answers, a closer look at those answers and their adequacy, the inevitable reconsiderations that grew from there. For a long time he lost track of the church, his office, and even himself. When he looked up two hours later, the sermon was done.

He would still need to time it, though that was hardly necessary. Long experience told him that it would come in at twenty minutes almost exactly, and he sat back to watch the pages as they slid smoothly from the LaserWriter. From nothing, something had emerged. It always seemed the most astounding of miracles, that inspiration had found him, a poor sinner, yet again. He smiled at the formulation — a bit self-consciously perhaps — and reached to the printer for his text.

He had just finished his proof reading when he heard footsteps in the hall. The Preacher was aware of himself putting down his text and turning in his chair. He was conscious of the greeting that formed in his throat. But most especially, he felt a keen pleasure fill him, at the sight of Em's smiling face as she leaned past the door.

NINE

For his appointment Mitchell was ushered back through a maze of consulting rooms to the physician's private office. Messner joined him a few minutes later, carrying a large manila envelope.

"Hello, Professor Chandler. Glad you could come in. First off, the news is good. The MRI is normal, just like the EEG and CT scan. It's all negative, right across the board."

"What about the amygdaloid complex? There could be involvement there."

"Nope, nothing. The pathologist checked the films and they're clean."

"May I?" Mitchell asked, pointing to the envelope.

"Yes, by all means, take a look."

Dr. Anthony Messner was a slender, earnest-looking man a few years Mitchell's junior, with a fresh patch of razor burn beneath his jaw.

"I'll admit, though, that you had me concerned. Dislocation in time, a sense of depersonalization, your original loss of consciousness at the Health Center — all were consistent, as you suggested, with some sort of lesion. Happily, that's not the case."

"What about a series of small ischemic incidents with interruption of blood flow?"

"It's possible, but there's no way to tell. I considered some kind of hepatic flare but your bloodwork is fine."

"There could be microseizures in the frontal lobe or hippocampus. There's nothing in these films to rule that out."

"Your EEG's were fine. It's the pathologist's opinion, and I concur, that brain function is normal." Messner permitted himself a small smile. "This is good news, Professor Chandler. You're going to live."

"A depth probe might pick up seizures missed by the EEG. The CNR levels would be useful as well. We could order the enzymatics to find out what they are."

Messner nodded. "We could do that. That's certainly something we could do. The insurance company willing, of course." He leaned back in his chair. "So how's the research coming? Family all right?"

"Everything's fine."

"Sex life okay? Any history of depression?"

With little effort to conceal his irritation, Mitchell shook his head.

"The headaches are most likely sinusitis, so let's go with Tetracycline." Messner leafed through his file. "For the other symptoms, I'm thinking paroxetine."

"You're suggesting an antidepressant."

"More of an anti-anxiety medication, actually, in your case. Normally I might have gone there first, but you came in so well-prepared that…"

Tactfully, he left the sentence incomplete. Mitchell and this lesser man had shared their intimacies: for an insurance physical the year before Messner had performed the requisite rituals, thumping his chest and listening to his heartbeat, palpating his prostate and looking in his ears. For matters of substance, Mitchell trusted himself. He went over the image, looking for a shadow he might have missed.

"Panic attacks are nothing to be ashamed of, Professor Chandler. You'd be surprised at how common they've become. You'd be surprised, too, at the number of people from campus, over the years, who have sat right where you are, having the same conversation we're having now. Lately we've been seeing good results with Paxil. Once an equilibrium has been re-established, I think you'll find an improvement."

Mitchell looked up from the film. "Re-establish an equilibrium."

"Most likely it's an imbalance you were born with. There's no need to suffer needlessly when the chemistry can be restored."

"Restore the chemistry," Mitchell repeated. "An interesting notion. Paroxetine enhances serotonergic activity, am I right?"

"Serotonin is certainly a factor."

"Would its impact be primarily pre- or post-synaptic? How is it related to an overall disinhibition of the limbic pathway?"

Messner's razorburn reddened. "Paxil is indicated not just for depression, but for more generalized anxiety. Especially where the symptoms appear largely psychogenic."

Mitchell leaned forward earnestly, MRI in hand. "That's why I'm interested, Doctor. This seems to be an area in which you have considerable familiarity. Perhaps you could point out the sites of this so-called psychogenesis. Or didn't the Glaxo salesman cover that when he brought by the trays of pasta for your staff?"

They regarded one another carefully, but not for long. Messner reached for his pad.

"Look, Professor Chandler. You're a bright guy. You've been in the fast lane a long time. It takes a toll. Let's try the Paxil and see how it goes." He scratched out the prescription with his fountain pen. "There may be some dryness of mouth, so I'd carry a pack of chewing gum. Any shortness of breath, be sure to give us a call."

He stood up and extended his hand. "Why don't you have Trudy schedule another appointment in a month or so. We'll see how you're feeling then."

The other patients, as he came back into the waiting room, looked up hopefully; when he turned out to be merely one of them, they returned to their magazines. Mitchell stood at the counter while a young girl attended to his paperwork. He thought again, as he had so often over the last two weeks, of Barquet, his mentor at Stanford. Barquet, who had gotten in early on recombinant sequencing, who over the last year of his life tracked the cancer that killed him, recording in his lab book the size and proliferation of tumor patterns, sending email updates to his former students right up to the end. Physical processes were physical processes, and there was little use in whining when there was knowledge to be gained.

How to account, then, for the fine feeling of relief that filled him as he came into the sunshine, a receipt for the co-pay and prescriptions in hand? Good news, Professor Chandler, you're going to live. It already seemed impossible that he'd doubted it. His EEG and blood work were normal. The MRI and CT scan were clean. If stress was a problem, there was always the Activity Center, where he could join the other profs pounding laps at the pool.

The doctor's office was at one end of a small strip mall shared with a hairstylist. A UPS truck idled peacefully at the curb. He had been going through a rough spot, perhaps, but that was behind him. He was Mitchell Chandler, who held the Brightbill Chair in neurobiology. He had been featured in *Newsweek* and twice on the *News Hour*; in another twenty minutes, he'd be back in the lab. His car was only a block away when a side street intervened. Mitchell looked at his watch. Instead of returning to his Triumph, he turned at the corner, moving into an old neighborhood of frame houses and overhanging maples, tucked away between campus and the tracks.

Prairie Grove lay tranquil around him. All was well and fully accounted for. A low afternoon sun warmed his neck and shoulders, and protruding tree roots jumbled the sidewalk beneath his feet. He knew this place, after all, with its flat terrain and unassuming homes, a dogged evenness among the the townspeople that Maureen found amusing. He could still hear her quick rejoinder at a dinner party when someone mentioned a neighbor's nervous breakdown. "How on earth," she had said, laughing, "could they tell?"

The area east of First Street had been a tradesman's neighborhood originally, built close to the railroad. As the University expanded the families moved away. It was an area that had become popular with foreign students, and Mitchell paused in front of a small house with worn shingles and weatherboard, a filigree molding beneath its eaves. Yellow flowers had been planted in a window box and a Warrior windsock hung loosely by the door.

He stood a long time before it as if trying to decide. When he moved on again, it was toward the sound of running water. An iron handrail rose up to meet his palm. The Mud Fork emerged from a drainage pipe and flashed briefly below the sidewalk, disappearing a moment later beneath the street. On a windless afternoon, he heard a rushing in the trees. Winter ice storms had torn the canopy above him, leaving large gaps of sky to pulse gently beyond the leaves.

A half block further on, in a small park, the creek reappeared, breaking free in a wide meander through the grass. A wooden bridge led to the other side where a small pavilion provided shelter, next to a children's playground in Warrior orange and blue. He sat down at the single picnic table, stained and sticky, anchored to the pavilion floor by a heavy metal chain.

It hadn't taken long to bring himself up to speed on brain states, especially with the BioMed library and expanding resources on the web. Pathology, as expected, shaped the literature — lesions were implicated in the vast majority of delusional disorders. Atrophy associated with senility brought increasing confusion. Psychosis and schizophrenia traced a more diverse symptomology, as gradually the terms began to blur. "Depersonalization" described the world at a distance, and "derealization" that same world gone strange.

There had been "deterioration of consciousness," too, which hardly seemed fair — he had barely strayed from First Street when the houses loomed above him, and a deep apprehension of loneliness mixed with curry filled the air. In front of the filigree house the image had been vivid: a gray carpet and faded floral wallpaper, a woman who stood crying in the hall. Someone was dead, he had known instantly, at the ice plant. From behind the house came the sound of children's voices. The ring of a long-gone streetcar came across roof tops from Springfield. At the corner window a curtain hung loosely in its frame.

He sat at the picnic table, breathing shallowly. A Dr. Pepper can lay in the weeds along the creekbank, not far from a pink flip-flop abandoned in the mud. From somewhere beyond the park came the growl of a chainsaw. The playground's jungle gym sat squat above the sand. A barrel topped by a cartoon bear's head stood at the edge of the pavilion: the idea was to deposit trash there by reaching in its mouth.

All experience, apparently, fell victim to its descriptors: the bear was "cute" and the playground "fun," the park "pretty," and the day safely "nice." He was suffering, in Messner's judgment, from "panic attacks," which 20 milligrams of paroxetine every morning would chase away.

He was hardly a naive empiricist — our senses yield not the world, but what helps us survive it, a hard-wired narrowing of possibilities continually reinforced. When trauma blocks habituation, perceptions seem novel. Seizures weave new interpretational schema, only rarely productive. Unmentioned, though, was what seemed more like *transparency*, a deepening apprehension of how things really were. Boundaries were far more porous than previously acknowledged. Development occurred within a larger structure that linked and defined. The park's ragged grass, loyal to its grassness, sparkled sentient, the soil beneath it swelling restless against its seams.

At the table, Mitchell assessed his situation. No trauma or disease had shown up on the lab tests. His reflexes and coordination were completely unimpaired. The currents that swept his legs and spine appeared largely epiphenomenal: when he refused to tense against them, the headaches went away.

The better question was how he could have missed it, the unifying fabric that spanned space and time. Messner might pause, as he ran his daily maze, to sniff the air. Researchers wasted lifetimes sifting baubles in the sand. It was a blindness that seemed almost willful as he sat at the park bench, especially when the creekbed had such clear bearing on the swingset, and the muddy flip-flop made reference to the leaves. Dutch elms from a half-century before echoed unevenly along Springfield, as if memory resided as much in the landscape as it did in his brain.

There was that special current, too — cognized crudely as destiny — that bore him steadily forward. How responsive was it to his individual consciousness? How large a factor his willingness to know? Instead of "panic," Mitchell felt a surge of excitement. He had waited a long time for a challenge his equal, a chance to follow the data as far as it would go.

He wasn't alone as he sat at his table: the city had commissioned a half-dozen concrete silhouettes of parkgoers, two-dimensional sculptures set out along the creek. A woman figure stood relaxed with her hands in her pockets. Two children bent in frozen wonder beneath a tree. A dark figure had already emerged from the culvert under Springfield, where the Mud Fork dipped underground on the far side of the park.

Even at a distance Max was clearly recognizable, with his heavy snout and white diamond on his chest. Collar slipped, the dog ran sleek and lively, darting at water's edge to splash with his forepaws, pausing to sniff at a milk bottle abandoned in the mud. When it couldn't be Max, with Manor Lake five miles away, abruptly it wasn't: a belly-white opossum trotted stiff-legged in his place.

Near the footbridge the opossum gave way to a large raccoon that veered from the water, climbing toward Mitchell along the bank. Twenty feet away, it rose on its hind legs to menace, hissing sharply through amber-colored teeth. Without hesitation Mitchell stood and approached it, barely making it to the grass before "raccoon" lost its hold. He watched as a harmless tree squirrel darted past him to a maple, scrambling up the trunk to disappear among the leaves.

By eight o'clock, the Campus Church was dark except for the front of the sanctuary, where spotlights sparkled in the acrylic of the podium. Spread out before the altar were a stocky guitar player with a Peruvian vest and graying hair in a ponytail, a teenaged drummer with shaved skull and a silver earring, a tall black man with an electric bass on his hip. All three were watching the little pastor as he strutted across the stage.

Beneath the spotlights, Pastor Randy reached out for the collection plates. He balanced them easily, microphone in hand.

"So that's about the long and short of it, the way it works. He who watereth shall be watered himself. 'Think not that you have received all that there is, for the Kingdom is without limit.' That's what the Bible tells us. That's the promise of our Savior who showed us the way."

For all the volume of his voice through the loudspeakers, the preening as he moved across the stage, his audience that evening was sparse. From the darkness beyond the spotlights, Mitchell counted barely twenty people. An older couple was near the front, staring straight ahead. Behind them three teenagers slumped together, exchanging whispers. There was a woman who still wore her Prairie Transit uniform, not far from a man in a custodian's blue work shirt. His collection safely stowed, Randy smiled out at them broadly, microphone cupped in his fist as he backed across the stage.

"That's Jesus Christ I'm talking about, in case you're wondering. We can't forget the Christ part just because we know Him. Just because we're proud to call Jesus our friend. See, 'Christ' isn't Jesus' last name. It's not like you go to the Nazareth phone book, and there He is, under the 'C's,' over on North Gethsemane. That's not quite the way it works.

"I'm gonna do a little teaching here, just a minute, so listen close. Anybody remember what 'Christ' means?" He held up one finger to the guitar player. "Now, Donnie, don't be saying. These other folks deserve to have a shot. Me and Donnie been together a long time, so maybe he's heard me preach on this a time or two. Maybe three or four times, Donnie, do you think? Since those days back in Dallas with the band?"

The guitar player said something Mitchell couldn't hear and Randy laughed.

"That's right, old friend, you said a mouthful. There's some things that bear repeating. Sure are. You can't hear them often enough. See, 'Christ' means the Anointed One. The One who was chosen by God. The One who sees the truth all the rest of us forgot."

As he strutted forward the congregation regarded him dully. "But the thing is, *we* can be anointed, too. 'Truly, truly' — that's John 14:12 if you want to check up on me — 'truly, truly, I say that he who believes in me will do the works that I do, and *even greater*.' Did you ever stop and think what that means? Do you see what it is the Bible says? It doesn't say we *might* enjoy the fruits, or that we kind of *hope* we will, or if we pray real hard, maybe we'll get a little help. 'Not one word of God is void of power.' Come on, now, I want to hear you say it. 'Not *one* word is void of power! Not one *word* is void of the truth!'"

The response was desultory, but Mitchell was barely paying attention — he had picked out Lee by then, near the front of the church. She was sitting alone, not far from her husband; there was the familiar rise of her cheekbone at the edge of the spotlight, a soft shine that reflected from her hair. Pastor Randy paused in mid-stride to peer out past the scaffolding, looking toward the darkness at the rear of the church.

"But then again, sometimes you run into resistance. I got interference right now, can anybody feel it?" He stood with his head cocked, staring back against the glare. "I got interference like there used to be on the radio — you all remember AM, don't you, how it cut out when you drove beneath the tracks? All that static when a storm's in the way? That's the kind of interference I got right now, the AM kind. You can always feel it when Satan draws near. Brrrr, that hand on my shoulder. Brrrr, that cold breath on my face!

"But the gates of Hell *will* not prevail. They will *not* prevail. They will not *prevail*, and that's the promise of Jesus Christ. Father God, give us power against the darkness! Give us strength against that evil by Your Name! I stand here only to announce victory! The battle is already won!"

The pastor had picked up the volume even as his clients remained unresponsive, their dullness settled cloud-like, a muddy brown, above the pews. Mitchell must have missed the cue, though, because they were already on their feet, moving forward along the aisle. The older couple ambled stiffly behind the Prairie Transit woman. One of the teenagers was shuffling to the front. The stocky guitar player cradled his instrument with one arm, lifting the other to wave slowly above his head.

"I can feel the Spirit move," Randy was shouting. "Hebbada heggah la oshi majanna. Hebba channa la magdeshaday!"

A piano chorded as they gathered beneath the stage. Mitchell followed Lee as she came forward to join her husband. Face raised, she swayed with the music, hands clasped tightly before her chest.

Pastor Randy made his way beneath the pulpit, stopping first in front of one person and then another, his voice only occasionally reaching out past the pews. The woman in the Prairie Transit uniform waited, docile, with her head bowed; a push from his palm dropped her quickly to the floor. The older woman fell, too, and the teenager; when the janitor proved resistant, Randy stepped back. "Break him, break him," he cried out. "Break him, sweet Jesus, right now!" When the man shook his head, Randy grabbed his shoulder and forearm, banged a palm against his forehead yet again.

Mitchell, though, was watching Randy's wife. Even at a distance he felt her singular appropriateness. He knew her beauty, her faithfulness, her depth. Hands tightly clasped, she was frowning as she looked back to where he stood. He was able to hold her effortlessly, peering back against the spotlights, until she finally turned, still frowning, away.

Pastor Randy had given up on the resistant custodian, moving on to the last of the group. The congregants felled earlier had begun climbing to their feet. In the shadows Mitchell found himself nodding. Even understanding was a part of the fabric, far less puzzled out than already known. Which was why the words, moving into place, seemed familiar, so fully formed that he found them on his lips.

"Marry me," was what they seemed to be saying. "Marry me, marry me, marry *me*."

TEN

Even though the church was a full fifteen minutes away in North Dallas, a much younger Lee Overmeyer had been slow to leave her apartment after work. There was always, it seemed, another reason to dally, which meant that she had a pink plastic trash can in hand when she met him, on her way to the dumpster at the bottom of the stairs. He was leaning against the railing on the walkway, a scruffy black-haired boy with sleepy eyes and a torn tee shirt, who turned slowly to greet her as she came out the door.

"Hi," he said, "I'm Randy." He glanced at the tag she still wore from the office with 'Missions Specialist' stamped in red beneath her name. "Nice to meet you, Lee. He leaned back to study her door. "So this is your place. I'm visiting a friend down the way."

She could have guessed the apartment he pointed to, one flight up, the screen door hanging loose beside an empty case of beer.

"I'm a singer," he said. "with the Stoned Lizards. You've probably heard of us. Last winter we opened for Aerosmith down at the Astrodome. You know the guy with a ponytail, comes around on a Kawasaki? That's Donnie, plays lead. Drummer's named Stan, looks like a speed freak. Tattoos all up and down his arms."

"I hadn't noticed."

"Most of the time we're downtown at the Ballroom. Or at Pete's on the West Side, if you get over that way."

'He isn't a believer,' Lee thought, but that hardly mattered: rock star Randy was the kind of boy she'd never cared for, altogether too pleased with himself in his shaggy hair and boots. Even so, she felt distracted by his prettiness — Randy was always a handsome man. She felt a stab of embarrassment, too, over the empty box of tampons that lay in the trash can under two crumpled paper towels and a box of Special K. Randy put his hand on her elbow.

"Maybe you can help me figure," he said, "how all this happened. How I came down a flight of stairs and past those apartments. How I ended up here outside your door."

As she moved past him, his fingers slid to her hand.

"Wait, Lee, this is important. See how the paint along the staircase is peeling? All those cars in the parking lot? That stupid macrame hanging down the way?"

In spite of herself, Lee looked around. The paint above the stairs had pulled away in long mahogany strips. Windshields from the lot below reflected painfully beneath the glare of summer heat. It was a heat that gray-eyed Randy seemed largely immune to, as she felt the sweat begin to trickle beneath her arms.

He held her hand easily as they stood on the walkway. "That dress you're wearing, what color is it? Light green? Maybe a mint color or cool green, do you think?"

"Just green," she said, and Randy closed his eyes.

"What's today? It's June by now, I know that much. What are we, the 5th or 6th?"

"The eighth," she said, and he smiled.

"Right. The eighth. We're at the Ballroom this weekend, maybe you can see us. The eighth of June, 1980. About six on a Wednesday afternoon. Your just-green dress and a clear blue sky. Stan's ugly Chrysler at the bottom of the stairs. These are things I'll need to remember, because it's the day that I first met my wife."

Annoyed, Lee pulled her hand away. She was twenty-two that summer, with her own apartment and a job at the mission office, plus a brand-new Sunbird in the parking lot below.

She had a boyfriend of her own, thank you, tall and athletic —— Lloyd was already, at that very moment, in Garland, pacing outside the church as he waited for her to arrive. She resented rock-and-roll Randy and all that he stood for, still slow to grasp he was talking about her.

"So, you from around here?" he asked, frowning. "Your folks live nearby? How about your favorite flower? Your blood type? Those are things I'll be needing to know."

Lee heard herself laugh. "You've gotten too much sun, mister. You'll have to find another wife somewhere else."

"I hope you like kids, 'cause I do. How about Harley for a boy? After my granddad. Or we could use your dad's name, I guess, if you like it better. As long as it's not something like Wendell or Marion. That's a mean thing to do to a kid."

"What about she? She could be a girl."

Randy rolled his eyes back in pleasure. "Oh, that would be too much, it really would. I don't even know if I could stand it. The two prettiest girls in the world and both of them mine."

Lee was used to comments about her attractiveness, usually from women. They said it without warmth, as a fact to be acknowledged, while men, for the most part, were afraid of her. That didn't seem to have occurred to Randy. When he came for her on Sunday evening he was recently showered and still smelled of shaving cream, ushering her to a battered Econoline that belonged to his band. He had suggested Putt-Putt, which sounded safe enough. The golf course was part of a nearby family entertainment center with batting cages and a driving range, a course for go-karts through banked bales of straw. Lee stood by the first hole, waiting, as Randy dug in his pocket to pay for the round.

Reprieved from the sun, families moved beneath a canopy of lights. Groups of gawky teenagers showed off for their friends. Putt-Putt was a popular destination for Christian Singles, and Lee halfway expected, on a Sunday evening, to see them there, the men whooping loud and competitive, the women chattering mindlessly in their wake.

Talkative on the ride over, Randy joined her without comment. Under pole lights a course was set out for her: a maze of Astroturf strips among bright, harmless obstacles, the route marked by squat numbered posts. They moved into place behind a family, the father and his chubby son in Dallas Cowboy tee shirts, the mother and daughter trailing behind them with their clubs.

Lloyd took his golf game seriously when they'd come with the Singles, frowning in concentration as he bent low to putt. Randy, on the other hand, played with indifference, unconcerned if he took three strokes or ten. By the fourth hole they had stopped keeping score. Lee was never, for an instant, unaware of him, Randy in his burgundy polo shirt a size too small for him, the blue jeans that fit snugly on his hips. She was never unaware of herself either, in her sun dress and sandals, of the two of them moving wordlessly beneath the lights. At the ninth tee, a fiberglass giraffe stretched its neck high above them, while they waited for the family ahead to play out the hole.

Her father and Lloyd were both tall men, forever scanning the world above her head. Jesus, too, liked to lean down in comfort, while wiry Randy was barely her height. He seemed to have been waiting all that time for her to turn to him. His eyes were calm as they looked into hers. There was a background of humidity and distant voices, a buzzing from go-karts as they circled on the track.

"Aw heck," the chubby boy said, "I missed it," and there was a hollow clunk of a golf ball as it bounced against a board.

Even Lee's own voice seemed to come from a distance.

"You need to know something," she said. "It's not the same for me as it is the other girls. I'm different."

"Good," Randy said, "so am I." He shook his head as he looked around the golf course. "I hate fucking Putt-Putt. Let's get out of here." She gave him her club and he threw it on the grass. A low picket fence lay between the giraffe and the parking lot, and just past the fence was the van.

It wasn't that Lee was indifferent to men: she had watched the boys carefully all through high school and Bible College, waiting for a partner in mission to make himself known. After college, still waiting, she had come to Dallas. Now, on a Sunday night, she rode with Randy. Cassette cases and duct tape cluttered the van floor between them. A stained mattress lay on the floor behind the seats. Randy slowed at a complex of storage units, rows of white garage doors behind concertina wire.

"That's ours on the end, 680. We were the first band to rent garage space to practice. Now you hear about it all the time." He checked his mirror as he eased into traffic. "There's an A&R man from Decca who wants to see us in Galveston. We got a recording session in Arlington at the end of next month."

Randy had big plans for himself and the Stoned Lizards, plans that he outlined in detail as they angled north from the metroplex. Rural mailboxes flashed by in the headlights. There were boarded up produce stands and dark clumps of trees. Randy talked eagerly of record deals and signing bonuses, promotional tours and fame, while Lee tracked the blackness of his eyebrows, his voice as it trailed off softly at the end of his words. She found correspondence, too, with his bare wrists and forearms, the way his hair had shined, on the golf course, like a girl's.

She had, with bulky Lloyd, come to dread the end of an evening, the inevitable moment when he would sigh as he leaned down to kiss her, tongue burrowing like a weasel against her teeth. Randy's arm had brushed hers twice in the course of the evening, the first time at Putt-Putt as she paused before the fence. The second was in the apartment house parking lot, on their way from the van to the stairs. When she slowed at the first landing Randy did too. He kissed her so gently that she felt herself tremble. It was her body that rocked forward to meet him, her own lips that parted lightly against his.

Lee was a successful single with her boyfriend and apartment, her job and her faith and her car. She wasn't aware, herself, until she had stood at the golf course waiting, how alien she still felt in her own country. How little she had ever warmed to complacent Dallas and its pastimes, to Cowboy Stadium and the Six Flags amusement park, to the shopping malls, freeways and golf. Even church had grown stale and predictable: she skipped services on Wednesday night to go out with Randy. Randy had his own world of guitars and dance halls, practice sessions and fame, but he broke away from it again two nights later to see her. He was in College Station all weekend with his music, but on Monday took her to Denny's for dinner. After that, by unspoken agreement, they headed west to Silver Lake. That was where the Stoned Lizards and their friends gathered in the evenings, along with the gaggle of girls that liked to party with the band.

She had met, early on, the other band members: Donnie with his Hawaiian shirts and fedora, tattooed Stan with his tank top and skinny arms. It didn't surprise her that Randy was at the center of things. Randy with his easy grin like he was never quite serious, his careless self-confidence as he moved through the group. He wore their attention comfortably, exchanging complicated handshakes with the men and hugs with the girls — girls younger than Lee, barefoot and in haltertops — girls who settled in again nearby with their cigarettes, eyes never straying from Randy for long.

Lee had long thought of herself as exotic: she spoke smatterings of two African dialects, had spent her eleventh birthday at the airport in Khartoum. This gypsy tribe had a different kind of strangeness, young people like herself but with long hair and insolence, slouching aimlessly with their boom box and beer. There was a purposelessness that kept her off balance, especially when Randy ranged away beyond the tables to the van. When he came back smoky-smelling and silly he settled beside her, one hand wrapped around a beer can and the other at her waist.

Sometime after dark Randy would stir at the table. When he stood up Lee did too. She knew then, like the girls knew and God knew, like Donnie and Stan and the rest, why she was there. She wasn't at the park because she enjoyed their company. She hadn't come to Silver Lake to share the good news of Jesus Christ. She didn't fool anyone in her prim skirt and blouse — they knew she had been waiting for exactly that moment, when Randy would walk her away from them, out along the lake. He led her through an adjoining picnic area, by that time deserted. With Randy's arm around her shoulders she raised her hand to his ribs. She felt beneath it the sharp tautness of his muscles, tried to contain within her own chest the crazy pounding of her heart.

On the opposite shore were the runways of DFW, the airport's lights reflecting toward them across the water. The air by the shore was still and warm. At any moment, she knew, Randy would turn to her. He would turn to her at last with his kisses. Even if his mouth tasted burnt for an instant from the cigarettes, right beneath was the sweetness of his tongue.

She didn't stop to question his ease and confidence, already famished for his lips and Randy-breath, the feel of him up against her in the dark. Sometimes when a surge of sound came across the lake he would pull away, distracted by yet another jetliner as it climbed to the sky. It was the first time she could remember being impatient with him, desperate only that he turn to her again. When they settled at one of the picnic tables his hands trailed lightly along her back, behind her neck, across her knees. She was so aroused that she was certain she had wet herself, the first time he slipped his hand beneath her skirt. She had the first orgasm of her life seconds later, twisting barelegged and shameless on his lap.

He wasn't a Christian, which should have made a difference — there was a warning about unbelievers that came courtesy of Paul. Pastors were stern about sex but the Bible left leeway, and Jesus had said nothing at all. Helpless, Lee grasped at what she could. It was agony when he spent a full week with his band in San Antonio and left for Galveston only a few days after that.

At this point a friend might have stepped in to offer caution, but Lee didn't have any friends. None that she would have trusted in matters of Randy, not when she burned with impatience the whole time he was away from her; not when she had seen the other girls at Silver Lake watching him. Another part of her, meanwhile, was practical. She took an afternoon off from the Mission Office to drive to South Dallas, emerging from the Planned Parenthood clinic two hours later with a starter pack of pills.

When Randy came to her apartment after Galveston she met him at the door. She had gone braless that night like the other girls, her skin alive as he unbuttoned her blouse.

"Are you sure, Lee?" he'd asked, and of course she was, with Randy — if not for her broad shoulders and breasts jutting like google-eyes between them, the plague of tiny brown moles that spread across her chest.

"Oh my," he said, brushing his lips across her skin. "Oh my, Lee, oh my, my, my."

Raised in the church, Lee had never had a conversion experience. Envious, she had watched others' transformation, and now her own turn had come. Within twenty minutes she and Randy had done it. Two hours later they did it a second time, and the next morning they did it again.

There was guilt but it couldn't deter her. They did it a fourth time later that same week when she met him at the storage sheds. They did it a fifth time when he came by after midnight, his hair smelling of cigarettes and sweat. One of the great luxuries, it seemed, that summer, was losing count. Everywhere she went their lovemaking clung to her, creeping out as she stood at the stencil machine with Mrs. Druckenmuller, making its way into the boxes of supplies that she packed for overseas. It radiated from wherever Randy had touched her: her shoulders, her breasts, between her legs. She had never imagined how much that special exercise would agree with her: her appetite when Randy drove her to the truck stop at dawn for a skillet breakfast, was excellent. She woke up every morning well-rested and refreshed. Her period, thanks to the pills, was much easier, regular for the first time in years.

Even AIDS, that summer, was still safely on the horizon, as if the same God who brought her Randy had decreed a last summer of freedom, just to see what His people would do. What Lee did was wait for Randy. Time, she had learned, meant nothing to him: he might say he would be by at seven and get caught up with his music; hours later she would hear him at her door. Other times he didn't come by at all. On a Saturday in late July he showed up at three in the morning. Their sweet hours before dawn merged into Sunday morning, and all too quickly into Sunday afternoon.

Made lazy by their lovemaking, Lee watched Randy from the bed. Naked, he stood at the closet, trying on her clothes — he was always on the lookout for something new to wear on stage. He tossed aside a fitted jersey in favor of a cotton blouse, its collar edged in lace.

Words bubbled up from her childhood, a phrase in Akan which she remembered as 'I love you.' It could have been 'God loves you,' instead — it had been a while — the words rising warm in her throat. Randy moved past the closet to her bureau, where he inspected a row of photos set out along the shelf.

In the first Lee stood on a sidewalk in petticoats and ankle socks. She was on the grounds of the mission headquarters in Ghana; at her back pressed a tangled wall of green.

"So this was in Africa? How long were you there?"

"Almost four years. We were in Accra, and then Sunyani where my father had his mission."

Randy had moved on to the next photo. "And here's your dad."

"He's with Peter and Josiah, two of his elders. That cinderblock shed was our church."

"No shots of your mom?"

"We're not really close. She wasn't happy in Africa. She brought my sister and me home before I started junior high."

"And that's when they split up?"

"My father wanted to stay with the mission. He was willing to give up his family, if that's what God asked."

There was a romantic quality to the story for church people, especially if you left out the subsequent divorce and Mim's years of wildness, her own sense of failure that a calling never came. But Lee had told Randy all of that and more. There was nothing that summer she could have kept from him: it was by knowing him she made acquaintance with herself. Randy liked his eggs sunny side up with a side of country sausage; hers she preferred scrambled and dry. He had slender toes that were long like a baby's fingers, while her feet were rounder and soft. She had always loved God and been grateful for His mercy, while Randy never thought of Him at all.

Randy stood with her lace-collared blouse unbuttoned and hanging open, revealing a brush of wiry hair across his chest. There was a dark line, too, below his navel, the thatch between his legs where his penis hung slack.

"Do you pray for me?" he asked, and she nodded.

"I do. I pray for you all the time."

"What do you pray?"

"I pray that God will bless and keep you. I pray that Jesus will find a place in your heart."

Randy yawned. He stretched in front of her, the hem of the blouse sliding past his belly to his ribs. "Well, I better get going. We got practice at four. You mind if I go over in your car?"

Lee didn't mind. She was twenty-two that summer but might as well have been fifteen, for all she knew of the world. Besides the car, she was already loaning him money, three hundred dollars for an advance on their recording session, another hundred and eighty when the van was in the shop. The money didn't matter — there were five thousand dollars in a mission savings account she had been building since high school. It was far worse to think of him out on the highway, unsaved in the rattletrap van. It terrified her to think of him unredeemed and lost for eternity, cast away from God's presence and love.

There was another reason, too, for loaning him the Sunbird: that way she knew when she would see him. He wouldn't get distracted like he had a way of doing, more and more as the weeks slipped away. She didn't even know where he lived that summer; sometimes a week might go by before he called her, or stopped in for a quick trip to bed. She *did* pray for him, fervently and with gratitude, because God's purpose had finally come clear. It was ingenious and designed to perfection: through her love Randy would come to know Jesus. He would be saved and Lee would still have him, their faith growing deeper through the years. The particulars were never quite clear, but in late August the band was at the Ballroom, Randy upbeat and happy when he came for the car.

She walked with him from the apartment to the walkway, kissed him goodbye at the top of the stairs. Before she went to sleep she set the alarm for one-thirty. When it rang she got up to shower and do her hair. She changed the sheets and fluffed the pillows and comforter, turned the lamp in the corner down low. After slipping into a fresh nightgown she waited in the living room, but careless Randy never came back.

He didn't come back that Saturday night to see her. All day Sunday he didn't appear. Mrs. Druckenmuller gave her a ride to work Monday morning. On Tuesday and Wednesday she stayed home. Late Wednesday evening the police called about the Sunbird. It had been side-swiped and left in a ditch east of Abilene, and she rode over the next morning with Donnie and Stan.

Stan's mood was dark as they labored along I-20 in the van. "Why worry about Randy when we're the ones screwed? He had time enough to grab the PA system before he left, plus Donnie's guitar and the amplifiers. I'm just lucky he didn't get my drums!"

Donnie was driving and Lee sat in the passenger seat, while Stan slouched on the mattress in back. "The little prick, we're all set to cut the demo and now he pulls this. He's crazy is what he is, I've always known it. He'll be in the pen before long, just like Dike." He scowled out at the mesquite along the interstate. "Just because he's the singer the chicks thought he was magic. They all lived for a little taste of Randy's wand."

Donnie glanced at Lee, but skinny Stan didn't care, and Lee didn't care about Stan. Without Randy, Donnie and Stan were just two boys from the Midwest with silly clothes and bad haircuts, short of money and a long way from home. In Abilene an officer with graying temples gave her the address to the towing yard. The Sunbird's front door was smashed in on the driver's side and a deep gash ran the length of the car.

Stan found Donnie's guitar in a Forth Worth pawn shop a couple of weeks later. By that time one of their musician friends had spotted Randy in San Marcos, where he borrowed fifty dollars before moving on again. He was traveling with a woman, a fact Lee barely registered. She hurried home from the mission office every afternoon to wait for him, determined to be cross about the car.

It was easy enough, she knew, for others to pass judgment, but they didn't know Randy the way she did. They didn't understand that God had picked him out for her; they hadn't held him close and met his eyes. Downtown she parked far from the office. At home she left the Sunbird under an elm tree, hidden away in a distant corner of the lot. It was only on the highway that the damage accused her, like an emblem for everyone to see. She made it past Labor Day and into the second week of September, still waiting for his knock on the door.

Randy was gone, though, and wasn't coming back. It was a realization that finally came to her in the middle of afternoon rush hour on I-35. Somehow she made it back to the apartment. Her hand shook as she tried to work the key. Afternoons, after a long summer, were finally bearable, but Lee didn't care because she wasn't going out.

She couldn't face the bedroom so she carried her pillow and comforter out to the living room. At some point she called the mission office, pleading a family emergency that had summoned her home to Virginia Beach. She hung up and sat back on the sofa. She had loved Randy but he didn't prefer her, and a sound not unlike a wild animal's escaped from her throat.

Lee had never been a crier. That was Mim, who had wailed every night at mission school until her mother finally came to take them home. Mim, who in Virginia Beach had stayed on the telephone for hours, giggling over boys, while Lee had been more level-headed. Now she lay on the sofa and wept. She cried because she was a fool and should have known better. She cried because Randy didn't love her. There was nothing she had to offer that was different than the other girls — not her love or her body or heart. Her mistake had been to think she was special, the way a person could believe almost anything if she wanted to enough.

"He will be all or He will not be at all." The words formed a refrain that still echoed from Bible College. The professor, with his reedy voice, had pronounced it passionately, striking hard on the lectern with his hand. "You never break God's laws so much as break yourself against them" — she'd said the same thing a hundred times herself. At some point Lee had brought her alarm clock from the bedroom. She could still remember looking at it just before midnight. That meant the whole thing took barely fifteen minutes, because by quarter after, all of it was gone.

It wasn't just Jesus and His sacrifice. It wasn't just God and His love. *All* of it fell away in those fifteen minutes. His power and goodness and wisdom. His redemption and judgment and Word. Once she was launched it seemed nothing could stop her. There wasn't any Plan or Commission. No Atonement had been made in her name. She had tumbled into a freefall through a lifetime of imagined meaning — a freefall that didn't stop until she was back in her Dallas apartment, faithless and emptied, alone with her sofa and the ticking of the clock.

Lee couldn't remember later if she even slept that night. She had no idea how the next hours could have passed. For days, it seemed, she sat without moving. At first she was *afraid* to move, still awaiting His anger, even in a world neither governed nor loved. For a time she felt certain she was dying, but remained, on the sofa, still alive.

Sometimes in later years she would feel a strange nostalgia for those lost weeks in Dallas. She had still pined for Randy, foolishly or not — her hands had become hers when Randy kissed them; she had first seen herself when she looked in his eyes. She missed Randy in her stomach, under her fingertips, in the cells of her blood. The foolishness she felt was her foolishness, the mistakes she had made all her own. When her heart ached, at least it was *her* ache, as she moved through the apartment alone.

God had left with Randy but that had its benefits: untended, she did as she pleased. She could eat toasted cheese sandwiches three days in a row if that's what she wanted. She watched television for hours on end. Christian programming seemed like the ravings of madmen so she switched to soap operas. Freed from God's love she slept exhausted and dreamless, through whole afternoons and far into the night.

Part of her still expected that the sofa would collapse and the floor fall away, that she would spin out forever and never come back. Instead, nothing really happened. Ungodded, people went about their business. Doors slammed along the walkway and there were voices on the stairs. An elderly man stood outside his door to smoke a cigarette. A woman walked her spaniel on a leash. When she drove the Sunbird to Safeway no one noticed the car door — there were a lot of damaged cars on the road.

She had rushed past herself in the bathroom mirror that summer, thinking only of Randy. There was a silly girl later on who had stood at the washbasin crying, with streaked cheeks and twisted, rubber lips. Now the woman in the mirror had begun to look back at her. Her skin was pale and her eyelids seemed bruised. Her hair hung lifeless and dull. Even so, when she finally took the car in for repair the week before Thanksgiving the service manager went out of his way to flirt with her, tall and handsome with coffee cup in hand. The PicQuik countermen paused, counting change, just to look at her. A new neighbor, well-dressed and with salt and pepper hair, had twice tried to engage her in conversation. He said he taught at a nearby community college, and the next time Lee saw a stack of catalogs she picked one up and brought it home. She lay on the sofa to consider the possibilities, moving from computer drafting through cosmetology and welding, from hospitality services to legal studies and math.

The days had grown short, which pleased her; she liked the browning grass and bare branches of the trees. She liked the soft press of her pillow and dark stillness of the night. In mid-December she was on the couch, sleeping soundly, when she was awakened by a knock on the door.

The light above the stove, with its distant vigil, had grown dear to her. The comforter was at her ankles as she stumbled across the room. There was a sense of floating unbound above the carpet, so she still might have been dreaming when she opened the door.

Even half asleep Lee knew him immediately. She knew him immediately, even filthy and disheveled, with a stocking cap pulled down to his eyes. He wore a ragged denim jacket and had a cast on his wrist. One of his front teeth had been broken in half. Even after a dozen weeks Lee's legs went weak at the sight of him, back at her apartment door again.

Another person might have recalled his thoughtlessness, had the presence of mind to feel resentful or betrayed. Instead Lee felt shy in her bathrobe, gummy-mouthed and uncertain as she unlatched the door.

"Is it you?" he said. "Are you really here? Can you ever forgive what I've done?" His smile puckered where the broken tooth caught his lip. "I was dead, babe, but now I'm living. By the grace of Jesus Christ, I've been saved."

"Randy," she said, trying out his name.

"Can you believe it, Lee? Me and Jesus. I know Him as my Savior and my Friend."

For a moment she wondered if he was kidding. It was hard to tell because his Randy grin was back. "He knows all about us already! He's got plans like you wouldn't believe. Would you get down on your knees to pray with me? Will you join me right here to praise His name?"

The winter air came in fresh through the screen door. Out past the walkway lay an empty Texas dawn. Across the room were her sofa and comforter, the pillow case still wrinkled from her sleep.

Randy had dropped to his knees. "God has a plan for me, honey, that you're a part of. There's so much that He wants us to do."

Gathering her bathrobe she slid to the floor.

"'I've sinned and I need Your forgiveness. I accept that Jesus gave His life for my sins.' Come on, babe, we've all got to say it. If you don't know the words, you can pray after me."

Lee knew the words. Her father's church had distrusted emotionalism, preferring a steadily deepening awareness of God's presence in our lives. She was skeptical herself of quick conversions or ecstasy; a Christian's life was the best proof of faith. In the end though, the theology hardly mattered: she would have confessed and accepted anything, robbed banks or rolled on the floor, she was that grateful to have Randy back again.

Lee knew too that God wasn't fooled, then or ever. What we barely glimpse He inhabits in full. And that was how, sifting patiently, He must have found it, the final prayer hidden deep in her heart. It was the one prayer she had never given up on: please bring Randy back again. Let me have him, let him love me, and God had heard her, no matter how much she pretended He was gone. With a last look at the sofa Lee bowed her head to follow Randy, close behind as he led them both in prayer.

ELEVEN

Her daughter and granddaughter would have had a fit, but Vera Eller was just as happy to be alone in the back seat while the men rode in front. It was hardly a prize anyway to be trapped up front like poor Walter was, with Austin Chandler holding forth in the driver's seat, as he guided his big Buick through the rain.

"And I'm not saying that young people can't have opinions, because they can. But damn it, it's Harry Applebee that I blame. He's the one who got them worked up in the first place. The Chief has been the symbol of this university for fifty years, and as far as I'm concerned, he can stay fifty more."

He scowled at Vera in the mirror. "It's an honor to the native people if you ask me. Everybody knows that. It's not like he's some silly gopher or wildcat prancing on the sidelines. He comes out, does his dance, and leaves. It's dignified from beginning to end."

On a rainy Sunday morning traffic was sparse, and Austin Chandler negotiated University with both hands clasped tightly on the steering wheel, his big chin jutting out at the world. Vera regretted having him down for the dessert. The berry pie, as good as it turned out, couldn't quite make up for two hours worth of Austin Chandler in her living room. Worse, now he had attached himself to them, calling at suppertime to see if Mindy had brought their paper or coming all the way down the block whenever Walter was in the yard. That morning he had insisted on driving them to church, forgetting that they had somehow managed to make it there on their own well enough all those years when he was too important to go.

"Like I say, Applebee is the problem. You'd think it was a political science class, not a church. Last Sunday it was the girl on the Holocaust. The week before that the gays. Today all those students about the Chief. It looks to me like Applebee has it figured pretty well. Get somebody else to come in and do the work!"

"I'm not sure it was worth it, all the wrangling on the gays," Vera remarked. "Dori's committee spent a year getting the resolution put together. There was meeting after meeting to talk it out. We had that big "Open and Affirming" sign painted for the front. And how many new members did we get? Not a one. Those two women from Danville attended just long enough to get everybody stirred up and then they never came back." She shifted under her seat belt. "Gladys says they may have broken up, which doesn't surprise me. That little Jeannie was cute as a doll, but Marta might just as well have been a man, with those suspenders and flannel shirts. And those shoes! If I wore shoes like that my feet would hurt for days."

Austin Chandler snorted. "Applebee just likes the girls, no matter what the persuasion. You see how he lights up every time that brown-haired one spouts off about the Chief?"

"The Jewish girl was the prettiest, if you ask me," Vera said. "Such a cute little thing with those deep, dark eyes. And what a sad, gruesome story she told! "

The weather was warm for mid-October, but a cold rain splashed against the windshield. They had often driven around after services over the years, with different people from the church, but so many of them were out at Cooke-Davis now, in a hurry to get back for their Sunday meal. For a long time there had been Nan and Jim Kelleher, who liked to eat at the Student Union. Wendell Unger wanted to look at new houses, so they headed west of town to where the doctors built their homes. After the Ungers they had driven around with the Doores, before they left for Arizona, and with Myra Snyder after Bill passed away.

All such nice people, she thought, which was why it seemed strange to be in the car with grumpy Austin Chandler, who hadn't even bothered to ask where they wanted to go. At Five Points they picked up the highway. Long after they had passed the National Guard Armory he was still complaining.

"Overall, I'd say he makes a pretty poor excuse for a preacher. 'What about this?' 'Aren't we called on to do that?' Anybody can ask questions for twenty minutes. The trick is to come up with some answers! That's how a man earns his keep!"

Vera had been trying to figure out where he was heading, and when they turned at Manor Lake she finally knew. She and Sally Springer had been out after Meals on Wheels to look at the new houses, and they'd picked out Mitchell Chandler's right away. It was a big one, which made sense, because Mitchell was flying high — there were months when you could hardly open the *Courier* without seeing his name. He had been on the campus TV station where several people saw him. There was an article in *Newsweek* a few years before. Even so, the old dean had to drag them out to Manor Lake just to brag on him, so he could be sure that they wouldn't forget.

"I can't see the attraction," she said, "of living way out here in the country. All winter long you fight the weather and all summer you spend your weekends cutting grass. And some of these places are all roof! I guess that's the style now, but can you imagine? That gray house looks like a barn! The Hinkleys had one just like it for their dairy cows when I was a girl!"

Austin Chandler ignored her and they wheeled past the golf course, past the big houses with their columned porches and coachlights, the cast iron mailboxes set out along the street.

"You know," she said, "you have to wonder why a young person would even want to settle back here in Prairie Grove. I'm glad Ronnie and Kate had the grit to make it on their own."

When Austin Chandler scowled, Vera was pleased; she knew that he wished she would just disappear so he could bully Walter in peace. After Mitchell, his family's achievements weren't much to brag about: Betsy, with all her husbands, was just a glorified secretary over at the Athletic Department, while Geoff had wound up in one of the Spanish countries somewhere, as far as he could get from his dad. Mitchell's house was on the left, a half a block ahead. At least she and Sally had thought it was Mitchell's house, but the old dean sailed past without a glance. There was a big pond at the center of the subdivision, surrounded by houses, and he followed the road around it to the other side. He slowed in front of a two story house, a showplace, really, with four separate gables, and a herringbone sidewalk from the driveway to the door.

"There," he said with satisfaction. "What do you think?"

Walter leaned forward to look. "Seems like a nice enough house."

"Right. That's the whole point. It's a *very* nice house. Do you like it, Vera?"

She hesitated just long enough to irritate him and shrugged. "It's all right, I guess. Might be a little dark on the inside. I thought Mitchell's house was over there."

"Mitchell?" Austin Chandler looked back at her in annoyance. "Who said anything about Mitchell? This is where that Randy Overmeyer lives. Quite a move up from Darryl Chapel, wouldn't you say? What does he have, a three car garage? Not bad for a man of the cloth."

"Well," Walter said, "people have to live somewhere."

"But everybody doesn't have to live out here, that's what I'm saying. Not while he plays Campus like fools. Maybe he could learn to pay his bills before he buys in at Manor Lake."

After they had studied the house for a while they wound back through the subdivision. At the highway Austin Chandler turned left instead of right, heading away from town. Less than a mile later he turned again to cross the railroad, and they left the highway behind.

With the harvest underway the two men were silent, scanning the fields. Wendell Unger had been an Ag man too, so sometimes after church he steered them into the country. He and Walter looked at the crops while she and Millie chatted. Vera could still remember when Millie turned to her and said the cancer was back.

"Oh, I'm so sorry, Millie," Vera had told her.

Millie was a full-faced woman who never cared much for fashion and wore her hair chopped close around her head. Their eyes had met for the longest time as they rode past the fields.

"I'm going to beat it, Vera," she said, "I really am."

And she did beat it for a while, like a lot of people, but it wasn't long before Millie Unger was gone. Cancer hadn't taken Jim Kelleher but a heart attack did, while he was outside one morning cleaning their walk. Vera couldn't help but fault Nan on that one, what with the paper full of warnings about snow shoveling, but then how to explain Phil Snyder at their granddaughter's wedding, when he slumped over, a dead man, in the pew? It was old age, she knew, which wore at everyone, but all Vera could think of was Millie in the back seat next to her, and the lost, frightened look in her eyes.

"Good grief, Austin," she said irritably, "where are you taking us, Danville? Are we going to see Marta and Jeannie ourselves?"

Austin Chandler had been off in his own world and he looked up startled, taken aback by the sharpness of her voice.

"Just a little farther here," he said. "Right down this road. There's something I want Walter to see."

They had turned north and were almost to the interstate, but just before they reached it he turned right onto a narrow lane. They came into a meadow where there were the beginnings of some kind of building, the wood frame half-collapsed in the rain.

"There you go, Walter. That's what your young friend has going for him. That's the new church he's been talking about. How soon do you think they'll start moving in?"

In the front seat Walter looked out through the wipers. Austin Chandler leaned forward above the wheel. "I just thought someone on the liaison committee ought to see it. The grand temple of Spirit Rising." He wiggled his fingers above his head. "'Jesus, Jesus, Jesus.' You hear how that boy shouts it, with his Explorer and a house at Manor Lake. Get in trouble, just call on Jesus. That's all a person ever has to do!"

Vera looked out, too, at the meadow, at the sagging lumber and cornfields and ditch. Rain drummed steadily on the car roof, and traffic moved along the interstate a quarter mile away.

"You know," she said, "I keep thinking about that Jewish girl who spoke at the church. Such a lively thing, and really, just imagine, losing all your people like that. You wonder how a person goes on. I wonder about us sometimes, too, with our friends. It's like a Holocaust, really, when you think about it. You look around and almost everyone's gone!"

Austin Chandler, his bad news delivered, was sitting back satisfied. He grunted derisively. "Sure better not let them hear you saying that! It's their tragedy and nobody else's! The whole thing makes them pretty touchy."

"Well, yes," she said, "and that was something special over in Germany, of course, with the meanness and all, but when you step back and think about it…"

He dismissed her with a wave of the hand. "Oh no, Vera, that's not going to cut it. Not at all. See, they're the ones who got the worst of it. That's what they want you to think, anyway. Nobody's ever suffered but them!"

He pointed again across the meadow. "Just look out there. There it is. Randy Overmeyer's folly. His pride and joy. You can't make a silk purse out of a sow's ear and a boy like that won't ever change his spots. It's not that easy. You can't walk away from things just because you want to. Just because some Jesus Christ comes and takes away your sins."

Vera might have argued if she'd known exactly what he was upset about, but then again, maybe not. Austin Chandler was always so sure of himself — his secret over at the Ag school — blustering away while the others lagged back. She couldn't help thinking about poor Edie, afraid of her shadow to begin with, cooped up with him all those years at the end of the block.

Walter was so quiet sometimes that it was easy to forget about him. If she had been paying attention she would have seen his ears redden, and the tell-tale way he had of shaking his head.

"That Jewish girl," he said, his voice quavering. "Those poor homosexual people that come to our church. Harry Applebee. That young Spirit Rising pastor and his wife." She knew by the way Walter stumbled he was angry. "We've just got to have some consideration," he said. "We've got to have a little consideration for what other people have to say."

His face was red by the time he finished and his eyes flashed with tears. Vera was embarrassed, of course, but she felt sorry for him, too. He was tender-hearted to begin with and it had only gotten worse through the years. Almost anything could set him off: a photo of their grandchildren with their band instruments, pictures on the news of calves trapped in a snowstorm — she'd already told him he couldn't watch the Olympics anymore if that's the way he was going to be. Earlier that week she'd surprised him in the TV room as she brought in their coffee. The little Chinese girl had lost out in the skating competition, which was a shame, of course, after all of that practice, but Walter, in his chair, had been crying, even as he turned away in the hope she wouldn't see.

He couldn't help it if he liked the preacher, a lot of the church people did. He liked the little pastor and his wife. He'd liked that Marta and Jeannie too, from Danville, always making a beeline to talk to them after church. In the front seat, he sat with his head down, stricken with an embarrassment that would last half a week.

Meanwhile, Austin Chandler had finally gotten what he wanted. That's how it was with people who needled: it wasn't much fun unless somebody cared.

It would have been easy enough to get stuck in the mud with Austin Chandler, and Vera was relieved when he finally got his big boat of a Buick turned around. They made it onto the county road again and from there to the highway. Vera was glad to see houses coming up around them as they drove into town.

It wasn't just the church people who had slipped away over the years, there were the department people too. Hal Bruder had been one of the first, and still such a young man, when he came into Walter's office after lunch. He was having trouble holding onto a piece of paper, he'd said, laughing as he told Walter about it. It seemed silly at the time but what he'd gotten was his death sentence — it was the Lou Gehrig just settling in. Walter was out at the Bruders' almost every night at the end, all the men were, but it was a hard way for poor Hal to go. There were cancers and more cancers as the years added up, the heart attacks and strokes, and now there was Alzheimer's with its pick of the rest. A cold wind comes a-blowing, like her dad used to say, and it had found her and Walter and Austin Chandler bumping across the tracks on a Sunday morning, the last of the berries on the vine.

She was glad when they finally turned on Washington Street, ready to get out of her church clothes and settled in with the paper. Even so, she couldn't stop naming the houses as they went along: the Yoeys and Bergethons, the Hendersons and Tolleys — all of them once neighbors and all of them gone. She considered Austin Chandler's fat head as he pulled over to let them out. She didn't care if he had been a dean, it felt a whole lot like a Holocaust to her.

Twelve

The auditorium at the Diven Center was well-appointed with blond trim and cranberry carpeting, the seats in a half-circle as they rose from the stage. Mitchell Chandler stood behind a podium, slide projector humming quietly at his side.

The annual Sterling Lecture was something of a star turn, sponsored by the University's Center for Collaborative Studies. After an introduction by the Center's director, a Hungarian biochemist named Radinsky, he had climbed to the stage. From it he surveyed the complex ecology of the scientific community, the patchwork of sport coats and tie-dyed tee shirts, camouflage and dreadlocks, the last of a season's hairy legs under baggy khaki shorts. It was an environment he had thrived in, unsentimental and competitive. He had achieved, in that fierce hierarchy, a spot at the podium, so they put aside their sack lunches and *Daily Warriors* to see what he had.

He recognized within the room a certain shared arrogance: they were able to do something others could not. Lesser people taught literature or sold real estate, guarded crosswalks and delivered mail, but only a few got to work at life's center, negotiating the fast-paced world of genome and cell. They shared a grid of interlocking suppositions, of evidence and trial, a system of explication so powerful that his presentation was already shaped before he stepped to the podium. It was so fully circumscribed, in fact, that he could — and a moment later did — leave his talk unattended, floating out into the audience from the stage.

There was much to admire from that vantage point: the quality of science and logic of his narrative, the confident march of slides across the screen. The slides themselves were an affectation, perhaps — most of his colleagues had moved on to Powerpoint. Only a handful were remotely his equals. He moved past irreverent Caldes with his cadre of graduate students, regal Bachelder in his seat by the aisle. He felt for the undergraduates, their pencils poised earnestly, when this was the last place in the world to hear anything truly new.

A rustle had arrived in the auditorium. Tissue from a salamander's neural pathway stretched above him on the screen. He would have known Brian's voice anywhere, low-key and hesitant as it rose near the front.

"Um, Mitch, I think the slides are out of order."

The auditorium seated perhaps two hundred and fifty. Another thirty or forty were gathered in the aisles. He looked out from the podium.

"I trust most of you have had a chance to meet Dr. Kirby, our Lab Director. Dr. Kirby played a key role in the original identification of the Lazarus gene and has been my principal collaborator for well over a decade. I appreciate his willingness to play straight man. Thank you, Brian, very much.

"Dr. Kirby, of course, is correct. Generally a slide of neural tissue taken *before* injury would be followed by one taken *after*. Before and after. After and before. Generally, too, we would examine the 'after' section" — he made quotation marks in the air — "for evidence of regeneration. That is, if we can speak with any real confidence of 'regeneration.' Or even of 'repair' for that matter, as a discrete set of processes, along the axis we like to call 'time.'

"Some of you can no doubt anticipate where I'm going with this," he added, his little joke, because he could already feel the grid of understanding as it roused itself against him. It had begun to coil, self-protective, across the rows of the auditorium, the tight web of agreement that locked perception in place.

"Not that genetic coding is irrelevant, of course. Far from it. As we approach the millennium it will receive enormous attention, especially through endeavors like the Human Genome Project. And that's fine. Somebody has to do it. It's just that it will be so much less *important*, ultimately," — his tone was casual as he tossed down the gauntlet — "so much less *interesting* than the structure that governs it, the deeper substrate that determines shape and form."

He bounced the red ball of his pointer across the screen. "The mistake is to see process as separate. It's far more interactive than we've been willing to believe. This won't be *seen*, of course, so much as intuited, especially since the regenerative state is, in a real sense, ever-present, bound by spheres of intelligence co-existent with our own."

Excited, he'd begun to talk faster.

"But here you can glimpse what I'm talking about. No, here, the next slide is clear."

His confidence was a shaping force in its own right, and he went on another five minutes like that, still excited, pointing to a simultaneity of event and non-bounded awareness, a flexibility of form as it meets space and time. Meanwhile he became increasingly aware that to his audience his words were pure gibberish. If not incomprehensible then deeply misguided — misguided, unfounded, simply *wrong* — and stabbing at his remote he began to move faster. A line of perspiration had broken out on his neck.

"There," he said, "the cells at the wound site. Can you see what they're trying to tell us? Can you see what it is they need to know?"

It seemed, though, unlikely that they could. Disdain formed the claws of the animal, and an annoyed sort of murmur had risen up among the rows. Just in time, then, he spotted what eluded him, half-obscured in the gap between the slides. He was toggling ever more quickly to catch it, slides flashing as the Carousel labored, when there came a loud pop from the projector and the screen dropped to black.

There were thirty thousand microbiologists active in the United States alone, give or take a few hundred. Investigative technique grew in sophistication every day. There seemed scant respite from that cascade of sheer *knowing*, little opportunity to really inhabit what they rushed to explain. For a moment, though, that knowing stood suspended, in favor of a deeper silence that lay just below. It was the one moment, in the Diven Center, where they still might have joined him, but by that time someone had located the lights. Radinsky bounded from his seat to the stage.

"Thank you, Dr. Chandler. That was very engaging. The Sterling Lectures are designed to stimulate thinking and this has been no exception. You've given us a great deal to consider. Yes, indeed."

The director glided to his elbow, managing to look disappointed as he glanced at his watch. "I doubt we'll have time for questions. Don't forget that Dr. Lillibridge will be here a week from Tuesday to discuss the post-translational processing of yeast-based proteins.

Individual conferences can be scheduled through the Center office."

"I'd like to continue," Mitchell said, "if I might."

Radinsky had stepped in front of him, arms stretched wide as he pantomimed bemusement. "Technical difficulties. It never fails. We type the genome but struggle with a simple tungsten bulb."

"Not a problem," Mitchell said. "I have a spare in my briefcase." He moved past Radinsky, who frowned.

"Yes, of course, Dr. Chandler, if you're sure you have the time."

Mitchell had little choice but to trust the current that had brought him this far, the momentum that bore him to his briefcase at the edge of the stage. His resolve, on its own, might have faltered — a simultaneity of event and non-bounded awareness? A flexibility of form as it meets space and time? — but he had already retrieved a small Kodak box and was carrying it across the stage. He held the box out to Radinksy, who reluctantly took it from his hand.

The flaps were glued tightly enough that the director had to struggle with them, prying at the cover with his thumbs. There was the usual strip of foam inserted for padding. Beneath lay a protective pouch, heat-sealed at the factory. Radinsky gave out a small grunt as he tore at the opening, reaching inside to pull out a grape.

It was small enough that only the two of them could see it plainly, he and Radinsky at the center of the stage. It was, from the looks of it, a simple table grape, still moist with dew, with a tiny bulge of translucent flesh where it had been pulled from the stem.

Radinsky looked at it, puzzled, and then at Mitchell. He looked again at the grape, lying briefly in his hand. Briefly, because what couldn't be a moment later simply wasn't. In a single motion Radinsky deftly palmed it, the grape dropping out of sight into the pocket of his coat.

Mitchell felt a giddy sense of lightness as he balanced on the stage. European-style, Radinsky was a heavy smoker, so his fingers smelled of tobacco as he eased the microphone from his lapel. There were a few final remarks of appreciation, another promo for Lillibridge and his yeast cells, and with that, the Sterling Lecture was done. The only thing missing, which didn't occur to him until later, midway across the Engineering quad, was the customary round of applause.

On a bright fall afternoon his lab team, like seconds in a boxing match, had fallen in behind him: Brian and Ginny, Prakash and Rene, while Nicole trailed twenty yards behind. Charlie Bates was nowhere in sight. Around him rippled the tell-tale murmur of their respiration, timed to a deeper hum settled in along his spine. Beneath their feet, the sidewalk coalesced calmly to sparkle, as two boys in pursuit of a Frisbee raced shirtless across the grass.

"Diffusion gradients," he said suddenly, "as mechanism. A bicoid protein providing signals for the cell. We need to get somebody on it as soon as we can." He turned to Brian. "Did you see how they tried to keep up with us? Did you see how they strained to understand? I hope I didn't go too far at the end and tip our hand."

Brian exchanged a quick glance with Ginny. "I don't think that's a problem, Mitch. Not on this one. I doubt that's a problem at all."

That awareness is in essence mobile was no longer at issue. He didn't need experimental proof, back at the BioMed Building, to let his attention range out effortlessly, traveling from his office along the hallway of his lab. Ginny had returned to supervise her lab techs as they cleaned out the incubators — despite their best efforts, the contamination had spread. Prakash heated a slice of pizza in the microwave. He watched Peter Edwards, his animal tech, salvage printouts from the recycling bins, to be shredded into bedding for the mice.

His own office, by contrast, felt increasingly cramped with its journals and grant proposals, the pile of Fed-Ex envelopes growing higher by the door. There was no end to the spinning coins that kept them all hypnotized — lab budgets and pathways, gel runs and committee meetings, the steady ping of emails that kept arriving at his desk.

The first he opened was a message from Radinsky thanking him for his talk. The director expressed hope for more cross-campus collaboration with the Chandler Lab. He trusted faculty could count on his influence with the NIH on the next round of funding. Only at the end was there an inquiry about his health.

Other colleagues, too, seemed barely to have made it back to their own offices before firing off messages. One tried to engage him on content, appealing for "greater specificity on the underlying mechanism for non-sequential models of development." Another claimed historical perspective ("For almost forty years the centrality of the genome in biological development has been clear. Yet you seem to imply..."). The tone ranged from chiding ("... one would have hoped, especially from a researcher of your eminence...") to the frankly hostile ("... came to your seminar expecting perspective on post-trauma reneuralation, only to be served warmed-over theosophy instead."). Mitchell scanned the inbox impatiently before closing down his mail. He could hardly be concerned with the chatter of frightened children, fluttering against a world they would rather not know.

From the mail program he moved on to Netscape. Ethernet had been installed just that summer in his office, so the Chandler Lab homepage formed up on the screen. Near the bottom was a synopsis of their research interests, with a cartoon Lazarus emerging just above. There were lists of publications and profiles of the lab team, schematics and institutional affiliations, a link to LazTec, where the stock was going down. With a click of the mouse, all of that disappeared. He called up, in its place, another website, pixels coalescing to spell out SPIRIT RISING on a deep blue background, its white letters above a bright shining cross.

He was already well acquainted with the Spirit Rising site's contours. A click on *Our New Home* produced the drawing of a enormous church building set out against a chalky background of landscape and sky. *When We Worship* listed services and prayer groups, with the last update almost three months before. Behind *What We Believe* lay the discipline's tenets, a dozen entries in Old English font. There was the primacy of the Bible and God in Three Persons. There was Adam's fall when sin entered the world. There was a Godly sorrow that ever worketh repentance, and failing that, the eternal Lake of Fire.

Who We Are, though, was where he was headed. A click there opened a digitalized photo gallery where a studio portrait of Randy and Lee Overmeyer came up to fill the screen. There was a shot of Lee as a child in a Sunday dress and white ankle socks, posed on a sidewalk before a tangled wall of green. Side-burned Randy crouched with a group of evangelists. The pretty couple served fried chicken in a park. There were other images but Mitchell scrolled past them, on his way to the one he had first seen only a few days before.

The genome's composition at its most basic level is unexceptional, four common nucleotides bound together to form a strand. The webpage too, in its elements, is trivial: a sequence of 1's and 0's on some distant file server's hard drive, a resultant spray of photons on the back of his screen. What mattered more was the pattern they achieved there, the photograph of a man and a woman that gradually took form. It was from someone's back yard, down south, in early evening. There were green grass and paving bricks, with woodland behind them, and what looked to be kudzu growing thick among the trees.

Lee he had known immediately, from the first time he saw her. Harder to recognize at first had been himself, the Mitchell Chandler who stood beside her on the screen. He was older and his shoulders had broadened. One arm was draped loosely around her back. His glasses were oval-shaped and his hair was graying; a small case that looked like a beeper was attached to his belt.

Lee was older too, so her loveliness had deepened. Her face was full and the makeup was gone. They looked directly into the camera, their expressions serene — even in the short time he had been coming to the image, she had begun to relax. They were finding comfort together, Mitchell and Lee, this middle-aged couple who stood in the shade. Absent from her hand was the sullen Bible; her left arm now rested at his waist.

That all existence is interactive was no longer in question. Even the grape that Radinsky palmed was, in the end, mostly flourish. Confirmation, for those who cared to see, of nature's inherent flexibility; a reminder that Awareness itself had its own agenda, bringing into being the forms that it pleased.

There was his own mind, alert and co-creative, a mind that only now had begun to realize itself, to catch the slightest glimpse of what it was and might know. Still unresolved were the limits of that power, as Mitchell brought his attention a final time to the screen.

Time was expressed digitally in the upper right corner, seconds flashing steadily past. Leaning forward, he rested his fingers on the monitor. There were voices from the corridor and the sound of glassware, a crackle of static electricity as his thumb neared the screen.

His first trial was unsuccessful, but Mitchell was patient. It had taken them nearly a thousand gels to catch Lazarus at work. He settled in before the monitor to come at it again. The seconds had reached zero and were again moving forward. There may have been a slowing at seventeen as they briefly resisted, before they returned, through the twenties, back to speed.

He came at it yet again, bringing himself fully to bear. The seconds were at the end of the forties before he finally caught up with them. The first perceptible lag came at fifty-one and fifty-two. The hum from the hallway grew sluggish. The sound of glassware in the labs died away. At fifty-eight, he brought process to a stop. Metabolism, mutation, osmosis: all were held in suspension while time took a break. It was a break that lasted a full second — a year, a lifetime — before Mitchell raised his thumb and let it go.

He sat back in his desk chair, breathing shallowly. *This is madness*, he thought, but even that fear, uniquely human, couldn't hold him. What he weighed instead was simple opportunity. He heard the sound of human voices as they returned to the corridor, the centrifuge as it climbed back to speed. He considered the short tether of understanding they had learned to clutch onto, the vast expanse of *More* that lay out beyond its reach. There was Lee too, waiting patiently for him — for their paths to converge — all of which made it that much more absurdly easy to finally step away.

Thirteen

The trip to Pinelands State Park took almost two hours, and by the time they had wound back through thickening woods to the picnic area, Austin Chandler's joints were so stiff he could barely move. His daughter Betsy, at the wheel, scanned the wide gravel parking lot. Finally she spotted a tall woman steadying a pennant on a stick. Five Boy Scouts lay sprawled on the ground behind her, their knapsacks around them on the grass.

"There's Shelly," Betsy said. "Looks like they're ready for the hike."

"Those young men don't look ready for anything," Austin Chandler commented, wincing as he shifted his legs. "Alertness is important in the woods."

Betsy turned to her sons in back. "Put those things away," she said, pointing to their Game Boys. "We're here."

Abel was dark like Betsy's first husband while Willy, from the second, took after his mother, square-faced and fair. Squeezed in between them was five-year-old Scooter, product of yet a third marriage, who had kicked a steady rhythm against his grandfather's seat the whole way from Prairie Grove.

The park was a narrow corridor of forest that flanked the river, grown up around a scattering of old strip mines. Abel and Willy were in line for a hiking badge and it was for their benefit that Betsy had herded them into the car that morning and driven halfway across the state. Austin Chandler had been brought along to watch Scooter, who, even before the car stopped, was already scrambling impatiently between the seats and across his lap to the door.

It was a relief to finally move his legs, and he was still straightening when Scooter darted past him into the parking lot. Two fishermen, attentive in their pickup, skidded through the gravel to a stop.

Betsy retrieved Scooter and as she scolded him he squirmed in her arms. Abel and Willy climbed reluctantly from the car.

On the trip from Prairie Grove Austin Chandler had been

wary. Through all of her various marriages Betsy had managed to stay disappointed in him, full of admonishments for failings past and present. Returning from the restroom he saw her at work among the Boy Scouts, sunglasses pushed back above her forehead. She wore a sleeveless blouse, her shoulders sprinkled with the tiny red bumps of a heat rash that trailed toward her breasts.

Embarrassed, he looked quickly away. He had never quite adjusted to his daughter's adult presence: she still lingered in his mind as a twelve-year old, sneaking up to hang over his shoulder as he read the paper in his chair. Somehow that peripheral girl-presence had been transformed into this confident, sandy-haired woman with bare shoulders and hiking boots. She had rousted the scouts from the grass and was directing his two older grandsons toward their places in the group.

He had never had time for Boy Scouts himself. He wasn't sure he had even heard of them as a child, bound to a steady circuit between a country schoolhouse and their hard-scrabble farm in the Adirondacks. Geoff, and even Mitchell, must have served a turn, because he remembered them in uniform at Warrior games, two fingers raised to their eyebrows in salute. It was harmless enough, he supposed, but he'd had more than enough saluting in the army, deferring to idiots while his life ticked away.

Now, though, the women were in charge, the Scouts listening without enthusiasm as Betsy gave them their orders. Timed as part of the badge requirement, the hike would be five miles each way, winding north along bluffs above the river. She produced a water bottle from the cooler for each of them. She went down the line with a bottle of sunscreen as the boys docilely held out their arms. As part of a series of warnings — the importance of staying together, a prohibition against using their whistles except in case of emergency — she led them to a low patch of green at the edge of the woods.

"And these," she said, "are stinging nettles. I'm pointing them out so you'll know to stay clear."

Beside him, Scooter craned his neck. "Oh, boy," he said, "you see them stinging nettles?"

"*Those* stinging nettles," Austin told him. "There's no reason to talk like a hillbilly. And pay close attention to what she says."

"Stinging nettles," Scooter repeated dreamily, savoring the words. "They reach out and sting you real bad."

Austin looked down at his companion, barely three feet tall and clad in a snug tee shirt and short pants, his bare knees already stained with grass. In his own day he had approached his grandfather carefully, unsure of the mysterious, rope-veined man who smelled of sweat and the chicken house, and brandished a stubble of whiskers like briars on his cheeks. Now young people expected adults to court their favor, joining them for games or a romp on the floor. There was a sing-song sort of tone, too, that people used with children, a dialect he had never mastered. He preferred to speak plainly, which had gotten him nowhere — in the handful of conversations he'd ventured in, over the years, with his grandchildren, he had ended up bickering like a ten-year-old himself.

He was able, at the edge of the parking lot, to keep Scooter on the grass, the boy darting to the restrooms and back again, glancing slyly over his shoulder. Betsy had just drawn up her troops for a final round of instructions when they heard Scooter's cry. He came out of the nettles wailing, small white blisters already puffing on his legs.

"Dad," Betsy complained, "You're supposed to be *watching* him."

"I did," Austin Chandler replied calmly. "I watched him learn something for himself."

The expedition was delayed while Betsy retrieved ice cubes from the cooler, glaring at him as she rubbed them on the boy's stocky legs. Another grievance was forming: though Scooter had been warned a dozen times on the ride up to Pinelands, he only just then understood he wasn't going on the hike. This insult added to his misery and he was left on a park bench with his grandfather, crying disconsolately as the others disappeared into the woods. When they were out of sight he stopped crying. For a long time he sat back on the bench, rubbing his legs thoughtfully with the ice cube.

The parking lot, on a sunny Saturday in October, had begun

to fill. Families carried coolers from their cars to picnic tables. A line of pastel balloons marked the site of a wedding reception. They walked over to watch a nervous young man in a bolo tie, the caterer apparently, supervise his two teenage assistants as they lifted a cake from the van. From there they followed a flagstone path to a shady stretch of bottomland. A forlorn refreshment stand was buried among the trees, surrounded by swarms of gnats and the smell of ripening garbage. As Scooter veered toward it Austin Chandler blocked his path.

"See that insignia there on the concrete slab? This was a WPA project from before the war. My father was in the WPA, and his father as well. They helped build Bear Mountain Park, along the Hudson River. It's hard to imagine now..." but Scooter wasn't listening, bumping at his grandfather's knees as he tried to get past him to the refreshment stand. Checked, he ran off in the other direction, toward a low stone wall that extended along the levee. A half-dozen men leaned above the water, tackle kits spread at their feet.

Scooter ran to each in turn, bouncing up onto the wall and peering into their bait buckets, full of questions as he moved down the line. He was too impatient to wait for answers, darting from one to the next until he ran out of fishermen. At that point he abandoned the levee in favor of a crushed gravel walkway that led out across a meadow, a mowed clearing between river and woods.

It felt good to Austin Chandler to stretch his legs in the sunshine. It felt good to be away from the crowded parking lot too, with its burden of leisure — young people seemed unsure of what to do with themselves, especially with the heavy lifting done. Wedding parties and lawn games had won out against the coal mines; men who should have been out building bridges or blasting tunnels were squeezed into shorts and tank tops, shepherding slack-eyed women with strollers back and forth across the meadow. Austin Chandler was just as happy when Scooter broke away from the walkway, darting onto a path that veered toward the woods.

It was a path that led, within a quarter mile, to a platform left over from mining days, heavy iron rings set in concrete along its base.

Beyond it, the trail turned to dirt. Scooter squatted to rummage through the weeds. When he stood, he held a sagging condom in his hand.

"Here, here, now," Austin Chandler said sharply. "Put that down. No, put it down, damn it, Scooter. Good. Just drop it right there. Now wipe off your hands. Go ahead, you can wipe them on your pants."

They had come into a brushy area thick with sumac, where he felt a familiar pressure against his bladder. He left the sumac to climb a few yards up the hillside, turning his back to unzip his pants. Scooter thrashed his way up to join him, giggling as his own stream sizzled against the ground. The boy left him there, climbing higher through the trees.

Austin finished relieving himself, an apt expression, really, because it *was* a relief, more and more so as the years went by, and he climbed behind Scooter gratefully, enjoying a rare freedom at being in the forest. The fresh feel of the Adirondacks came back to him, the honed blade of his father's ax as they tramped through the woods. There was something uncomplicated about men together. He often labored beside his father a full day with barely a word spoken; he and Geoff had stood together for hours as they worked on a motor, leaning under the hood of one or another of the family's cars.

Scooter was ahead of him, climbing, and at the top of a low ridge they came across what seemed to be a trail. Austin Chandler was surprised at how good he felt — short of breath, perhaps, but still moving easily — his muscles loosening as he followed Scooter through the trees. Ahead of him the boy slowed. "Grampa, will you buy me a Coke?"

Austin Chandler shook his head. "You're asking the wrong man. I don't purchase soft drinks."

"Come on, buy me a Coke. Please?"

"It won't do any good to wheedle, Scooter. Your mother left juice in the car."

"Yeah, but I'm thirsty now. We can stop at that food store and get a drink."

Scooter had picked up a stick, using it to whack tree trunks as they walked. They continued along the first ridge before crossing to another, eventually dropping to a narrow water course where the air felt cool. After a time they began climbing again. Near the top of the next rise Scooter slowed, feet shuffling heavily.

"Come on, Grampa, let's go back. That way you can buy me a Coke."

Shouts from the river and meadow had disappeared behind them. Austin Chandler was enjoying the thick feel of woodland, the quiet in the air as they moved through the leaves.

"You know," he said, "I was thinking of your Uncle Geoff back there a little ways. I was remembering when he was about your age, the year he turned five. Your grandmother had a party planned, but he looked sad when he came down for breakfast. When we asked him why, he cried and cried. 'Because I'll never be four again.' That's what he told us. Can you imagine? Sad because you're going to be five? Your Uncle Geoff was a different kind of boy. He wanted to dig a hole behind the house so he could live like Bugs Bunny. That way he'd never have to leave."

He would have found it difficult to express how good he felt with the forest around them. The class at the church didn't hurt, with its practice at noticing: he was aware as he walked of the balance of his muscles, the dry, loamy smell of the earth. They might have gone another ten minutes before Scooter balked again.

"Come on, darn it, Grampa, I'm *thirsty*!"

Austin Chandler stopped beneath a sycamore. "All right," he said, "you're thirsty."

"Yeah, and I'm bored, too. I'm sick of this stupid hike. Let's go back."

"Wait a second, one thing at a time. Let's just stop and think a minute. Anybody can get a drink of water. Anybody can buy a Coke. There are other things you might want to explore."

"Like what?"

"Well, like the fact that you're thirsty."

"I already said that I was!" Scooter kicked at the ground. "Come on, let's go back!"

"Can you wait a minute? Would you wait a minute, please? Just wait? Wait? All right, thank you. I want you to try something. Take a deep breath and close your eyes. Both of them, Scooter, it's an experiment." He felt a surge of impatience, but the Swiss boy, in class, never hurried them, his voice always measured and calm. "Are they closed? Good. Now take a minute just to experience things. See what it is that you find. Is your mouth dry? Is there a tightness in your throat? No, keep your eyes closed. That's how it's done."

With the boy beside him, Austin Chandler considered his own heavy tongue and pulsing temple. There was a light-headedness that settled in with his eyes closed; finding his balance, he rocked slowly on his feet.

"Just stand quietly a minute and take an inventory. Make sure you get all there is. Then you can say, 'This is thirst.' You'll have a much better idea of how it feels."

Scooter threw up his hands in exasperation. "Jeez, Grampa, I already know how it feels. It feels *thirsty*. When I'm thirsty, I like to drink Coke!"

Austin Chandler looked around at the leafy hillside, the press of underbrush and thick stand of trees. "Well, I suppose we could turn back any time now. Which way is it to the trail?"

"It's back there," Scooter said irritably. "Or over that way. Maybe it's back over there."

"Well, it can't be all of those places so we have to think. I remember coming past that fallen tree. We know the river's on our left. It's important to maintain a sense of direction. You've got to pay attention when you're out in the woods."

When they returned to the fallen tree, though, the trail had disappeared. Farther on there was another downed trunk, but nothing like a path. They came back a hundred yards along the ridge.

"This isn't right either. I don't think we came along here." Austin Chandler pointed to his right, down the slope of a ravine. "I guess we'll just head downhill. That's something to remember in the wilderness. Go the way the water flows and eventually you'll come out."

Downhill should have been easier, but the slope was steep with a thick layer of underbrush. When he looked back at Scooter the boy was concentrating hard as he waded through the brambles, wincing as they tore at his legs. After that there was another rise to negotiate, with more underbrush as they struggled to the top. The forest seemed thicker than he'd remembered, with wide snags of tangled fallen wood. Austin Chandler struggled to keep his feet as they descended again, sharply, grabbing at roots and branches as they slid through the leaves. Abruptly the slope gave out and he scrambled back from a dropoff. As the boy slipped past, he seized him tightly by the wrist.

"Ouch, Grampa," Scooter complained, "that hurts." As he rubbed his arm, they looked at a crescent-shaped pond a hundred feet below their ankles. It was one of the old mines, now flooded from the looks of it, the water a dark metallic green. Pine trees closed in thick around it, and away from the water rose sharply away.

"Come on, Grampa. We've come far enough. Let's go back to the car."

But Austin Chandler didn't know the way back to the car. He didn't know the way to the river either, not from where they sat on a cliff thick with underbrush, a crescent lake below and the forest pressing in. He needed to think, which wasn't so easy — his brain felt thick and clotted with age. Fatigue had already set in as they climbed the last hillside; now he led them back up again, Scooter thrashing in his wake. They had just reached the top when he stumbled heavily forward, a sapling whipping hard against his shin.

His skin, when he pulled up his pant leg, looked like another man's entirely, pale and hairless, the flesh split by an angry red slice. It was hard to catch his breath and his glasses kept slipping. His heart thudded thickly in his chest. For a moment, he heard what sounded like a motorboat, the sound floating somewhere beyond the trees.

"Hey," he called weakly. "Can you hear us?"

The strained sound of his voice was greeted by silence.

"Hey," Scooter demanded shrilly. "Here we are! Answer back!"

His cheeks were dirty and his fine hair lay matted against his scalp. "Oh, great," he said, "now we're *lost*."

"Not lost," his grandfather puffed, "just disoriented. We don't know exactly where we are."

"Come on, we'll go down over there."

"No, that's not it, damn it, let me think for a minute. When I get my bearings we'll be all right."

He had spoken too sharply but was still struggling against breathlessness and the ragged pounding of his heart. He just needed to gather his wits. If he was patient logic would reassert itself, but for a long time that logic stayed away. Finally he pointed to his right.

"Come on," he said, "we'll go up here."

At the top of the next ridge he leaned against an oak tree to vomit, a surprise rush of scrambled eggs and bile. Scooter watched wide-eyed beside him. As Austin Chandler straightened he heard the sound of an airplane, flying free high above them, and he wiped his sour mouth with his sleeve.

The woodland couldn't last forever if they moved east from the river, and for the next two hours that's what they did, thrashing across hillsides and ravines. When they stopped to rest the earth seemed to reach for him; if he lay back on the leaves he might never get up. Recriminations had settled in with his breathing. He thought not just of his countless mistakes through the years but of their witnesses — Edie and Betsy, Mitchell and Geoff — and now Scooter who sat back against a tree trunk, chubby forearms resting on his knees.

"Did you ever think what would happen, Grampa," he asked, "if the ground wasn't here? And there was like this glass beneath us so we could see down below? Did you ever think about that?"

Austin Chandler shook his head. "No, I never did." He climbed to his feet. "Come on," he said, "we'd better keep moving. We'll come to some kind of road if we keep going this way."

That was the theory, anyway, which within another quarter hour was borne out. They came first to a small clearing with a fire ring and beer cans; next, to a narrow, weedy lane, and finally to a road of black asphalt, recently oiled. The forest ended at the edge of the asphalt: before them was a wide field of soybeans, and beyond it a distant grain elevator pushing up against the sky.

A hundred yards along the road they came to a sign: 'Pinelands State Park, 3 miles.'

"Come on," Scooter demanded. "What's it say?"

"It says we've got a ways to go still, but we're on the right track. We'll meet your mother a little farther down the road."

His foolishness still nagged, but paled against a feeling of plain relief as they stumped along the shoulder. He felt a surge of affection for the boy who trudged in front of him, an admiration for his stocky legs, stippled with scratches and dirt.

"Doing okay?" he asked as Scooter slowed by the roadside, a frown of concentration on his face.

"My feet are hot and my legs hurt. My hands feel heavy on my arms." He closed his eyes. "This is *tired*, Grampa. This is what tired feels like."

"I'd say it's tired, all right."

"And umph, this is *sweaty* too. I can feel it all prickly on my skin."

Gradually Austin Chandler had become aware of his own aching legs and blisters, the dark band of sweat that soaked his sport shirt and pants. No cars passed until they had come to the park again, where a mown path led back to the river. The concession stand was closing but by hobbling intently across the flagstones he made it in time. Scooter took the Coke and tipped it up gratefully. "Umm," he said, "that's spicy. It's wet and cold. This Coke here really tastes good!"

Water from a nearby fountain, by contrast, was warm and tasted of sulfur. After Austin Chandler drank he dampened his handkerchief, wiping first Scooter's face and then his own. He rinsed the handkerchief and squatted with difficulty, washing the boy's legs as best he could. The blisters from the nettles had given way to a latticework of bright red scratches from the brambles. Scooter winced as his grandfather cleaned them, intent on the Coke in his hand.

They'd barely made it back to their park bench before the Scouts began to emerge from the forest. They appeared one by one, spreading out to throw their packs on the grass. Betsy came into the picnic area looking flushed and annoyed. Scooter rushed up to greet her.

"Mom," he said breathlessly, "Grampa barfed!"

"Willy," she said, "that's not where your pack goes. Pick it up and take it to the car. Abel, Mrs. Gresham can use help with the cooler. Come on, get moving." She looked more closely at Scooter and then at Austin Chandler. "You two look like you've been rolling around in the dirt all day. Where in the world have you been?"

"Mom, Grampa and I have been walking. We walked and we walked and we walked."

"Abel, make sure the other boys get some too. There's enough for everybody. John, give that bottle to your mother."

"Mom, listen!"

She turned wearily to Austin Chandler. "Dad, do you mind riding in back on the way home? I want Willy up front with me. Come on, boys, use the bathroom so we can go."

"Mom, Mom, come on! Listen!"

"All right, Scooter, you've got my attention. What is it? What's on your mind?"

"I want to come hiking again soon sometime, maybe tomorrow. Me and Grampa had *fun*. We were out in the woods there and we walked and we walked, and we…" It didn't seem clear to him exactly what it was they had done, slogging up and down hillsides, but by that time he had caught sight of the sandwiches. He ran off to join the older boys who cuffed him easily aside.

The wedding cake was gone and the balloons had been scattered. The families were packing to go home. As Betsy wound back through the park Austin Chandler sat crammed into the back seat with Abel, already lost in the Game Boy, with Scooter squeezed in between them. Juice boxes and potato chip bags lay scattered at their feet. Betsy was sunburned and looked tired as she glanced in her mirror, but now that she had her father captive she settled in to talk.

"...but now that his family's out here he just ignores them. He's gotten so *strange* anymore. Maureen hardly sees him at all."

"Mitchell is a busy man with an important position. He had that Sterling affair earlier in the week. He has a conference in Europe, I believe, later this month. Sometimes a family has to understand."

"He's an asshole, Dad. That's the bottom line. Mitchell's never cared about anyone but himself. Maureen is about ready to throw him out."

In his own fatigue what came to mind was a Katzenjammer Kid sort of image, a comic strip Mitchell tumbling out the door to the street. He didn't pretend to understand his daughter's attitude about marriage, her own readiness to trade up when a better model came along. There was her salty language too, but the boys didn't notice — they possessed a kind of tensile strength that alloys often had.

"And whatever happened at Cooke-Davis? I thought you were going to talk to them about an apartment. You can't just hole up forever on Washington. Ever since Mom died, you've let the place go!"

Austin Chandler might have defended himself but by that time they were back on the interstate moving high above the prairie. All around, the view was unbroken; they made their way smoothly past fencerows and farmhouses, the broad fields with the harvest half done. He thought again of hearing the airplane as they slogged through the forest, its serene glide above them out of sight beyond the trees.

How foolish his struggles would have seemed to that distant pilot, how frequent his missteps as they thrashed far below. From high above all the choices look easy, far from the pull of brambles and thick, jumbled trees. The strip of woodland was narrow but he had managed to get lost in it. He still wasn't sure where it happened, the point where his attention lapsed and the path slipped away.

Scooter would learn soon enough not to trust him. For the time being though, he lay back under his grandfather's arm, head lolling heavily against his chest. They were out of the woods but the boy was still walking, legs moving fitfully, his fist tight on Austin Chandler's pantleg as they sailed high above the fields.

FOURTEEN

'All things work together for the good of those who love the Lord and are called according to His purpose.'

Pastor Randy Overmeyer sat in his and Lee's small office at Campus Church, considering the passage before him. He had found it that morning in a desk drawer, stuck behind a box of staples — a good sign, because God's ways of communicating with him had been growing more and more obscure, to the point where they seemed to have entirely disappeared.

That the verse was in his own handwriting didn't matter: Randy couldn't remember when or why he had written it. He couldn't have known he would find it again at this particular moment, and he tried the passage again.

"All things work together for the good of those who *love* the Lord." He certainly counted himself among that number but it was hard to see how things were working for the good. A vibrant, growing ministry had, in less than a year, almost vanished. Attendance had dwindled to the point where he could no longer service the mortgage on the new church lot, let alone pay the back rent still owed to Campus Church. His credit cards, at their limit, were useless, and calls from bill collectors formed a constant source of tension between him and Lee at home.

'All things work together for the good of those who love the Lord, and are *called* according to his purpose.' Randy's head ached and the text swam in tight circles. "All things work together for the *good*," he murmured, feeling for an opening. "All things work *together*. Work together for the *good*. Work together for the *good* for those who *love* the Lord and are *called* according to his purpose."

He sat back and sighed. There had to be a reason for their difficulties, a reason that would become clear once God revealed his plan. A plan that even then was in motion, the very point he'd been arguing with Lee a few weeks earlier when they looked up to see the tall man at the rear of the church. At least God's throws were coming closer: it wasn't quite a stranger, but Geoffrey Chandler's brother Mitchell, wandering in from the street.

Randy heard footsteps in the parlor and sat back to listen. "All things work together…" he murmured, in search of his rhythm. 'That very morning I was sitting in my office, about ready to give up, when I found this verse from Romans in my desk. I was studying it, wrestling with it, even *doubting* God's power to help me, when one of His agents showed up at my door.'

"Come in," he called out cheerfully. "Ask, and it will be given, seek and you'll find. Knock or just come on in!"

A stocky boy with tangled blond hair and a dirty Metallica tee shirt pushed the door open. An oversized wallet stuck out from his back pocket, linked to his belt by a heavy metal chain.

"Hey there," the boy said, "how's it going?"

"As long as I walk with Jesus, everything's fine. It's when I go my own way that trouble settles in. How about you, brother? Does God have a place in your life?"

The boy was older than he'd seemed at first glance, with a half-smile under a ragged, wispy beard. A collection of muddy tattoos covered both of his arms.

"I'm not really here for me."

"If not for yourself then who are you for? If only for yourself then what's the point? Jesus has a way —"

"I'm here for Mickey Ellrod over at Prairie Motors. I've come to take back your car."

"My car," Randy said.

"The Explorer. I'm here to pick it up. That is unless you've got twenty thousand dollars lying around somewhere you want to give me. Otherwise, I'm gonna need the keys." The boy looked slowly around the office. "Kind of tight quarters you got here. Be nice when you have that new place by the interstate. Mickey told us all about it. He used to be one of your elders, is what he said. Anyway, he holds the note on the Explorer, and I guess God told him he'd better get it back."

The boy rubbed along his bicep with his hand. "Funny, I saw one that looked just like it a couple of blocks from here, same model and color, license plates registered to you. Only it was parked back behind a sorority house, kind of out of the way. Like maybe nobody would even know that it's there."

Randy rose slowly to his feet. "I know you, don't I? You look familiar."

"You've seen me, but you know my girlfriend better. She used to go to Spirit Rising when you were out at the Lamplighter."

"Okay," Randy said. "It's coming back to me. Charlene Wiltgen, am I right? And you're Darrin. Or Loren, maybe. No, that's not right. Don't tell me, it's…"

"Jaron. Hey, that's pretty good. Jaron Price. I'm surprised you remember. You told Charlene to stay away from me if I wouldn't come to church."

"So how's Charlene?"

"Can't really say. She moved with the kids back to Carbondale. She's living with her folks down there."

"That must be hard, a man without his family."

"Oh yeah," Jaron said. "It's real hard. I cry myself to sleep every night." He laughed. "You're the one I ought to get down on my knees to, for getting that bitch out of my hair."

His laugh hung between them as Randy came around the desk. "You liked that beer quite a bit if I remember. What was it, PBR that you drank?"

"Hell no, not that hog piss. Coors Light's the only beer for me."

"Oh, that's right. I guess I forgot. Coors Light. The old Silver Bullet. I'm sorry to be asking, but I'm kind of a curious person, Jaron, is what it is. There's always one more thing I want to know. Right now I'm wondering about those Silver Bullets, and how many more you plan on shooting in your life. You know, looking out ahead. What do you figure?"

The boy shrugged. "I don't know. A hell of a lot, I imagine."

"And that's fine, Jaron. It really is. Jesus didn't turn the water into Dr. Pepper, now, did he? He didn't make Lipton iced tea." As Randy came closer the boy backed away. "There's nothing wrong with a little something to drink now and then, I don't care what the Baptists say. It's just that after a while that old beer kind of loses its fizz. Sooner or later it's not quite as fun. Am I right?"

Jaron looked back at him uneasily. "Maybe. Who knows?"

"I do," Randy said. "And you do too. You know exactly what I mean, every word of it. Your woman and children live halfway across the state and you don't even care — that's how empty your heart is. But, hey, that's okay, too. It's your heart, your life, your soul. Nobody says otherwise. Just don't count on the beer, that's what I'm saying. Not when it comes to the emptiness. The more you try to drown it, the better it knows you; the faster you run, that's how fast it catches up."

"I came for a car, not a sermon."

Randy lowered his voice. "Don't lie to me, Jaron. I won't stand for it. You could have wired that damn Explorer half an hour ago. You could already be back at the car lot playing grabass with the salesmen. We don't need to stand here all morning playing games. There's something else that brought you through my door."

Uncomfortable, the boy licked his lips. "I can't let you keep the Explorer, Randy. I don't care what you and Jesus have to say."

"But what do you say? That's the question. What do you have to say for yourself?"

"I say I came for the car."

Randy had, from the first days of his ministry, liked the sassy ones. The farther a person came to meet Jesus, the deeper His love got to go. The boy's voice sounded almost wistful as he stood with his clipboard, as if he was about to say goodbye to an old and trusted friend. And, in way, he was: it was one of Randy's gifts to see before him the false Jaron, weathered and lifeless, like a brittle shell that was about to give way. He could see the real Jaron, too, right beneath it, still tender and looking for a hand. When he went to reach out, though, he could barely raise his arm.

"You just have to…" he said, and faltered. He tried again but the words slipped away. He had brought hundreds of people to Christ through the years, through altar calls and on street corners, in living rooms and city parks, but instead of recalling their faces, radiant with gladness, he could see only their backs as they all turned away.

"Jaron," he began again, but nothing came. It was as if a barrier had been raised between them. It was as if God's love was a joke and had never existed; as if they were two talking animals, only briefly alive. When Randy looked for his strength, fatigue was what found him and he reached in his pocket for the keys.

"Here," he said. "You can have them. That little clicker there goes to the door."

Caught off balance, Jaron looked back at him blankly.

"Go on, take 'em. Tell Mickey it pulls to the right at stop signs. He might want to have a look before he puts it on the lot."

Not quite believing his reprieve, the boy reached out his hand. Randy gave him the keys and turned to his desk. He closed his Bible and recapped his pen. He slipped the verse from Romans back in the drawer. When he looked up, Jaron was still in front of him — buoyed by his good fortune he seemed reluctant to leave.

"Hey Randy, you still play music? I remember seeing you over at Allerton one Sunday with the Lizards. I was thirteen, maybe, trailing around after my older brother. What was that one tune you did, 'Twisted Summer'?

Randy nodded.

"Man, I loved that song. You guys could rock! Hey, you want me to give you a ride somewhere? I'd be glad to."

"No thanks, Jaron. You've got things to do. I'll be all right."

The boy hesitated, pasty face coloring. "Come on, man, why don't you let me take you home at least? It's a long walk from here to Manor Lake."

Randy looked around the small office, at the boxes Lee had been packing up and moving to their garage. He thought of the distance that had grown up between them, the way they argued almost every time they talked. He lifted his sportcoat from the chair.

"All right," he said, "I'll take you up on it, if you don't mind making a swing out that way."

Outside they moved through a steady flow of young people on their way to class. Jaron was in good spirits, strolling with the self-conscious swagger of a town kid. Randy, in his sport coat and slacks, didn't fit in any better, and the students spread wide on the sidewalk to let them pass.

The Explorer was squeezed between a dumpster and a spreading mulberry in the sorority house parking lot. Jaron gunned the engine for the benefit of any co-eds who may have been watching, spinning gravel as they surged to the street. It had been a long time since Randy was in the passenger seat, and he looked out on campustown. Among the bookstores and taverns there was even a church or two, the Newman Center and Baptist Student Union, the Presbyterian Campus Ministry with its red brick and vines. Jaron lit a cigarette as he settled behind the wheel.

"Did I ever tell you," Randy asked, "how I first met God?"

"The time you OD'ed down in Dallas? I guess I heard it a couple times. Maybe more, and I barely came to services a month."

Randy nodded. "Probably so. It made an impression. Wake up in the hospital like that, tubes all down your throat, it's something you remember. Find out you died three times and are still there alive."

A good testimony has multiple uses — sometimes he touched on his lostness, sometimes on the dangerous snare of drugs. The disillusion of rock and roll fame was a popular theme. The story had gained through countless retellings its own life and purpose, a finely tuned example of the saving grace of Jesus Christ. The less serviceable parts lost their seats at the table, and over time he had almost forgotten them himself.

Among the things misplaced, and harder to express somehow to the struggling sinner, was the simple pleasure of those days back in Dallas. The pure and undiminished *joy* there had been in being Randy Overmeyer, a joy that sometimes seemed barely containable within a single body. It had been a Saturday night after closing at the Ballroom, a time to relax after the crowd had gone home. There was a glow from the jukebox and a wide, empty dance floor, a big booth in the corner of the bar.

Lee's Sunbird was out in the parking lot, but another girl had found a place beneath his arm. She claimed to be nineteen but was probably younger, smooth-skinned in her tank top and tight pair of jeans. He could still remember the click of her heels as they floated across the dance floor. They had already shared a joint, necking at the bar, and Randy loved the way her nipples pressed out against the tank top, her giggle as he brushed them with his palm. He had his other hand wrapped tight around a tequila sunrise, and a wide silly smile on his lips. There were plenty of reasons to smile: the A&R man had been calling from Los Angeles, Stan had finally mastered the backbeat on "When We're Loving," and their first recording session was two weeks away. He couldn't possibly imagine feeling any better, at least until he got to the booth and saw lines of powder on a mirror.

"Coke?" he asked hopefully, but Stan shook his head.

"Naw, just angel dust. Frog's trying to get rid of it." Stan had already done his part, from the looks of it, and so had Donnie, who sat back, dazed, with a white residue on his moustache, a stringy-haired little toughie perched smoking on his lap.

"Maybe I can be of service," Randy said, and bent to the mirror.

"Let the good times roll" was the phrase he'd been singing, a new song by the Cars that had been going through his head. He took the first line and the second, leaning low across the booth. "Let the good times roll," he sang, but the melody stumbled, as the first wall of buzz hit his brain. He straightened in the booth to find his balance, before leaning back for the line that he'd left.

"Wow, Randy," Stan said admiringly. "That was a *hit*."

'The godly sorrow that bringeth repentance' had been Lee's line in their Statement of Faith. Randy couldn't remember being sorrowful at all. Incredibly stoned, yes, and unable to stand — at some point he'd found himself on the dance hall's filthy carpet, the girl in the tank top sitting cross-legged at his side. He felt her finger as it ran lightly across his forehead, a puff of breath as she leaned low to kiss his cheek. She wasn't there a little later when Stan's voice floated in. "Hey, dig it, Randy is *gone*." Someone poured beer on his forehead which struck him as funny, the cool trails of wetness dripping past him to the floor.

The odd part was that he had never much cared for angel dust. For all its plain kick-in-the-head power, the high was jarring and discordant, with a sharp chemical meanness always lurking close at hand. When the meanness reached out for him Randy was agile, skipping past. Jagged cartoons laced his mind with their strangeness, and when he'd had his fill, he pulled free to look around. The dance hall's slowly ebbing energy formed a pool far behind him. For a time he glided low over Dallas, circling the business district twice as he headed out of town. Almost immediately, it seemed, he was back at the Astrodome, where a narrow runway stretched out from the stage.

The Stoned Lizards hadn't been the first or even second choice to open for Aerosmith. Negotiations had been conducted without ceremony, and the band dressed in a small umpires' locker room far from the stage. During sound check they received a series of warnings, the most emphatic of which had been about the runway — it was designed for the headliners, not them.

Six months later there was little reason to hesitate, and Randy threw down his guitar as he came across the stage. It must have been then, when he stepped onto the runway, that he left his own heartbeat behind.

Left behind, too, were the whirl and dizziness. As he bounded up the incline, his whole mind was clear. The crowd pumped their fists as they called out his name. At one time he would have gladly stopped to listen, but that time was over. He'd reached the tinted panes of the Astrodome roof, still climbing higher. Meanwhile, back in Dallas, a man's body struggled. A body that someone, it seemed, had finally noticed. A body that was half-dragged across the dance floor to the fire exit, doubled into the back seat of someone's car — a drama increasingly irrelevant as Randy moved up the runway, marveling at the great and glittering space that spread out on every side.

'So this is where the music comes from,' he still remembered thinking. There were jingles from commercials and African drumbeats, songs from Mrs. Pilcher's fourth grade classroom back in childhood Prairie Grove. He found the new riff for "Bitch Nation" he'd been working out with Donnie, fully resolved after teasing them for days. And it wasn't just melodies that found a place in that spaciousness: all that was and ever could be — traffic lights and blood vessels, shop vacs and earthworms — was enfolded neatly around him, poised and formless as the music slipped away. The silence deepened as he edged along the runway. It was while he was inching higher, still in his tight pants and feather boa, that he looked up and met God face to face.

In the passenger seat of the Explorer Randy shifted in his seat. It was a sunny day in the middle of October. All along Lincoln Avenue maples flashed a brilliant red and orange. The marquee outside the Baptist Student Union had held a warning for students: "God grades on the cross, not a curve." Outside a frame church close to campus another message waited: "Exposure to the Son Can Prevent Burning." Jaron downshifted, racing the engine. A marquee two blocks further on made its stab, barely trying: "Most of us give God credit; few of us give Him any cash."

Looking out his window, Randy pondered the signs. By this time he should have had a marquee of his own installed by the interstate. The one he picked out would have been bigger than any of them, with bright lights like a football team's scoreboard, and a rolling text so he could run messages just as dumb. He would have kept shrinking God, too, until He was easier to manage, little more than a killjoy high school principal, slow-witted and wise-cracking, set against a cartoon Satan with barbed pitchfork and curling tail. And maybe that was all right. Maybe he really was supposed to spend his days poring over carpet samples, deciding whether a church balcony should have six rows or eight. Or maybe, just like always, he was guided, and had only forgotten why God brought him back to life.

It wasn't that he had ever misled people — everything he said in his testimony was true. There really was God's goodness and power. There really was the saving grace of Jesus Christ. At the same time, truth got shaped to ministry and rarely the other way around. As the years went by his witness had grown leaner and more effective. The harder to express parts faded further from memory, until Randy had almost lost track of them himself.

There was much from that runway, high above the Astrodome, that surprised him, things so completely clear that he never forgot. God wasn't mad at any of them. There was no reason, in His presence, to be afraid. He had wanted Randy's help, which at the time sounded reasonable — it appeared they'd done business before. That he would come back to Dallas and marry Lee was a part of it. That they would return to Prairie Grove and start a ministry of their own. Back on earth, of course, the details grew sketchy, but from high above, the whole plan was clear.

Even as Randy mulled it over, though, his attention was wandering. There was God, but he remembered something else. He kept trying to look past His shoulder, toward the end of the runway, until God finally stepped aside so he could see for himself.

It's one thing to have a Creator of the universe. To have a single path stretching out through the world. At the end, though, Existence keeps going. What Randy got to see was the Rest of the Story — all that went on after God fell away.

It was a Vastness that still had the power to chill him, like a searing flash of ice that spread out from his chest. Even that barely recalled glimpse was enough to overwhelm him, throwing Randy back hard against his seat. His breathing grew shallow but his vision was sharper: as they turned onto University he had remembered how to see. There were *cars* that nosed in at the cross streets. There was *sky* that spread out above the trees. Visible, too, was a crackling white current settled in along the railroad, flashing out behind sagging storefronts and weedy vacant lots. From Five Points the old highway took over, and a couple of miles later they reached the entrance to Manor Lake.

"Bear to the right here," he said as they came past the coachlights.

Randy had encountered not just Memory but a familiar feeling of steadiness. He was alive to the hum of their tires and a wide, curving pavement, the cardboard houses spread out around the lake. Jaron had lapsed into silence, his good humor gone.

"There's things about Charlene you don't know," he told Randy, scowling. "Only one of those kids is even mine."

"Take this next turn, where you see the construction site. We're the fourth house down on the left."

"She's hard to live with but people don't see that. She's like another person entirely as soon as we're alone."

"Right there, the house with the gables. The one with the three car garage. " He turned to the boy, who had pulled over along the curb. "Jaron, I need you here with me. Don't worry, there's nothing you have to do."

"I want to love my family but I can't! It's like the shit you were saying earlier. When I look inside, all I see is that emptiness! It's like sometimes I'm already dead!"

"Shhh, shhh," Randy said. "Jesus loves you. That part is never going to change. We got something else here that's going on around us. A battle raging we can't even see. Don't be scared, just give me your hand a minute. I need someone solid at my side."

Jaron nodded, his fingers cold as he took Randy's hand.

"Father God, I'm here with Jaron in Prairie Grove. He's a good man and he's eager to love You. Do what You can to set him right." The boy's hand jerked involuntarily. His eyes were clenched and his half-smile was gone. "But right now I need help for Your servant Randy. Give him strength in the power of Your name. Keep before him the terms of our covenant. Help him recall why You gave him second life." Randy felt the welcome tug of his eyes rolling up behind his lids. "Abba de gadda," he said, "la mah lay kada. Ana da gala lay sahda la dah."

There was always a moment right at first when he tried to guide things, impose his will on what God had to say. That was before the Full Spirit surged to fill him, before his mind went blank and fresh words filled his throat. For all the time spent on thought, it's not at the heart of things, and the heart is where God leaves His mark. And sure enough, before long there it was. Even bleached by the sun and his spotlights, obscured by earth and ambition and time, his task had come back. It joined the deep sense of calm that had already settled over him, the great relief of finally knowing what to do.

He turned to Jaron, who still clutched his hand. "You can say amen, Jaron. The prayer is over."

"Amen," the boy said beside him. His face was drained of blood and his lips were trembling. "I don't want to drink no more, Randy, I really don't. While you were praying, I could see it all happening! I could see my life trickling away!"

"Shhh," Randy said, "it's okay."

"Mickey's back on pills again. People don't know it but he is. He's like a crazy man all day at work."

"Shh, shh, it's okay, it really is." Randy waved his hand past the golf course and tidy lawns. "We live in wild times and places. Great armies clash in combat all around. People can't help but be caught in the middle."

"I don't care nothing about the Explorer, just keep it. Somehow you and Jesus got to help me! Somehow you need to help me find a way!"

"It's okay, Jaron. Come on, let go." Randy twisted his fingers, trying to loosen the boy's grasp. "Go ahead, do your job. Take this back to Mickey at the lot. After that, you can find us at church. I got a feeling we're going to be there a lot."

He stood in front of his house as he watched the Explorer go. By the corner, it was already unfamiliar; a moment later, it had never been his. Back instead, just in time, was his excitement — after so long in hiding, the Resistance came clear. The battle had drawn close and Randy was ready; as he looked toward the golf course, he felt himself smile.

FIFTEEN

On an early October morning they had the women's department to themselves, Lee waiting in a wicker chair outside the dressing room while Barbara tried on a jumper. The jumper had been cute on the hanger, but when Barbara came out it looked wrong.

"I don't think this quite does it," she said doubtfully. The mirror's three reflections didn't help: the fabric bunched at the waist and clung tightly to her hips.

"Why don't you try that blue linen one? A bright color would look nice against your skin."

"Do you really think so? I guess it doesn't hurt to try."

This time the dress hung more loosely, but its shapelessness had a matronly feel. After a spin in front of the mirror Barbara shook her head.

"Clothes don't like me," she said forlornly. "Maybe it's just as well. Royce would go through the roof if I paid this much for a dress." She pulled at the shoulders. "It would just be nice someday to try on something that fits."

"I can't wear V-necks like you do. They always make my face look too long."

"Lee, please," Barbara said, "You're so pretty it isn't funny. How about this dress with the sea shells? That would be colorful enough."

Lee had come up to stand behind her. "I'm thinking more along the lines of silk pants with a long flowing top. When a woman has good height she really ought to show it off."

Meeting her eyes in the mirror, Barbara blushed. "Well, maybe so. Let me get this stupid thing off and we'll go take a look."

Lee found her place on the wicker chair again, half hidden among the clothes. She had been suspicious when Barbara first called, the morning after the Women's Prayer Circle, inviting her on an expedition to the Amish colony south of town. More than anything else she had gone along to re-establish herself: her breakdown had felt like a betrayal of both Randy and their faith. Barbara never mentioned it. Instead she seemed nervous herself as Lee climbed into the car, a battered Oldsmobile with sheepskin seat covers, and a stuffed tiger on suction cups stuck to the window in back.

Tentatively, on the ride down, they began to talk. They talked more freely as they shopped in the souvenir shops, strolling past rough-cut shelves of honey and peanut brittle, refrigerators filled with summer sausage and tins of Shoo Fly Pie. By the time they had doubled back to an outlet mall near the highway, Lee knew the frequency of Barbara's periods, details of Royce's feud with one of his supervisors at the processing plant, all about a boy named Allen she had been in love with at sixteen. Incredibly, Lee found herself talking as well. Not carelessly, to be sure, but with increasing ease: she touched lightly on her long estrangement from her family, how disappointed she had been when her mother had abandoned the mission and brought her and Mim home.

All at once, it seemed, they were back at Manor Lake, curving past the golf course to her house. Parting shyly, they met on Saturday for a movie. The following Thursday, for Women's Prayer Circle, they ventured across the street to the Warrior Jitters coffee shop. They ordered tall lattes and settled in among the students, where they talked the whole morning away.

Barbara's motive, she gradually realized, was friendship, an experience Lee felt little acquainted with. What women did together, apparently, was talk and listen, agree and sympathize, and then talk and listen some more. Simple acknowledgements — Randy's stubborn insistence that they move up to campus, her resentment toward the church elders who had abandoned them — seemed the currency of the exchange, and each small expenditure felt like a new kind of freedom, as if she were setting down burdens she had carried all her life.

This wasn't to say the admissions weren't painful, especially about their shared hopes of motherhood. As time went by though, an odd thing happened: the more Lee revealed of herself, the more real Barbara became. Barbara had delicate hands and a frank open gaze; she possessed an unassuming honesty that Lee deeply admired.

They both avoided baby showers and pregnant women; both had experienced deep bouts of shame that they worried would never lift.

It was easier to understand, too, under the influence of that honesty, how her own faith had been distorted. Randy loved Signs and Wonders, the healing and tongues, a ministry that had never suited her at all. She recalled with a deep shudder the altar calls, the fervent prayers as they rose up around her, the laying on of hands and slaying in the Spirit, as some of the times when she felt most alone.

It had taken a toll on her, too, her role as the pastor's wife — and before that, a missionary's daughter — the one whose faithfulness was always on display. Perhaps that's why it felt so good to sit invisible in the women's department waiting for Barbara. That sense of peacefulness only deepened as they walked through the mall. They settled after a while near a splashing fountain. The concourse on a weekday morning was deserted: two Penney's sales girls talked together in sportswear, while a white-coated woman at Eyemasters worked on her nails.

After a while a young woman came out of Osco, chatting on a cell phone as she pushed a stroller. Barbara waved at the little boy who rode in it. He looked back at her with interest, half-standing to watch until they moved out of sight. Barbara didn't say anything but Lee felt a sadness for her anyway. She felt a sadness for Barbara in *her* heart, the kind of thing that happened, she was learning, with a friend.

It was impossible to overstate how deeply she had been affected by Barbara's friendship. And it wasn't just friendship, she knew, but ministry: Lee marveled, as she drove home, at autumn's brief majesty. She felt a renewed appreciation for the cycle of seasons, an agreeable smallness to her will within the world. At Manor Lake she went upstairs to change her clothes. The house was cold — with money running out, they'd been trying to economize — and seemed to her more excessive than ever. Its kitchen alone dwarfed their house in Sunyani, the master bedroom as large as her father's whole church.

The walk-in closet, too, seemed newly obscene to her, with the wall of Randy's suits that filled up the left side, her own clothes clogging hangers on the right. Even in the first year after seminary, with Randy earning eight hundred dollars a month as assistant pastor in Oklahoma, he had driven them back every month to Dallas. A Neimann-Marcus charge card had performed the miracles in those days, the clothes a reflection of God's pleasure in them both. She thought of Randy, finally humbled in Prairie Grove. She felt for Barbara, unwilling to give up. She thought of her own hopes too, with what seemed to be tenderness. She would be thirty-eight in the spring, her birthday two weeks before Randy's, and she was finally ready to accept that a baby wouldn't come.

With that assent came both freedom and opportunity — looking in the mirror, Lee could acknowledge a certain attractiveness. It wasn't meant to burden or indict her; it was just one of the many ways that God found to do His work. From her side of the closet she chose a simple gray exercise outfit, a tapered jacket and pair of matching pants. She pulled on white socks and gym shoes. Mother or not, her tastes were still feminine: the jacket had pink trim and there were poms on her socks. She left the gold chain around her neck. Business-like, she dropped her keys into her pocket and trotted downstairs to the door.

Outside, the neighborhood basked in sunshine. There was a green cast to the lake behind their house. She passed, at the end of the block, a lot where a house was going up: there were pickup trucks and the rattle of hammers, a portable toilet with an Indian on the side. Behind the lot lay the stubble of a bean field: a crop had come and gone while she was wrapped in herself.

At the corner Lee crossed the street to the golf course. Like the mall it was largely deserted. She climbed through the rough to a fairway, where a swirl of gnats hovered, summer-like, in the sun.

Beyond the fairway there was a small shelter for the golfers. When Lee came around the edge of it he was already there, sitting at the end of a wooden bench.

"Hello, Dr. Chandler."

"Lee," he said, without rising. "Lee Overmeyer. Hello, Lee

Overmeyer, hello."

"Hello," she said needlessly again. "I thought I might be early but you're already here."

The shelter was made of pressed metal and open on three sides. Before them were more small trees and a series of fairways, with the Manor Lake clubhouse low in the distance.

"Actually," she said, "it worked out well for us to meet here. I don't think I realized we were neighbors. Which house is yours?"

"Over there," he said, pointing past the shelter.

"Oh, really? You're on the lake? Randy and I are, too, but on Sunset. We live in the house with the…"

"Gables," he said, "and tin roof above your porch. The three-car garage and a herringbone walk."

"That's right," she said, feeling herself color. "You know the neighborhood very well." A pair of golf carts glided soundlessly near the clubhouse. "We've lived in Manor Lake almost two years and I've never been out here. Do you and your wife play? We don't, unless you count miniature golf, and that was a long time ago."

Mitchell Chandler didn't answer. He wore a blue sweater and slacks, and was watching her closely.

"I received your emails," she said quickly, "that came to our web site. You've been very persistent, which is good. I'm sorry we never responded. My husband, of course, is in charge of our men's ministry, and normally I would have passed them on to him. But Randy…"

Lee paused, pulled at by old habits of dishonesty. "But Randy has been preoccupied by problems at the church. Problems that have become quite serious, unfortunately. So I finally decided to see you myself."

She felt a certain nervousness, which was understandable, alone with a strange man in the middle of the day. It wasn't a rendezvous, though, but an opportunity to witness — for the first time in her life she had something to share.

As Mitchell Chandler looked back at her from the bench, she remembered their first meeting in the sanctuary, the powerful aversion she had felt at the time. A month later, she could see him much better. A University person and a professor, certainly, but for all of that, just a man. A man not unlike herself, with his pride and arrogance; he watched her with the same measuring gaze she had felt in the alleyway, as he had stood waiting for her to open her eyes.

"So I'm pleased you want to learn more about our church. Pleased, but also surprised. A Spirit-based ministry can be confusing. For all the power that's generated, it's easy to feel disappointed. It's easy to think God doesn't care when our dreams don't come true.

"I know that you wanted to talk to me in particular. Your emails made that very clear. But I wasn't someone, at the time, who could help you. That's the real reason I didn't respond. I wasn't sure what our ministry had to offer you. I wasn't sure what it had to offer me either, really, to tell the truth. It wasn't clear I had anything to say.

"You see, Dr. Chandler, I know what it's like to be doubtful. You may not think so, but I do. Please understand: I know God exists and that He created us in His image. I know Jesus died for our sins. I don't expect you to believe that, of course. Not yet. It can take a whole lifetime to fully understand."

Somewhere inside, Lee felt herself wince. What grated most was the sound of condescension, a superiority she no longer claimed. It was wrong to see herself as special, especially when God's love lay in the opposite direction, within a shared brokenness that healed and renewed. She wasn't going to have a baby and Jesus suffered on a cross: for the first time, her faith's equation added up. God's world, exactly as it was, felt finally right to her, a rightness barely containable as it swelled in her chest.

"I had been going through a difficult time when you saw me that night behind the church. I was angry about so many, many things. There was something I wanted very badly. I couldn't understand why God wouldn't answer my prayers.

"But before that there were other things I wanted badly. And before that there was always something else. There was a reason I needed to be chastened. There were lessons I still had to learn!"

"You stand here only to announce victory."

"No, please listen, Dr. Chandler. There's a point to things. That's what I came to tell you. That's all anybody really needs to know. It's not just nothing, like you think. There *is* a God and He never wants to hurt us! He *loves* us so very, very much. Otherwise…"

She paused because only then had it become fully clear to her, so powerfully she felt tears in her eyes. "I mean, otherwise…"

That her words failed at that point hardly mattered. She felt a wave of real compassion as it rose to fill her — compassion for Barbara, for herself, for all of them, fellow travelers in a damaged, suffering world. The professor sat silent with his head down. On impulse she moved to his side. When she laid her hand on his shoulder he closed his eyes. He rocked to his feet then, to point across the grass.

"Manor Lake," he said, looking at her intently. "Do you see what I mean? Can you understand what I'm saying? This isn't a manor. That's not a lake. It's just a pond they fill with a pipe."

Still moved by the power of her own understanding, Lee could only look back at him. His eyes shone with an intensity that bound her. She was silenced by his tallness at her side. She felt herself beginning to tremble.

"Steady," he said, "I won't hurt you. Don't worry, everything's fine."

His voice was calm like a doctor's, and after all he *was* a doctor of sorts — that's why they called him Dr. Chandler. She stood helpless as he reached to embrace her. His lips against hers were chilly, his long arms alien as they wrapped around her back. He kissed her again before stepping away.

"Okay, listen," he said, "this is important. Forget about all of that bullshit. All of it. There aren't any lessons to be learned. You don't need to be chastened or curbed. Go home and take care of what you need to. Stop the paper and give away the cat. Then come with me. You can be just as free as you want."

Paralyzed, Lee stood before him, mind racing. Before she could catch up to it he drew her close. "No," she said, "that's not what…"

"You're easy," he said, and kissed her again.

His lips were less chilly and his arms strangely welcome — it was only with a surge of will that Lee broke herself free. She backed carefully away along the bench. The golf course with its autumn greenness shimmered, prickled by tiny flags against a pale prairie sky.

At the edge of the shelter she turned to run, breaking from its shade onto a wide, empty fairway. She found herself fleeing dreamlike, legs churning and gym shoes flashing, the poms bouncing wildly against her heels. As she ran her body took over. When her heart raced it was to help her go faster. The perspiration on her neck served to cool her as she ran. She bounded into the deeper grass that bordered the fairway and down through the grass to the street.

As she approached their own corner a tough-looking boy with tangled blond hair came gliding through the stop sign. He was driving an Explorer that looked like their own. She finally slowed as she passed the new home site. Still flushed and panting she came along the sidewalk, to where Randy stood waiting on the curb.

Sixteen

The knocking came a long way to find him, and for a time Austin Chandler lay motionless, waiting for it to go away. When it didn't his sleeping mind had little choice but to rouse itself, beginning the long climb toward being awake. Landmarks emerged: there was a white patch on the wall that came from the streetlight, the outline of Edie's armoire and press of his pillow, his heavy body as he shifted on the bed. The numbers on his clock radio bobbed blurry until he'd located his glasses: 2:35.

He had already found his feet, it seemed, hobbling stiffly through the dark. The knocking came again as he hurried along the hall. Somehow he negotiated the stairs. He pawed for the knob in the darkness, twisting it sharply to pull open the door.

No one was there. No one waited on the front porch or walkway. No one hung back beneath the paw-paw. At that hour Washington

Street lay empty. Down the block a single porchlight was burning, where a small panel truck sat parked at the curb.

It didn't take long to identify the problem. He had removed the screen from the storm door a couple of days earlier, replacing it with a glass panel for winter. The door was old, and under the extra weight rode heavy on its hinges. That meant the wind, gathering in the threshold, could catch it, creating a knocking sound as it banged against the frame. Irritably, he reached for the handle, the door resisting as he pulled it into place.

His bed was still warm and it was a long time until morning — the thing to do was climb upstairs and go to sleep. Instead, Austin Chandler took note of the silence, the threshold's metal flashing as it pressed cold against his toes. There was a thudding in his chest from his rush down the stairs. The same wind that had rattled the storm door scattered leaves along the pavement, and the glow of the streetlight lay pale across the grass.

It wasn't just the church class, with its emphasis on noticing. That had been one of his advantages early on when he was still at the University — the ability to see things as they were. He was little swayed by idle hopes or wishful thinking, an ability that should have meant something as he moved through the ranks. He had done well, he thought, in his interview for Vice Provost, confident of the charts and diagrams he'd worked on a month.

There were handicaps, to be sure, like Edie's fragility, the kind of thing that still made a difference at the time. Geoff's hijinks with Randy Overmeyer hadn't helped him much either, with the break-in on the front page of the *Courier* for everyone to see. There was the University's long prejudice against Ag men. There was a lack of appreciation for the hard work he'd done. It was a litany of complaints that even he had grown tired of — in his experience, failure lay mostly in the man.

In the end he just hadn't had it, the kind of thing that often stays hidden until late in the game. Not even on the short list, though, that was the hell of it, but he had pulled up his socks and got on with things, through all his years in the dean's office before retirement, and Edie's long illness after that. Mitchell was marching through Hopkins and Stanford, the NIH and Chapel Hill, while he *hadn't even made the short list*, a slight that had endured through the years to jab at him like a thorn buried deep in his flesh.

He considered the darkness, stretching out past the paw-paw. The only one still bound by that failure was him. It was difficult, in the end, to let go of it, to turn his attention to the moment instead. A gust of wind pressing against the storm door left behind only silence. The floorboards creaked when he shifted his weight. He could have gone to bed but remained in the doorway, wide awake in the middle of the night.

Around him his own neighborhood lay cool and uninflected, barely known after he'd lived there fifty years. On his way to campus he had seen other men on similar forays: Lilley downtown to his paint store, Peters out to peddle insurance, Art Watley who worked for the state. There had been the Yoeys, at one time, and the Bergethons. A family on the corner with a boy sweet on Betsy — it seemed to him Porter was their name. All must have have slipped away while he was taking care of Edie, tracing his narrow circuit from the basement where he soaked her bedclothes in Clorox, back up to the bedroom with his bucket and mop.

Edie was gone, though, and didn't need his attention. Moving along the dark hallway, he had checked off the bedrooms: Betsy's, next to theirs, was the closest, followed by Geoffrey's, and Mitchell's at the end, past the stairs. Geoff had been the one with the nightmares, whose winter colds always settled in his chest. Now Austin Chandler was unlikely to be summoned. He had hurried, half-asleep, along the hallway. He had come down a flight of stairs to pull, eager, at the door. He wondered who he had thought was knocking, and what kind of difference it could possibly have made.

None of it lasted, nothing mattered, no one judged. It was a stark way of seeing things when you came right down to it, and he found himself thinking of the Swiss boy. It wasn't impossible that Stefan was awake even then — if not at that very moment, then almost certainly on other nights, somewhere in town — looking out through his own door to the darkness outside. The boy seemed insubstantial at first glance, in his sandals, but he knew the emptiness and that meant a lot. He wasn't afraid to face things as they were. Austin Chandler felt the deepening chill of his toes against the flashing, watched the street light's glow stretching pale across the grass.

Failure, he tried again, but the sting was gone. He rested his knuckles against the glass of the storm panel. He felt the heat in his fingers as it slowly drained away. This is nighttime, he thought, in Prairie Grove. A man called Austin Chandler looks out to the street. Simple reality was all that met him there: shadows clung to tree limbs along the sidewalk. A locust pod tumbled to the ground. All the while, the wind — like Spirit — kept working at the storm door, so he reached out a final time to check the latch. With it secure, he closed the front door behind him, and climbed back upstairs and went to bed.

SEVENTEEN

From where he parked on Sunset Mitchell could look across the water to his own house, with its pitched roof and wooden deck. The days had grown chilly enough that Maureen, as she got out of the van, wore her leather jacket, a silk scarf tied loosely around her neck. He followed her long stride as she walked to the house. When she came out again the boys were with her. Kai climbed into the van while she went back for Nick, who stood complaining by the door. When they were loaded she backed from the driveway. The van disappeared and reappeared as it moved behind houses, making its long curving way to the gate.

They were strangers though, and had been for years. Prairie Grove, too, possessed little that held him, save for the resolving current that brought it into existence, a low hum that meshed deftly with his heartbeat, kept time with workmen's hammers at the end of the street. As shadows lengthened the hammers fell silent. The last pickup had just pulled away from the construction site when he saw her car. It slowed as it passed, turning into the drive.

Lee Overmeyer climbed out with a bag of groceries. He had ordered a skirt but jeans seemed to fit better. She wore a man's navy pea coat open to the waist. There could be a wool sweater, too, if she wanted it, a leather key chain that dangled from her hand. When she saw him on the driveway she pulled the groceries to her chest.

"Stay away," she said, "and leave me alone."

"Lee," he said simply as she flushed.

"And stop calling. I know it's you. If you keep it up I'm calling the police."

"Why don't you complain to your husband?"

"Don't think I won't."

"I do think you won't. Did you ever mention you came to see me at the golf course? To give voice to the wonders of the Lord?"

"I made a mistake. Go away and leave us alone."

"I see you. I know you. I always have."

"Please," she said. "Please go away."

"Come on," he told her. "It's time to go. There's nothing left for us here."

Even their squabbling took on a certain intimacy, voices low at the edge of the garage. His intent was more than enough to hold her there, the same intent that had delivered for him a car and a driveway, this woman named Lee who only then met his eyes.

"Where would we go?" she asked, honestly distraught.

At least that was what she might have said, if not "What do you know?" or "Bear wood is slow" — phonemes had begun, in recent days, to leak meaning. She didn't flee but stood motionless, the groceries between them. He lifted his fingers to her cheek. It was only then that he saw Randy had joined them, standing on the low front porch a few feet away.

Trim in sport shirt and slacks, he watched them back, like two children, apart. He seemed to have just finished eating something, lower lip bulging as he ran his tongue across his teeth.

"Professor Chandler," he said. "Good to see you." He came down from the porch. "Or is it okay to call you Mitch?"

"This has nothing to do with you," Mitchell told him. "Go inside."

Randy strolled toward them on the driveway. "Got some groceries there, honey? That's great. Sure is. Got us a few cornflakes for morning? A little coffee, a little bacon, a little beans?"

"This has nothing to do with you," Mitchell repeated sternly. "Go back in the house." When the other man held out his arm, Lee retreated to his side. Randy gave her shoulders a squeeze and she moved past him to the porch. As the door closed behind her, Randy turned his way.

"Been out in the garden?" he asked Mitchell easily.

"Pardon me?"

"Looks like you forgot to use your gloves."

Mitchell joined Randy in looking at his hands then, unfamiliar and alien-looking, as if they had only just then sprouted on his wrists. The fingernails were dirty and his knuckles were raw. There was a deep slice across the center of his palm. Randy watched him with interest.

"There's fall things, I guess, that people do. Mulching or squlching or whatever. I'm not much of a yard man myself. For some reason people like to see the pastor with his hands dirty. I've never really known why that is."

"Shut up," Mitchell said. "This has nothing to do with you. Maybe for once you could just shut your fucking mouth."

Shrugging, Pastor Randy stepped aside. "I'm not in your way, go talk to her." He cupped his hands to call toward the door. "Honey, Mitch here has something to say!"

"This has nothing to do…" Mitchell began again, but Randy shook his head.

"No, Mitch, that's where you're mistaken. I know you don't think so but you are. It's not my wife you're looking for. It's not my wife you're after, but me."

The hum was non-local but at every moment present, spreading across the golf course and fields. It had grown over time more persistent, at odds with a low kind of groan settled in along the street.

"You don't know," Mitchell told him in dismissal. "The highway and railroad. The grass and the trees. This isn't a manor and that's not …"

"A lake," Randy said, nodding toward the water. "The river runs a full mile north of here. They fill up that pond from a well."

As they stood on the driveway energy coursed the length of Mitchell's body, rising in great surges along his legs. Two doors down a garage door ground open, and a man in a Warrior windbreaker emerged pushing a lawnmower. He kneeled to check the height of the cutting blade, unscrewed the gas cap to peer inside the tank.

The green Lumina had become a more constant presence. It was the same car he had first noticed six weeks earlier on Sixth Street, on his way to the alleyway and Lee. The driver, at the time, had barely acknowledged him, lifting his wrist as Mitchell passed to check his watch.

Now the Lumina was back, nosing slowly past the golf course. It often glided past to take the lead on the highway, showed up along the country roads that he negotiated late at night. That's where the hum grew loudest — Mitchell had almost caught up with it as he crawled through a bean field, stubble slicing sharp against his hands. When he broke free it was to glide high above the ditchbanks, sometimes accompanied but often alone.

His body ached and his mind felt unsteady, worn by the deepening struggle to remember what was real.

"It all is," Randy said, nodding. "All of it's real, and that's just the beginning. 'Everything' was only a word to me fifteen years ago. I couldn't even have imagined what *everything* was."

As he moved to join Mitchell he dropped his voice.

"You know that far country and I do too. Jesus makes three. There's a reason He went down to the underworld. He wasn't on Easter vacation. He wasn't buying postcards for people back home. It was more of a business trip, really, that He went on, those three days after Calvary when He left us all alone."

"Shut up," Mitchell said. "I don't want to hear it."

Randy laughed. "Oh, I don't imagine you do. Not at all. I didn't either. When I met God high above, that's one thing. That's the part we all talk about in church. His love and His beauty and wisdom. His goodness and power and grace. It's the rest that kind of kicks you in the stomach. It's All the Rest that really blows your mind apart.

"You know what I did when He brought me back, Mitch? The very first thing I did? I *ran*. That's exactly what I did. From Dallas I took off through West Texas. I looped through the Valley and back up to Laredo. From Laredo I took off across the plains. The whole time I never stopped running. I ran until I couldn't run another step. If it hadn't been for a lay Pentecostal preacher in Dalhart, an old man who came across me in a barroom, I wouldn't be here. He pulled me off that bar stool and down to my knees."

The man with the lawnmower had set in on his yard. A blue Suburban pulled in just beyond. The driver got out, reaching back for his briefcase.

"God's love isn't all I saw there, not by a long shot." Randy nodded past the man and his lawnmower, past his neighbor with the briefcase, past the wide lawns as they curled around the lake. "If they knew what I saw, they'd come down and kill me. They'd come out of their houses, Mitch, and tear us limb from limb."

They might have been any two Prairie Grove husbands standing together on the driveway. The temperature had begun to drop as evening settled in. When Randy turned to Mitchell there was excitement on his face.

"I wasn't sure, until you came forward, what was happening. I couldn't understand what had stopped us in our tracks. The Opposer is near and the circle is closing. You don't know how glad I am you finally brought him to my door."

Mitchell had already broken away and down the driveway to his Triumph, squeezing back in behind the wheel. The car's interior reflected a week's steady occupancy: the floor was littered with fast food wrappers and scraps of note paper, credit card slips and empty soda cans, the jacket that he pulled over himself to sleep. He had walked quickly but Pastor Randy was right behind him, leaning in at the window as Mitchell reached for his key.

"We'll be at the church every night, so that's where you'll find us." When the Triumph's motor rose between them, Randy pushed himself away.

"I know you don't think so, but I can help, Mitch. I really can. I know all the demons you're fighting. I know every last one of them by name."

EIGHTEEN

Vera Eller paused, rake in hand, to consider their progress. Even without a solid freeze the leaves had been falling, and on an overcast Saturday morning she and Walter got to work. Their system, developed over the years, was simple: Walter raked while she stood by with one of the city's leaf bags, swooping in to fill it when he'd built up a pile.

The city had been out earlier that week to dig up a gas main in front of the Williams' house. The hole was still there between a mound of dirt and a metal sawhorse, its yellow light blinking. A row of plastic pylons had been set out along the street.

Walter had on his white tennis hat and an old Warriors sweatshirt, and she was wearing a woolen car coat and baggy pair of jeans. It was a good thing they had their rakes, because otherwise people might have thought they were homeless people, wandering around the lawn. On a Saturday morning traffic on Washington was light. The day was gray and cold, clouds pressing low above the trees.

Neither of them was as lively as they once were, but in a couple of hours they had the front yard nearly done. When Walter finished under the old sycamore, he set to work on the magnolia. A chiming from the courthouse sounded muffled, and it felt like they were the last people left in the world.

Lacey had hobbled out to the porch at mid-morning to hang her Warriors flag and they waved to one another across the Tolleys' front yard. As she steadied her leaf bag Vera was thinking back to their old apartment on First Street, the first winter they spent in Prairie Grove. Washington Street was still a cow pasture in those days, and she had worked at the glove factory while Walter went to school.

It was still dark when they set off in the morning, Walter walking her down First Street to Springfield, under the train viaduct and up the other side. He hurried from his lab to be there every afternoon at the end of her shift. There were plenty of things to be frightened of — the lingering depression and faculty wives, a war in Europe coming on — but for some reason she had been afraid of the viaduct, and was reluctant to go under it alone. She was homesick their first year of marriage, and at night had crept close to Walter. He may have been a Skinny Minnie but was warm even then.

He had been up late the night before, working on another article for the archives. When he finally came to bed she crawled over, but he was too hot to lie next to, restless and murmuring in his sleep. She slept uneasily herself, dreaming of the Cooke-Davis retirement home and its rows of apartment doors, its wide hallways as quiet as the tomb. She was glad when the night was over and a gray dawn filtered in through the blinds.

Walter had uncovered something beneath the magnolia. It turned out to be the shoot of some poor plant pushing up, fooled by the lateness of the frost. He left off his raking to study it, squatting to poke through the leaves. Vera leaned on her own rake as she surveyed the yard. She had made a nice tuna salad early that morning and had a can of soup set out by the stove. The Warriors came on at twelve-thirty. When they got finished with the leaves they could turn on the radio, and enjoy their lunch while they listened to the game.

The yellow light in front of the Williams' was blinking in its offbeat sort of way and the chiming came again from the courthouse. Walter raked carefully around the confused plant at the base of the magnolia, and she moved in closer with the bag.

Her eyes weren't worth much when it came to seeing at a distance, so what Vera picked out first, down the block, was a black smudge that sat in front of the Chandlers'. After a moment it began moving toward them. The engine grew louder and a small sports car came into focus, weaving erratically back and forth along the street. It picked off one of the pylons in front of the Williams' before veering their way. When it hit the curb just past their drive, the motor died, leaving the car's stubby back end sticking into the street. Mitchell Chandler climbed out from behind the wheel.

Vera had hardly needed to worry about their work clothes — the Chandler boy was the one who looked a fright, unshaven and disheveled. Mud caked his shoes and his pant legs were grimy; his sweater could have been chewed on by a dog. As he came across the sidewalk he looked at them wild-eyed, like they both had just sprouted extra heads.

Peering through fogged glasses, Walter smiled. "Hello there, Mitchell. This is a surprise. How are you doing?" He used the rake for leverage as he climbed to his feet. "Looking for your Dad? I imagine he went over to the Quarterback Club to watch the game. It's in East Lansing so kickoff's an hour early."

Mitchell regarded him coolly before turning to Vera. "You're wondering about my hands," he said, which took her aback, because she had just been looking at them, at the dirty gauze wrapped in loops across his palms. She wondered how he had gotten himself into such a state with his clothes all dirty, his hair tangled and covered with straw.

He looked around the yard like they'd managed to disappoint him. "Is this the best you can come up with, raking leaves?"

Walter blinked behind his glasses. "Well," he said, "I suppose it is. This time of year they're always a concern."

Mitchell seemed to think that was funny, smirking as he looked past them to the house. "This time of year they're always a concern. Raking the goddamn leaves. Can't you see through all of the bullshit? Can't you open your eyes five seconds and *see*?"

He was talking to both of them but kept his eye on Vera. Unhappy with what he saw, he slowly shook his head.

"40 to 7," he said, turning to Walter. "Does that mean anything to you?"

Walter pulled at his ear. "Well, not much, right offhand. What would that be, 5.7 or thereabouts?"

Mitchell smiled. "5.714."

"It could be a constant, I suppose, although not one I'm familiar with. There might be some kind of friction coefficient that's close."

"A constant." Mitchell nodded knowingly. "You like those constants, don't you, Professor Eller? You like things that stay in their place. Look there, where the city's been digging. Those pylons lined up along the curb. Can you follow me? Do you catch my drift?" Still smirking, he shook his head. "That's all right. You can't see it. Don't worry. Most people never do."

He turned to Vera. "Iowa, Ohio, Nevada. How about that?" He spoke slowly, as if she were a child. "Iowa, Ohio, Nevada. That's all I'm going to say."

"Mitchell," Walter said, "something's gotten you all worked up. Why don't you relax a minute, and things will look better."

As he reached out his hand, the Chandler boy recoiled. "Don't touch me," he screamed, "I'm poison!"

"Oh, for heaven's sake," Vera scoffed, "you're not poison."

"I'm poison!" he screamed again like a crazy man, and with a sudden lunge snatched the rake from Walter's hands. He swung it wildly in front of them. "Get back, I said, damn it, I'm poison."

"Watch how you handle that thing," Vera snapped, as Walter moved in front of her. Eighty years old and capped by a silly bonnet, he still slid without hesitation between her and the rake.

"You've got a screw loose," she pronounced from behind Walter's shoulder. "Somebody's going to be locking you up."

"We're about done here anyway," Walter said soothingly. "Why don't you come in for a cup of coffee? We saw Maureen down at the grocery store a couple of weeks ago. We couldn't believe how those two boys had grown."

But Mitchell wasn't listening. He'd caught sight of the blinking light on the sawhorse by then, his lips moving silently as if reading along. The flag in front of Lacey's hung limply. The streetlight needed painting and her cheeks had grown cold, but wherever Vera settled to think, Mitchell was right behind her.

Before she knew it he was pointing at her.

"You know," he said quietly. "Just like I do. Don't try to deny it because you do."

If he meant the state names that was hardly a feat, especially after all of her crosswords. Iowa, with its four letters, was the street just north of them, followed by Ohio and Nevada before you finally got to Main. But that wasn't what the Chandler boy was driving at. There was something else that he seemed to have in mind.

Houses along the street rested dream-like in the stillness. A yawning sort of depth stretched out, empty, beneath the sidewalks. Vera thought of the little green car she'd seen idling earlier at the corner, when she'd glanced up a moment from the leaves.

An eerie feeling came over her and they regarded each other with care.

"Just admit it," he said. "Don't play dumb all the time. Just forget the fucking Warriors and come alive!"

"Do you want to listen to the game?" Walter asked, brightening. "Come inside for a few minutes and sit down. I can look up that constant if you like. I've been wanting to talk to you, anyway, since your talk at the church. Could glutamates be blocking the outgrowth? Do you think calcium might have a role?"

The Chandler boy, though, studied the rake. All at once he hurled it past them, sailing it in a high arc across the yard into the magnolia. He looked around, uncertain, before finally settling on the leaf bag they had just finished filling. He wrestled it away from Vera and with a grunt launched it toward the street. It split open on the curb and spilled out on the sidewalk. He began running then, from bag to bag, kicking and tumbling them, scattering the leaves across the lawn.

Vera felt the eerie feeling disappear, replaced by a feeling of satisfaction. Kate and Ronnie may never have been in *Newsweek* or on public television, but at least they weren't running around a neighbor's yard like a three-year-old, making a mess of a whole morning's work.

Even as the Chandler boy wore down, he kept to his task.

Eventually all but the last bag had been emptied, the leaves spread in ragged piles across the lawn.

"You're asleep," he snarled, gasping for breath. "And the sad thing is that you like it. But hey, that's okay. Keep on raking, folks. Just keep on raking those leaves!"

With a hearty kick he split the final bag open, shuffling back and forth until its leaves had been scattered. Back in his car he banged forward twice against the curb, stalling, until he finally thought to put it in reverse. That shot him backwards across the street — he was lucky there wasn't any traffic — where the car stalled again. He finally got the little rattletrap moving, and went careening away down the block.

The neighborhood was so quiet that Mitchell might never have been there, except for the leaves that lay spread out all around them, along with the brown, shredded remnants of the bags.

Vera had always liked autumn, even with all the raking. She liked the way the chill numbed her cheeks and made her nose run, a chill that even then worked its way through her shoes. She had her trusty car coat and warm pair of gloves. There was fresh tuna salad and a waiting can of soup. If she brought the radio out they could hear the first quarter — it was always nice to catch the Warriors before they fell too far behind.

She did feel sorry for Walter, who always had an eye out for the young people, even when they acted so wild.

"Is there somebody we should call?" he wondered, tugging nervously at his collar. "What should we do?"

Vera had reached high into the magnolia; by stretching on tiptoe, she reached the handle of the rake. With a tug she brought it tumbling to the ground.

"Well," she said, "probably the best thing is to start on that far side. Then we can gather them all back this other way."

NINETEEN

The Preacher was in his Campus Church office late Monday morning, at work on the weekly bulletin, when Libby McNeil called to tell him about Dori Maple. He wrote down the details and hung up the phone. He closed his PageMaker file, and after brushing his teeth in the church lavatory, came back to put his Bible and a writing pad in his briefcase. The Justice Coalition had a meeting scheduled for later that afternoon, so he taped a note to his office door in case he didn't make it back.

He knew immediately upon arrival at the emergency room that he wouldn't be returning to the church. Libby was already there, along with the Nesbitts and Joanne Meyer. They murmured to him the details — Dori alone in her car on North Lincoln, the brick wall at Hutchins Van Lines — before moving aside as if one to let him pass. Dori's husband Ralph sat at the far end of the waiting area beneath a television, where a commercial for Burger King flashed silently above his head. He looked like a patient himself, gray-haired and gaunt, a portable oxygen tank beside him on the floor.

"Ralph," the Preacher said, "they just told me about Dori."

"Oh, fine," Ralph said. "Just fine, Harry. How are you?" When he turned his head, plastic tubes tugged at his nostrils. "I guess Dori had trouble with the car."

"I'm so very sorry. I know this is a tremendous loss."

"The doctor says it must have been a heart attack. Probably dead before she even hit the wall." He looked up at the television as if for confirmation, but the commercial had given way to a TV courtroom, where a beefy man in suspenders waved his hands in the air.

"Come on, Ralph," the Preacher said gently. "Let's go home."

The Maples lived only two blocks away in an older neighborhood that Dori had, over the last dozen years, tirelessly defended, organizing opposition to each new hospital wing and parking lot as they spread out among the houses. The Preacher drove them there, helping Ralph with his oxygen as they went up the walk. The comfortable clutter of the Maples' small living room was well-known to him from deacons' meetings and fellowship dinners, with Ralph's recliner and Dori's worn armchair in front of the fireplace, their dining table pushed back against the wall. A roast was defrosting in the sink. Walter Eller arrived a few minutes later, followed by a young police officer who came by with two bags of groceries that he'd salvaged from the car.

While Walter put the food away the Preacher coaxed Ralph through the first of the obligatory phone calls, to their daughter Anne whose family was on the east coast, and to Dori's sister who lived in Duluth. Dori had organized the "Getting Things in Order" workshop at the church a couple of years earlier, so in the top drawer of her file cabinet he found a folder with funeral arrangements and a list of Ralph's medications, a safety deposit box key and a copy of their wills.

In the living room Ralph was rehashing the accident with Walter.

"… so it couldn't have been the brakes."

"Probably not," Walter agreed.

"That means it was a heart attack, just like they told me. Said she was dead before she even hit the wall."

There was a rhythm to everything, grief included. Over the first hours those involved were most often simply stunned, unable to process their loved one's absence from the normal flow of life. And for a time that flow went on — throughout the afternoon the telephone rang steadily for Dori. A member of the Rent Council needed the time for a committee meeting. There was a hearing before the Zoning Board later in the week. The Preacher and Walter took turns fielding the phone calls, and came back to the living room to sit with Ralph.

"Oh, well," Ralph was saying, "maybe basketball will be better." There was a hiss from the oxygen as he shifted in his chair. "They have that new boy from Moline who could probably play forward. Billy Hedrick saw him last winter down in Carbondale. Said he looked pretty good."

Shadows fell across the room as afternoon moved into evening. At seven they went to Denny's for dinner, where Ralph talked about his service on a destroyer in the Pacific. He and Walter reminisced about the old interurban that had run before the war. Back at the house Walter made coffee in the kitchen.

"Dori's sister was going to come in November," Ralph remarked. "Now there's hardly any point." He rubbed his knuckles. "Looks like another long season," he said, returning to the Warriors, and Walter, pouring coffee, agreed.

About nine o'clock Walter took the car home for Vera, leaving the two of them alone. From outside came the sound of a siren. When it had dropped away the Preacher leaned forward in his chair.

"Ralph," he said, "I find myself wondering what you're feeling. You know that Dori's gone. She won't be coming home."

Ralph nodded.

"Do you have any thoughts about that? It's a tremendous blow for you, I know. It's a tremendous blow for all of us. I'm wondering if there's something you'd like to say."

He waited.

"For Dori to go so quickly like that, so unexpectedly, makes it difficult." The Preacher paused again, feeling his way. "You must be very angry," he said, and Ralph looked up at him, surprised.

Ralph and Dori weren't University people, which was somewhat unusual for Campus Church. Dori's father had been a railroad man until the roundhouse closed down, and Ralph had managed a small grain elevator a few miles from town. A pack of cigarettes weighed down his front pocket and a tattoo from navy days lay faded on his arm.

"God's promise isn't that we won't experience loss. Hardship comes to us inevitably in life. I don't have to tell you that. I know you loved Dori very much."

After another long silence he opened his briefcase and took out the Bible. Ralph glanced at it warily before looking away.

"I can't tell you what to believe. No one can. But I do know that God won't forget us. He won't forget you and he won't forget Dori. He won't forget Anne and the girls."

Ralph sat in his recliner as he looked across the room. There was the hiss of his oxygen and the ticking of the clock.

"The Lord is my Shepherd…" the Preacher began, but that was all the further he got before Ralph began to cry. Tears welled up, sliding down his cheeks to drip onto his shirt front. Tears that made his nose run and the oxygen tube slippery — the Preacher gently eased the tube out, draping it across the arm of the recliner. A moment later he reached out his hand. Ralph clasped it straight on as if in greeting, grinding the Preacher's knuckles sharply under the fierceness of his grip. The Preacher let them ache as he leaned forward with his head bowed. They sat together like that, Ralph weeping silently, until Vera dropped Walter off again a little after ten.

After Ralph went to bed they heard him for a time moving back and forth to the bathroom. Eventually the old house was quiet. Walter had taken the couch and the Preacher the recliner; before long Walter was stretched out, his arm across his eyes. Soon he was breathing deeply, fast asleep.

That he and Walter would be spending the night at the Maples' had been, like so much at Campus Church, simply understood: with no family in town, Ralph wouldn't be left alone. The Preacher wasn't used to coffee so late at night and he sat fully awake, roughing out Dori's eulogy. He would miss her too, he knew, a feeling that would visit him much more profoundly later on when his own tasks were done.

As it was, he was still at work and had been since early that morning. The church members, too, had been busy: arrangements were in place to pick up Anne at the airport. Dori's many friends were in the process of being called. Schedules had been changed and casseroles made; by the next day there would be a steady stream of visitors to the house. During those first awkward hours, though, no one had to worry: they all knew the Preacher was there.

A heightened self-awareness had its positive aspects: sometimes he was able to appreciate his usefulness to the people he served. One thing he had learned to do was listen carefully, valuable in a congregation where so much — especially the deeply felt — went unspoken. The church members were people of wide experience and accomplishment. They had raised families and buried their parents; they didn't expect him to tell them how to live. Instead, he listened for the tell-tale hesitation in an otherwise normal conversation, had grown proficient at following up with a discreet inquiry later on. As death approached, people often sought him out. It was his job, after all, to be there, the one who stepped forward even as others backed away.

He had learned that release, in the end, could lie almost anywhere, even in an old psalm half-remembered from childhood, its iambic cadence reassuring like the beating of the heart. His work required a certain skillfulness, to be sure, and creativity, even if they were most often known only to himself. Perhaps it was only natural that he wished someone were with him. That someone might have seen him as he went about his work that day, that someone would understand what he did in the world. God knew, of course — at least that was the usual formulation — but the someone he imagined had a more definite presence, both human and deeply alive. The Preacher felt a pang, not quite surprise or even embarrassment, when he realized he was thinking of Em.

It wasn't so unusual that Em would come to him — she was seldom that far from his thoughts. Much of it, of course, stemmed from the amount of time they spent together: the Justice Coalition campaign was a success beyond anyone's expectations. There had been articles in the *Washington Post* and the *Wall Street Journal*. ESPN was preparing a short feature for later that month. As he and Em emerged as spokespersons he was ever more impressed by her coolness and maturity, a grace under fire he admired very much.

So it was understandable that the Preacher might imagine Em nearby as he sat in the recliner. That she might come to mind as he drove home, the next morning, to shower, and again on his way back to church. There was a message from her on the answering machine when he got to his office — she had scheduled a Thursday morning interview with one of the Chicago sports stations, a presentation for a political science class on Friday afternoon. He marked the dates on his calendar. She had left a second message only a half hour earlier.

She was on her way to a calculus test and had just called so he could wish her luck.

The Preacher was stiff from the night on the recliner, but otherwise felt a sort of ease as he moved through his day. Buoyed by a sense of privilege he returned to Dori's eulogy — he thought of the dog-eared *Daily Devotional* that had sat by her arm chair, the copy of *Vagina Monologues* that lay underneath. In late morning he caught up with Grace Susaki, the graduate student who served as their music director. Grace thought the organist could come up with something from Mahler, a composer Dori had always loved.

By late morning his remarks were largely done. At noon he took a break for lunch. In the normal course of his days, Em often joined him, and out of deference to her vegetarianism he had begun packing peanut butter and the occasional Gardenburger. When she didn't arrive he ate his sandwich alone.

Tuesday afternoons were most often reserved for hospital and home visits, but the Preacher spent the rest of the day in the office, catching up on tasks set aside the day before. Even so, he followed his Tuesday evening custom of having dinner at the Student Union. He had often found it pleasant, after a day with the sick and elderly, to eat surrounded by young people, and on his way back to his office he passed Lincoln Hall. Em had a seminar there Wednesday afternoons in anthropology, where he had joined her a week earlier for a presentation about the Chief. Afterwards she hugged him in the hall.

"We do such a good job," she said, "you and I together. How can they help but agree with what we say!"

Back at church the Preacher closed down his computer and locked the office. He took a final glance into the sanctuary on his way out the door. He wasn't surprised to find Randy Overmeyer camped out there with a half-dozen of his Spirit Rising people. Regular services seemed to have given way to some kind of vigil where they sat in a small circle of folding chairs beneath the pulpit. A murmur of prayer came toward him above the pews. He watched for the longest time, unsure of the attraction, before he went out to the alley and his car.

When he was hired at Campus Church the Preacher had agreed that the church could sell the old parsonage. The small townhouse that took its place was entirely adequate, part of a quiet complex on the west side of town. He brought in the day's mail and set it on the dining table. He turned on the lamp in the living room. When he checked the answering machine its message light was blinking.

There was a call from a credit consolidation company and two inquiries about Dori's service. There was an invitation to the Schallers for bridge on Friday night. An interfaith ministry conference set for the weekend had been canceled, and would be rescheduled for sometime in the spring.

Em's message was next to last, left earlier that afternoon. "Hi, Harry," she said, "how's it going? Sorry I missed you at lunch. I wasn't feeling well after the test so I came on home. It's probably just a cold. Call me later on if you get a chance."

The final call was from Father Mitch at Saint Patrick's. The abortion issue aside, they'd become good friends over the years, and often went out for dinner or a movie. It sometimes amused the Preacher — especially given the deep distrust of Catholics that had pervaded his childhood — to consider how priest-like his own life had become. He traded his shoes for slippers and pulled on a sweater . He gathered newspapers and cans for recycling. He stood at the kitchen sink, thinking, as he scraped carrots for lunch the next day.

"Call me," Em had urged, and he considered it. He considered calling but that wasn't all. He wanted to get in his car and drive back to campus. He wanted to park at her house and go up to the door. He was sorry to hear she wasn't feeling well. He was wondering how her math test had gone. He had a pack of chamomile tea bags above the stove in a cabinet, and chamomile was good for a cold.

The Preacher, at the sink, closed his eyes. He ran the garbage disposal and wiped down the counters. He made out a grocery list for later in the week. Fortunately his bank statement had come and he spent twenty minutes on his checkbook. There was a letter too, owed to an old friend from seminary; a reply in careful longhand took up most of an hour. At nine he found "Nova" on his small Motorola. It was barely ten when the show ended — still early for college students — and the telephone was on its stand only a few steps away.

He had become accustomed to walking Em home after Coalition meetings. She often took his arm as they strolled through the leaves. She seemed to save a place for him when they gathered at the Wigwam, and the beer had just begun to warm him the first time he heard it, a coaxing voice that now filled his mind. What it said was that anything's possible, even with a girl barely a third his own age. Her hand, when she squeezed his, was often chilly, her breath warm against his neck when she hugged him goodbye.

He could hold her, the voice whispered, insistent. He could reach out to Em and pull her close. The Preacher turned off the porch light and came back to his bedroom. He slipped off his sweater and shirt. In the bathroom mirror he considered his body. He was fit enough, certainly, for a man his age. To some he might even appear boyish, in his serious sort of way. if not for the age spots along his wrists and forearms, an unappealing slackness to the flesh across his chest. He brushed and flossed as he stood at the washbasin, taking special care around a troublesome crown.

His bachelor pajamas were in the top drawer of his bureau and the Preacher undressed and put them on. Filling a water glass, he carried it to the bedroom. A telephone was on his nightstand for emergencies. Nearby lay a small stack of books. He wondered if he had put out the recycling. When he remembered he had, he climbed into bed.

The voice was there too, though, more powerfully than ever, the telephone an arm's length away. He could reach out, even then, to call her; nobody but Harry Applebee had the power to stay his hand.

On top of his stack of books was the most recent *New Yorker*. Beneath it was an offering by Jack Good, a theologian he admired. The Preacher slid past them to an old volume by Paul Tournier, whose meditations on guilt and grace had largely fallen out of fashion. Settled under the sheets, he read until sleepiness found him. When it had, the Preacher turned out the light.

In the dark his torment continued. He could kiss her, the voice kept insisting. She was waiting even then for him to take her in his arms. "Please God," he thought, "protect me from my foolishness," and realized only then that his prayers had begun.

The Preacher had more than enough occasion to pray professionally. That he might pray alone felt vaguely embarrassing — was it something that Em would ever do? Would Meg or Carrie or Salim? It seemed unlikely, but he wasn't Carrie or Salim. He was fifty-five and not twenty-one. His nightly prayers were a childhood habit that had lasted a lifetime, preserved in those first moments after he turned off the light and lay quietly in the dark.

If it was a child's habit, then it made sense that he so often began, like a child, with his surroundings. It seemed only natural that he start there: the Preacher felt genuine gratitude for the comfort of his bedroom, for the softness of his pillow and freshness of his sheets. He gave thanks for engaging books and the intimacy of lamplight, for the deep pleasure that reading had always brought. He prayed for the students in the Justice Coalition, whose example of good-natured faith seemed so effortlessly provided, who had given such joy and renewed purpose to his life.

He still prayed for his parents too, reflexively, wherever in space-time or fading memory they endured. He felt grateful for their humility and unquestioned love for him, for the many kindnesses he had received at their hands. He prayed for Ralph Maple in his small house near the hospital. He prayed for the members of his congregation — for Walter Eller and Joanne Meyer, for the Nesbitts and Schallers — for the many people who had begun as his employers and now were his friends. He gave thanks for their indulgence of his failings, their patience with the many peculiarities and weaknesses that he had.

He prayed for Em again too, this time specifically, holding her special spirit in mind. Inevitably he thought of Clare and the years of their marriage. He thought of the deep depressions that had so often plagued her, praying she would find peace in the years that lay ahead. He prayed for Lee Overmeyer as she searched for understanding. He remembered his and Clare's own painful struggle with childlessness, their deep sense of betrayal when a family never came.

Night after night the Preacher returned to these well-worn pathways. Often he sought, then, to expand the frontiers of his gratitude, moving on to people more troublesome in his life. He saw Vera Eller, enduring his Sunday sermons with her arms folded, deeply unimpressed as she sat with Walter in the pew. He bumped past Austin Chandler's scowl at the back of the church. He prayed — the acid test — for the Republican leadership, for the drunken fraternity boys who had shouted at Em.

In this way he finally arrived at Randy Overmeyer. For some reason that lonely vigil still resonated; even at the edge of the sanctuary he had found it hard to pull away. It was something he didn't fully comprehend, but that seemed not to matter: Randy Overmeyer was with him as sleep settled in. Please grant him, the Preacher asked, peace and wisdom. Grant him courage and endurance and faith. In all his battles, he prayed, please be with him, and please, gentle God, give him strength.

TWENTY

Lee rarely used the big tub in their master bathroom, with its jacuzzi jets and shiny fixtures, but in late afternoon she filled it and sat back to soak. Her toes were a steamy pink when she rested them against the porcelain. The leg she extended from the water glistened, thanks to a pack of blue bath salts Barbara had given her for the occasion. Barrenness had its benefits: her belly was flat and her hips narrow, her nipples as small and lightly pigmented as a girl's.

Her infertility had been hard on Randy, too. The forced-march intimacies had taken a toll on their love life — luckily there were plenty of books at the Christian bookstore about rekindling excitement in a marriage. A long bath beforehand had been one of the recommendations, followed by a quiet dinner with candlelight. "Men are visual," one author had counseled, and after her bath Lee pulled on a pair of bikini underpants that Randy had always liked.

Economy at that point hardly mattered so she had left the house thermostat on high. The hallways were warm and the bedroom lights low; she slipped on a robe to come down to the kitchen. Randy came in the front door while she was checking the oven; she followed his footsteps as he went quickly upstairs. That was another drawback of a big house — they had been able to avoid one another far too long. She heard the shower in the guest suite as she came back to their bathroom. She was a long time there, putting on makeup and brushing her hair. She dabbed perfume between her breasts and along her neck. Finally she slipped out of her robe, pulling on a simple cotton shift that hung halfway down her thighs.

When she came into their bedroom Randy was already in his white shirt and slacks, standing at the mirror as he straightened his tie.

"Hi there, handsome," she said, "how about some dinner? I've got meatloaf tonight and mashed potatoes. There were even a couple of ears of sweet corn I found at the store."

"Hey, hey," he said, "all my favorites. Too bad I'll have to pass tonight, hon. I'm fasting."

"Fasting? Are you sure? I said meatloaf, sweet guy, and mashed potatoes. I've got a coconut pie for dessert." Lee slipped behind him to wrap her arms around his shoulders. "I don't mind fasting, though, as long as I get a taste of neck now and then. Or maybe just a tiny bit of ear."

The nip of her teeth was designed to get his attention. Her breasts were loose beneath the shift and her thighs and feet were bare. She rubbed her knee against the back of his leg.

"I love you too," he murmured, intent on his tie.

She slipped her tongue into his ear.

"Come on, babe," he said, "I've got to get going."

When he shrugged his shoulders to free himself, Lee held on, dropping her arms so they wrapped around his ribs. "I've been missing you," she said, and slid her hand to his stomach, past his belt to the inside of his leg.

"Come on," he said. "I love you, too, honey, but this is serious. You need to get ready if you're coming. They're waiting for us over at the church."

Lee pressed down a surge of irritation — this wasn't any easier for her. She smelled, on Randy's cheek, his familiar aftershave, saw the slack look of fatigue on his cheeks. Finally he met her eyes in the mirror.

"Don't go," she said.

Even with his serious vigil face, Randy smiled. "What do you mean?"

"Just that. Don't go. I want you to stay here with me."

She felt like a child again at the Accra airport, saying the one thing she never could have asked. She wasn't a girl, though, anymore, she was a woman, alone with her husband in their bedroom, in a cotton shift that rode high across her legs. Randy reached up to loosen her hands.

"We can't give in now that we've almost made it. We can't step back when the breakthrough is near."

Lee spoke carefully to keep the edge from her voice.

"Randy, babe, listen to me. I love you and believe in you. I always have. But Spirit Rising is over. You've got to understand that. That part of our work is done."

"We can always count on God to do His part. The answer lies somewhere in ourselves. We've got to locate the last pockets of our unwillingness. We have to be ready for the moment when it comes."

"No," she said, "we're done at church. It's over. It really is." When he looked back at her with his gray eyes she softened. "We're not going to have a baby, honey, either, and that's the truth of it. Our time has passed. Maybe we can start thinking about adoption. There are a lot of babies out there who need a home."

Lee felt relief once the truth had been spoken, a release from the long years of lying to themselves. Randy, on the other hand, just looked back at her, as if the fact of their childlessness had completely slipped his mind.

"We contend not against flesh and blood," he said," but against principalities and powers. Satan and his armies draw near."

Lee felt her stomach drop. "Oh no, Randy," she said. "Not again."

Half-naked beneath her shift, she felt the pointlessness of seduction — Randy was excited but not about her. Beneath the fatigue his eyes were sparkling, and his old Randy grin had returned.

"It took a while but I finally remembered. I know what I'm back here to do! You must have thought I was out of my mind, buying that land by the interstate. Letting go of the Lamplighter and moving up to campus. Up on *campus*, Lee, can't you see it? That's where God needs me. That's where the battle line's drawn."

Stiffening, Lee backed away. "You promised all that was behind us."

"Can't you see how it all goes together? God brought us back here for ministry. He put the new building in my mind. We both knew it wasn't time, but He insisted. He brought me to the meadow again and again. And now we're up on campus, don't you see? Can't you see what it is He had in mind? There's nothing else left to distract us! All our best soldiers are in place!"

Lee kept her voice even like she was speaking to a child. "That's not the way it works."

"You remember how it was in Oklahoma. You saw how the Opposer made his move."

Randy had been an indifferent student in seminary; if she hadn't written his papers he would never have gotten through. The music of the scripture was what attracted him, the odd phrase he might pick out and use. That lack of grounding had finally caught up with them in Ada during his stint as Assistant Pastor. His restlessness and boredom might have been factors, too — Randy wasn't designed to be assistant anything. He was in charge of church outreach and pastoring the youth group, while she worked at the local K-Mart, trying to keep up with bills.

They were living in a small house south of town surrounded by woodland. They had been in Ada less than a year when Randy heard the call. It came to him suddenly and without warning — one evening at dinner he had simply dropped his fork and gone out to the car. That summons, she quickly learned, could come any time, high noon or the middle of the night. She would awaken in bed to find him dressing in the darkness, reaching for his jacket on the way out the door. Hours later he might make his way back again, pale and exhausted, to where Lee waited, terrified, at home.

"I'm not going back to that craziness," she said bluntly. "You knew that before we came to Prairie Grove."

"But can't you see, babe? The job wasn't finished like I thought it was. It was just another battle in the war! When we pulled away, we were only getting closer! There's something here that He wants us to do! Why back to Prairie Grove? That's what I wondered. Why up to campus, I must have asked a million times. How could our ministry just collapse like that? How could they all turn against us like they did?"

Lee felt a wave of exasperation. "We came to Prairie Grove because that's what you wanted. We moved up to campus because you only listen to yourself. And people turned against us because they were tired of pretending! That's why they quit coming to church!"

"I suppose you never felt it either," he said, "when we were filled with the Spirit."

Even in her anger, Lee hesitated — there were times, it seemed, when she had. There were times when the air crackled alive as she stood next to Randy, when a healing current flowed like fire from his hands. She could have dismissed the battle, too, if she hadn't experienced it, if only she hadn't met the Opposer herself that lost summer in Ada, one week when it followed Randy home. She felt it lurking at the end of the aisle as she priced hairspray at K-Mart, pooling along the highway as she drove south from town. It lay low among the trees that pressed in around their farm house, resting behind the shower curtain and in the corners of their room. For whole nights they had stood up against it. For whole days they sat thrown back, side by side, in their living room, barely able to move as the world came undone.

"I've felt things," she said to him slowly. "I've felt things just like all the other poor fools who come to Spirit Rising. They feel it because they're ignorant and don't know any better. They feel it because they're afraid to grow up. They get lost and don't know what to do about it, so they come to Spirit Rising and roll on the floor!"

"Why, then, all this resistance? Why can't we have the baby we want?" His eyes narrowed as he nodded, looking sly. "Why do you think that professor came to find me? What do you think it was that brought him to my door?"

"Randy, wake up! Are you really that blind? He came to see *me*, not you. He came to see *me*. He never once thought of you at all!"

At least Mitchell Chandler had been flushed out between them, the reason for a deep shame that had plagued her all week. He had reached out on the golf course to hold her. He had leaned down and kissed her on the lips. And now her cotton shift and poor stab at seduction, while Randy could only look smug.

"The demons were what led him to you. Don't think I can't see them at work!"

"You don't see anything, Randy, that's the problem! Demons didn't lead him anywhere. I'm a woman and he's a man. Maybe he came to see me because he wanted to! And maybe I'm happy he did!

"He thinks you're a fool just like I do. He thinks you're a big joke prancing around up in front. God doesn't need Pastor Randy to fight His battles! There's no Opposer out there standing in our way!"

"Get thee behind me…" he began, only to be cut off when she struck him in the chest.

"Don't even think it," she said. "Don't quote scripture to me. Don't you dare say a single thing. Don't say a word after all we've been through!"

She had seen countless others overtaken by the Spirit; she had stood empty among them as It seemed to pass her by. Something *did* surge up now to fill her, the purest rush of anger coursing hot through her arms. The second time she hit him Randy winced. When she swung for his head she made contact a third time, fist stinging as it glanced off his ear.

"Spiritual Warriors!" she snarled. "Spiritual Idiots! You were play-acting and everybody knows it. Everybody but you. You drive around eastern Oklahoma. You park the car someplace and pray. There's nothing out there except your imagination! There was nothing else out there at all!"

When she swung again, Randy caught her wrist. "I'm going," he said. "If you need to find me I'll be at the church."

"You're *crazy*. You really are. You're crazy and selfish and wrong. Crazy, crazy, crazy," she accused, and with each clear pronouncement swung her fist. As he closed to restrain her, they wrestled, staggering across the room. Finally Randy flared and shoved her sprawling across the bed.

"Crazy," she managed another time, struggling to her elbows. As she scooted forward her shift caught on the bedspread. The burning in her face had spread to her chest. When she kicked out Randy seized one of her ankles. Grabbing her shoulders, he pinned her hard against the bed.

Lee had finally found his temper and she was glad. They leaned together a long moment, panting, before he caught hold of the shift and dragged it past her hips. With a twist, he had it over her head. He dragged the bikini bottoms down, too, past her ankles, but Randy barely had her naked before Lee was on him — crazy, crazy — her forehead banging hard against his jaw. In the end, though, Randy was stronger. Safe within that knowledge, she brought herself fully against him. She fought without measure until she was rocked back and entered, only giving in when she had been pierced deep and held.

In the beginning there was Randy and there was Lee. Lee had never for an instant been afraid of him — when Randy got ahead, she touched his shoulder to slow him. The press of her palm led him back to her again. Her nails, sharp against his spine, drove him forward. A tap from her fingers brought him easily to bay. She tugged at the buttons of his dress shirt, seeking the brush of his chest against her own.

She had always loved his compact size and heedless ways. She had never minded waiting late at night in Dallas for him to come to her, loving the wind on his collar and the liquor on his breath. She had relied, too, every day of their marriage, on his faithfulness: when Randy had come to Jesus, he came all the way. Even that Lee could hardly hold against him — all that really mattered was that he had been there to claim her, had been waiting outside her apartment on a stifling summer day. His blindness, too, had its advantages, bearing him unerringly past her willfulness and moods. She let him in, and why not, he was Randy, her husband — the stranger who knew her best of all.

He rose up between her and all that would consume them, the insect earth and an endless, empty sky. Afterwards she lay listening to their hearts. The pulse beat a cadence she knew the words to: Randy and Lee, Randy and Lee, Randy and Lee. Randy and Lee as two hopeless sinners, Randy and Lee by a Savior redeemed; Randy and Lee in their bedroom together, briefly joined as they traveled through the world.

TWENTY-ONE

"We've cleaned out the last of the trays and Ginny and Bea have been sterilizing the units. Once they're clean we'll get back in production." Brian consulted his pad. "The NIH follow-up proposal is due on Friday. If you want to sign off, we'll Fed-Ex it tomorrow."

Mitchell nodded and clasped his hands. He brought his thumbnails together at his lips.

"Prakash is moving on. He's hooked up with Baylor in their infectious disease program. Nicole is going with Bachelder. She'll move over at the start of the year."

He watched as Brian hazarded a glance from his notes. Brian had kept up, for almost two weeks, a steady stream of emails, taped a dozen messages to Mitchell's office door. Late on a Wednesday night he had finally caught up with him. Met with silence, Brian essayed his own limited thespian repertoire. A gradual softening around his eyes was meant to signal concern.

"Um, Mitch, I wondered if you might want to play racquetball sometime. I wouldn't mind a chance to get out of the lab. Might even lose a couple of pounds." He patted his stomach and frowned. "I remember when Karyn and I split up, just before we left Chapel Hill. You were there for me, Mitch, and that was important. You were there when I needed a friend."

Long-absent Karyn had appeared effortlessly in the office, a stringy girl from the Piedmont who packed a thermos for Brian's lunches, cried at the airport when he went out of town.

"What did I do?" Mitchell rasped, his voice unreliable.

"Well, I was up at the lab one night right before Christmas. I guess you knew we'd been having trouble so you came down and found me. I was hurting and you knew it. Things had gotten way out of hand. You told me I'd have to buck up."

"Buck up?"

Brian nodded. "I'll always remember it, how much that meant to me. And that's what I did. I took care of business with Karyn. I got my focus back on work. I—"

"Buck up," Mitchell repeated. "Are you sure it wasn't 'buck down' or 'buck over?' How about 'get a grip?' Maybe 'Don't take your eye off the ball'?"

The silence that spread out between them had an anchoring feel, like the agar that held gel runs in place. He had never, it seemed, in fifteen years, really *looked* at his colleague, at the damp portals that formed his eyes and mouth. At Brian's lashes, long and girl-like behind his glasses, the rosy symphony of capillaries that brought blood to his cheeks. For some reason, the voice was more familiar, even with its new tone, low and direct.

"Okay, Mitch, let's cut the bullshit. I don't know what happened to your trip to Copenhagen and I don't care. Washington and the review panels, that's your area. What I do know is that our goddamn media are shot. The grad students are bailing. We haven't run gels for a month. I'm not going to let this lab slip away."

"Well," Mitchell said, "I guess we'd better buck up, then. Maybe we can buck up and see how it goes."

Brian's anger was bracing as it flashed across the desk. "I hate you, you bastard, I really do. I hope you lose your goddamn family too, and see what it's like." He paused as he licked his lips. "Maureen is ten times better than you ever deserved. And that signaling protocol is a ticket to the shit pile. We should have retooled three years ago when stem cells were coming on."

Anger deeply felt is so pale as to be almost colorless. It spread out from a band of orange around Brian's ample middle, a gathering of blue at the base of his throat. They both courted Maureen when she was a post-doc and Mitchell had won. Since then, they had co-authored sixty articles. They had coordinated millions of dollars in funding and built two different labs. What Brian had wanted, though, was to have Maureen naked, to move his penis back and forth between her legs. It seemed like the strangest of notions, but no stranger than the two of them fully clothed and folded into chairs in the office. No stranger than that shared history between them, never mentioned, unacknowledged through over a dozen years of reading gels and tracing pathways, puzzling over the tiny slice of process that kept them all fed.

"The Southwest," Mitchell said suddenly, as it came to him. "The University of New Mexico, in Albuquerque, have you been there? Big cottonwoods and brown adobe walls." As clearly as inappropriate Karyn had appeared among them he saw a second Brian, a few years older, in a lab. Sunlight broke through a recessed window. There was a seminar room down the hall. A black mountain lay low on the horizon, and from a nearby interstate came the rumble of trucks.

"Albuquerque, that's good. You'll be the star there. A better wife than Karyn, by a long shot. A family of your own, how does that sound? People love those long desert nights. Buck up, buddy, and it will be okay."

"Listen," Brian said, "you look like shit. Do you know that?"

"Maureen didn't choose you. She could have, but she didn't. This reticence thing you do is getting old. It's time you were out on your own."

In the stutter step of the evolving moment Brian had found his feet. He loomed large, in the narrow office, above him, big fists doubled at his side.

"So what are you going to do, Brian? Are you going to *pound* me? Are you going to *beat me up?*"

It would have been welcome, in a way, if he had. The boundaries of "Brian," though, were already in dissolution, giving way to a cluster of confetti in bright red and green. Even after the confetti had moved away, with the slamming of his office door, its Brian-field hovered, resonant within the same space where "Mitchell" found form. The soft hum of his computer brought him back to the keyboard, and the task he had begun before Brian came in.

The screen was filled with emails from his inbox, two weeks of unread messages that he moved through with efficiency, steadily deleting until all of them were gone. His files were next: data and memos, proposals and articles, patches of binary code on a spinning magnetic disk. Off and on, yes or no, right and wrong — the hard drive was what he was after, at the base of the chassis beneath a simple metal flap. He had just pulled it free when his body spoke up. 'Come on,' it was saying, 'got to go.'

There was much that still bound him to his office. The smooth surface of his desk and a seductive computer screen, stacks of journals and printouts on the shelves. He felt a sharp nostalgia for all that held them captive; another twenty years, and he might have made it through. Instead he used a hammer, its head wrapped in a lab towel, to smash the hard drive. He finished just in time, his body insistent. The constriction had increased around his head and shoulders, part of a growing pressure that finally brought him to his feet.

Along the hallway were refrigeration units and cabinets for storage, lab rooms and display boards, fluorescent lights and the soft gleam of tile. Metabolism whirred on in the animal colonies: tiny lungs respired and lipids formed membranes; drops of urine were formed and released. Contracting cinderblock walls squeezed him helplessly past them, down the metal staircase and across the lobby to the door.

Earlier that evening the first wave of an autumn storm front had soaked the streets of campus. His car was nearby along the curb. As he came along the sidewalk Mitchell knew to be careful — one false move and the fabric tore away.

Locomotion, if cumbersome, was effective. The front seat of the Triumph re-emerged to contain him, a refuge of leather, stretched canvas and steel. With a turn of the key the small engine came to life. He made a large circle, bumping his tires across the median, and under a scatter of rain headed back the other way.

Though little honored, the question endured of what's really "out there" in the space beyond our senses and ourselves. Whatever it was included influence and energy, tendencies and residue, a cascade of vibrational frequencies that helped matter find form. And ever-present, the mind's earnest effort — ahead of him rubber cones had been set out on the pavement, and two rain-ponchoed police officers motioned him to a stop. An orange glow lay ahead above the treetops. When he rolled down the window there was smoke in the air.

The first officer had just bent to his car when brakes squealed behind them. There was a shouted curse as a pickup passed them by. The policemen were abruptly gone then, the damp street deserted. Mitchell sat alone, heart pounding, behind the wheel.

That's when he caught sight of the Lumina, ahead at a stop sign. As he accelerated to catch up some deeper Mitchell offered counsel: come on, old buddy, buck up.

Neighborhoods blinked away only to re-establish themselves, as traffic lights blinked cryptic encouragement and street signs made suggestions from their poles. It was by strength of will alone that Prairie Grove still prevailed. A white current sizzled, unrestrained, along the railroad. A blaze from beyond the tracks had engulfed the old roundhouse; he saw it from Five Points where he glided to a stop. Wearing out, he was lucky to spot it, the neon-lit Chief Cheehaha motor court barely a half block away.

In the parking lot the Lumina waited. Turning to Mitchell, the driver nodded toward the office, and when Mitchell hesitated, nodded again.

He had grown grateful for suggestions from other entities, more and more as his will slipped away. Otherwise there was nothing to guide him. Nothing but his mind trapped alone with no exit, winding ever more deeply back into itself. Luckily his body, dense and plodding, knew the way. He made it to the office door and reached out to pull it open, only to step back as a huge man in a paisley dew rag wrestled a lounge chair across the threshold. He winked out at Mitchell beneath his load.

"Hey there, bro, right on time! Thanks a lot."

Two pale strips on the office floor marked where the lounge chair had rested. There was water damage on the ceiling, with several tiles missing. A fat man behind the counter looked back at him without interest.

"You want a room, I need the cash up front, my man. You got thirty bucks or are you wasting my time?"

"Credit card?" Mitchell croaked.

The man climbed to his feet. "Lemme have a look," he said and held out his hand.

Mitchell slid his hard-working credit card from his wallet, reliable everywhere and always for a tank of gas or candy bar, at any of a dozen convenience stores as he made passes through town. It had gotten hard enough just to manage his signature; he despaired at the blank registration form that lay between them on a pad.

The man squinted at the card. "Mitchell Chandler?" he said. "Why didn't you say so? A room for two, I already have you down."

Dumbly, Mitchell watched him sort through a drawer. The countertop beneath his hands was solid. The man and the office seemed real.

"Who paid?"

He had found his voice again and the man looked up. "How's that?"

"Who reserved the room?"

The man studied him a long moment before shrugging. "Dunno, maybe you did. Or maybe it was the woman who called a little while ago. Jerry took the call. You can ask him when he gets back from the dumpster. You got number 14, straight back on the left."

Outside, the Lumina was gone. Slowly, Mitchell inched the Triumph through the parking lot, past puddles and rose-painted doors. At the back of the lot, the man with the chair had finished at the dumpster. He was on his way back to the office, bloody slashes across his face.

"How you doing there, bud?" he asked, puffing happily. "You okay?"

Shrinking back, Mitchell moved to his room. The rose door was swollen and clung to its frame. By banging with his shoulder he finally pushed it free.

Inside there was a faded carpet, heavily worn, with a wide stain near the bathroom. A night table striped by cigarettes sat at bedside. A panel closet stood empty in the corner, with two misshapen hangers and a roach trap on the floor.

Of the room's previous occupants much remained. Quarreling voices and the daze of intoxication, confusion and rage, a smell of cigarettes and mildew in the air. When he looked out the curtains the fire had come closer — the National Guard Armory, too, was in flames. In the parking lot a smooth-faced Jerry bent to a police cruiser. Straightening, he pointed toward his room. As the officer turned Mitchell retreated from the window, dropping the curtain as he backed quickly away.

By moving to the margins he had finally reached Center, the place where the world found its form. His mind clawed at the edge to find balance. A loud rush and buzzing filled his ears. Somewhere within it was the burr of a telephone. The ring came again as the din died away. Before it could ring a third time Mitchell reached for the phone.

"Hello," he said eagerly. "Lee? Lee, is that you?"

The receiver felt sticky against his ear. The sound that greeted him was high-pitched and uneven, like the squeaky voices the lab techs assigned to the mice. Somewhere in the distance a man lectured on vectors. There was a discussion between two workers about the best sealant for pipes. As their voices faded the line remained open.

"Lee? Is it you? I'm here waiting in the room. Can you come over and meet me right now?"

It was pathetic, really, the hopefulness in his voice, the narrow slice of consciousness still guarded as his own. The line lay noncommittal in his hand. *Got to go*, but his options had narrowed: the only path left stretched within and beyond him, out past experience itself. Past purpose and understanding, confetti and time — once the membrane was pierced only absence remained. Nothing he knew as something had yet claimed existence: there was only Silence, deeply furrowed and alive.

Conceptualization still occurred, elemental and self-reflective; it was only with its help that he distinguished the universe, the tiniest of a thousand ripples that soon fell away. Otherwise there was only Vastness stretching out before him. All that was or ever would be returned there — he looked from a narrow ledge where he found himself clinging, shrinking back as he scrambled to keep his feet.

At stake, clearly, was the last of Mitchell Chandler. Whatever lay before him was both intimate and alien, restless and complete. As fully as it manifested form, it was inclined to extinguish: utterly, forever, without a trace. Puny as it was, his dread kept him upright. The tracklessness beckoned but he fought his way back. He would have given in then, to its deep lure and terror, if he hadn't found Randy Overmeyer beside him on the ledge.

"Don't," Randy said, and shook his head.

The little pastor's hair was swept back from his forehead; he still wore his white shirt and tie. No better anchored than Mitchell, he grinned with excitement. What lay before them was remorseless and profligate. Deep within its furrows lay a gentian purple glow. As Mitchell moved a final time toward it the pastor caught his arm. Randy reached out for him when Mitchell would have yielded, seizing his elbow tightly in his hand. He held on to it as long as he needed to, for all of the hours or minutes it took for time to reassert itself, for the reassembly of nightstand, stained carpet and bed. Even when Mitchell was back, he felt that grip at his elbow, the pastor's fingers merging with a sharp cramp in his arm as he stood in the motel room, receiver clutched tightly in hand.

TWENTY-TWO

The sanctuary was dark except for a single floor lamp near the front of the church. The small group gathered there sat with their heads bowed, in a circle of folding chairs between piano and pews. Mitchell was halfway down the aisle when Randy stood to meet him.

"Welcome. We've been waiting for you."

By focusing on the little pastor he made his way forward, arriving uneasily at the edge of the circle.

"I haven't been sleeping well," he said, and Randy nodded.

"I don't see how you could. Nobody in this whole town is sleeping right."

"I found the Lizard People out near the airport. I know how they act to control us. They're in our brains and there's nothing we can do."

He might have gone on but he saw Randy smile.

"That's what they say when they find out you're listening. They like to pretend that their hands are on the wheel."

"That's not even..."

"The half of it."

"Not a thousandth."

"Not a millionth, brother. Believe me, I know."

In a world lacking logic or platform, Randy's voice was calm. He stood easily in his white shirt and tie.

"It's all right, Mitch. You've come to the right place. All of us are happy that you're here."

"She's not," Mitchell said and pointed to Lee.

"Lee Overmeyer" had stood up as he came down the aisle. A

stocky man with a ponytail joined her, still cradling his guitar. Others took form around the circle: an older woman in a floral dress and a skinny girl by the piano, a boy with tattoos and dirty blond hair. When Randy reached out to him Mitchell recoiled.

"Stay back," he warned, but Randy shook his head.

"I won't abandon you, Mitch. That's one thing I promise I'll never do. There's nothing secret that shall not be made manifest; neither is anything hid, that shall not be known and come abroad."

He had made it through a collapsing landscape to the sanctuary; a loud drone and buzzing filled his head. At the edge of the lamplight it was hard to keep his feet. One of the folding chairs was open and he found his way to it. Randy sat down to face him, knees inches away.

"I'd like you to give me authority here, Mitch, to work with you. I'd like to speak past you to the intruders within."

Helpless by then, he must have nodded.

"Satan," Randy pronounced, "you have no power here. Demons, I rebuke you, in Jesus' name. Jala hawa, dah-jessa mahalla. Hada kalama ja dah."

In a world without rules even "strange" lost its strangeness: he had released himself to another's agency, a confidence superior to his own. What sustained that confidence mattered less than its presence — Randy had taken charge at the edge of the lamplight. For a long time Mitchell sat mindless, a voice near his ear. As time went by it grew steadily more intimate.

"Coma, coma," Randy was saying. "Abba je ladda, kasadda ji lah."

That he found the words meaningless seemed unimportant — the conversation wasn't really with him. And over time the buzz fell away. The dark space around them let go of its menace. The current in his spine settled down. The high walls of the sanctuary came back into focus, followed by pulpit and floor lamp, a rough-hewn cross with brass casters in its base.

Randy rocked back in his chair. "Victory is won, Mitch. I stand only to announce it. You've been restored to full life among men."

"I have?" Mitchell thought, but even the question felt familiar, not unlike something he would ask. His mind had returned to his skull again, where it peered out, safely separate, through his eyes. Something important, it seemed, had taken place. The woman in the floral dress was crying. The boy with tattoos had gone pale. There was an attractive woman among them, smooth-skinned, across the circle, and with a sudden stab of recognition he saw it was Lee.

Not Lee as a cloud of confetti. Not Lee as his Intended One either — it seemed he barely knew her at all. She was attractive but with a distancing coolness. Her arms were folded tightly across her chest. Her shoulders seemed wide for her body, and an open collar made her face look too long.

"… and that's when they take hold, at an unguarded moment. When you're defenseless and can't keep them out. Twelve strong demons held power within him. I had to track them down and call each out by name."

Randy laughed, loose and giddy, in his chair. "Did you see, Donnie, how hard they held onto him? Did you see how I had to work to gain their trust? Look out now, the Spirit's not through with me. There's things It still wants to say. Yadda dala gantage, matandi. Yadda dala ta ganda la say."

If words were still meaningless, the sharp calmness was not. His own mind was clearly coming back. He was Dr. Mitchell Chandler, with a lab at the University. He had been on NPR a half-dozen times. He was well-known in his field but surrounded by strangers — strangers with bad haircuts and troublesome complexions, who seemed to be gathered in his mother's old church. Carefully, he climbed to his feet.

"… so a lot of pastors yell, but I never could see it. Those spirits are scared bad enough as it is!"

Still talking, Randy stood up to join him, sliding one arm easily around his waist. Mitchell's mind was still tender, his reactions unsure: he dropped his own arm to the smaller man's shoulders. There was a pleasant warmth from their ribs pressed together, the presence of solid Randy at his side.

"Of course there's another piece of business still before us. I'd hate for Mitch to come all this way — it's hard to believe, but people do it — I'd hate for you to come this far, Mitch, and let it slip away."

Mitchell nodded vaguely in agreement. The pews stretched away toward darkness. The church people and chairs held their forms. Against that resurgent flatness the questions kept mounting. Was he really shed of Maureen? What had he done with his hard drive? Weren't the NIH follow-ups due in the fall?

"You know what I'm saying," Randy said, but Mitchell didn't, for once the slowest student in the group.

"Without Light the darkness comes quickly. Once the house is swept, it needs to stay clean."

From behind them came the sound of a piano. When Randy held up his hand it chorded to a stop.

"Thanks, Mary Kay, but we won't need the sound track. Mitchell has to know he's decided on his own. And that's what you get to do, Mitch — make a decision. You get to decide which direction you want to go. You can't measure it, you can't prove it, you can't eat it. You can't drink or explain it away. All you have to do is say the words after I do. 'Lord Jesus Christ, I really want to know You. I give myself to You right now.'"

"Randy, it's not that easy." Lee's voice, as it broke in, was angry. "You have to love Christ to take Him as your Savior. You have to give yourself up to follow Him."

Mitchell and Randy still leaned together like best childhood buddies. On her feet too, Lee glared across the circle, but Randy, unruffled, turned to him.

"Not many people, Mitch, get to see what you have. Even fewer can find their way back. But my wife is right in what she says just like always. There's a new life that comes with Jesus Christ. If you like your old one, it's waiting there for you. The deliverance was yours free of charge. Go home and forget that this happened. Pretend that you don't really know. Maybe you can get real *involved* again and see if it carries you. That's what a lot of folks do."

Randy's hand was already at his shoulder; light pressure was all it took to bring him smoothly to his knees.

"We may be a bunch of dumb bunnies," Randy said, "but we love you. Jesus does, too. It's okay, Mitch. It really is. God works not with persuasive words, but in Spirit and power, that our faith be not in men's wisdom, but the power of God."

It was that much harder to think, head bowed and on his knees. But thinking wasn't really the issue. The breach before him resided somewhere else. Memory had little weight in a material universe, but the images held power nonetheless. He saw his mother's casket at the front of the sanctuary. He remembered the gentian purple glow lying restless between the furrows, felt the strong grip of Randy's hand when he might have slipped away. He found himself dogpaddling alone in the Prairie Grove swimming pool, a child, at twilight, in summertime, out near the middle where the water got deep. He watched his father beckon, near-sighted and irritable; saw Geoff crying in fear as he clung to the chain.

"Come on," Randy urged, "this is a *dynamic* sort of thing. You've got to say the words, honey, you really do."

There would be plenty of time later for "reasons" to accumulate: six weeks of madness that left him exhausted, the chaos that had seized his world and mind. There was the touch of Randy's hand at his collar, the incongruous 'honey' as he finally stepped aside. In the end, though, it made little difference. The real surprise came when he was *met* there. He was met there by Something that loved him. Something he knew in an instant was real. An entity, a force, an impulse, a name— Something that Cared for him, in particular, Mitchell Chandler — the one thing he had never imagined, even once, to be true.

Mitchell had barely begun to say the words before he found he was weeping, unaccustomed tears splashing from his cheeks to his hands. He would try later to recapture that moment, but all there seemed to have been was a first sense of certainty, a reorientation that began deep inside. He floated unresistant above a simple chording on the piano — the skinny woman was playing again — the sweetest sounds he had ever heard in his life.

He was aware of praying voices around the circle. At some point he wept shamelessly again. He wasn't blind to Love because he knew it when it filled him, love for the woman in the floral dress and the ponytailed guitar player, for the boy with tattoos and for himself. There was some kind of hymn the group sang around him. After another prayer they all sang again. When the song was finished they came to greet him one by one.

"Christ be with you," said the woman in the floral dress.

"God bless you," said the ponytailed guitar player.

"I love you, man," from the boy with tattoos on his arms, who hugged him tightly, with tears in his eyes.

The skinny piano player, too, stood up to embrace him, shoulders sharp and bony beneath his hands. In this way he came at last to Lee Overmeyer. Even more than embarrassment he felt a deep surge of gratitude. He could see what she had tried to tell him that day at the golf course! Instead of opening her arms though, she looked back at him, expressionless, before turning away to walk up the aisle.

The rest of the group was gathering chairs and pulling on their jackets. Randy reappeared at Mitchell's side.

"I don't think I want Mitch to be alone just yet. He still looks a little dazed." He turned to the guitar player. "Donnie, you mind tagging along with him a while?"

"Glad to do it," Donnie said, straightening from his guitar case.

For the first time Randy seemed worn to Mitchell, looking up the aisle as he slipped on his sport coat. "I think I'll get my wife and take her home," he said. "When the Opposer comes against one, he does violence to all of us, no matter who a person might be. No matter how she stands with the Lord." He brightened, shaking his head. "Did you see how I had to convince them? Did you see how I called out their names?"

He reached for the floor lamp. "Maybe somebody can take this back to the parlor. I don't think we'll be needing it anymore."

The blond boy raised his hand. "I'll take care of it."

"Jaron" Randy said, "I felt you with me. I'll never forget how you stood at my side. Mary Kay, can you smell the new sweetness? Can you feel what a difference there is? Let's try a regular service this coming Sunday morning. We'll see if the good folks here at Campus will give us another month."

As he started up the aisle Mitchell trailed close behind. Randy turned to point him back the other way.

"Go with Donnie," he said, "it's okay now. It really is. You're in the Body of Christ. Nobody can do you any harm."

Mitchell was reluctant, though, to leave Randy's side. When he finally backed away Donnie was waiting. He followed him from the sanctuary out through the foyer, past the dark parlor and down the front steps. Outside the storm front had passed. Donnie had an old Fairlane with rusted out fenders; on the sidewalk he fished for his keys. When he'd stowed his guitar he slammed shut the trunk.

"Okay," he said, "all set."

"What are we supposed to do?" Mitchell asked, and Donnie laughed.

"Whatever you want, Mitch. This is your night. I'm just along for the ride."

The storm had left in its wake a clean sort of dampness. The world, in a dissolving mist, brimmed with possibility, but with his first steps Mitchell headed instinctively toward the parking garage, tracing the same route he'd walked a thousand times. He broke free to venture forward along the sidewalk. A skim of oil lay along the gutter, colors swirling. The parking garage wall cued its coarse code in brick. Mitchell felt a clutch in his stomach as he paused at the corner, reluctant to step off the curb.

"It's okay," Donnie said. "Don't worry. He's holding you safe in His hands."

And it seemed there really was a stable axis for the evening, for the campus world with its freshness and resonance, for a pristine beauty that took away his breath. They came past Arby's and the Campus Corner. The Kopy Kat was firmly in place. A window at Hair Benders showcased bottles of hair gel, its long row of chairs stretched resilient past the glass.

Streetlights left a sheen on the pavement. Parking meters weren't just in place but deeply appropriate, the shop doors both meaningful and true. After another block they turned to file along a side street, past fraternity and sorority houses where exhibits for Homecoming had been set up on the lawns. Goalposts wrapped in orange and blue were surrounded by spotlights. A fiberglass Chief Cheehaha bopped a cringing Badger on the head. Groups of students pressed around them on the sidewalk, bobbing hopeful and eager and loved.

They came at last to the taverns on College Street. The doors to the Gridiron, at midblock, were propped open. A sort of podium had been set up on the sidewalk, where a thick-shouldered boy in a rugby shirt checked student ID's. Caught up in his brisk efficiency he was slow to spot them in the crowd.

"Can I help you gents?" he asked, and Mitchell shook his head. Donnie stood beside him, paunchy and graying. Small drops of moisture sparkled lightly in his hair. They were harmless enough, middle-aged and marginal, but the boy couldn't help glancing back at them a second time and yet again, shyness peeking out between his scowls.

Around them was the smell of peanut shells, wet leather and perfume. The rattle of a snare drum floated out from the stage. Mitchell's eyes traveled to the marquee above the entrance where 'TONIGHT: ARRIVAL' was spelled out in block letters. He blinked and glanced down at Donnie. Donnie, with his musician's small smile, simply nodded: it was another of Life's many riffs to be acknowledged and enjoyed. Reprieved from his smartness, Mitchell laughed.

"Hold on," Donnie said, back at the Fairlane. He rooted past his guitar case in the trunk. "Here, this is for you."

With a sinking feeling Mitchell saw it was a Bible. "That's okay," he said quickly, "I'm fine. I'm sure I won't need that tonight."

"Here, Mitch. I want you to have it."

The Bible was thick, its cover worn smooth. A dozen yellow Post-It notes stuck out along the side. Uneasy, Mitchell held it in his hands. " I can't take this, Donnie. It's yours. I'll stop and pick one up tomorrow."

"Hey, it's not a rabbit's foot, man, it's a Bible. It doesn't matter whose it is. The words are what count. You have a phone number where I can reach you? In the morning I'll give you a call."

Mitchell reached slowly for his wallet. "I can give you one of my cards, I guess. My office is over at BioMed Complex. For the time being, though, you can get me at the Chief Cheehaha. It's off University a half a block, near..."

Donnie nodded. "I know where it is. Hey, cool card. Maybe I can come by your lab sometime and look around. I always liked science in school."

"Look," Mitchell said. "Let me give this back to you. It's not really the kind of thing..."

Donnie held up his hands. "Uh-uh, Mitch, it's yours. You're going to need it. Try Matthew or Luke to get started. John might be a little intense. I'll call you at the Chief before noon."

With a clap on his shoulder Donnie left him on the sidewalk. Mitchell watched the taillights of the Fairlane as they moved away down the street. The Bible in his right hand felt intrusive — he had been able to push from his mind for a time what had happened. A madness that for weeks had seized him. A casting out of demons at the front of the church. A relief, a decision, a breakdown; finally an acceptance of Jesus as he wept on his knees.

All of which was true and still felt essential, even if he was unclear as to exactly what it meant. The world was restored and resonant, full of sweet logic and truth, but it was still a mystery what "Jesus" had to do with it. Or, for that matter, the Bible itself, thick and heavy in his hand.

Randy, though, could probably tell him. Randy, he was certain, would know. With that assurance Mitchell could look out toward the Math Building, the upper floors of the BioMed Building half-hidden in the mist. Transcription, translation, and thus protein. Protein, in turn, forms the cell. All nature was as it should be, active and orderly, only informed by that same Something Else that lived through and defined him, beyond any power of his own to deny or disdain. *God is*, he thought — the strangest of propositions — but it was what he was left with on a campustown sidewalk, Bible in hand: confounded, delivered, born again.

TWENTY-THREE

On his patio in Zone 10, with his friend Leif beside him and Maribel's small bunny hopping through the grass, Geoffrey Chandler remembered himself at six, bent over a piece of construction paper in his first grade classroom. He had drawn a crayon diamond and was engaged in labeling each of its points with names. Dad and Mom were at top and bottom while Mitch and Betsy provided balance on either side. As he considered the elegance of the formulation he was surprised by Mrs. Murray, his hearty, big-breasted teacher, who had from the first day of school left him speechless with fear.

"Why Geoffrey," she cried, "what are all those other people doing there? That's a fine kite, but they didn't draw it, you did! Do you need help writing out your name?"

He didn't and shook his head. He was forced to weigh, though, as she hovered, his own name, long and unwieldy. The points of the diamond were taken. He knew instinctively it didn't belong at the center. Finally he blocked out GEOFFREY at the corner of the paper, floating untethered all by itself.

"I think we'll do Panajachel after market day in Chichi. And then a couple of nights in Xela with a visit to the springs. The Hungarians last year seemed to like it." Leif pulled a last drag from his Bravo. He was Norwegian by birth but had lived in Guatemala since childhood. Well past sixty, he still favored the Ladino custom of leaving his shirt half unbuttoned, the better to display a thatch of white chest hair across a narrow, brownish chest. His half-dozen languages came in handy for a tour service he ran, leading groups of travelers to Chichicastenango or the ruins at Copán. His English was British-accented and effortless, but with Geoffrey, in recent years, he had begun lapsing into a cowboy sort of dialect, picked up watching reruns of old westerns from the States.

"And then I reckon we'll saddle up for Flores. There's a new hotel not far from the plaza. It's run by a South African couple who promised good rates."

Spanish-speakers appropriated names shamelessly, but while John went to Juan, and Mike to Miguel, Leif had resisted translation. So did Geoffrey, for that matter. There had been a brief stab at Geofredo early on and some long-time customers at the shop still called him Don Fredo. Celia, like his daughters, called him Papi. It seemed a strange thing for a grown woman to say, especially as she paused, going out the door in her business suit; when she tapped his knee impatiently in their old Volkswagen van to point out a break in traffic; when she rolled up close in their tiny bedroom, whispering it sleepily in his ear.

"Another pilgrimage to San Simón?" he asked.

"The Hungarians went crazy for it and the Czechs might, as well. They like their icons, the stranger the better."

Leif had begun, a year earlier, taking groups into the mountains above Quetzaltenango, and in March Geoffrey had closed the shop and gone along. Their objective was San Simón, the vestige of an early conquistador murdered by the Maya, his spirit returned to earth via a department store mannequin dressed in cowboy hat and sunglasses and paraded through the streets every day to its shrine. Villagers traveled from all over the region for rituals that were vaguely Catholic but, with the burnt sacrifices and grain alcohol offerings, clearly something different, both ancient and strange.

It was the first time he'd ventured into the highlands in years and the whole trip felt wet and depressing. He had missed Celia and the girls, for one thing. He had missed his workbench with its line of fuel injectors, the cool metal logic of their parts. He had missed his patio, where Leif lit another cigarette and Mari's bunny hopped before them through the grass.

"Business all right?" Leif asked.

"It's steady, and with Asia struggling, that's a surprise. For the last couple of years the Koreans have kept me going. They're running a half-dozen bulldozers at a factory site near Esquintla. Martín has one of their injection units in the shop right now."

Leif raised his eyebrows. "Martín as in Cristina's *novio*? Wedding bells, Geoffrey?"

"Could be. He's from a good family. Celia was nineteen when we got married. Cris will be twenty next month."

"I ran into a cotton planter over near Morales when I was there with that Swiss group. Said he was having trouble with his irrigation pumps. I told him he ought to look you up."

"I did a unit from Rio Dulce a couple of years ago, rode over on the bus one weekend to pick it up."

"You need to get out on the Internet, Geoffrey. That's where business is being done. You should have seen the Hungarians whenever we found a connection, lining up to send their emails back to Budapest. Why don't you call that Peruvian who set up my web page? He can get you ready to go."

"You're probably right. I'll have to get hooked up eventually."

He would have to eventually, but for a while could put it off — Guatemala was a country where the modern lagged behind. Only a couple of months before Celia had sold three hundred manual typewriters to the government, finally tracking down a factory in Brazil that still made them. She found it on the Internet, of course, but Geoffrey was resistant. It seemed of little advantage for him and Leif to be sending emails, when they got to sit in the sunshine every day after lunch.

"I need to pick up Mari," he said, and stood up.

Stretching, Leif climbed to his feet. "Yup, partner, time's a-wastin'. I'd best be moseyin' too."

As they went through the sliding door Geoffrey used his leg to block El Gato, the family cat who spent his days watching the bunny through the glass. Leif followed him through the house to the carport, and down their narrow driveway to the street. They parted there, Leif chugging away in his ancient Fiat and Geoffrey on foot, walking beneath high concrete walls topped with shards of broken glass. At the corner he was met by the busy Avenida, with its brightly colored buses, blaring air horns, and exhaust.

The patio was a place of refuge from the chaos of the capital, a place where pigeons cooed in early morning among the bougainvillea, and city traffic seemed a hundred miles away. After dark there was the steady rattle of firecrackers to celebrate somebody's birthday, a strange custom for a country so long plagued by gunfire. And for a time, during the worst years, it had been gunfire, as the government's ceaseless campaign against the villagers spilled into the capital and a violent settling of scores took over the nights. Celia's family, turn-of-the-century German immigrants, were no longer prosperous, but an uncle had been kidnapped as he came out from breakfast, and a cousin was gunned down on the street. One morning Geoffrey had come across a headless body in the gutter along the Avenida, as he hurried Cris and Rosa to school.

The worst of it took place in the countryside, merciless and unrestrained, but gradually the violence ebbed away. Not totally, of course, but some of that dark tension lost its grip on the capital and a kind of relief slipped into their lives. In their bedroom, too, a fragile carelessness returned, the result being Maribel, ten years younger than Rosa, and in her first year at the primary school where Geoffrey was headed to pick her up.

In the bright autumn sunlight he joined a growing group of women on the sidewalk, young mothers and older sisters, grandmothers and servant girls, all of them there to fetch the children who milled in the schoolyard. He was watching for Mari, light-complected like her mother, and he felt a familiar helplessness fill his chest when he spotted her breaking free from the knot of other students. She stood at the gate to look for him, impossibly small in the white blouse and blue skirt of her uniform, shoes scuffed and one sock drooping, dragging the same worn book bag that Rosa had carried to school.

"*Papi*," she exclaimed, her eyes big. "*Vimos una víbora. Alguien la trajo del campo!*"

"Honey, pull your sock up," he told her, taking the bag. "What kind of snake was it, did the teacher say?"

"*Ay*," she said, shrugging dramatically. "*Era bien larga.*" She stretched her arms out to demonstrate. "*Así. O no. ¡Más bien, así!*"

Of all their daughters Maribel was the most resistant to English, even though he and Celia tried to speak it at home. Cris and Rosa, when his mother had been alive, made occasional summer trips to Prairie Grove, and now Rosa was in Houston for college. He supposed they would have to work something out for Mari, too, once she was older. In truth, though, he could barely imagine being apart from her, enjoying, as they walked, her casual dominion over the busy Avenida, the squealing buses and piles of rubble on the street. Chattering next to him, she already had her eye on the *tiendita* they frequented, a dark little store with a wooden counter, and bright bottles of soda stacked around a thick block of ice.

"The world is getting warmer," she lectured him in the doorway. "If it gets too hot, the snakes will all die."

They drank a soda there, sitting on boxes near the counter, before walking the rest of the way home. As they came up the driveway, she ran ahead to her bicycle. Geoffrey unlocked the chain and lifted the bike down, pushing it ahead down the drive.

He had taught her to ride only a few weeks earlier, running behind her along the narrow lane of the cul-de-sac. Now she rode in expert circles on the pavement as he watched from the shade by the door.

For a long time, it seemed, they'd had no choice but to live carefully. Now that the city had calmed fads from the States were making inroads. About the same time as the Internet, a psychic from Los Angeles arrived and spent a profitable week doing readings for middle-class women in the capital. Celia's sister Grisela had made an appointment for his return visit; flush from her deal with the typewriters, Celia went along. As part of the reading she brought photos of the family — Cristina and Rosa on the patio in swim suits, her mother and father at their anniversary, Mari on her first day of school.

Celia had recapped the session afterwards, at home in their bedroom.

"… so music will be more important in my life. I might end up doing some kind of writing, too. I'll know when the time comes. I'll know because he told me that's my gift in life. I've always known exactly what I want."

Geoffrey nodded.

"Cris is practical, like me. He liked what he saw in Martín. He said we'll be grandparents by the end of next year."

It had been early on a Saturday evening as they lay together. Her father guarded a secret disappointment. Her mother had been a Prussian soldier in a previous life. Rosa wouldn't be returning to Houston after the school year, which didn't surprise him — the girls grew bored quickly in the States. Among the scattered photos was one of him, bearded and frowning at his shop.

"So what did he say about me? That I'm a monster?"

Celia smiled. "He said my husband would always love me, which was nice."

"That's true enough," Geoffrey said. " I could have told you that and saved the thousand *quetzales*."

"It's all part of my incarnational blueprint. My Higher Self keeps everything in line. I'll probably have another business of some kind after the typewriters. Mari feels closest to her dad."

Celia still had on the pretty gauze skirt she had worn to the reading, draped loosely over smooth legs and sturdy calves, the blue veins that first began to bulge as she carried their children. As he trailed his hand lightly along her hip, she switched into English.

"It was funny, really, because he looked at your picture the longest time. Finally he nodded and gave it back. He said, 'Your husband is a lucky man. He's come to terms with himself. That's something I don't often see.'"

Leaning back beside her, Geoffrey laughed. He'd laughed, but the next morning, at the shop, considered the assessment. He thought of it again that afternoon as he sat with Leif on the patio. One of many things his adopted country possessed was a tolerance for pondering, respect for the private spaces in a neighborhood or mind.

He lit a cigarette in the carport, leaning back against the wall.

He could barely imagine sometimes that Celia had stayed with him, but Celia, like the man said, was practical. She knew that brooding was what some men had to do. He had gone through whole years of it, it seemed, angry and resentful, but there came a time when he raised his head and looked around. That's when he'd found Celia waiting. That's when he remembered Cris and Rosa, dependent daily on his presence. That was about the time, too, when they were given Mari, who six years later rode in circles before him, calling out as she came past the drive.

"*Mira, Papi. No, ¡a mí! ¡A mí! ¡Mírame a mí!*"

"I see you, honey," he called and pushed away from the wall, coming down through the carport to the sun.

He didn't need a psychic from LA to point out his good fortune. The mindless violence in the end had never touched them. In a country full of hungry cats and dogs, Mari's bunny hopped safely through the grass. Celia loved him despite his moods and melancholy, and over time he had gained the confidence of her family, gradually mastering both a language and a trade. With the weather so temperate, days ran seamlessly together, the hours as well: when Celia got home, he would head to the shop. First, though, he watched Mari trace a final circle on the pavement — his heart in her hands — before climbing high on her pedals to glide up the drive.

TWENTY-FOUR

The Swiss boy's voice had grown deeply familiar to him, the words floating somewhere behind his brow.

"How willing are we to face the basic facts of the world, our sensations as they come to us and go? A deeper stillness, never far away. And isn't that stillness reliable, like the earth beneath us, providing ground for all that we know?"

It was near the end of a Thursday afternoon Senses Alive! class and Austin Chandler lay with his eyes closed. He had, that afternoon, pondered the shifting weight of a bean bag. He had come to standing and sat down again. Now he lay quietly on the floor. At some point the boy's words dropped away. In the vacuum Austin Chandler felt the press of his sweatshirt, heard Olive Giesseking's congested breathing a few feet away.

Libby McNeil's face floated through his mind. She had told them before class that her daughter's MS had worsened; even as her face faded he heard the quaver in her voice. A damned shame, he considered, for someone so young, and he felt the knot in his chest as it tried to loosen, a warmth spreading from his stomach to his legs. He settled into a silence so profound that he might have been napping, when Stefan rang his bell and the meditation was done.

Even then Austin Chandler lay a time without moving. With a grunt he came back to sitting. Libby, across the circle, kept her eyes closed. Marge Cobble had a wistful look that made her seem young. It was a time that the Swiss boy, to his credit, didn't rush. A jumble of voices came toward them from the sanctuary — apparently Randy Overmeyer's group was still in business. Austin Chandler let the irritation rise up within him and slowly drift away.

"I have an announcement," Stefan told them. "I must be away for a few weeks."

Austin Chandler's classmates nodded and Mary Kerwin raised her hand. "I hadn't said anything, but I'm going to be out of town myself. My granddaughter is getting married in Connecticut."

This caused a flurry of interest around the circle.

"Isn't that nice," someone said. "Connecticut!"

"Is that Karen's daughter or Cheryl's?"

Mary smiled with pride. "It's Cheryl's oldest girl, Amanda. Karen lives in Florida, but they'll come up for the wedding. Steve's flying in from Austin."

"Steve's in Austin? That's where the Buddinger boy is! I wonder if Steve has his address?"

"Wait, wait, wait!" Austin broke in. "Wait there just a second, Stefan. When are you leaving?"

"Very soon, on Saturday morning. I won't be back until the end of the year."

"What about the class? We're scheduled to meet twice a week. I mean, not that it matters, but that's what we signed up for. Until December 12, like it said on the flyer. I think we deserve an explanation."

Stefan hesitated. "Okay," he said, "I will tell you. I have good news. I met someone. I'm in love. I want to take Tanya to see my family."

Two months earlier Austin Chandler wouldn't have felt his wrists stiffen, noticed the hard cords of muscle as they tightened across his back. Stefan blushed as the women began to coo.

"Oh, that's lovely, Stefan."

"Is she a local girl? Did you meet her here?"

"Your family will be so glad that you're bringing her home!"

"Yes," Stefan said, his blush deepening, "it's true. I am in love. I can hardly believe it sometimes. Everything..." he gestured around the parlor, with its worn carpet and chairs, "...everything is so beautiful with this person in my life. Would you perhaps like to see a picture?"

Of course they did, and Stefan dug through his bag. Exclamations followed a silver-framed photo as it was passed around the circle. When it came to Austin Chandler he found a pretty young woman smiling into the camera as she leaned against a tree. Anger squeezed tight around his throat.

"But what about us?" he persisted. "We still have a class here. We signed up for fifteen weeks and that's what we should get!"

Stefan frowned. "Perhaps we could start again after Christmas."

"But that wasn't the agreement! We're just getting the idea when you decide to run off. You're a talented young man, but there are things you need to learn. Professionalism is one of them. It's just not very professional, the way you're doing this, breaking off in the middle of the term."

The boy looked back at him with interest.

"It seems that you're experiencing disappointment," he said, and Austin Chandler flushed.

"I'm not disappointed, damn it, just, well, it *is* a disappointment, the way you've arranged this. There's the scheduling, too. I've got this all set on my calendar. The afternoons are blocked out for the rest of the fall!"

Stefan nodded thoughtfully. "That's true. We did agree to meet. Perhaps you, Austin, could lead the group in my absence. You seem very engaged. You're the first one here every week."

As the boy looked back at him Austin Chandler wondered if he was being mocked.

"We explore our relationship with our thoughts and the world that surrounds us. That's all we do. I think you would be an excellent leader. That way the classes could go on."

"Why, yes, Austin," Billie Morrison said. "I can come if you still want to meet."

Olive Giesseking nodded in agreement. "I can make it too. Five weeks are all we have left?"

"I'll miss those two sessions for Mandy's wedding," Mary Kerwin was telling him, "but after that, I'll be back. Of course, Austin, we'll come to your class."

"It's not *my* class," he said irritably, "it's his. I just think we ought to see it through."

Marge Cobble had come by often near the end to see Edie, taking her to the beauty parlor or out for a drive. "We'll be happy to come," she said, "if you want to keep meeting. We all enjoy this too."

"No, no," he said, "it's all right. We'll wait for the professor to come back." He waved his hand in dismissal. "Let's just forget about it. Not a problem. It will be good to have the afternoons free."

"Well," Stefan said, "then it's settled. I have your phone numbers. I'll let you all know when I return."

"That's just wonderful, Stefan. We wish you every happiness in the world."

"Let us know if you decide to get married. Maybe we could do something for you at the church."

"Well, we'll see," he said, unable to keep from smiling. "That may very well be part of the plan."

Austin Chandler kept his head down as he gathered his blanket.

By the time he finished the women were gone. As he approached Stefan the boy was bent over his bag.

"Well," he said, "congratulations. You've found yourself a handsome young lady."

"Thank you, Austin. I'm very pleased."

"Not so much detachment these days, I'd imagine. The world looks a little riper to grab."

"I feel very fortunate. Tanya is a remarkable person."

The boy was so slight and sexless that Austin Chandler could barely concede the girl to him, especially one so pretty and at ease with herself, leaning back smiling against a tree. He and Edie had been inexperienced on their honeymoon, uncomfortable and fumbling, so embarrassed the next morning they could barely speak. He pressed on with Stefan, his tone conspiratorial.

"Some things are worth holding onto, I guess. Is that what you're saying? Stave off that emptiness a little while along the way?"

Stefan smiled. "Well, I guess I am feeling some attachment these days." He straightened as he shouldered his bag. "But that's only to be expected, isn't it? You have had a family. Now maybe I will have one, too. If so, I would like that very much. And really, Austin, does it change anything? Isn't our task still to encounter each moment as it comes to us, whether that moment is bitter or sweet? Shouldn't we attend as fully to our happiness as we do to our pain?"

Austin Chandler nodded, not really listening. He followed the boy into the entryway, slipping through a stream of Spirit Rising people on their way to the sanctuary. When Stefan paused to zip his jacket he decided to take the chance.

"Say there," he said, "I wanted to ask you something. You know those different points in the body you talked about a few weeks ago? Where the energy is centered and all that? Not that there's any real proof, of course, but I may have experienced it. A kind of fullness right here in the chest. Do you think maybe the area could be opening up some, like you talked about that one day in class?"

The words came out in a rush at the end, hopeful and silly, but Stefan, as always, listened carefully. Balancing his bag, he nodded.

"It's possible. The unfolding of the heart chakra can be very dramatic." He looked back at him in the half-light of the entryway. "But if you'll pardon me, I wonder if you've had a checkup with your doctor lately. That might be a good thing to do. Especially if you feel discomfort in your arm."

He pushed open the door. "I'm sorry but I have to go. Tanya is waiting. Please take care of yourself, Austin. I hope to see you again."

Austin Chandler stood alone with his blanket. He zipped his own jacket and pulled on his stocking cap. As he pushed open the door a guitar squawked in the sanctuary. Three more Spirit Rising faithful passed him on the steps. Prayer groups and faith healing, God in heaven and the burning pits of hell — it was almost as bad as passing bean bags around a circle, or imagining there was something special in your chest.

"This is foolishness," he thought, with a trickle of pleasure — for once he had gotten the naming exactly right.

Outside the air was crisp and cold, and Austin Chandler stood at the bottom of the steps. He looked past campustown to the Math Building and BioMed Complex, the Engineering Library and Physics Lab. At least the University was a place where you had to know something, with little patience for vague hopes and dreams. A place where evidence mattered; a body of understanding carved out step by step. For over forty years he had been a part of that enterprise. He'd made contributions of his own, as small as they were. Mitchell, of course, had done even better, and as Austin Chandler turned he was startled to see him there, coming toward him on the sidewalk.

"Hello, Dad."

"Mitchell," he said warmly, "it's good to see you. Did you break away early? How are things going at the lab?" He felt a quick rush of pride. "Are the Ag boys still sniffing around? I know their operations aren't the most prestigious, but give them a hearing. In a state like this they've got the power of the purse!"

He was determined not to give advice, which wasn't necessary anyway. Mitchell knew what he was doing. Already he was beginning to dress better, with pressed pants and a sharp black blazer. Grad students could afford to be sloppy, while the top men had to dress to fit the part.

Mitchell nodded toward the church. "Are you attending services at Campus?"

"Oh well, you know," Austin Chandler said lightly. He shrugged, blanket bouncing in his arms. "Several former colleagues attend. You may remember Walter Eller, down the block. He's a member here. Several others come too, when they can make it. I'm happy to help out with rides from time to time."

Mitchell looked at the old building appraisingly, the concrete steps and dark heavy doors.

"Campus Church," he said. "I remember how Mom used to love it. The people were good to her here." He paused, looking thoughtful, "I wonder if they really know Jesus? Do you think they really know who He is?"

It had been so long since Mitchell asked his opinion that he was caught off guard. "Well," he ventured carefully, "some might. They've been at it an awfully long time."

"Hey, Mitch," a young man called out as he trotted up the steps. An older woman, passing by, touched his arm. Too, there was what Austin Chandler had been doing his best not to notice: the thick Bible he carried in his hand.

"Mitchell," he said, "you've got to be careful. They play rough at the top levels, I'm sure you know that. You can't afford to give them extra ammunition. You can't let down a minute or they'll pass you right by."

He waved toward the church.

"All this is fine, in its place, but don't get distracted. Everybody has troubles at home. Don't do anything foolish, that's the main thing. Keep your head and you'll come through all right."

He had vowed not to give advice, but there it was anyway: look out, be careful, avoid mistakes. What else could any father say? It seemed like so little, finally out there between them, but Mitchell was peering back at him intently. Austin Chandler shifted, uncomfortable, with his blanket. He didn't know why everyone had decided to turn the cow eyes on him, the old biddies in class and then Stefan in the entryway; now Mitchell in his sharp pants and blazer, eyes glowing wet and intense.

A girl leaned out the church door above them. "Come on, Mitch," she called, wagging her finger playfully. "Randy's getting ready to start."

Mitchell waved but he watched Austin Chandler. A stricken sort of smile spread slowly across his face. "Dad," he said, as if trying it out. "Dad, Dad, Dad." Before he could retreat Mitchell had already seized him. Tall like Edie's people, he wrapped long arms around his shoulders, their foreheads banging as Mitchell drew him close.

"Dad, Dad, Dad. God bless you," he whispered. "May the Lord guide you and keep you in His sight."

Austin Chandler tried his best to pull away, but Mitchell was stronger. They wrestled there, together on Sixth Street, until his son finally deigned to set him free. With a last squeeze on his shoulder Mitchell left him on the sidewalk, hurrying with his Bible up the steps.

TWENTY-FIVE

Cold weather had arrived and Mitchell watched his breath as he scanned the traffic. When a car slowed in front of the Clark Station a ragged interval opened up, allowing him a space to trot across the street. A sidewalk on the other side led him past the Autoplex to McDonald's, a half block away.

For three weeks he had followed the same routine after awakening in his room at the Chief Cheehaha. He waited in line behind others to order, slipped into a small booth he'd staked out as his own. Layered before him were the crisp disks of his breakfast — English muffin and settled egg, a crescent of pink flesh that lay glistening in between. Careful, he thought, but the world kept its order. Grateful, he bowed his head to offer thanks.

He had heard early in the semester, barely paying attention, grad student complaints about an early morning prayer group that was meeting in the BioMed Building. It was in his own darkened microscopy lab that he'd found them, eight people huddled in a circle holding hands.

"No, please," he said, "it's all right. You don't have to leave. I'd like to join you a while, if you don't mind."

He'd had little reason before to notice Christians; now it seemed they were everywhere. Jerry at the Chief Cheehaha had come to God in the penitentiary. Churches clogged the streets of Prairie Grove. Skinny Jana, one of his lab techs, kept a Bible on her desk, and she was the first person he picked out in the prayer circle. There was Bernadette, a secretary from Grants and Contracts, and a postdoc from China named Liu. He recognized Chet Davis, who ran the supply room. He was surprised to see a professor there as well, Heimowitz from BioChem, and they regarded one another cautiously as Mitchell found a chair.

"Welcome, Dr. Chandler," Jana said — apparently she was the leader — and with that they returned to their prayers.

In the center of the microscopy lab was the polished column of a Hitachi 700, an electron-scanning microscope he'd gotten with NIH money a couple of years earlier. Three mornings a week they gathered beneath it to pray. Mitchell and Chet had spoken, on occasion, in the hallway, usually to exchange meaningless banter about the Warriors. Now they shared something more profound. Liu was homesick and scared. Bernadette had trouble with her daughter. Heimowitz blustered in department meetings but discouragement stalked him, and they put their hands on his shoulder as they prayed. The group prayed for Mitchell, too — Jana and Bernadette, Heimowitz and Chet — an act of kindness that often moved him to tears.

Around him at the McDonalds were other customers, sleepy-eyed with their breakfasts. He watched the countergirls with their lazy, rote courtesies, two young African-American boys slouching stoic in their booth. He wondered if they felt the power that filled them. It was the very thing that he, for a lifetime, had been blind to, a force that he now knew as Love.

He hadn't been so far off, in his weeks of insanity: there *was* something that connected supernovas and birthday cakes, lawn shears and retroviruses — the same Life that helped his right hand, back at the motel room, guide his toothbrush, his fingers as they knotted his tie. It bore him, too, on a Sunday morning, east from Five Points on the highway, out to the brick columns at the entrance to Manor Lake. He followed the pavement's wide curve to his own house, where the windows were dark and the family van gone.

He let his car idle before turning off the engine. The lake, under low clouds, was gray. Beyond the golf course the bean fields were bare. As Mitchell waited five minutes, and then another ten, he felt a growing sense of relief. The first he saw of Maureen was when she pulled in beside him, just as he was reaching for his keys.

She wore, as she climbed from the van, a new hair style, tinted red and cut short like a boy's. She came to his window.

"Sorry I'm late. I had to drop the boys off at Betsy's."

"I'd hoped to see them. I thought maybe they could go with us."

"I don't think so," she said, and shook her head. "Wait here, I've got to go pee."

He noticed as she came close that her face had broken out; he was surprised that their separation had cut a wake. He squeezed from the Triumph to stand on the driveway. The screen door was ajar and Max nosed his way past it to the porch. When he saw Mitchell he ambled toward him, tail wagging. It wasn't long before Maureen was back.

"Are you sure we have to do this?"

"Yes," he said, "if you don't mind too much. Why don't you get in and we'll go."

It felt strange for them to be together again in the Triumph. They seemed bigger than when they were courting fifteen years earlier, winter coats binding as they shifted in the seats.

"So how are the boys?" Mitchell asked.

"All right, I think. Kai wet the bed for a while, but that's over now. It's always hard to tell about Nick."

"And you?"

"Mitchell, let's just go if we're going. Don't make this any harder than it is."

The growl of the Triumph was subdued as they wound toward the highway.

"I called John Darden. If we file here, division of assets shouldn't be a problem. We can split the court costs right down the middle."

"I've been thinking," he said. "Maybe we can work something out."

She frowned. "Look, Mitch, don't hold back on Laztec. Don't try to finesse us on the shares. It wouldn't be fair to the boys."

"That's not what I meant," he began but didn't finish. He had changed in ways she would never understand. She looked out the window as they picked up speed along the tracks.

"How's the lab going? Brian said you were coming back around."

He cleared his throat. "So Brian's still crying on your shoulder?"

Beside him Maureen bristled. "He's my friend and he was yours too, not so long ago. If not for him that whole lab would be history. I know it's hard to believe, Mitch, but the field goes on without you. Proposals get funded and papers come out even while you're on vacation. Even while you're running around with your little pals, witnessing for Jesus. Is that what you do? Do you stop people on the street corner and try to save their souls?"

"Hey, listen," he said. "You don't know the first thing —"

"Of course I'm still wondering when I'll find out about the other woman. There is one, isn't there? That's the only thing missing so far."

Chastened, he retreated into silence. The Love that always seemed so self-evident early in the morning, especially after a second cup of coffee, was little match for the tension between them, sculpted with such care through the years. He wasn't perfect, he reminded himself, only saved, reassurance that struggled against the power of Maureen's disdain as she sat beside him in the Triumph. He had been resistant when Randy insisted that he call her, after Bible Study a few days before.

"What you need to do, as soon as you can, is bring your wife."

"I don't think so," Mitchell told him. "Maureen hates religion of every kind."

"You're a man, Mitch, and responsible for your family. Invite her on Sunday morning. You might be surprised."

Now Maureen rode beside him across campus.

"They're not going to dunk me, are they?" she asked as he parked on Sixth Street. "It seems a little cold for that."

Mitchell shook his head.

"Or stone us? But it would be me who got stoned, I guess. Isn't it the women they like to keep in place?"

"I really don't know," he admitted. "So far I'm kind of feeling my way."

When he reached for the Bible she smiled. "Do you carry that everywhere you go?"

"Come on," he said. "We're late as it is."

It occurred to him that she was probably nervous. He was nervous too, with Maureen beside him: University people had begun to venture out, on a Sunday morning, with their newspapers. Across the street they crowded into the Warrior Jitters coffee shop, while he and Maureen climbed the steps to the church. From the sanctuary came eager shouts and the sound of clapping hands.

She drew back instinctively at the door. He would have drawn back too, but there were ushers to greet them, a young woman with rubber bands on her braces and a tall man in a sweater vest with thin wispy hair.

"Hello, Mitchell, God bless you."

"Hey there, Mitch. I wondered where you were!"

Someone else grabbed his shoulder from behind, and he and Maureen were propelled forward, down the aisle toward two seats near the front.

The projection screen loomed high in the choir loft, flashing a sandy beach and wide tranquil sea. The rough cross stood above them on the stage. The Spirit Rising congregation was lively and growing again: there were easily eighty people who surrounded them, swaying with the music, shouting out with their hands in the air. Maureen, at his side, gave a little dance step, and Mitchell, defiant, raised his hand.

"Did I ever tell you how well praise becomes you? You all look so *good* when you raise your hands to God." Randy swept down, trim and beaming, from the stage. "Can you feel the Spirit here among us? Can you feel the new freedom in Prairie Grove?

"Jesus!" called a woman in front of them.

"Jesus, Jesus!" cried a man across the aisle.

He felt Maureen stiffen beside him. Apparently the scripture lesson was over, the offering, too, because already people streamed past them to the front. Randy leaned close to the first man who whispered in his ear. Tucking his microphone under his arm, Randy reached out his hands.

"Sickness be gone, I command you. God wants this man healthy right now. In the name of Jesus Christ I bring the Spirit to bear!"

They had arrived too late for the singing, which was just as well — the words on the screen were often cryptic, full of Calvary's triumph and the blood of the Lamb. The Bible, too, had proven largely indecipherable, despite his best efforts to make sense of what he read. What never wavered was his faith in Randy, just then moving into the healing and praise session at the heart of the service. Mitchell spotted Lee next, alone near the front. Shy around her now, he had kept a safe distance, while she never once looked his way. Instead they were both watching Randy.

The man with the secret illness had collapsed on the carpet, and as Lee moved to join her husband more people crowded in.

"It's not the gall bladder," he was shouting, "it's the gall. You've got to give up that hatred right now!" Another woman fell before him. "Not by me, but by Jesus Christ you're delivered. Howday bradda, ma howla jah la!"

Not everyone was caught up in the excitement: an older man

with slick hair stood sullen across the aisle. Two small boys pushed a toy car along the pew. Their mother, a heavyset woman with hoop earrings, fell writhing to the floor. Mitchell shifted in his seat, growing deeply uneasy, as Randy moved past her down the line.

The difference, of course, was Maureen. It was hard not to see the spectacle through her eyes, stylized and meaningless; she hadn't looked around on a narrow ledge and found Randy still there. Randy, who knew the contours of his madness, who had found the demons within him and sent them away. Who had introduced him to a Force they were enjoined to call Jesus, rising up among them to enliven and explain.

That was the theory anyway, and over three weeks Mitchell had kept to his narrow circuit, moving from prayer group to office to church. He had stayed close to other Christians, his understanding still fragile. He went to church because he knew he'd find Randy, and in Randy's presence the whole notion still held.

And he had, almost certainly, felt something. He read the Bible every night in his motel room, alert for hints of the depth that he'd seen. He bowed his head without hesitation with the prayer group, had come to services Sunday mornings and Wednesday nights. He had withheld judgment as people cried out around him, still humbled by the simple fact that all of them *knew*.

He was no longer crazy, though, and that made a difference. There had been a characteristic flatness to the prairie landscape as they came in on the highway, a familiar cast to experience as connection drained away. Others now claimed Randy's attention. All around him they called Jesus' name. Who were they and how did they know him? What was he doing in church? He couldn't look at Maureen, but felt exposed before her and in the very midst of a serious mistake.

The altar call seemed to go on forever, well-rehearsed in its ecstasy. A dozen people at the end still lay at Randy's feet. Slowly they climbed from the floor. Lee had returned to her seat. The band members were reaching for their instruments, but Randy, up front, wasn't done.

"Oh, I could feel the Spirit this morning. I can feel Jesus with us right now. See, when people look for God they get in a hurry. 'I don't see it!' That's what they'll tell you. 'I don't see it. I *can't* see it. *There's nothing there!*'"

Randy laughed as he came forward, panting lightly.

"There's a Bible story, maybe you remember it, about the man who was so crazy they locked him in chains. When the chains broke he fled to the wilderness."

He had picked out Mitchell by then, above the pews. "Maybe some of you have been to that wilderness. Maybe somebody out there's seen it besides me.

"Jesus and the demons, that's easy to remember. He drove out the spirits and made the man whole. It's the second part we tend to forget about. Where the people got scared and drove Jesus away. Drove Him away! The Son of God! But that's what the Bible says they did."

Randy had reached the head of the aisle, only a few feet away.

"There was this other time, too — everybody's heard about it — when a storm came up on the sea. The disciples ran up to Jesus who was sleeping like a baby. Taking a snooze at the front of the boat. He rebuked the wind and waves, and the storm died away. End of the story, am I right?" Randy shook his head. "Nope, not by a long shot. The disciples were *afraid*. That's what the Bible tells us. They were afraid because the storm went away!

"They were afraid! They were *afraid*! Isn't that just like us sometimes? Isn't that just the way we are? While the storm rages we long to be free of it. We want the wind and the waves to go away. But when they do, that's when we really get worried. We're more afraid of the *cure* than the sickness. We're more afraid of the *calming* than we are of the storm!"

Even before Randy started down the aisle Mitchell's unease had dissolved. The sharp surge of doubt passed away. Even now, Randy bothered to find him. He had read his private thoughts as if etched on his shirt front, picked out the very doubts that plagued him from far across the room.

"You worry you're ill at ease with your family? Jesus wasn't a family man Himself. You take things too hard? So does Jesus. That's why He cares for you and me."

By that time he was at his side but Mitchell kept his head down, both grateful and relieved. Randy had turned off his microphone so his voice was soft, resting gently above him.

"You know that hopefulness you had as a little one? I mean real little, you'll have to go back a ways. Can you see that precious heart, the way it trusted? Those little feet standing brave in the world? Your trust wasn't ever mistaken. All of that love is still there."

Mitchell had already noticed that Randy could get carried away sometimes — a downside of his confidence — going on long after the point had been made. The description was no longer right on target. He was describing, it almost seemed, someone else.

When Mitchell looked up Randy was moving past him in the pew. He was sliding past to Maureen, who sat with arms tightly folded, face a bright crimson as she stared at the floor.

Randy put his hand on her shoulder. "You're not a burden. You're not a bother. You're not forgotten. There's a place for you here in the world."

Without the microphone his voice was intimate. Bewildered, Mitchell stared at Maureen, who had tears in her eyes. A great heat came off her body, next to his in the pew.

"If you're ready to accept Him, He's right here to meet you. You can invite Him to join you today."

At some point the piano had begun playing. It chorded softly but Maureen shook her head. Randy leaned back above her, relaxed against the pew.

"You sure? No time like the present."

She shook her head fiercely.

"That's okay," he said. "I needed to ask. But this isn't Final Jeopardy no matter what they tell you. I don't care what the other pastors say. God goes on forever and so do we. That's what Jesus came to tell us. That's why they hung Him on a cross."

Randy clicked his microphone on as he moved back to the aisle.

"But don't we ever get *tired* of hoping God will find us? Aren't we *glad* that He never gives up? I'm glad, Mary Kay, aren't you? Aren't you glad, Margaret, that Jesus touched you? Aren't we all glad that His love is alive?"

People had come to their feet around them. The man across the aisle was still grim as he raised up his hand. Lee Overmeyer seemed to be in her own world, far away from them, but otherwise everyone *did* seem glad, shouting and laughing, their hands raised high in the air.

"Oh, there's glory. I feel it around us. There's freedom in the sovereign rule of God! Can you feel the air, how it's charged with His power? Can you smell the sweetness now that Satan's on the run?"

Mitchell couldn't clap and hadn't stood; he was just turning to Maureen when she pushed past him to the aisle. She hurried back along it to the door. The band had started to play as Randy danced to the front.

"I love it so much when we share in God's victory. Didn't you wonder, Donnie, if we'd be able to do it? Didn't you wonder if we'd ever prevail? Donnie says he never did. All right, then, I didn't either. At least not much. Hardly ever. Oh, maybe once or twice, a long time ago."

He rocked back, studying the band. "There's nothing else to do here but play a little music. I've got to feel that guitar in my hands. You think you can keep up with me, Donnie, now that we're old and feeble? Think there's some kind of *praise* song the rest of us can play? What's that key you're in, Mary Kay, D major? How about a little lower, can we all find a B? That's not everybody's favorite but it suits me. It always helps to find the place where your voice likes to be."

A red electric guitar was waiting near the pulpit, and Randy laughed as he pulled on the strap. Before he plugged in he came up the aisle. He leaned close so that Mitchell could hear.

"Better go to your wife now, Mitch. She needs you. We've got things covered in here."

Mitchell stood up. He gathered his coat and Maureen's. People all around were dancing and clapping, singing God's praises as he came up the aisle. The entryway was empty and so were the steps. Maureen wasn't waiting at the Triumph. He finally spotted her past the parking garage, alone on the corner, holding herself tightly against the wind.

TWENTY-SIX

There wasn't much left of the old farmstead that Walter had grown up on in Indiana, but he liked to go over and poke around when he could. Vera didn't mind — it was nice once in a while to do things the way she wanted. On Friday night she stayed up late watching some silly movie on TV and on Saturday afternoon set in painting baseboards in the kitchen. She had gotten past the stairway and was working her way toward the refrigerator when Maddie came in the back door.

"Grandma, what are you doing on the floor?"

Her voice could still jar Vera — sometimes it was hard for Maddie to know when she was talking too loud.

"Oh, hi, honey," Vera said, looking up so her granddaughter could see her lips. "I wanted take care of these while Grampa's at the farm. Are you hungry? Do you have time for something to eat?"

"There's a dance for one of my sorority sisters up near Chicago. She's getting engaged. Do you want to come with me?"

"Oh, I don't know, honey..."

"I've got a motel room up there. Grampa's gone anyway. Come on and we'll have some fun."

Vera climbed to her feet. Sometimes it took a while to get the blood back into her legs, but she could see Maddie was impatient. "All right," she said, "let me get this brush in some water and I'll gather a few things."

Less than twenty minutes later they were in Maddie's little Honda climbing onto the interstate. Vera couldn't help being excited, settled into her seat: instead of crawling along the kitchen floor with her paintbrush she had ended up out on the highway with their Maddie Girl, one of her favorite people in the world.

She could tell Maddie was excited about her dance. The first of their grandchildren, she would have been special to them anyway, but Vera could still remember her as a little girl, so sweet and eager, with those big hearing aids banging against her chest. She drove with the music so loud that it buzzed against the dashboard, but once Vera had turned down her own hearing aid they got along fine.

They passed Rantoul and the big truck stops at Onarga, sailed through Kankakee and over I-80 as they came into the suburbs. The dance was at a Holiday Inn in Naperville, where girls from Maddie's sorority had all gotten rooms. It would have been nice for her to be bunking with one of them instead of her grandmother, but apparently they were already paired up. While Maddie was showering, Vera ate a hamburger they'd bought on the tollway. They hadn't come any too early; by the time Maddie had put on her dress and makeup it was nearly nine o'clock.

Maddie looked so nice when she went down to the dance. She was a pretty girl to begin with, and with the improvement in hearing aids and the way she cut her hair, you could hardly see them. Her sweet, eager look had gradually given way, though, over the years, to an expression that was tougher and wary. She liked the handsome boys, too, which made it hard. She had brought one named Scott over for dinner in September, a boy just a little too sure of himself for Vera's tastes, with a sloppy sweater and sideburns, and a cruel sort of shape to his mouth. Maddie had watched him with such hungry eyes it made Vera's heart hurt to see it, the way she hung on the few words he said.

But Maddie was up there to have fun with the other girls on a Saturday night. After a few minutes Vera ventured down to the lobby herself. Her family had never had much when she was young, and she enjoyed standing off to the side near the conference rooms, watching the young people as they came and went. The boys were loud and wise-cracking, the girls like china dolls in their makeup and clingy dresses. Maddie was as pretty as any of them, which made her feel good.

She bought a couple of postcards at the front desk and a Coke from the machine, got ice in the bucket and settled in the room. She drank the Coke while she wrote the post cards, and was just sitting back to enjoy some television when she heard the key in the door. Maddie barely made it inside before her whole face crumpled. Something at the dance had gone wrong, and she curled up on the bed where she cried and cried. Vera sat beside her, patting her hand, and all of a sudden they were packing again, the curlers and nail polish, the Q-tips and Maddie's stuffed bear. Vera dropped the post cards off at the desk, and before long they were in the front seat again, heading back through the night to Prairie Grove.

Disappointment isn't easy for anyone. Vera felt sorry for her, but Maddie had turned off her hearing aids, moving into a separate world where a grandma couldn't go. Vera couldn't even get her to come in for a few minutes when they got back to Washington Street. She took her suitcase, gave Maddie a hug, and said goodbye.

She had just gotten inside when the phone rang. It turned out to be Mr. Williams, the colored man who lived across the street.

"Mrs. Eller?" he said, "I'm sorry to bother you. We're concerned about Mrs. Butler."

"Lacey?" she said "Why?"

"Her newspaper is still in front and her dog hasn't been out. She hasn't been at the window, either, as we've come and gone. Usually we can see the curtain move."

"Well," Vera said, "let me see if I can raise her. Thank you so much for letting us know."

When Vera looked at her watch it was almost midnight. She felt a pang of guilt as she dialed the Butlers' number. It was odd that she hadn't heard from Lacey, but she'd been busy with the baseboards and then ran off with Maddie without a second thought. While she let the phone ring she rummaged through a tangle of keys in the drawer beneath the microwave. There were far too many for the neighbors they had left: there were still keys for the Tolleys' and for Helen Meade's house, a set for the Scullys who had been in Arizona for years. There was a key for the Ag barns at the University and another for the side door at church. Finally she found Lacey's on a Western Bowl key chain. Vera took it with her and went back outside.

Without her jacket the night was chilly, with a bright blanket of stars stretched high across the sky. Taking a chance, she hurried past the new woman's oleanders and across the lawn to Lacey's. As she came onto the back porch she could hear Jasper at the door. When she'd pulled it open he almost knocked her over coming out. He crouched with one leg raised at the edge of the driveway, a faraway look in his eyes.

"Hoo-hoo," Vera sang. "Lacey, are you here?" She stood in the doorway, waiting for stupid Jasper to finish. Luckily he didn't run off on her, instead scampering back inside. There was a closed-up feeling as she followed him through the house. In the bathroom she found Lacey still in her nightgown, flat on the floor with her eyes open, a thin line of vomit on her chin. Her skin was cold and her muscles stiff. Her poor ruined legs were thrown out in front of her, and Jasper climbed back and forth across them, panting happily. When he darted past again Vera kicked out and missed — all they needed was for him to get underfoot and trip her, so that she ended up on the bathroom floor too.

There was an afghan in the living room that Mary Tolley had made, and Vera covered Lacey carefully, tucking it under her chin and loosely around her legs. With a dampened washcloth she wiped off the vomit off her chin. When she came back to the living room there was a rap on the front door and she opened it to find Mr. Williams. Vera unlatched the screen door to let him in.

"She's gone," she said. "It looks like a stroke."

"Oh, I'm so sorry," he said. "That's too bad."

"Well, yes," Vera said. "It is too bad. It really is an awful shame."

Mr. Williams had clearly been settled in for the evening; he had on a green tee shirt and faded pair of sweat pants while Vera still wore her traveling clothes, a trim navy pantsuit and vest. They stood together in Lacey's living room looking at her rundown sofa, the TV tray and recliner, a half cup of coffee sitting cold beside the chair. A moment later she heard Mr. Williams in the kitchen, his voice soft as he talked on the phone.

Whatever he told the emergency people, it was the right thing, because the ambulance arrived without sirens, its red light flashing in a wide circle across the lawns. The police came too, and before long a whole group of sturdy young men in windbreakers had filled up the living room, broad shoulders bumping as they went back and forth down the hall.

"Yes," Vera was explaining, "we're her neighbors. My husband William and I live two doors down." She pointed at Mr. Williams. "And this is Mr. Walters, who lives in the Manner house across the street."

The names were confused but she was clear in her own mind, embarrassed that she had left Lacey's underwear on the shower rod in the bathroom, her dirty coffee cup still sitting by the chair. The police and paramedics went about their business and in barely any time at all Lacey was wheeled out the door.

A policeman consulted with Mr. Williams. "Is there someone we should call?"

"Oh, yes," Vera broke in, "there's her daughter Lindy. I'll take care of that. She only lives an hour away. Bill will be harder — he and his mother were never close. I'm not really sure what the problem was."

The policeman and Mr. Williams looked back at her and she realized they didn't care about Bill. Or about Lindy either, except that she needed to be called. Her number was beside the telephone, an old Princess with a lighted pad and spongy keys, lodged into a crowded niche above the trash can. While the phone rang she looked at Lacey's kitchen. The poor thing had been so worn out at the end she couldn't get to the dishes; there was a whole stack of them sitting in the sink.

Vera never knew what Lindy held against her mother. And maybe, by that time, it didn't matter. She was sleepy-voiced and irritable when she answered the telephone, but Vera had barely gotten the words out when Lindy started in. "Oh no! Oh, God, no!"

she screamed. "Please God! Please, God, oh no!" shrieking so loudly that Vera had to hold the receiver away from her ear.

Mr. Williams was still in the living room. "Will you be all right?" he asked.

"Oh yes," she said, "I'm fine. Thank you for calling me. I think I'll just wait for Lindy. I don't want her coming into an empty house."

Mr. Williams still hung around by the door while she assured him a dozen times he could go. When he finally left she set to work in the kitchen. Why Lacey had never gotten a dishwasher was a mystery — it was more sanitary, Walter had read, and handy, too — it kept things out of the sink. When the dishes were done she swept the floor and wiped the counters, using an old sponge Lacey must have had a hundred years.

She got the underwear down from the shower rod, cleaning out the laundry hamper, too, while she was at it, filling a bag she could take home and wash. She was just picking up the last of Jasper's toys when Mr. Williams knocked at the door.

He had showered while he was gone and wore a dress shirt and nice pair of slacks. It was kind of him to clean up like that, in the middle of the night, but the stupid dog was right there at the door. Vera didn't have time to warn him, all fresh-shaven and smelling so nice, before he'd reached out his hand for Jasper to nuzzle with his snout.

"I'm so sorry," he said again, as they sat in the living room. "I know you and Mrs. Butler were close."

"We were," Vera said. "We were neighbors for over fifty years. This was the edge of town back then, if you can imagine. Cows came up to a fence that ran right behind our lots. The Butlers' Lindy and our little Kate liked to go out and feed them grass."

"Mr. Butler already passed on?"

"Almost twenty years ago, from lung cancer. At least Lacey didn't suffer like he did. It's a shame how so many people do."

It was the kind of thing Vera had often heard older people say when she was a girl, but it had taken years before she really understood. She could still remember looking across at the Butlers' late at night to see the light on, and poor Ted up walking the floor. He'd walked and walked, but the cancer kept up. She remembered Lacey's mother all those years in the nursing home, and the way Walter's dad had dragged on at the end.

Fast or slow, death found its way to everyone. It would be hard to count the number of nights she and Walter had spent in somebody's living room, sitting with the family and looking at the walls. It was hard to know why Lacey, on hers, had kept the wood paneling, especially when it made rooms so dark. She thought of Maddie in the motel room, curled up in tears. She thought of the sandwich from the tollway and how much she'd enjoyed it — it wasn't all soggy like sandwiches could be.

"It's been a sad year for the football team," she remarked. "Do you think basketball will be any better?"

Mr. Williams shook his head. "I'm sorry, I don't follow sports."

"Oh, that's too bad," Vera said. "They confused me too, at the beginning. When we first came I didn't know one ball from another, but gradually you get it figured out." She noticed she was twiddling her thumbs and tucked them away. "Football's not my game anyway, but I try to keep up. Now basketball, that's another story. Oh, how I love to beat that Bobby Knight!"

About that time there was another knock at the door, but instead of Lindy it was Mrs. Williams, who was wearing a wool skirt and pretty cotton blouse. She'd brought over a crumb cake, warm from the oven, and Vera hurried to the kitchen to make coffee. The filters were where Lacey always kept them, high on the shelf above the stove.

With all of them dressed up it was almost like they were having a party together in Lacey's living room. They were a little shy at first, but the crumbcake helped, and before long they were getting acquainted. Mr. Williams was from Mississippi while his wife turned out to be from Dominica, down in the Caribbean. She was such a pretty girl, with a musical kind of accent that made Vera smile. They'd met at the University of Wisconsin where both went to school. As they chatted together Vera's only regret was that Walter wasn't there.

He was always so interested in young people and their lives.

It had turned out to be quite a day: first the baseboards, then Maddie and Lacey, and finally coffee with the Williams in the middle of the night. It was too bad Lacey couldn't be there too, but it was hard to imagine — she'd lost all interest in entertaining when Ted passed away.

"How do you like your gazebo?" she asked.

The Williams exchanged glances and he nodded. "It's all right."

Mrs. Williams had the prettiest skin color, with large brown eyes that she turned on her husband.

"Do you have picnics out there?" Vera went on. "It seems like it would be nice in the summer."

"We don't do anything with it," Mr. Williams said and they smiled.

Mrs. Williams was blushing. It was harder to see with her complexion, of course, but the blood came to her cheeks as Mr. Williams took her hand.

"I always wanted one," she said in that pretty, lilting voice. "I remember seeing it in *The Sound of Music* when I was a little girl. If I ever have a house, I said, I'm going to get one. I wanted a gazebo of my own."

"Well," Vera said, "that's reason enough, I guess. It looks very nice, what we can see from our yard."

"Maybe we can have you and Mr. Eller over to sit with us sometime when the weather gets warm."

Vera smiled, too, as she nodded, because it *was* a pretty thought, all of them sitting together in the shade. But it wasn't very likely — when nice weather rolled around again they would be out at Cooke-Davis. Mrs. Ormsbee had called that morning while she was mixing the paint. A two bedroom expanded had come available, on the second floor like she wanted, and before they were halfway through the crumb cake Vera had decided. She had about decided on her curio, too, instead of the bookcase, if Walter thought only one piece would fit. The small desk where she did the bills could go in the second bedroom. Her stained glass plate would look pretty in the window, early in the morning with the sun shining in.

Their dining table was too big and she wondered if the Williams would want it. They were such a sweet couple and she hoped they liked the neighborhood. She hoped they would be happy like she and Walter were, when it had been their turn, with the Tolleys and Butlers and Meades.

The Williams, young as they were, had spent nights like this before. They didn't have the uneasy look that people have when they're new at it. They didn't mind sitting quietly when the conversation died away. Her own thoughts kept drifting to Cooke-Davis. The Schallers were already there and liked to play bridge. Old Doc Hanson had an apartment, too, like the Fullers. Joanne Meyer was right behind them on the list. She thought about the new couch Walter had promised to buy her — she'd like something a little lighter that didn't show dirt.

Vera had been in Lacey's house hundreds of times over the years, but it had already begun to feel unfamiliar. It wasn't too much longer before there was a flash of headlights. When the car pulled back along the driveway Vera stood up. The Williams stood up too, to greet Lindy, as she came in sobbing through the door.

TWENTY-SEVEN

The Warrior Jitters coffeeshop, on a late October morning, was crowded, with an autumn smell of coffee in the air. Lee watched Barbara make her way carefully among the tables, brow wrinkled in concentration as she balanced their tray.

She delivered their drinks, her cappuccino and Lee's cup of mint tea, returning to the counter for a small plate and a fork.

"A lemon bar. Just today, to celebrate. Have you noticed? Six pounds and counting."

"You're lovely," Lee told her. "You really are."

Lee had staked out a table near the window for them and couldn't help smiling as she looked at her friend. Although attendance had picked up at services the Women's Prayer Circle was still in hiding, a time reserved for the two of them alone. With Barbara beside her almost nothing was daunting. One Thursday morning they had ventured to the Student Union, and a week later, they made a tour of the quadrangle, watching young people hurry past them to class. Inevitably they ended up at the coffee shop, undercover among the faculty and students. Barbara had sampled a half-dozen drinks before settling on her favorite, a tall cappuccino with a full head of foam.

Barbara wore a loose top in bright red which flattered her. There was a pleasant murmur of conversation from the tables around them, a clank and hiss of the espresso machine a few feet away. Barbara ate daintily, wiping her mouth with a napkin; her clear enjoyment of the lemon bar brought tears to Lee's eyes.

"What?" Barbara said. "You've got something on your mind."

"I do. There's something I want to tell you. But let's pray for a minute first. We don't have to bow our heads, God will hear us." She reached across the table for Barbara's hand. "Precious Jesus, thank you for this amazing woman. Thank you for letting her guide me in the wonders of Your love."

Embarrassed, Barbara dropped her eyes.

"You're very important to me. I want you to know that. I thank God every day for bringing you into my life."

Barbara smiled, her heavy features coloring. The fine hairs on her upper lip had trapped a thin line of foam.

"All right," she demanded, "what is it? Somebody here's swallowed a canary. Come on, Lee, I want to know!"

"You're not going to believe it."

"Is Randy going ahead at the building site? Is that it? The Spirit was so strong on Sunday I could hardly believe it. I felt it right down to my toes!"

Unable to keep from smiling, Lee shook her head. "It's not Randy. Well, it is Randy too, but it's me. Randy and me."

"So tell me. Come on!"

"Can you keep a secret?"

"Lee!"

"Oh, I know that you can, I'm sorry. You're the very first person I thought of to tell. After Randy, of course. He had to know."

Barbara's eyes were wide. "What is it? Come on, tell me."

"I don't even know how to say it. It's a miracle, really. I'm pregnant."

Barbara gasped. "Are you sure?"

"I had been feeling strange for a while. There were signs, but I didn't dare trust them. Finally I bought a kit here on campus."

Every detail of the afternoon was still powerful in her memory. It was as if Barbara had been with her even then in the Walgreens on Fourth Street. The aisles were crowded with college girls buying lipstick and greeting cards. As if in a dream, Lee had moved to the women's aisle, with its bright array of pregnancy kits spread out on the shelf. She waited in line behind a student with zinc lozenges, a bus driver who bought a Milky Way. The sales clerk rang up her purchase with indifference, calmly chewing gum as she slipped it in the bag.

"You know how it is. You pee in the cup and stick the strip in. You see what color it turns."

"But sometimes the tests aren't reliable. I remember once I..."

"I saw the doctor Tuesday morning. I'm pregnant, Barbara. I really am. We are. Randy and me."

Barbara's wide forehead was creased with concern. "Lee, be careful. A lot can still happen early on."

Lee looked back at her friend with tenderness. "I know things go wrong, but this is different. It's too early, I know, but I can tell. I already feel him inside."

It was a relief, first of all, that she and Randy had rediscovered their intimacy. It could have been that first night or later the same week — it was hard to know when new life had taken hold. She had forgotten pregnancy was even possible, especially for her, attributing to Randy's returned attentions the light spotting in her underwear, the way her breasts had felt swollen and alive.

"Of course I'm happy for you," Barbara was saying. "Just be careful. I made it into the third month once, before I..."

Lee stiffened. "That's not going to happen. I'm going to have a baby, Barbara. I really am."

Across the table, though, her friend's face had fallen, cheeks blotched as if someone had slapped her.

"What's the matter? I could hardly wait to tell you the news."

"I'm sorry," Barbara whispered, "it's me."

"What do you mean? I know it's you. You're my friend and I love you. You know better than anyone else how hard it can be."

Barbara shook her head. She studied a last corner of lemon bar on the plate. "It's me, Lee. It's my smallness. My ugliness."

"What do you mean? You're so lovely, I wish you could see that. You're one of the most beautiful people I know."

Barbara nodded, twisting a napkin in her lap. When she looked up there was pain in her eyes.

"But what about *my* baby? What about a baby for me?"

"You'll get your baby, Barbara, I'm sure of it. God has a plan for all of us. In my case I just wasn't ready. He needed to reach me and that was through you! You're such a big part of this, please understand!"

"What about me, though? I want a baby too! You'll have yours, but what about me?"

"Maybe Randy's right and the resistance is gone now. We'll break through to the abundance that's ours. That's got to be it! It's the only thing that makes sense. We'll keep praying and trust God to answer. You'll get your baby too, wait and see!"

She spoke with real feeling, but Barbara shook her head. When Lee reached across the table she pulled her hand away.

"No," she said firmly, "I won't. It's not going to happen. God has His favorites like everyone else." The bitterness in her voice made it harsh. "Why shouldn't Pastor Randy heal you? You're his wife. Why wouldn't he bring the Spirit to you?"

"That's not how it…"

"Why shouldn't God answer your prayers? You're the pretty one. Don't even say it, because you are. You've got the pretty husband, the pretty house, the pretty life. Now you'll have a pretty baby too." She winced around her tears but in the end couldn't help it. "Goddamn you, that's all I can say, Lee. Goddamn you and Pastor Randy straight to hell."

Barbara had seemed to grow ill right before her at the table. Her face was twisted, made unlovely by pain. She seemed unsure of what to do, finally struggling to her feet. Her voice trembled as she reached for her purse.

"Don't touch me, Lee, please, don't talk to me. I hate you. I'm sorry, but I do. I hate everything in this whole stinking world."

Evidence of that stinking world was all around them, not least the young co-eds slouching slender and fertile, the professors smart and laughing with their friends. Barbara's heavy hips, on the other hand, were a handicap, bumping tables left and right as she gathered her coat. The foam mustache had dried gray above her lip. Her pain, in the narrow space, became audible, a sob and groan that made others look their way. She jarred the table again, spilling the festive cappuccino. Another effort to get free sent the sugar bowl tumbling, and their silverware clattered to the floor.

"I hope your baby *dies*," she hissed and burst into tears, truly stricken by what she had said. The coffeeshop customers looked on as she fought through the tables. Finally she broke free to the doorway, where a silver bell jingled merrily in her wake.

Lee was still in shock as coffee dripped past her to the floor. She was on the verge of tears herself, but the patrons quickly rallied. Two professors tracked down the sugar bowl. A girl from a nearby table knelt to retrieve the silverware. A woman behind the counter hurried to her side with a bar cloth and a young man in a tattered scarf reached to straighten Barbara's chair.

There was a moment when everything changed for Lee at Warrior Jitters. Something had shifted and it wasn't the baby — she wouldn't forget the look on Barbara's face or her gray flecks of mustache, that sad, lonely rush to the door. There was her own self-regard and glib reassurance, her failure to heed another's pain. In the end, though, it was God who was shameless. Men young and old smiled with kindness across the tables. The woman from the counter brought a fresh cup of tea. *She* was the one they felt sorry for. They all felt sorry for *her* and never mind Barbara, another angry woman with a weight problem, unattractive and not particularly pleasant; unhappy with herself and with everyone else.

Even then, though, when Lee could have followed, she didn't. There was little she could have said, for that matter, to defend Him — it's the way He did business here on earth. Fairness wasn't part of the Plan. Humans were still animals, even gathered in a coffee shop, and the circle formed around her felt largely instinctive. God's favor, men's protection, the women's care — they were advantages she had little choice but to accept now, a mother among them: after all, she had life within her and Barbara did not.

TWENTY-EIGHT

The battle is most fierce at the edge of a breakthrough, and Randy had known they were close when the outlook grew bleakest, and his own resolve and memory were all he had left. The final point of resistance, though, had little to sustain it: the twelve strong demons that had seized Mitchell Chandler, hiding out there, reluctant to grow. Once he freed them God's will could gain traction, and his own life begin to make sense again.

He had been on his way to a Wednesday night service when Lee told him about the baby. The first thing he did was hug her; the second, fall to his knees.

"God, thank you," he said, "now and always, for Your bounty. Thank You for answering our prayers."

It was all he could do not to rush to church and shout out their victory, but Lee had begged him to keep it to himself. It took some convincing, but Randy gave in. The people flowing back into his services didn't need reminders. They all knew the Spirit was back. They raised their hands high, awash in His glory and filled with the force of His love.

The Opposer, on the other hand, prefers chaos. Its favorite

targets are hopefulness and meaning, human plans and a point to the world. Confusion had reached for Randy too, those dark months at the church. Months when his prayers had sounded like pointless mumbling, his shouts of praise like the barking of a dog. That's when he had looked over to see Lee standing steadfast beside him, the only proof of God's love he was ever going to need.

The lies were tiresome in their sameness, once he got to know them. That the Holy Spirit flowing through him was an illusion. That Lee didn't love him and her own faith was gone. He could always tell the darts coming from Satan — they were the ones that hit closest to home.

Life on earth from high above can look easy. Randy had seen it for himself years before on a runway, with God looking down at his side. It's a little different back on earth where death seems to matter. A little different down below where mistakes still have meaning, our bodies dense and the sightlines less clear. Where we trace a distant orbit in our own separate capsules, out of contact with Mission Control.

That doesn't keep all Spirit from lining up for a shot at it, ready to enter restless life as it forms far below. Randy could still see Dike beside the trestle with his battered helmet, a towel wrapped around his face as he straddled the bike. Ralph and Tommy stood impatient beside him, eager for their own chance to push off the edge. Pumping hard, they dodged stumps and car batteries, boulders and broken glass, bound for the wall of brush at the bottom of the ravine. They liked to hit it full on, heads down and legs churning. They liked to be staggered and buffeted, pulled at and knocked, searching for the branch finally strong enough to tear them from the seat.

Randy had gotten a good look at that endless cycle from the runway. Dreamer or dreamed, it formed the same story: there were angels and aliens, the real and imagined, One among Others at play with Himself. This God divided Light from the Darkness. He encompassed life and death, swarming demons and Saviors, the slice of All the Rest where human beings made their homes. Randy had smiled as they looked out on His handiwork, and all the thousand million sparks where those different realms touched.

God had been talking as they looked out on the universe, explaining the role Randy still had to play. It's possible that Jesus had been there too and he just didn't notice — there was a lot to take in at the time. At any rate, Randy had been happy enough to find a place for Him in his testimony, and over time they had learned to respect each other, gradually coming to understand what the other one did. Randy saw the hole in people's souls, but Jesus could fill it. If Jesus needed help, then Randy pitched in. Jesus brought eternal life but only people made babies, and that's what he and Lee, that autumn, had done.

The runway had been a good vantage point. From it Randy had seen the many conflicting currents in the universe, bearing them through life as God's promise played out. He had come to know Spirit at work in their lives. More than anything else though, what he remembered was the Voice. A Voice he had known the instant he heard it high on the runway. A Voice that had come to him ever since with instruction, hastening and chastening like the hymn used to say. The same Voice that guided and sustained him. The Voice that gave him direction in the world. And best of all, a Voice easy to recognize, since it had always sounded so much like his own.

TWENTY-NINE

Austin Chandler preferred to be behind the wheel, but it was Walter's car and he insisted on driving. By daybreak they were well into Indiana, wide fields of corn stalks and bean stubble stretching out on either side.

He had been surprised at Walter's heavy foot on the gas pedal: by seven-thirty they were an hour past the Wabash, and by eight had turned onto a black-topped county road that ran along a creek. They came past an earthen dam and reservoir. Walter's place was a couple of miles further on, a cube-shaped farmhouse with fiberglass shutters. Two aging maples stood in a side yard, and there was an abandoned hog lot grown up in grass.

"Well," Walter said, "this is it. The center of the Eller family empire."

"Looks like a good day. Why don't we drive out to the woodlot so I can get a sense of the job?"

Walter turned off the car. "Let's take the groceries inside and use the bathroom. Those trees aren't going anywhere soon."

Austin Chandler felt a surge of impatience — you had to light a fire under old Eller to get him to move. Walter was no spring chicken himself, so he had ended up pitching in quite a bit that fall, helping trim the Ellers' evergreens and clean out their gutters. When Walter mentioned he had some pruning at his old place in Indiana he'd insisted on going along too.

It was good to have a task ahead of them. More and more in recent weeks he'd felt sluggish in the morning, plagued by angina and a stubborn fatigue. His arthritis had grown worse and his sleep was uneven. The feeling of heaviness seldom left his chest. But now, at least, he was wearing his old jacket and heavy boots. At the Hardees in Danville there were plenty of loafers sitting around with their sweet rolls, while he and Walter were headed outside to work.

The wood lot was a quarter mile from the house on a rise overlooking the reservoir. A glaze of frost still covered the grass as Walter guided his old Plymouth up the hill. He parked just below the steepest part and they ferried the equipment from there.

Walter moved with ease, bounding up and down the hill like a mountain goat, while Austin Chandler grew quickly short of breath. The chainsaw he'd seized from the backseat was heavy, and a full can of gasoline banged painfully against his knee. He had to stop a half-dozen different times on his way up the incline, his heart pounding hard by the time he reached the top.

Breathing heavily, he dropped his burden and looked around. The trees Walter had set out were still young, fifteen or twenty feet high, set out in neat rows across the rise. Someone had built a vacation home on the far side of the reservoir, where a mown path led down to a boat dock. A line of black stumps poked up near an inlet, and slabs of gray slate lined the bank at water's edge.

He was still trying to regain enough breath to give orders when Walter came back from the car with the last of the tools. He pointed toward the trees with his lopper.

"If you take that first row, Austin, I'll take the second. Go after the lower limbs, as high as you can reach."

When he wandered the woods with Scooter, barely a month earlier, Austin Chandler had felt his body move into gear as it responded to the physical, the feel of a slope rising up beneath his legs. It was harder to get loosened up with the weather grown colder, especially when the grass dragged so heavy at his legs. He'd worked a lopper many times but the motion felt awkward, handles heavy as he set in among the trees.

After a quarter hour he began to move better. Even at that he grew easily winded and knew that Walter slowed along his own row to accommodate him. It was an embarrassment but there was nothing to do about it; by the end of the first hour they'd both shucked their jackets, slowly pruning branches in the sun. When they came to a limb too big for the lopper Walter fired up the saw.

"All this work," Austin Chandler puffed, steadying himself against a trunk. "Hardly worth the man-hours for the return you're going to get."

Walter looked back along the row they'd just finished. "Oh, probably not, but the pruning makes a difference. In another thirty years this will be a fine stand of trees."

Left unspoken was that neither of them would be there to see it — at the end of the next row they came across the matted skeleton of a groundhog, losing shape along the fence. Scattered clouds moved high above the fields. A small flock of geese floated in a cove on the reservoir, where the sound of their squabbles rose up beyond the trees.

In late morning they took a break, drinking from a jar of well water Walter had filled at the farm house. Stretched out against their separate tree trunks, they looked out above the cove.

Walter pointed to the geese. "They didn't even bother to go

south last year. Wintered right there along the shore."

"Damned stupid birds. Not every year is going to be that mild."

"I tried to tell them but they didn't want to listen. Maybe they'll pay more attention to you."

Austin Chandler glanced over, suspicious, aware he was being kidded. Walter Eller, though, wasn't out to get him. He could have mentioned Mitchell a dozen times — there he and Maureen were every Sunday, waltzing in with the Spirit Rising bunch — but never seized the advantage. He had casually slowed his own pace, as they worked, to match his. "This is friendship," he thought, with a tug beneath his breastbone, as the few leaves above his head rustled lightly in the breeze.

The sun's warmth had found its way through his shirt and heavy work pants, balanced by a deeper cold pressing up beneath the grass. There was the echo of a train as it sounded at a crossing. It was a long time before they saw it, a snub locomotive pulling a dozen silver grain cars. With the lower branches gone their view was unobstructed — the train made a long loop across the horizon before passing out of sight.

He awoke to find Walter above him, oiling the hinge on the lopper.

"Okay, Austin, coffee break's over. Time to get back on our heads."

As they moved through the trees Walter was a thoughtful companion, pausing every few trees to look out across the reservoir. In early afternoon they ate the lunch Vera had prepared for them, turkey sandwiches with fresh sliced tomatoes, crisp carrots in a zippered plastic bag. She had sent along a tuna casserole too, for their supper; back at the farmhouse Walter heated it in the oven. Afterwards they rocked in the small living room, pleasantly worn out from a full day of work. He had been the weaker man, but that seemed not to matter. There was a pleasant stiffness in his forearms from the lopper, an ache in his shoulders that finally felt earned. It wasn't long before they nodded off, both dozing in their chairs.

They were like a couple of old draft horses then, in the narrow hallway of the farmhouse, shuffling back and forth as they settled in their stalls. Austin Chandler drew the room across from Walter's, small and spare with a battered bureau and metal frame bed. Vera had sent along fresh sheets to go with a pile of blankets, and he'd barely hit the pillow before he fell fast asleep.

He had long plunged into sleep like a diver, launched into a dark sea of forgetfulness that carried him safely to morning. Lately, though, that refuge was unreliable, and for a time he bobbed just beneath wakefulness. Sleep and memory were so interspersed they were hard to distinguish, with tree limbs and the flash of a lopper blade, the taste of well water fresh and cold against his tongue. They sat in living room rockers, the night dark around them. Walter was unpacking, yet again, Vera's tuna casserole, a tray of deviled eggs in their Tupperware bin.

Edie, too, had tried her best to take care of him. Early in their marriage, when he was headed off to some Ag conference or other, she'd gotten the notion that she would help pack his bag. An idea from some woman's magazine which made him impatient — when he found out what she'd done, he'd mocked and taunted her, dragging the clothes out of the suitcase and throwing them on the floor. It was hard to know what he had been after back then, crazed like an animal, an animal set loose on poor Edie who barely made it through the day in the first place, hanging back in the doorway as she tried not to cry.

Maybe he was asleep because the groan surprised him, a sound rising deep and mournful from his throat. He lay motionless, still hopeful he was dreaming, but soon heard a rustle across the hall. There was a creaking on the floorboards in the hallway, and a moment later, a figure at the door.

"Austin, are you all right?"

Walter's whisper came softly in the moonlight. It would have been easy enough to answer, but Austin Chandler lay back rigid with his eyes closed, head pressed against the pillow.

"Austin, are you awake?"

He was ashamed of himself certainly, a hundred times over, but that didn't explain some other embarrassment, more profound, that kept him silent. He couldn't bear, it seemed, that this other man would attend to him, that Walter had been concerned as he came across the hall. He tensed against that felt presence above him, resisted a sag near his arm on the bed. Satisfied that he was alive, Walter slowly straightened. He reached down to pull the blanket across his shoulder. He stood a moment longer looking out at the barnyard, before he turned away and went back to his room.

Austin Chandler was able to exhale then, the crisis averted. He was alone and unbroken by the darkness. He hadn't suddenly lost his head and clutched Walter by the hand. Poor Edie came to him again, still vivid in memory. He saw her across the crowded junior high school gym at one of Geoff's concerts, and the stark look of fear on her face.

Geoff was no musician which was why he played baritone, hidden away at the back of the band. Near the end of the program Edie had gone out to the restroom. It was something she seldom did alone and she must have miscalculated, because before she could get back, the concert was done.

It was a small enough venue, especially thinking back on it, with parents and their children milling slowly toward the door. Geoff frowned as he made his way toward them, dragging his instrument case. Not far away Betsy clowned with her friends. Mitchell had been there too, looking bored and aloof — who would have guessed he was the one who would weaken? Meanwhile Austin Chandler was watching for Edie. He caught a glimpse of her near the bleachers, panicked and desperate; he saw her relief as that fear dropped away. She had seen him, too, by that time, right where he should be. She had picked out Betsy and Mitchell and Geoff. She wasn't alone anymore, adrift among strangers, she had found her family and could finally relax.

There were others he might have married, but Edie had seemed to think well of him, had been willing to trust him to lead them through the world. He thought of how happy she always was to see the grandchildren, how much she had suffered at the end with her brittle bones and fragile skin. Even then she felt safer beside him, took comfort from his heavy presence in the bed. When he'd turned one morning to find her there, cool and stiffening, he knew that their Edie was gone.

He wasn't a child, of course, but it had still surprised him how quickly the heat left her body. How little was left once the cancer won out. Austin Chandler lay in a house not his own, awake in the moonlight. He felt the press of strange blankets against his chest. He thought of the deep sense of calm that had come over him in the tree lot, leaning back with Walter in the sun.

His senses, thanks to the church class, were active: there had been a low call from a bird along the fencerow and in the distance the rumble of a train. There was a mown path on the far bank above the boat dock. His work boots lay thrust before him on the grass. What he had felt, though, most clearly, was his *absence*, a clear sense of the world once he, too, dropped away. In an empty wood lot there had been a rustle of tree leaves, a quick flutter of wings as geese took flight above the shore.

It wasn't something he cared to shrink from once fully awake. What was it, this awareness, ever-present, crowding in to fill the space behind our eyes? What to make of that tireless watchman at work late at night? They were hardly profound questions, but his nonetheless — it seemed only fair that a man got to ask. You couldn't see around the corner either way, really — the Swiss boy was right — there was only that attention, and around it uncertainty. Uncertainty and guesswork, a moment and memory, the gentle rumble of Walter's snoring as it resumed across the hall.

It was hard to put your finger on, exactly, what it added up to, but Austin Chandler was willing to try.

"This is life," he thought, and pulled the blankets around him, deciding that was about the best he was ever going to do.

THIRTY

It was just as well Walter had gone to the farm because cleaning out the basement went faster without him. He was a good enough worker but sentimental, stopping to remember every old paper or snapshot they pulled from a box. Alone Vera could really make progress. They had started a pile each for Ronnie and Kate, another for Goodwill and the sale at the church. The smallest was for their apartment at Cooke-Davis. So far there was only a piano stool of her mother's that could serve as a plant stand, and a cherry end table Walter had salvaged from the farm.

The first thing she did after he left was tackle the closet beneath the stairs, pulling out two more styrofoam coolers to add to the church pile, along with an old crock that had belonged to her mom. They hadn't disagreed that much, really, on the sorting, except when Walter wanted to find a home for something Vera would just as soon have thrown out. When he started yet another pile for the Williams she finally complained.

"He's at the University and she works at home. They don't want our old junk."

It turned out, though, that Walter was right: Mr. Williams took the lawnchairs and croquet set, and Mrs. Williams liked a cut glass punch bowl they'd received as a wedding present. It was a pretty enough bowl but Vera was through with it, with the ginger ale and sherbet and their stickiness. She could drink somebody else's punch the rest of the way. The Williams had wanted the dining table, too, even if it was too big for them — maybe they were about ready for a family of their own.

She took an hour off at noon to watch *The Young and the Restless*, one of her guilty pleasures when Walter was gone. She ate a peanut butter sandwich while Katherine cried her eyes out — Derek was such a pill, which she never seemed to learn. After the show Vera returned to the closet. There was a pegboard from her old kitchen that went to the garbage and a stack of board games the church could try to sell. She found a box with two pocket fishermen and a bulky red camp stove, along with an old army poncho so musty she threw it out.

In the big trunk that Walter had taken to college she found her brother's gold star. It was such a sad thing, really, to think back on, Hal lost at sea with all those other boys when the *Indianapolis* went down. She came across her old ID badge, too, from the glove factory. That was a happier memory, at least, to go back to, working the line with the other girls while Walter went to school. There was an index card she must have made while he studied: across the top was written *Things Walter Likes*. She had tuna casserole on the list and hot beef sandwiches, hand cut noodles and fresh rhubarb pie. Kate would have eaten canned spaghetti every morning if they let her, while Walter liked fried eggs and toast. She remembered making Pigs in a Blanket one weekend for Sunday supper; when little Ronnie heard the name he'd laughed and laughed.

By mid-afternoon she was finished with the closet, moving on to the shelves behind the furnace. A couple of hours later, she climbed upstairs to take a break. It was already getting dark so she went to look for the paper. Mindy must have gone out for some sport again, because the *Courier* was nowhere to be seen.

As she stood looking out the doorway something moved that caught her eye. When she looked down she saw it was a spider, at work on a web in the space between the doors. A first long strand stretched from door hinge to threshold, with another anchored high against the frame. It seemed like a bad time to start but the spider was determined, swinging out across the doorway and back to the hinge.

Even though it was barely five Vera realized she was hungry. She foraged through the cupboards for a can of chili, another pleasure best savored alone. Walter dearly loved chili too, but it didn't care for him, which meant she was the one who had to suffer. She left the can on the counter while she got the coffee pot going, for a cup with the six o'clock news.

She usually left the thermostat low to keep Walter moving, but there wasn't any reason not to be a little more comfortable when she was there all alone. Warmth had been in short supply when she was a girl in Dakota, with the wind always rushing down the coulees, a single coal stove in the kitchen to keep them warm. She could remember the jiggle of lanterns and the children with their fevers, the winter as it raged all around. Sometimes it seemed a miracle they'd even survived.

She not only survived but had raised her own family, lived in a house with a good furnace she could turn up if she liked. Late nights working in the basement had made her sleepy, so Vera went back to the living room. She slipped off her shoes and lay down on the couch. She had one of Mary Tolley's afghans and wrapped the end around her ankles. Just as she was getting settled the furnace came on.

She had thought she would rest her eyes a minute, mulling over a clay planter she'd come across beneath the stairs. Cooke-Davis or the pile for the church sale — she would have decided but Vera was asleep. A teacher from their little country schoolhouse had handed her a pencil, and someone she didn't know wore a black woolen shawl.

She almost came awake but sleep was insistent, and it wasn't long before Vera gave in. The furnace went off and came on and still she wasn't finished, lying back with the sofa so comfortable and the afghan tucked tight around her legs. She slept and dreamed, and then slept and dreamed some more, but it's funny how time plays its tricks. She couldn't have been out more than fifteen minutes, if even that, awakening to the same winter twilight outside the windows as when she had first lain down.

The light above the sink shined through the doorway from the kitchen. As Vera lay on the sofa, a last dream was vivid — there was a big hotel where Ronnie was presenting a paper and she and Walter had come along to watch. The rest of the family seemed to have drifted away, the way they do in dreams, so she stood alone in the hotel's spacious atrium. Glass elevators glided up and down around her and there was a hum of ventilation in the air.

An oriental man had set up shop near the fountain, tending a cauldron over an open wood fire. He wore a long burgundy robe, its edges trimmed in yellow like the Tibetan monks Gladys had invited to the church. Everyone had been all excited about it, it seemed, except for her. She hadn't cared for the incense that filled up the sanctuary, a frog-like moaning that had given her the creeps.

In the atrium, though, she edged closer to the cauldron. The man stirred what seemed to be a stew with different parts of an animal, a pale liver and shiny hooves that tumbled to the surface, a flash of snout and glistening, pebbled tongue. The man fished out something that he wrapped in canvas and handed to Vera. Inside, she found a grayish chunk of meat. It was attached to a length of bone, rusty-colored and jagged, with a small patch of hide that still clung to the flesh.

"Is it beef?" she asked, and the man nodded. He seemed to find the question significant, looking back at her solemnly, but Vera was still puzzled by the meat. For tougher cuts some people liked marinades — she had a recipe from Mary Kerwin that her daughter liked to use. Braising worked too, if you had a while, but she had just about decided on her trusty pressure cooker. She was less certain about the meat's grayish color. It had been a long time since she'd used food that wasn't fresh. A mushroom sauce would help but she used canned soup for her gravies, which was more salt than Walter should really have.

It was while she was considering the options that Vera came fully awake. Even though it was still twilight she felt surprisingly groggy, her muscles so stiff she barely made it to her feet. She hobbled to the bathroom and then out to the kitchen. She lit the stove and found an opener for the chili, still trying to balance a half-light from the kitchen window with the stiffness in her legs.

The coffee was a mystery too, steamed into a black syrup at the bottom of the pot. When things don't line up a person starts to wonder — old people especially — but about that time she heard a banging outside. It was the garbage man on his way up the driveway. She wasn't senile so much as well-rested — she had slept the whole night through on the couch.

The garbage man was a gloomy, bearded boy in a denim jacket, with a slender set of headphones pulled over his cap. She watched from the window as he loaded the pegboard, along with the trash bags Walter carried out before he left. She was a little sheepish, of course, and in need of her coffee, but otherwise Vera felt cheerful. She had the chili for breakfast while she worked at her crosswords. With the leaves gone she could see the sky better, watching it turn blue beyond the garage roof and trees.

About then it occurred to her that she ought to sweep the front porch, at least, so the Williams wouldn't worry. She carried the broom through the living room to the door. When she pulled it open she found the spider in the threshold, still hard at work on its web.

Maybe the night had been milder than she'd thought it was. Maybe it stayed warm in the space between the doors. At any rate, the spider was making progress. It had managed to spin its wide web above the threshold, each ring inside the next as it spread across the frame. She looked past it to the For Sale sign that stood in front of Lacey's, the sycamore across the street that Ronnie had loved to climb. Morning traffic had begun to pick up along Washington and there was a light on at the Williams' in the back of the house.

This had been her world and Vera stood to consider it. She took a moment to watch the spider, too, with its spinning — the web that it built was almost done. It was a marvel, really, complex and well-anchored, individual strands shining brightly in the sun. Luckily she had the broom right beside her, and with a flick of the wrist the whole thing was gone.

THIRTY-ONE

They had agreed to meet at one o'clock, and Austin Chandler parked his Buick at the University golf course and crossed to the stadium. The state police were at the intersection directing traffic. Vendors stood along the sidewalk hawking programs, and a loudspeaker echoed from the field. The only thing missing were the people. The crowd that had milled along the concourse in August, boisterous and hopeful, had by mid-November largely disappeared, leaving behind a handful of diehards like himself.

He picked out the signs and banners of the anti-Chief contingent from a hundred yards away. On previous Saturdays he had given them a wide berth, but now he came along the concourse toward the group. Thirty or forty strong, they were mostly young people, joined by a few faded rabble rousers not much younger than he was. There were church people like Sheila Williams and Nesbitt from Horticulture, Libby McNeil at the center of the group. Harry Applebee stood nearby talking to a stocky boy in a khaki campaign vest, along with the young brown-haired girl who had spoken at the church. When Applebee spotted him he broke away and came over.

"Hello, Austin. It's good to see you."

"Looks like you've got a good turnout. The naysayers are more faithful than the fans."

"Yes, I'm proud of their commitment. The University needs to know the issue won't go away."

"I've got your ticket right here. Why don't I give it to you now and we can meet inside?"

"Oh, no, I'll go in with you. Could you wait a minute? We're just finishing a conversation with the press." He started toward the group but came back. "Sure you don't want a sign?"

"No, thanks. I'll let the rest of you handle it. The poor Chief has suffered enough."

With that weak attempt at banter they separated, and Austin Chandler moved to the edge of the concourse. After another poor night's sleep he had awakened congested, with a heaviness in his chest he still hadn't shaken. When the protesters roused themselves to chant, their shouts dribbled harmlessly along the concourse, and the few scattered fans simply ignored them on their way to the gates.

They might have devoted themselves more profitably to their studies, but otherwise the young people seemed harmless enough, pink-cheeked and smiling with their signs. Applebee's face was animated as he stood with the brown-haired girl; the old fox did a poor job hiding the glow that came over him whenever she was near.

He nodded at Nesbitt, whose placard read "Stop Organized Racism." Libby and Sheila stood at either end of the Coalition banner; they waved mittened hands in greeting as he stood near the grass.

The reporter, in his field vest, was a year or two older than the rest of the students and wore a professional-looking camera around his neck. He spotted Austin Chandler just as he was finishing his interview, and a moment later came over to join him.

"Excuse me, I'm with the *Daily Warrior*. Are you a football fan?"

"I most certainly am," Austin Chandler replied. "A great fan of the Chief as well. He's an Eagle Scout, perhaps you haven't heard that. It's one of the requirements for the job."

The stocky boy checked the settings on his camera. "I imagine you've seen some changes at the University through the years."

"Indeed I have. All this…" — he motioned toward the field house and golf — "has been added since I came to campus. Back then there was only the stadium and cemetery. And the University Farms, of course, where you see the dairy barns. The golf course is part of some new rec program the College dreamed up. Hard to see how that gets anyone fed."

His complaints, though, on a cold day, left him winded, and his voice sounded hoarse and strained. His angina, too, was acting up again, with a jab so sharp it brought tears to his eyes. The brown-haired girl trailed over to where they stood.

"Thank you for coming," she said to Austin Chandler. "Your support really means a lot."

He might have objected but there was hardly any point to it — let people think what they pleased. Even his many opinions felt thick and unwieldy, while the same invisibility that had calmed him in a country tree lot felt vaguely unsettling, especially on a day so cold and bleak. The brown-haired girl looked at him with what seemed like kindness — no wonder Applebee was sweet on her — before rejoining the others. When the angina struck again Austin Chandler shifted uncomfortably. The boy, camera poised, seemed almost to be herding him — not such an unpleasant feeling, really, on a November afternoon — and he moved along the concourse, a little closer to the group.

Vera had been surprised, as Walter steered them through campus, by the lightness of the traffic. The year they almost made the Rose Bowl seemed another lifetime entirely, when the sidewalks had been clogged around the stadium, and big motor coaches from Chicago lined up along the street. Now they glided easily through the Ag Campus to the Law School, and the parking lot where Walter left the car.

When Lindy brought over Lacey's tickets Walter's first thought, of course, had been to give them away. He tried the Williams, across the street, and the Schallers, even Mindy when she collected for the paper. When nobody wanted them they decided to take a break from housecleaning and go to the game themselves. Vera retrieved a Warrior scarf from the Goodwill pile in the basement, dug out her good wool slacks and a stout winter hat. Their stadium bag, bound for the church sale, got second life. She packed their blanket and a thermos of coffee, an extra sweater and two pairs of gloves.

It had been years since they had been to the stadium and she was excited. They came across a forlorn band of tailgaters near the law school parking lot. There was a man farther on who sat listening to his radio. The sidewalk ran past the cemetery, and when they came to a breach in the fence she and Walter turned in there, following a gravel road that wound back among the trees.

It was such a pretty spot, really, so close to campus — she remembered thinking that when they were at Della Mercer's service the summer before. Della was down with Bob at the far end, while Marla and Bill Tucker were closer to the fence. Through the empty branches Vera saw the smokestacks of the University power plant, their white plumes of smoke rising high against the sky.

Walter had left the road to make his way among the gravestones, and Vera had to pay close attention to make sure she didn't trip. They backtracked a time or two, once almost to the road, but Walter seldom stayed lost for long. Under a large oak tree he found what he was looking for, the square piece of granite that bore both their names.

Vera hadn't seen the stone since they'd picked it out at the quarry, and it was a little sobering to see the big 'ELLER' etched in block letters across its surface, with "Walter" and "Vera" in tidy squares just below. The trees had been full for Della but that was in summertime, and even beneath her hat and parka Vera felt a chill. There would be snow by the first of December, and all the long, icy months after that.

She never would have found the plot on her own, which was why they were out there: Walter wanted to get directions written down for the kids. He had tried to show Ronnie when he was in town for his reunion, despite Vera's warnings. The welcome dinner was on a Friday evening and Ronnie had come home all excited, with his name tag and pretty suit and tie. Walter was determined, though, and all Saturday morning he walked him through the papers. Ronnie hung in well enough through their accounts and annuities, the living wills and arrangements for their services. When they finished, Walter took him out to find the plot. With Kate she wouldn't have worried, but Ronnie was softhearted like his dad. They had barely left the gravel road when Ronnie broke down.

"But I don't *want* you to die," is what Ronnie said to him, all grown up and with a family of his own, sobbing like a boy as Walter held him in his arms. All of which Walter reported dutifully afterwards, but Vera had found it hard to get cross. It *was* kind of sad how things ended up in life, and there wasn't much any mom or dad could do to take the sting away. They'd had such a good time together through the years. Nothing lasts forever, though, and that's the truth of it, no matter how much a person wishes that it would.

Their plot had a good location at least, not far from the oak tree, and a good deal closer to Fourth Street than she remembered. It was another case of Walter thinking ahead, making sure they didn't wind up out at Meadowlawn like so many of the church people, or at Hillsdale, halfway to Rantoul. They were in pretty exclusive company so close to the stadium: there must have been a dozen deans and vice-presidents lying around them beneath the grass.

It was good that they would end up at the University, one of the best things that had happened in their lives. She had been terrified of all the smart people those first years on campus, but gradually she had learned to make her way. She read the *Courier* and followed the news programs, had gone over her bridge hands while Walter studied at his desk. Even then it would sometimes get the best of her, all the things to keep track of, the cards a big mishmash in her head, but that was when Walter would put aside his books. He would put aside his studying and come over to join her, sitting with her on the bed while they laid out the hands. He was learning too, so they went through it together, the point count and bidding and lead. She thought of him waiting outside the factory door every night when her shift ended, so she wouldn't have to go under the viaduct alone. She saw their two names etched together in granite and on impulse stepped up to take his hand.

Sentiment wasn't her strong suit and Vera knew it. Maybe those early years in Dakota had squeezed it all out of her, the cold of winter and summer's wind and drought. Walter was scratching away on his notepad so she caught him by surprise. He blinked at her from behind his glasses, with those pretty hazel eyes, and all she could think of was how lucky she was. What a good husband he had always been to her, hard-working and considerate, patient with the children and gentle with her. She hoped that Maddie would find the right person too. She hoped she would hold out for a good man, a clean man — a man who would take her into account. It was a hard thing to see when you were younger, but made all the difference as the years added up.

All in all they'd done pretty well. She looked at the gravestone, but try as she might Vera couldn't imagine them beneath it. It's possible that she just didn't care to, with so much on her mind — they'd been busy shopping for a new couch for their apartment at Cooke-Davis. It would be the last time she set up housekeeping, so she was taking her time; she had been thinking blue for the curtains but might want to go lighter, to take advantage of their window on the east. She looked forward, too, to a wing full of neighbors — when they went out to measure for the curio people were headed back from dinner. They must have spent a full half hour in the hallway just visiting. The meals, too, after all her years in the kitchen, would be a pleasure — that morning, they'd gone out for the early lunch the dining room served on game days. They'd had their choice of chicken strips or a nice taco salad, with streamers above the tables, and everyone around them in bright orange and blue. When they all stood together and sang the Warrior Loyalty, it had been a job to blink the tears from her eyes.

Walter was hurrying to put away his notebook and pencil, worried that he had upset her the way he had poor Ronnie. That wasn't likely though, because she wasn't Ronnie — Vera had already picked out the rattle of snare drums on Fourth Street, a flare of trumpets that came toward them through the trees. She squeezed Walter's hand again, this time in excitement. If they cut across the graveyard they could still catch the band. They could climb up to Lacey's seats and get settled, and then they'd see what the Warriors could do. Probably not much, but at least at halftime the Indian would dance, and Vera always got a kick out of that.

When the Preacher saw Austin Chandler on the concourse he felt his heart sink. Somehow he had almost managed to forget that gruff voice on the telephone earlier in the week, calling up with an extra ticket to the game. It was an attempt to reach out, he had realized, from a lonely parishioner, but the Preacher would have much preferred to walk back across campus with the Coalition members, find a place at the Wigwam close to Em. Instead, as gametime approached, he was making his apologies, shaking hands with Salim and Libby, leaning close to Em as she hugged him good bye. He felt ashamed of himself, of his own disinclination to join the old man at their margins, a Warriors stocking cap pulled down past his ears. When he looked back near the gate, Em had turned back to the young journalist, but several others waved merrily as he followed Austin Chandler inside.

The Preacher wasn't a sports fan. During all his years in Prairie Grove he had never been inside the stadium. They made their way across a cavernous entryway, past refreshment stations to a steep concrete ramp. Pigeons swooped and dove under a cloudy skylight as he and Austin Chandler wound their way higher beneath the stands.

The "Memorial" part of the stadium's name had never really registered on him, either, not until the ramp opened onto an open balcony with a row of columns that ran the length of the stands. Each pillar had the name of a University boy killed in World War I, a conflict that even in the Preacher's youth had been fading from memory. When Austin Chandler paused beside one of the pillars and bowed his head the Preacher did too, until he realized his companion was only catching his breath.

From the balcony they came out onto the field. The Preacher was impressed in spite of himself by the sheer size of the undertaking, a brilliant artificial turf marked in white below them, the dozen footballs that spiraled through the air. Bumping higher among the bleachers the Preacher glanced back toward the field. Armies in brightly colored uniforms conducted drills on the carpet. A fleet of golf carts glided soundlessly on the track. Men consulted clipboards and gestured with authority, as the marching band formed its ranks at one end.

He knew they were approaching their own section when people began to greet them. Austin Chandler waved at two seats among a crowd of older men sitting relaxed in their bright orange and blue.

"Hey, Austin, back for more punishment?"

"Where's that rascal grandson of yours? I brought him a candy bar."

"This is Harry," Austin Chandler said, puffing heavily. "He wants to see what suffering really means."

"Well, he's come to the right place," one of them said, amid general laughter. Arms unfolded to shake the Preacher's hand and someone slapped him on the back. He settled into place next to Austin Chandler, the chill of the aluminum bleacher pressing up through his pants.

A part of him, of course, was still back with Em, who in a few minutes would disband the group on the concourse. He had decided, earlier that week, that he should simply talk with her about their friendship. An old-fashioned option perhaps, but necessary — she had seemed increasingly distracted in recent days, at least for Em. Her visits to his office had grown less frequent, and her pretty face was often thoughtful when she glanced his way across the group.

He was happy to see that she was back to her old self on the concourse that morning. He felt proud to be with her as the young journalist asked questions. The boy had a maturity and confidence that made for a pleasant interview and the Preacher had watched Em as she talked. He allowed himself to imagine her in the stands with him instead of Austin Chandler, the two of them sitting close as the spectacle unfolded. It was new to him too, the *game* with all its pageantry and self-importance, the national anthem and high authority of the press box, a growing excitement as kickoff drew near.

It was an excitement that quickly faded once the game was underway. The two teams had lined up to face one another, the Warriors in orange pants and blue jerseys, the opponents in crimson and white. Even to the Preacher's unpracticed eye the home team seemed at a disadvantage — the Warriors were smaller and less swift than their opponents, and few of their plans seemed to work. On offense, their runners were almost immediately tackled, while the crimson-clad team was unstoppable, scoring the first three times they had the ball.

The crowd was sparse and clustered near the center of the bleachers, with scattered groups of spectators spreading out toward either end. Remnants of a student card section waved in gentle chaos across the field. At the beginning of the second quarter the Warriors finally mounted their own drive only to stall at midfield, on fourth down with a yard still to go. The verdict around the Preacher was unanimous, even as the men climbed dutifully to their feet.

"Better not," said a voice behind him.

"Never make it," said another, and he was right. The ball had barely been snapped when the opposition swarmed into the backfield, burying the Warrior quarterback beneath a bright crimson wave.

Austin Chandler sat impassively beside him, arms folded as he watched the action. It was unclear to the Preacher why he had been invited — his companion had barely spoken — and he began to entertain more seriously the idea of leaving early, slipping over to the Wigwam before the end of the game. As the first half wound down he watched the men around him make their way to the restrooms. A few were back for the beginning of the halftime show, where the marching band tried to simulate the Internet, with a small contingent of cornet players running back and forth between the groups. All had returned, though, in time to see the band form a large block W that moved north to the goal line. The marchers doubled back in the endzone, and Chief Cheehaha broke from among them to a roar from the crowd.

The Preacher had seen, of course, the ersatz war dance countless times. It figured prominently in the videotape the Coalition used for its teach-ins, the same tape he and Em took along to show in class. It turned out to be even worse in person, if that was possible, as an undergraduate in a feathered war bonnet traced circles on the field. The men around him, though, watched intently. During the dancer's final frenzy the Preacher stole a glance at his companion, who stood motionless, frowning at the field.

Mercifully the whole affair was soon over, and the Chief joined the band members in retiring from the field. As offensive as the display had been, the Preacher was glad to have seen it — he could call Em later on to report. It wasn't as if they couldn't see each other, something he needed to stress when they talked. It had already occurred to him that she might like the symphony. It would be fun to go out for a movie. One night, summoning his courage, he had even called her at home, the old house on campus that she shared with her friends. He had heard her name casually shouted out along the hallway, a babble of young voices as he waited on the line. He thought of how easily she'd colored on the concourse, her eyes on the young journalist, a boy that he, too, instinctively had liked.

The crimson team scored twice more in quick succession after halftime, so the final outcome was no longer in doubt. His companion remained silent beside him, but instead of rushing off to the Wigwam the Preacher sat back among the men. As play went on below he found himself thoughtful, part of a larger mood of contemplation that had settled in across the stands. He looked out toward the Ag barns and empty fairways at the golf course, the campus fieldhouse under a low winter sky.

It was contemplation that seemed appropriate enough for Warrior fans, given the fortunes of the ball team, with the mammoth stadium nearly empty and the game almost done. He thought of the high hopes that seemed to accompany each season, the resignation that settled in as events ran their course. When he thought of the human mascot, first to mind was its simple wrongness. Sooner rather than later the Chief would have to go.

Even so, it wasn't impossible for him to imagine the spectacle's attraction, especially in a community so reserved and stoic. In an era where sports, not religion, embodied our sense of the cyclical, provided metaphor for our hopes and disappointments, accompanied us reliably through the seasons of our lives. A stylized ritual acted out weekly before the faithful, hinting at a deeper importance and glory still to come. He thought of two buckskin arms raised at the end in benediction, a gesture disturbingly reminiscent of his own.

Inevitably, he came to the question: what is it we grasp for in our pursuit of the religious? What deeper intuition sustains our daily lives? The season was lost and winter approaching; only a few remained around him in the stands. Inevitably, too, he considered his congregation, steadfast and dwindling. He had never once doubted they were faithful, even if what they were faithful *to* was never completely clear. Certainly affiliation could have been forged with a more successful endeavor. Why a religion with human failure at its center? And how to explain that peculiar choice of faith itself with the ecstatic so elusive, and year after year only losses seemed to mount?

It no longer embarrassed the Preacher that he came to understanding as if building a sermon. Through a posing of questions, their answers always partial — the opposition had scored yet again, to make the score 40-0, the Warriors pinned near their own goal line as the season ticked away. There was one failed play and then another, before on the third try a small halfback broke free.

He briefly stumbled but managed to find his feet again, sprinting hard toward the far side of the field. Closed off, he swung to his right. Squirting between two would-be tacklers the boy burst into the open, angling toward the near sideline and picking up speed.

There was little about football that attracted him. The money wasted every season could find much better uses. The young halfback himself was deeply exploited, caught up in a sports program both cynical and corrupt. Still, the Preacher felt a surge of excitement. Arms pumping, the boy was at midfield and still gaining speed. The small crowd rose as if one, the Preacher among them, cheering wildly as he crossed the thirty yard line, the twenty and ten. Rolls of toilet paper unfurled from the upper deck as he reached the goal line. The smothered crack of the ROTC cannon echoed through the air.

With the extra point the score became 40-7, and the Preacher turned, still cheering, to his companion. Austin Chandler was on his feet but he wasn't applauding. Instead, he moved forward to the aisle. He might have reached out, but seemed to decide against it, tumbling past the Preacher head first down the steps.

For Austin Chandler, the angina had continued to plague him as they climbed the ramp to the balcony, where he was so short of breath he barely made it to their seats. After fifty years of watching the Warriors the whole affair — the ball game and music, the colors and crowd — seemed to be happening somewhere far away from him, trumped by a growing tightness in his chest. Slowly, he felt the pain ease. It didn't reappear until the middle of the Chief's dance when the tightness came back again, settling in for the rest of the game.

The aisle at the stadium was a row of steps, steeply pitched, between the bleachers. It wasn't clear where he thought he was going as he moved past the Preacher. After an initial surprise at being no longer upright he felt a surge of irritation: the only thing to do was get back on his feet. This, however, he couldn't do. The arms that should have pushed him up lay numb and unresponsive, as the heavy feeling in his chest spread to his stomach and legs.

In the Senses Alive! class they had come to standing and sat down again, taken note of the ball bearing's special preference for the floor. Only now could he feel gravity's true power, the casual ease with which it held him to the ground. Pantlegs and winter boots filled one corner of his vision. A scatter of popcorn lay forgotten between the seats. His hope was to lie forgotten too, but that was too much to ask. Faces were already pressing in, anchored by a chubby girl in an usher's vest, her breath in cloudy puffs as she crouched at his side.

The earth itself, finally, had reached out to claim him. As a child he had risen defiant against it, crawling with determination across a yellow braided rug. He had fallen then too, but not so heavily — he felt an ugly knot on his forehead where it struck hard against the steps. When human hands turned him, the cool air was pleasant. The upper deck's heavy girders blocked out half the sky. Someone covered his legs with a blanket and someone else slipped a sweater beneath his head.

His glasses had been lost but nearsightedness no longer plagued him. The Preacher appeared, mouth moving silently, and it was hard to know what it was he'd held against the man, complaining bitterly about him for months on end. On the contrary, Applebee seemed eminently decent, his face full of kindness and concern. Concern for an Austin Chandler who was sorry to see him replaced by a young man in a dark paramedic's jacket. The boy's face was girded for duty and his movements well-practiced; plastic-clad fingers found their way to his neck.

His hearing was acute but had come to lack focus. There was a car horn that sounded on Fourth Street, a distant shout and the medic's shuffled boot. He looked for Edie and the children but they were no longer with him, leaving behind only a sense of strangeness they had ever shared the earth. This is dying, he thought, grateful for the Swiss boy's patient tutoring, and with that, all the naming was done.

There was a body, to be sure, to be accounted for: a body that he had driven like a sulky beast through a lifetime, whose thankless task was finally at an end. A body best entrusted to others now that he was finally through with it, to the chubby usher, the Preacher and the paramedic, all three stepping aside as a stretcher bounced their way. His knees no longer ached and fatigue lost its power. Geoff no longer seemed so far away. He had even managed to slip free of his irritability, the flimsiest of garments, but one of the last of many layers to go.

The physical was what now seemed unlikely, pulsing frantic and dense and concerned. A pulse that bore away with admirable dispatch his many failures and foolishness, his resentments and endless mistakes. It was such good news that he found himself running barefoot across a grassy meadow to tell his mother, on a porch already dissolving as memory fell away. Life ended, had finished, was over and done, and now his real travels began.

Thirty-two

Jana ran the lab prayer group with brisk efficiency.

"And these signs, too, shall follow. God longs to gift those who follow His will."

Melinda, from the dean's office, took the first turn. "I just need to know that He loves me. Sometimes I feel so all alone."

"Precious Jesus," Jana prayed, "be with Melinda. Fill her right now with Your Word."

Bernadette, near the door, was crying. "My daughter's wild, I can't keep her at home anymore. The boys use her, I know they do."

Mitchell's head was bowed but he knew the others' voices,

following them as they rose up beneath the high column of the Hitachi, the heavy compressor at the edge of the room. As the murmur faded he felt Jana turn his way.

"And you, Dr. Chandler? How can God help you?"

He hesitated.

"He is with us now and always. Are there pressures at work that assail you? Do you question His wisdom or plan?"

"No," Mitchell said, "I don't. Actually, I'm thinking of my family. I hope I can learn to be with them again."

The hum of prayer resumed.

"Precious Jesus, teach us the ways of Your love for us."

"All-loving God, be with Dr. Chandler at home."

Their prayers rose around him in the room. It was hard to know exactly what to make of them, hard to know what to make of Spirit Rising and the Bible, the healing circles and altar calls, all the covenants and prophets and psalms. Even "Jesus" had proven oddly elusive, the bearded stranger the rest knew so well. Maybe He was a stand-in for that Something Else that Mitchell had first encountered in the sanctuary. A powerful feeling of being *lived through* that seemed only to have deepened rather than fading away. It was undiminished later that night at the dinner table, where Maureen waited for the boys to grow quiet.

"All right," she said, "let's take a moment together before we eat."

She no longer blushed as violently as when she had first suggested it, his second night home. She bowed her head only to raise it. "Nick, settle down. This is a time to reflect, which in your case wouldn't hurt."

An ever-active God made all things more possible. They'd said nothing at all about her experience at Spirit Rising, but Maureen went back with him the following week. The next Sunday she brought along the boys. A few days later he'd come back to Manor Lake.

Mitchell watched his wife across the table. Her complexion had improved and she sat with her head down, face calm and her hands in her lap. Unrugged Kai clenched his eyes, lips moving, the way he'd seen people pray at church. Nick leaned back in his chair to watch the ceiling fan, idly rocking the table with his foot. He turned to regard Mitchell coolly, and then, very slowly, shook his head.

Even Nick, though, liked the new evening regimen. Once they'd cleared away the dishes and cleaned up the kitchen they settled around the table for games. Mitchell had rescued Sorry and Uno from the old house on Washington, one Saturday morning when his father wasn't home. There was something reassuring about shuffled cards on a tabletop, the low-tech clack of a wooden marker being moved around the board. With Game Boys banned they tackled a jigsaw, teasing out a natural bridge that formed an arch in yellow sandstone, a hundred shades of blue pieced together to make the sky. Gradually the boys warmed to the puzzle's discipline — it helped with the strange shared embarrassment of being together. While they got ready for bed Mitchell stood with Max on the driveway. He watched the sky as Max sniffed at the bushes; there was a sharp jangle of the dog's collar, in the dark, when he sneezed.

The promise was for a life more abundant, of something more beyond his mind and the cell. When he stopped at the boys' bedrooms they raised their arms to hug him. He often remained a few minutes beside their beds. He was still sleeping in the guest suite and turned off lights in the kitchen, checked the back door before starting down the hall. He stopped in, on his way, to see Maureen. She had files stacked around the wicker chair where she sat in her bathrobe, drinking tea. Mitchell found a place across from her on the edge of the bed.

"I don't think it hurts them that much, the church services. Maybe they'll have more perspective on the way people live."

"Maybe so," he said.

"It's good to be exposed to different systems. That way, at least, they'll know their options. They can decide for themselves later on."

He nodded and they sat together in silence. For as long as he could remember, a certain distance defined them. Distance and the most basic of agreements: what the world was and what it could be.

Together they had watched their sons at the table, heard their squeals of laughter as they spun down their cards. At Spirit Rising there was an emphasis on family, support for a marriage they'd both thought was gone. Maybe that's what Maureen was thinking about, as they sat together in the bedroom, if not the tumult that rose up weekly in the sanctuary, the cries of people around them calling out Jesus' name.

"I'm not sure I can believe this, Mitch. I think you should know that."

"I'm not sure I can, either. It really is the most unbelievable thing."

Maureen put down her cup. "We've been so lost," she said, and reached out her hand.

She had reached out only to brush his cheek with her fingertips; instinctively, Mitchell recoiled. He recoiled, but was learning resilience, and came back, resolved, to her touch. Without her glasses she seemed new and unknown to him, this woman whose bathrobe gaped open as she leaned forward, who described a consciousness coexistent with his own. Her eyes held a secret that drew him closer, in past the speckled blue of her irises, her pupils a smooth glossy black. It was within that darkness, beyond a defining lens, that It waited — trackless Silence with its gentian purple glow. An unimagined vastness, a resonance, a hunger, a depth, and despite his best efforts, the demons were back.

The demons were there, but so, too, was Assurance: he could let go and not slip away. He slid his palm past the robe to her breast. She laid her hand on the back of his neck. Softness had formed up to meet his fingers. There was the press of another's lips against his own. This much — and more — he had learned to give in to, so Mitchell left himself behind and went out to meet his wife.

There had been scant evidence of the season's final football game as he drove to campus. The boys wanted to go skating so Mitchell dropped them off at the ice rink; his first thought of the Warriors came when he parked his car on Sixth Street, and heard in the distance a tinny fanfare from the band. When he got to his lab he borrowed Ginny's transistor radio and took it to his office. The Warriors were behind, when he turned it on, by three touchdowns, with the second quarter only barely underway.

It wasn't unusual that his father would come to mind when he considered his lab. There was a logic and discipline to the world of science that came naturally to him, and for that he was grateful to his dad. Even Spirit requires proximate influence, and their new work on chemical gradients had shown considerable promise, enough that the next round of funding was assured. Grad students had moved on but others were coming, as the enterprise continued to evolve, like a living thing itself.

Brian was away more and more as they entered the season of job interviews. The lab deserted, Mitchell set in on his email. He had simply ordered another hard drive and installed it in his computer, and within a week his new inbox was full. The current, as he slipped in, bore him easily: he responded to a dozen different queries from his review panel, weighed an invitation to chair a session that summer in Madrid. In an hour or so he was done. The boys would be calling so he switched the phone to the microscopy lab, where, the morning before Chet had told the prayer group about his dream.

"It was so *real*," he'd explained. "That's why I remember. There was a barbecue, like we have in the summertime. The neighbors get together and cook burgers on the grill. The moms and dads were drinking tea on the patio, and the kids were out playing in the yard.

"I wasn't really with them, though, that was the strange part. I was on my neighbor's roof, watching high above the yard. And that's where I saw Him. Jesus was up there too, and He was crying. 'Look,' He said, 'how happy they are. They think they're doing just fine. Some may even go to church now and then. But none really *know* Me, and most never will.'"

Chet looked slowly around the circle. "That really chilled me, I've got to tell you. But when I woke up it was more like a sadness. I thought how many people are just like my neighbors. I felt bad when I saw Jesus cry. All He wants is for people to love Him. It hurts Him to see souls being lost."

Jana wasn't sympathetic. "It's easy to forget that's a choice we make. Those people all know what it is they need to do."

"They think they've got time when it's already late!"

Jana shrugged. "He that is not with Him is against Him. He that gathers not with Him will scatter abroad."

Bernadette's voice rose up sharp with satisfaction. "By hard and impertinent hearts they have stored up His anger. Let them find out for themselves how they fare beyond His name."

"My yoke is easy," Mitchell ventured, "and burden light. Randy says God's love is extravagant. There's nothing we can do that would make Him turn away."

A silence fell over the room and the others looked back at him uncomfortably. Mitchell knew they had never quite trusted him — Heimowitz or Jana, Bernadette and Chet — he had soaked up their prayers when he'd needed them; this was one of the first times in the group he had spoken up.

"Randy says it's hard to love God if you haven't ever met Him. We can't love what we don't really know."

The others shared glances around the circle.

"That sounds about like him," Chet said. "Word has it Pastor Randy's riding high again. I guess he'll finally get his church east of town."

"He's a little weak on end times," Heimowitz grumbled and Jana laughed.

"Randy likes the triumph of the cross but he forgets about judgment. There's a price unbelievers have to pay."

"Unclean," Bernadette added, small eyes shining. "All our righteousnesses are to him as dirty rags!"

But Mitchell was no longer listening — he had begun to find himself, in the prayer group, growing bored. Jana's Christ was tough-minded and scrupulous in His reckoning. Chet's Jesus was easily hurt. Mitchell had begun to relax, though, his madness instructive: he knew now that our personalities only skim the surface, topography of something more enduring that rests just below. He knew his father's world, unresponsive and empty, at best, a puzzle to be solved. He thought of his lab mice, their destinies ever-present — if only they could decipher them — in the tangle of shredded lab reports where they lived and moved and bedded down.

Maureen had grown restless at Spirit Rising. She was already considering Campus Church if she could rekindle the Sunday school — apparently some of her friends had expressed interest as well. Mitchell, loyal to Randy, was torn. The Presence he had met never left him. He listened closely to what Randy had to say. But more and more as the group prayed he had his eye on the Hitachi. He looked past it to the scanning laser microscope at the edge of the room. He listened for the clank of glassware and morning voices in the hallway, sounds of the Chandler Lab slowly coming back to life.

On a Saturday afternoon the microscopy room was empty. He found the switch on the laser microscope; while it warmed up he went down the hall. In the animal colony, there were a half-dozen large salamanders, including one with a stump where its tail should have been. Victim of one of Nicole's transections, it was on a rock in its aquarium, crouched and wary as Mitchell drew near.

The salamanders' gods walked the earth in white lab coats; the animal was docile as Mitchell picked it up. A week after injury the stump was still raw. Even so, it was beginning to elongate, and Mitchell used a sterile scalpel to harvest cells at the wound site, a tiny heartbeat pressing flat against his palm. He spread the sample on a slide and let the animal go.

It had been years since Mitchell was at the bench himself. Even so, he knew their faith's careful rituals. He knew that Nicole would already have inserted, within the salamander genome, a tag marking Lazarus, protein that would fluoresce under the right kind of light. The electron microscope, for all its power, took only snapshots; for living cells he needed something else. In the microscopy lab he came past the Hitachi to the laser microscope, attached to a computer at the edge of the room.

The microscope was familiar in concept at least, if not its particulars, especially after his lifetime in the lab. His own movements, as they came back, felt deeply practiced. It took only a few seconds to position the slide on its mounting stand, make sure of fluorescence with a mercury arc. Finally he turned on the laser. A gray smudge appeared before him on the computer screen, as the hum of mechanism, like morning prayers, filled the room.

Nothing we call known ever arrives unmediated. The laser microscope accesses not so much tissue as the light shining through it — through and within it — a precise band of photons passed through a series of filters, each narrowing the scope of what gets to go on. And even that small remainder is broken down and digitized, interpreted by layers of software, rearranged to make sense on the screen. He picked out the outline of a cluster of cells. He chose one and brought the image still closer, his fingers moving quickly on the keys.

What emerged was an array of green dots set against a deep black background. Stingy with its secret, the salamander was active at the wound site: the dots marked new proteins in the cell. For years Mitchell had probed Lazarus' mystery, frustrated and demanding, eager to identify process and move on. Only now did he lean close to consider it, the wide galaxy before him on the screen. He tapped at the keyboard, seeking better resolution. A new dot suddenly emerged there set out against darkness. A moment later another one formed.

The first microscope was attributed to Galileo in the seventeenth century. Since then four centuries of optics, advances in stain agents and cellular processes, a better understanding of light waves as theory kept pace. And all of it, in the end, essential. All tirelessly pursued so he could arrive at this moment, when it could finally be experienced through His eyes — Our eyes — life in the cell taking shape.

Where nothing had been before, new structure existed. Amino acids found partners and protein was formed. Head bent to the screen, Mitchell felt a tingle on his neck. There was a familiar electric rush along his spine. It was a vantage so intimate as to seem barely permissible, a glimpse of a restless universe caught in the act of expressing itself — eagerly, helplessly — over and over again.

Beyond that narrow focus, too, the Rest never rested. Ginny's radio had been barely a murmured presence in his office, distantly attended to as the Warriors lost out. The score had been 40-0 when he finished his emails, and stood at his desk to turn it off. The image itself didn't catch up until later: a boy running as if pursued beneath a low winter sky. The odd ratio of 40/7 that had first visited him in the church alcove, as he stood above Sixth Street almost three months before.

Even then, it's unlikely the final score would have resonated — there's a lot, in a complex world, to keep track of — if his father hadn't come to mind one last time as he sat before his screen in the microscopy lab. Austin Chandler was there too, it seemed, and again quite distinctly, skeptical and dismissive, with silver glasses flashing, just as Mitchell, leaning back, heard the phone ring and reached across the table to pick it up.

THIRTY-THREE

Geoffrey Chandler had happened onto the sports bar two years earlier in an upscale hotel in Zone 9, where he was delivering a diesel injector to a coffee grower in town for the weekend. There had been no answer when he rang the hotel room so he strolled across the lobby. The sports bar was to one side, with soccer balls and baseball bats on the walls as decoration, and a half-dozen television monitors spread out around the room. A small dark man in a maroon service uniform mopped the floor near the restrooms and a Ladino in a white dress shirt was behind the bar cutting limes.

Otherwise the place was deserted, and he sat down on a barstool to order a glass of orange juice. A football game from the United States was running on a large-screen TV in the middle of the dance floor. When Geoffrey looked up from his orange juice he found his father, in a faded sport shirt and graying beard, directly across from him, frowning out from a long mirror that ran the length of the bar.

It was the one place, of course, his father would never be: at a tavern in the middle of the day. Still, they did look uncomfortably alike, and not just because the faded shirt had once been his father's, bounty from one of the periodic CARE packages his mother sent from Prairie Grove. It wasn't his bulk either, although he had inherited the same broad chest and thickness across the shoulders, early hair loss and a propensity to frown. What struck him most was the *solidity* of the man who looked back at him, the fuel injector wrapped between them, like a baby, on the bar.

The hotel's chilliness had been strangely detached from the concrete chaos of the city, with its bright buses gliding soundlessly beyond the windows, the clouds of exhaust that trailed behind them in the sun. Snowiness on the TV screen turned out really to be snow, swirling above the teams as they struggled on the field. The first thing that came back were the helmets, a distinctive maize and blue that belonged to Michigan. Next he made out the looming outline of the stadium, realizing only then that the game was being broadcast from Prairie Grove. Far behind in the fourth quarter, the Warriors had begun to rally. Outside was a brilliant sun and tropical sky, but the Warriors scored two quick touchdowns in a snowstorm, yet another in the closing minutes of the game. He had long since forgotten the coffee grower and his fuel injector, caught up in the delirium of a small distant crowd. Geoffrey found himself cheering along when the Warriors recovered a fumble, again when a field goal won the game. Alone in the sports bar he had found himself with a lump in his throat; when he tried to swallow it down, warm tears filled his eyes.

Over the succeeding two years he had thought, now and then, about watching another game. Martín was still inexperienced though, and the workload was heavy. They got Rosa packed and sent off to school. In time, he had forgotten the Warriors completely, which is why it was strange that he would awaken, on a Saturday morning in mid-November, with the notion of going back to the sports bar again.

Maribel had a birthday party in Vista Hermosa and he wouldn't pick her up for several hours. Cris and Martín were headed to the beach. Calibrating an injector at the shop took longer than he'd anticipated, and in mid-afternoon Geoffrey finally closed the shop. He drove to the hotel in Zone 9 but the sports bar was gone. Even from the outside, he could tell the difference — there were red neon guitars hung over the club's wide entryway, a 50's-style Chevy sedan half-buried in the wall. He went inside anyway, but the only television was tuned to a Mexican variety show and he came back outside to the car.

As Celia's business picked up they had bought another VW, an ancient Rabbit that he used around town. With Mari only halfway through her party he circled through the city. He came past his shop behind its heavy steel shutter. He was held up near the market by some kind of demonstration, locked in traffic as students marched on a cross street. Eventually the group passed, en route to the National Palace, and traffic started moving again.

Mari, when she climbed into the car, had a small stuffed parrot she had been given as a party favor. Water balloons had been part of the entertainment, and her blouse and hair were completely soaked. She chattered happily as they wound through the city. Eventually they arrived at their street, where the carport was empty — Celia had taken the van on business, early that morning, to Xela. He lifted the bike down for Mari and went in to find her another blouse. On his way back he came past the telephone, where the answering machine's message light was blinking in the dark.

His sister's voice had the tone of command. "Geoff, this is Betsy. Call me. Make it collect if you have to, but call. I need to talk to you as soon as you get home."

On a list taped to the back of a cupboard door he found his sister's phone number. He dialed international access and then the country and area codes, circling in toward her house in Prairie Grove. It was always something of a surprise to see how little really separated them: on the first ring, Betsy picked up the phone.

"Geoff," she said, "Daddy's gone."

His first thought was one of simple curiosity: where had his father been and where had he gone? His next impulse, as he heard

Betsy sobbing, was to feel a pang of sadness. It had always pained him to hear his sister cry.

"Betsy," he said, "I'm sorry. I really am."

"Geoff, damn it, you don't need to apologize! He's your father, too!"

He started to apologize again but instead fell silent. He leaned toward the doorway to check Mari on the street.

"Would you think about coming home for the funeral? Please? It would mean so much."

"Well," he said carefully, "I'll have to see."

"Geoff, Dad's gone. There's just us now. And, my God, Mitchell's gotten so strange. I'm afraid I'll lose track of you both!"

"All right," he said, "I'll talk to Celia. I'll see what we can work out."

"If it's the money..."

"No, it's not the money. I'll look into flights this evening and see what I can do."

When he hung up Geoffrey poured himself a glass of water. He had Mari's small blouse in his hand. From outside came the sound of her singing, as she turned wide circles in the sun.

He paused in the kitchen with his water. The article about Mitchell from *Newsweek* was still on their refrigerator, scotch tape yellowing, along with pictures of Betsy's three boys. He thought of their small kitchen in Prairie Grove with the linoleum glistening, a fresh smell of cleanser in the air. He thought of his mother's determination to perform the many chores of motherhood, her uncertain tremble as she held him in her arms.

He had loved his mother and wished life could have been easier for her. His father's impatience with him, on the other hand, had been fortunate — otherwise he might never have come across his own life so many miles away. With the passing of the terror tourists had returned to the capital, straining under backpacks, but it was childhood Prairie Grove that now seemed to him exotic, with shuffleboard at the Ellers' on summer evenings, popcorn and cider on cold autumn nights. There was a burlap bag he had knelt in with other shepherds at a manger. There was Betsy in the choir loft with chicken wire wings. There were the thunder and lightning that shook the windows in springtime, his father sitting calmly with the *Courier*, unimpressed by the storm.

He put down his glass and went out to the carport.

"*Mira, Papi*," Mari called as she circled. After a while she glided up to join him, panting as she straddled the bike.

"*Papi está triste, ¿verdad?*"

He nodded. "*Algo triste, mi amor.*"

She nodded in sympathy, her sweet face long and solemn. She patted his arm. "Papi's sad," she informed El Gato, who sat licking himself at the edge of the carport. She patted his arm and pushed off again, sailing easily away.

"*Papi está triste*," she sang, and Geoffrey did feel sadness, a sadness he felt disinclined to push away. It seemed of a piece with the life he had carved out for himself, of a piece with his love for Mari, with the unbearable pride he felt in Rosa and Cris. Of a piece with another world, too, now safely behind him — he had managed to hold out long enough until all of that was gone.

As Mari circled he watched the busy corner, waiting for Celia. He was waiting to go into their bedroom and tell her about his dad. It wasn't long before he saw her slowing on the Avenida, saw the old van as it turned and came wobbling toward them, coughing and sputtering, carrying her back to the place where they lived.

THIRTY-FOUR

Walter had been up half the night working on his piece for Austin Chandler's memorial service so Vera let him sleep until almost eight while she put a layer of meringue on her butterscotch pie. She was ready to eat someone else's cooking and looked forward to Cooke-Davis. The dining room was more of a restaurant, really, a nice one, with the women in their pantsuits and the men in coats and ties. She just hoped they didn't wear out their good clothes long before they got there, getting dressed for funerals every other day.

Walter wanted to get to church early so he could go over his talk with the Preacher. When they got there Renner's hearse was parked by the Behavioral Sciences Building, ready to back onto Sixth Street at the end of the service. Old Austin Chandler's casket sat in the front of the sanctuary, and Vera went downstairs with her pie. She got the lights on and sponged off the serving tables, made sure the plates were all clean. By that time Sheila and Libby had arrived; while they counted out silverware she climbed the rear staircase. The back entrance doubled, in the old church, as handicapped access — at Betty Maxwell's funeral, poor Mr. Hensley had hobbled all the way up the ramp only to find the door locked. It was too slippery for him to get back down again, so he spent the whole service standing outside in the rain.

When she pushed the door open Vera found a bearded man in a heavy winter parka leaning back against the railing.

"Why hello, Geoffrey," she said. "It's nice to see you."

He was smoking a cigarette, so it was just as well he was out of sight — to some of the church people, he might as well have been waving a bomb. Vera was glad Walter didn't smoke and she wouldn't have wanted Ronnie or Kate to take it up, but he seemed so peaceful, outside by himself. Geoffrey was always her favorite of the Chandler children anyway. He'd fallen in with a bad crowd in high school, but that happened: some boys needed a little rough and tumble as they grew.

"Did you get the clipping from the *Daily Warrior*? I have one for you if you don't." Vera rummaged in her purse. "Walter came up for extra copies as soon as we heard. Here, why don't you take it."

"Thanks. I'll put it on the refrigerator." Geoffrey smiled as he glanced at the photo. "I never knew my dad was so opposed to the mascot."

"Well, it surprised me, too, to tell the truth. The poor Chief doesn't have many friends left. It's a good picture, though. Both of us thought so. It's nice to see somebody besides the Preacher with his face in the news."

The photograph had been in color, in the center of the front page: Austin Chandler in his parka and stocking cap, surrounded by the protesters with signs in their hands. Sheila Williams and Bob Nesbitt were in the picture, and Libby, too — Libby had told her that Billie Morrison was planning to bring her Hawaiian Surprise for the after-service dinner. Billie always insisted on browning the coconut when she got to church which made the burners a mess. It hardly mattered because you left it out on the serving table, and by the time people got back from the cemetery the whole thing was cold.

People were starting to arrive for the service, the women carrying cake pans and serving dishes. Vera knew she should go downstairs and help, but she enjoyed standing in the cold air with Geoffrey, their breath in small puffs as they talked. With his whiskers and roughened fingers he reminded her of her cousin Louis, a mechanic in Fargo, who'd run a shop there for almost forty years.

"Your brother and sister are glad you're home, I'm sure," she commented. "I saw Mitchell and Maureen last Sunday morning going in with the Spirit Rising people. I wonder how they like it there?"

Geoffrey shrugged. "What's not to like? He knows a Power that guides and comforts him. He says he and the Creator are one."

Vera had spotted Billie by that time on her way to the front entrance. "There she is with that coconut thing when she was supposed to bring salad! All we're going to have are desserts!"

"He says we share a single mind, looking out on the universe. He says God lives through us as He comes to know Himself."

"Well," Vera said, distracted, "I'm sure that's true." She reached for the door. "If you'll excuse me, Geoff, I've got to catch Billie. If she gets her hands on that stove we'll never get it clean."

Geoffrey had been glad to see Mrs. Eller again, and when she left he studied the photo from the *Warrior*. He was just refolding it when the door banged open and Mari appeared, her face unhappy and tears pooling in her eyes.

"What's the matter?" he said. "Why aren't you downstairs with the other kids?"

"*No me gustan por nada*," she told him. "*Son necios todos.*"

"They seemed nice enough to me. Don't you like that big sandbox?"

"*Papi*," she said despairingly, "*No me entienden.*"

"That's because you're speaking Spanish, honey. They don't know what you're saying. People don't like what they can't understand."

She sighed heavily and fell back into his arms. Somehow in packing he'd forgotten a jacket, so he had ended up in his father's parka, the same one now memorialized in the clipping. He opened the coat and zipped it around Mari as she leaned against him. Together they watched students stream past the alley in their winter caps and scarves. It was a sight that captivated them both, Prairie Grove in winter, with the bareness of branches and sharp chill in the air.

He had just lit another cigarette when he saw a familiar figure picking his way through the parking lot. He recognized the black crown of hair and light step along the sidewalk, the quick trot up the ramp to the door.

"Hey, Randy," Geoffrey said, and Pastor Randy paused.

"Geoff? Geoffrey Chandler? Well, praise the Lord, look who's back from the jungle. I thought maybe I'd see you inside. I was awful sorry when Mitch told me about your dad."

Geoffrey nodded.

Randy tried to look sorry, which hadn't grown any easier for him over the years. Luckily he spotted Maribel, her head poking out from the parka.

"Hey there, Precious! Is this lovely young lady your daughter?"

"This is Mari, my youngest. I've got two older girls, seventeen and nineteen."

Randy shook his head. "That's so wonderful, praise God for His blessings. You know…" He looked around. "I'm not supposed to say anything, because I promised, but God's found a new way to bless us. A way that caught me by surprise. My wife is expecting. We're going to have a family, me and Lee. It's like Jesus says, 'To those who have, even more will be added…'"

"And to those who have not?"

Randy spread his hands. "What can I say? God is God and has His own way of working. It's a little easier, though, when you know how He sees things. How He's just waiting there to answer our prayers."

Geoffrey felt Mari shift beneath the parka, her small body pressing warm within his arms. Randy favored her with a wink as he flashed his wide grin. "But then again," he said, "that's the whole problem. Most of us never ask Him for nearly enough."

Lee Overmeyer wasn't beside her husband that morning, but still in her nightgown, lying back lazy in their bed at Manor Lake. Once the collections picked up again she'd bought a new flannel nightgown, and a big comforter she liked to burrow under in bed. She had begun to sleep later in the mornings, awakening to the sound of Randy already downstairs, whistling along with the Christian radio station as he made himself breakfast. The very first thing she did, when she heard the door close behind him, was go down to the kitchen and turn it off.

She pled morning sickness to escape church services and Randy was happy to oblige. She was, in fact, often nauseous in the morning, but even that felt sweet and intimate. Kneeling next to the toilet was exactly where she should be, knees cushioned by the bath mat and bare ankles on the tile. Warm air from the furnace blew extravagantly across her and in the distance lay the rumpled covers of their bed.

It wasn't so different from the freedom she had felt years before in her Dallas apartment, except this time she wasn't alone. She was going to have a baby — the pronouncement still thrilled her — and while Randy was clearly a part of it, bursting with pride and enthusiasm, what she longed for was the company of women. She'd begun to call her mom again at the apartment in Virginia Beach. She even tracked down Mim late one night, a disappointment — her sister was a Christian again and going to services, deeply sorry for the life she had lived.

The person she thought of most often, though, was Barbara, who wouldn't return her phone calls. She was right, God did have his favorites. Lee had realized by then that He would keep on blessing her, over and over until she finally gave in. Meanwhile Barbara got nothing. It was like a game to Him, the disappointments and suffering, and in return, He expected their love. He liked gratitude, repentance, submission; He hovered close around, ever hungry for His praise.

In any case, she was through with excuses: God was her Master, but He would never be her friend. Oddly, she was no longer afraid of Him, now that she had something even God couldn't touch. It felt older than He was, motherhood — what comforted her weren't a rod and staff, but a warm bedroom and pillow, a tiny heart that grew strong deep inside. Someday that life would be on its own, but for now she was watching, determined to protect it from His Love and Plan just as long as she could.

The first the Preacher had seen of the *Daily Warrior* photo was when Em and Meg brought it by his office Monday morning. "A Lonely Vigil," is what the caption read. Austin Chandler wore a scowl that could pass for determination, as he stood beside the Coalition members with their banner and signs.

"We never really knew him," Meg said sadly. "And only an hour or two later he was gone."

Clearly moved, Em could only shake her head. "It all seems so powerful, somehow. The protest is the last thing he did!"

"Yes," the Preacher said, "I suppose it was." He paused. "It's ironic, because Dean Chandler wasn't really what you'd call a supporter. It was more that —"

Meg pointed to her sleeve. "We're going to make armbands for the service." Salim put it out on the listserv and Shirley's canceled class. Everybody's going to be there."

Em put her hand on his wrist. "It's just so important when older people recognize — even somebody cool like you, Harry — when you understand how much things are going to have to change."

"Well," the Preacher said, "thanks, I guess. I'd better get to work on my remarks, then, so I'll be ready for the service tomorrow."

He was in his robe at the back of the church when he saw her the next morning coming into the sanctuary. The young reporter from the *Daily Warrior* was with her, and they came over to greet him as they passed.

"Harry," she said, "you remember Sterling from our interview. Sterling, this is Harry."

The boy extended his hand. "Pleased to see you again, Sir. Em's told me a great deal about you."

The Preacher had often imagined Em coming to services, imagined that she would have a chance to see him someday at work. When the processional began he walked to the front with Walter. With the Coalition members in attendance it was a rare day for Campus Church, as most of the pews were filled.

"We are here to celebrate the life of Austin Chandler," he began when the time came. "As I listened to Walter's description of his many achievements I couldn't help reflecting on what a great era of accomplishment this has been. How much our world has been shaped by Dr. Chandler and his peers. It seems important that we acknowledge that stewardship, especially since so many young people are with us today. They are in the process now of defining their own lives, and are the ones to whom the next stage of the human drama belongs.

"Dr. Chandler's appearance in Monday's *Daily Warrior* was a surprise to many of us. It is certainly among the ironies of life that the influence we have on others is far-reaching, even if much different than we imagine or intend."

Gentle humor was a part of his rhetorical style. It didn't hurt, either, in facing life's many lessons; his eyes passed over Em in the pew as he spoke. He must have known already on some level that she and the young journalist were intimate. Seeing them together again only confirmed his impression: there was Em's self-conscious flush and the boy's quiet confidence, the new world they had entered that held only two.

It seemed, sadly, more of a father's perception than a lover's. And not quite a father's either; perhaps an uncle's or a friend's. He might have searched his feelings for envy or the pain of exclusion, but he was in the pulpit, the service in his hands. The moment belonged to Austin Chandler, not him, and the Preacher looked out at the many faces, expectant, in the pews.

"Austin Chandler," he went on, "wasn't active until very recently in the church. Nevertheless he was known to us in many ways. He was a father and husband, a neighbor and colleague, and for almost two decades an administrator as well. I have sometimes noticed, in recent years, in myself as much as others, a certain discomfort with the roles that we play. Modern psychology has had its influence, of course, and there's a sense that these many roles represent a "false" self, while the "true" self lies hidden just below. There has been much concern about the masks we wear. Many of us have labored diligently to find our way beneath them, in pursuit of a self that's more real.

"And yet, for all the attractiveness of this approach and for all the many insights it has produced, I wonder if perhaps we haven't lost sight of the power of our roles. If perhaps these same roles, our masks, if you will, aren't in themselves important expressions of who we are. If the masks don't serve to *reveal* as much as conceal us; if they aren't as reflective of Spirit as our more private reckonings, and the doubts that often rise up to assail us late at night."

The Preacher had found his cadence by that time, a gradual, practiced merger of message and tone. As usual during his sermons, though, Vera felt her mind drifting — the poor man's head was always in the clouds. Walter had done a good job on his part, considering what he had to work with; her own task began when he came back to join her, keeping watch so he wouldn't go to sleep. Walter seemed alert, though, nodding along with the Preacher, so she took the opportunity to look around the church. There was a pretty good turnout, especially with all the University students. She saw Mitchell Chandler and Maureen with their two boys up front. While Randy Overmeyer was beside them, his wife was missing. They hadn't seen much of her lately at the church. Walter had been concerned but Vera wasn't worried — a pretty girl like that usually landed on her feet.

After the service the Chandler family took a moment around the casket. It was a surprise to her the one who broke down there, Geoffrey Chandler with his beard and rough fingers, eyes red as the family backed away. The rest of the congregation was already outside, spreading down the steps to the sidewalk. A Prairie Grove police car idled in front of the hearse while behind it were one of Renner's limousines and Austin Chandler's old Buick. The pallbearers formed up in the entryway. Walter wasn't supposed to lift heavy weights, but Mitchell and Geoffrey were on either side of him and they could handle most of the load. Geoff's little girl from Guatemala — Vera had heard her jabbering in the playroom earlier — hung back with Betsy and her two older boys at the edge of the steps.

The youngest one, Scooter, wasn't with them. Betsy had told her before the service that he was impossible all morning, so he'd been banished during the service to the quad with his babysitter. Vera first saw him, blond head bobbing, in front of Warrior Jitters, straining against the girl's hand at the back of his collar. They crossed the street just as the pallbearers started down.

It seemed a shame sometimes to have the church so close to campus, especially on occasions like this. There the students were, all laughing and lively, when right in their path was a hearse. The church people, at least, were prepared for it, lined up as the casket came by. Scooter was climbing past them, fascinated; she watched him put a forgetful step forward and find only air. In the next instant he was tumbling forward, head over heels down the steps.

It was a fall that would have killed any one of the rest of them: there was a collective gasp as he landed on the sidewalk, a stunned silence as he lay unmoving on the ground. All at once, though, Scooter raised his head. He let out a piercing scream, his face red and contorted. His distress was so great that even the pallbearers faltered. Luckily Geoff had the front end on the rollers, and Renner's men took over from there.

A half-dozen of the younger people had reached Scooter on the sidewalk. Others who couldn't move as fast arrived a moment later, and soon there were more than enough hands reaching down to pat his shoulder, smooth his hair and help him back to his feet. Scooter found Betsy among them and, weeping, buried his head against her leg.

When it appeared that he was all right, a murmur of relieved amusement ran through the crowd. Scooter must have heard it because he raised his face to complain.

"This is hurty," he told them, indignant. His lower lip trembled as he held up his palms. "These are scrapes. This is hurty. This is *pain*."

None of them on the church steps doubted it, and there's something about a child's cry that commands attention, so fully that Austin Chandler was loaded up while they attended to the boy. Things have a way, at the end, of going quickly — the patrol car's lights twirled a lazy circle as it edged from the curb. Renner's men moved into the street to block traffic. The family jockeyed at the doors of the limousine, and soon the whole parade was underway.

Vera stood at the foot of the steps to watch it go, enjoying the young people in their arm bands as they hugged and parted, joining the jostle of other students who had reclaimed the sidewalk. She climbed back to the alcove and looked over campus. The paper said there might be snow flurries later in the day. Inside, she joined Sheila and Libby, who were staying behind too, in the basement, with the food.

Walter would be one of the last ones past the serving table — the way people liked to talk to him he always was — so she uncovered the butterscotch pie and cut a slice. She started small but on second thought made it bigger. Walter had always been a man who liked his pie. She stashed it away for him where she wouldn't forget it, high in a cupboard beside her purse.

The Chandler plot was out at Hillsdale so there wasn't a hurry. They checked the covered dishes in the oven and scoured Billie's spatter, wiped off the counters and sink. Then Vera sat down with the other girls and a fresh cup of coffee, to wait for the living to return.